Hume's Fork

a novel

RON COOPER

Hume's Fork

a novel

RON COOPER

bancroft
press

Copyright 2007 by Ron Cooper
All rights reserved.

No part of this book may be reproduced in any form or by electronic means, including information storage and retrieval systems, without written permission from the publisher, except by a reviewer, who may quote passages in a review.

All the characters in this book are fictitious, and any resemblance to actual persons, living or dead, is purely coincidental.

Published by Bancroft Press ("Books that enlighten")
P.O. Box 65360, Baltimore, MD 21209
800-637-7377
410-764-1967 (fax)
www.bancroftpress.com

Cover and interior design: Tammy Sneath Grimes, Crescent Communications
www.tsgcrescent.com • 814.941.7447

Cover illustration: Rocky Shepheard

Author photo: Sandy Pell

ISBN 978-1-890862-50-3 (cloth)
LCCN 2006935333

Printed in the United States of America

First Edition

1 3 5 7 9 10 8 6 4 2

For Sandra

Hume Family Tree

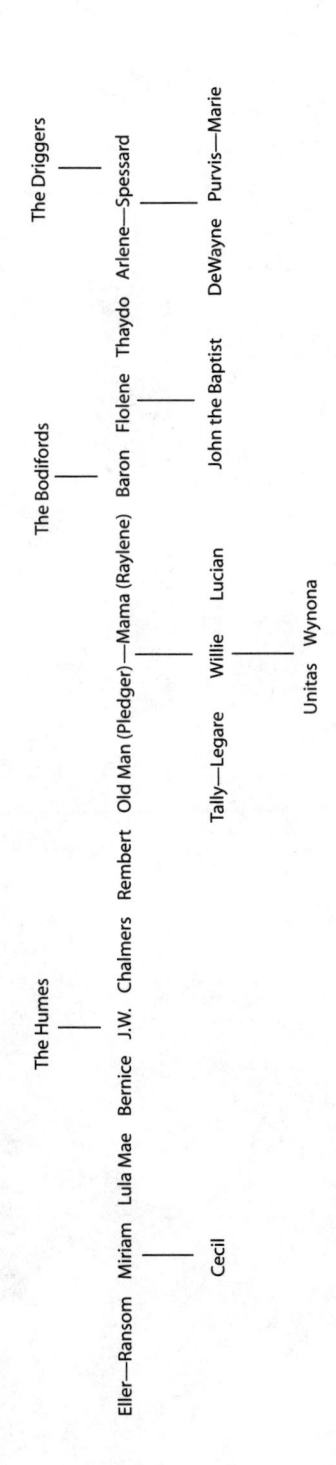

The Humes

Eller—Ransom Miriam Lula Mae Bernice J.W. Chalmers Rembert Old Man (Pledger)—Mama (Raylene) Baron Flolene Thaydo Arlene—Spessard

The Bodifords **The Driggers**

Cecil

Tally—Legare Willie Lucian John the Baptist DeWayne Purvis—Marie

Unitas Wynona

Unspecified Humes: Pudge (cousin); Booger (Strom Thurman) (cousin); Markley (Anchorhead) (cousin); Uncle Lum (Christopher Columbus) (cousin); Stetson, Levi, and Grace (cousins, Uncle Lum's children)

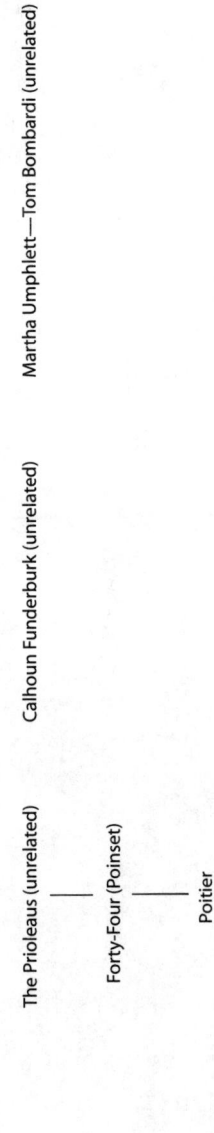

The Prioleaus (unrelated) Calhoun Funderburk (unrelated) Martha Umphlett—Tom Bombardi (unrelated)

Forty-Four (Poinset)

Poitier

ONE
The Ontological Argument

The dinner plate, which arced towards me in parabolic elegance, spun just slowly enough that I could make out two blue birds circling above what I supposed to be a pagoda. I was sitting on the mauve futon which Tally, against my objections, bought to replace the vinyl sleeper couch—it was ugly, sure, but I had been relegated to it enough nights for a fondness to develop. Though she had whipped the disc in a shoulder-forward, girl-throwing way that a grown woman should have been embarrassed about years ago, Tally's overhead release and extended follow-through managed a jai alai hurler's manipulation of centrifugal motion.

My previous underestimation of an argument for the existence of God was now replaced by a more serious underestimation of Tally's arm, and I had to laugh. For her to think she could actually hit me a good fifteen feet across our low-ceilinged "family" room (as she, childless, called it) with a Blue Willow plate, and me only on my third beer, was ridiculous enough. More absurd was her apparent expectation that the plate would hook right at my forehead, so I refused to dodge.

The episode had been caused by an even more fundamental underestimation: her reaction to my announcement that I had decided to go without her to the philosophy conference that week. Slapping her eighty-nine-cent Walgreen's flip-flops across the terrazzo floor to the bedroom, cussing me through gritted teeth for an hour, even yanking open the chifforobe Mama gave her and feigning to pack her "I've-*had*-it" suitcase—all this I would have called typical, creating in me that usual sense of trapped despair to which I have become so accustomed that I sometimes mistake it for comfort.

But winging a piece of her prized china collection at me, due to my admittedly last-minute decision to go on a four-day trip, was so unexpected that it overwhelmed my ordinary fear of her. I actually felt the urge to chuckle, and leaned into the plate like a pitch. Another man might have ducked, then beaned his wife with his half-empty bottle of Coors. Or he might have set it on a coaster and inquired into what was really bothering her. Me? I sat smiling like an other-forehead-turning Jesus, realizing I had finally taken all she could fork out, and had lived.

I remembered having the same feeling once before. A hurricane hit Charleston when I was an undergraduate. I didn't answer the phone when my worried folks called, hid when they showed up to take me inland, and ended up riding the sucker out. I had just read a Walker Percy novel for a Southern Lit course in which the protagonist has an epiphany during a hurricane, and I thought I could use a storming. Granted, I was drinking a steady stream of cocktails at the time, but in the midst of the wind and broken window and rain gushing in, I really did feel as if I had nothing to lose.

Tally's plate found its mark just above my left eye before landing on the coffee table. It wobbled a few seconds, then settled to face me as if ready to present a meal. I stared at its two flying lovebirds and noticed a yellowed chip on the rim just above them, which explained why she had examined three or four other plates immediately following my announcement before calmly selecting this one. That decision made me laugh even more. What would she have done had I ducked, not giggled, took the hit despite evasive maneuvers, and crumpled to the floor in a most unmanly way? Gasp, run to help me up, and fetch ice? And what would I do? Apologize, bemoan doing so much to cause her such distress? I could not fully unpack the implications of this moment, but I was sure I had met some sort of horizon, some boundary experience that might redirect my life. Or else I was drunker than I thought and could not have evaded the plate had I tried. Either way, I had called five years of her bluffing, and I had won by just sitting still.

I promptly phoned Grossman. I would explain later, I told him, but he should swing by and pick me up in the morning on his way to the conference.

Two philosophers in a ten-year-old Volvo station wagon with bald tires and no rear-view mirror crossing Tampa Bay is hardly noteworthy, unless you know they are heading south on the Interstate towards Sarasota to go north to South Carolina.

"Where are you going?" I said. "You need 275 North—turn right."

"This is the way I know," Grossman said.

"But we need the Howard Franklin Bridge."

"Unsound. The Skyway's state-of-the-art." He stuck a pinkie with a too-long nail into his right ear and shook his arm as if trying to widen the hole.

"Didn't it collapse a few years ago?" I asked.

"Rebuilt. That's why it's so strong."

"OK. Then what about the causeway through Clearwater?"

"Too long."

"And going south through Bradenton isn't?"

"I know this way. It's how I came." He removed his finger from his ear and inspected something on the nail.

I realized he meant he would drive east through Manatee County, then north to I-4 through Orlando to I-95. It was the reverse of the route he had taken when he first drove from New York to St. Petersburg two weeks after getting his driver's license and buying the used Volvo. In his four years at AmWorld U., Grossman had strayed from his campus/apartment/grocery store axis only once, when I dragged him snook fishing. He waded out twenty feet into the water, only to scare up a sting ray and shit in his bathing suit.

Even among philosophers, Grossman was a nut. Two years earlier, when I mentioned I was thinking of driving to the Keys to try to hook a bonefish, he showed me his list of 600 or so North American bridges, of which he had probably seen five, along with their specifications. So I had no right to complain about his route to South Carolina, but in my defense, I had decided just the day before to go to the conference, which made it too late to book a flight. I could not leave Tally carless (even though I imagined she was still too mad to drive), and Grossman was going anyway. Further, his leaving the county needed my witnessing, and that itself was worth his route amendment and phlegmatic driving style, and the fifteen-hour trip.

Grossman and I both started teaching at AmWorld U. when America World Enterprises of Orlando theme park fame bought a bankrupt Cordle College. The Cordle president had been caught in a sex scandal involving several male students and a missing couple of million dollars. Even with pictures, the old boy somehow got away clean and rich, but enrollment at Cordle plummeted. Sinecured faculty, whose only previous worry had been white St. Pete Beach sand in their drawers, now found little to fill their scrambled-over résumés. AmWorld freed some noosed necks by giving an endowment to Cordle, changing the name to America World University West Campus, and issuing early retirement tickets to three-quarters of the Cordle faculty.

The AmWorld U. main campus in Orlando, which used to be the University of Central Florida, now churned out almost entirely School of Entertainment Studies graduates, most of whom were on a work-study plan that had them don furry animal costumes at the theme park when not in class. After receiving their degrees, most went to work full-time at the very same jobs, and for the very same minimum wage, at the very same theme park, the only careers for which their degrees seemed suited. In its first three years, AmWorld U. began to make money, and thus caught criticism from the rest of higher ed, so it wolfed up Cordle College to establish academic credibility by having a second campus that demanded the high standards of a traditional liberal arts college. Announcements went out calling for the best and brightest of academe to apply, but somehow they got me.

We crested the Skyway. A few hundred yards west, officially outside Tampa Bay, a few snowbirds sat on upended paint buckets, probably baited up with fiddler crabs and trying to feel the pianissimo of a sheepshead alongside the pilings of the old bridge. The local joke is that the sheepsheads are so nervous that you have to set the hook *before* the pulse comes through the line.

It was a long way up, down, however we were getting there, and I needed something to kill the silence, so I asked Grossman something I'd always wondered about—how a seriously talented philosopher like him wound up stuck at a rinky-dink college like AmWorld U.

"I already told you," he said. "Right when we started teaching together, when I couldn't fit my key into my office door lock, and you helped me—"

"Just remind me, all right?"

"They interviewed me at the APA in New York."

That much I knew. Grossman was only in his mid-twenties then, but already he'd managed a Ph.D. from Columbia and a string of articles in the toughest journals in the country, which pretty much outshines my entire career. I was never sure if he knew it (ending up here, he couldn't have), but Grossman could have had his pick of nearly any school he wanted.

I'd already been able to piece together the fact that Grossman had bummed around Columbia and taught as an adjunct after finishing his Ph.D., because, being a savant geek, in addition to a lapsed Hasidic Jew disinherited by his jeweler family when his interests turned from God to Gödel, he had no idea what else to do nor even that something else should be done.

Me, I was desperate for any offer and applied to AmWorld U., as I had to forty other colleges, fudging on my training and specialties to meet their descriptions and hoping to bluff my way through the interviews. Tally was pulling for me to get this job, because her parents had retired and moved from Atlanta to Lakeland, about an hour or so from St. Pete. The AmWorld reps at the American Philosophical Association conference that year were looking to fill four openings with specialties in logic, philosophy of language, philosophy of mind, and philosophy of religion. Since I had just completed my Ph.D. at Rutgers, which had recently wooed three big names in philosophy of mind to its department, the reps assumed that I did philosophy of mind, which I did not, but as I talked about my training in phenomenology, using phrases like "contents of consciousness" and "noetic intentionality," it all sounded like the same stuff to them. One interrupted with, "Then you do philosophy of religion, too, right?" I was not sure what they had misheard—maybe I mentioned the philosopher Gadamer and he thought I said "God"—or whether they threw existentialism in with religion, but I said, "Of course."

"What I mean," I said to Grossman, "is why didn't you get snagged by some good school?"

"I didn't want to leave the city, but my professors at Columbia negotiated with the people here. They said they had talked to my uncle in Ithaca, and I would live with him." He was smoking a Chesterfield that I did not know could still be found, pinching it between the tips of his thumb and ring finger as if the little cylinders had never become familiar in his hand, blowing the smoke out the window, and squinting to read the mileage signs. My sense of smell seemed especially acute, and the smoke was strong and stiff.

"Wait, I'm confused. Ithaca?"

"I was confused, too. The Cordell representatives could not recall anything about my uncle, and they were talking about St. Petersburg." He picked something from the tip of his tongue, probably a bit of tobacco, and examined it before wiping it on his sweater. "They asked me a couple of questions. One of the men said he'd heard about me. Then they offered me the job."

"Hold on a minute—did you say Cor*dell*?"

"Yes. That was the former name of AmWorld."

"No, Saul. It was Cordle. Listen, you said you have an uncle who lives in upstate New York?"

"Uncle Morris—my only relative who doesn't live in the city. Why?"

"You dumbass. They were talking about Cornell University in Ithaca, New York. Cor*nell*. You could be teaching half your load now for double the salary." Something finally made sense. The AmWorld reps had landed Grossman on their first cast, and they got a twofer in him (logic and philosophy of language) and were still celebrating their efficiency when they interviewed me, who specialized in none of those fields (and was good in no others) but was mistaken for another double talent. Only a half hour into the trip, and I had made a major discovery.

"You never told me that, Saul, because I sure as hell would have remembered it."

"I did tell you, Greazy, and you labeled me a dumbass that time as well. Then I asked about your background, and you just said, 'Hard to say.'" He looked out the window with a jerk. "Is this it?"

Grossman always expected his interlocutors to know just what he was talking about, even when he revived a conversation from exactly the point it had broken off years before. Usually, he did the breaking off—something suddenly occurred to him, and off he would go. Tally hated that about him almost as much as his incessant teeth-picking, followed by intense scrutiny of the extracted morsel.

"Is this *what*?"

"Is this the South?"

"Don't start that shit." I figured this query was related to his remark to me years earlier that living in the South did not seem so bad, and I corrected him, saying that St. Pete and much of Florida, for that matter, were not the South. He had looked confused and jotted something down in the little notebook he kept in his breast pocket. One side of his office desk was stacked with the little notebooks he had filled over the years. I had always assumed he was making notes for some logic proof emerging in his head. Once, when he had left a notebook in a classroom, I picked it up to return to him, but thumbed through and found this sort of thing: "Quantified Logic seminar each Tuesday at 1 o'clock pm. Many television channels. Juanita the cleaning lady speaks Spanish. After 10 o'clock pm is late. Music next door is very loud. Wittgenstein's deontic logic—?"

"I want to know when we're there," he said. "You're the only Southern person I know, I think, and Charleston is the real South, right?" He knew me more than a year before I revealed to him that I was Southern. My accent (resilient despite my post-college attempts to dispel it) and tastes for bluegrass and snuff were no clues to him. He knew only that I had gone to Rutgers for my Ph.D. and assumed I was a New Jerseyan.

I was the only Southerner in the Letters Collegium, except for one historian from El Paso who claimed Southernness when convenient, but I called him western. Not that my roots ever made much difference to me; I had just grown sick of being drilled on all things Southern as if I were W. J. Cash. The literary types were the worst. They expected me to wear white suits and have mint julep breakfasts and say, "Yes Suh, we shall rahz again," and offer a speech on the nobility of the mule and the proper preparation of the hoecake. They could not pass me in the hall without informing me how much they adored Flannery O'Connor and how proud I must be of my rich heritage. I would explain that I had indeed grown up an hour from Fort Sumter—in a trailer. And they would laugh and laugh.

The knot on my forehead from Tally's aerial attack the day before started to ache.

"Charleston, for all its beauty," I said, "is just another tourist trap that has somehow convinced the world that it is not. I could stand on the corner of King and Broad, and New Yorkers like you would gladly pay five bucks a pop to hear me say, 'Shut my mouth.' Now who's the carpetbagger?"

"I don't know."

I immediately felt bad. Grossman might be the most brilliant person I have ever known, but he never knows when someone is making fun of him. Besides, I needed to remember how terrified he must have felt, not only driving his car for maybe the dozenth time since he had gotten it, but actually driving it hundreds of miles. Worse, he was surely mortified about having to read a paper at the American Philosophical Association conference. Despite penning an article every couple of months in a top philosophical journal, writing two books since coming to AmWorld U., and receiving good enough student evaluations—they were charmed by a self-absorption they took to be shyness—he had never presented a paper at, nor even submitted one to, a refereed conference. This presentation was now a requirement for tenure—the personnel office had mistakenly used "and" instead of "or" in the list of tenure requirements. He and I were both up for tenure, and the APA conference at Charleston happened to be the nearest one for Saul, a non-flyer. He had submitted a paper to the APA that I knew would be placed on the program, and he had elicited a half-promise from me to accompany him.

My yearly submissions to the APA since grad school had all been rejected. I had published two articles harvested from my dissertation, which I was still hawking to university presses. And I had read several papers (well, several versions of the same paper) at second-rate conferences. Students liked me, and I had not actually slept with any, and while the administration and everyone else probably knew I would never have an idea that would light any philosophical fires, they still thought I would do. So, tenure was within reach, but I needed something to seal it up. A paper presented at the APA would do it, and I sent in one in which I attacked another philosopher's attack on a famous philosopher's version of the ontological argument for the existence of God. Lo and behold, I got a letter saying my paper had been accepted and placed on the conference program for presentation.

It was the saddest day of my life.

※

The ontological argument comes from the 11th-century monk Anselm, who said that if we define God as that which nothing greater can be conceived, and if we agree that existence is greater than nonexistence, then QED, you got your God argued into existence as pretty as pi.

For centuries, philosophers have roundly rejected the argument for various logical technicalities. Chauncey Hartley, now a hundred years old and retired from the University of Chicago, built a grand career defending it. Hartley claimed that Anselm's second version, which the old monk probably did not distinguish from the first, restated the second premise—*necessary* existence is greater than nonexistence (and also a whole lot better than plain old existence). It was thus immune to the attacks. To claim that God or anything else exists is to assert a contingent fact that is settled only by empirical verification. But to say that God exists necessarily is not to state a *contingent* fact, and that changes the metaphysical ballgame.

I had not really cared about Hartley's argument until I read an article in *Philosophical Review* by a guy named Bishop from Duke, who claimed to find once and for all the chink in Hartley's logical breastplate. I thought the chink was too slight to expose Hartley's argument to any real danger, and my paper argued that the Duke guy was making too much of it. My paper addressed only the one point made by that one critic, not whether the base argument really worked or not. The last paragraph of my paper stated that, despite my defense of Hartley on that particular point, I still thought the argument was weak for other reasons. Sitting on the futon in the moments before Tally's flying plate, I wondered if I should leave that part out when I read the paper at the APA conference, because the damn argument was beginning to sound pretty good to me.

Four months earlier, when the congratulatory letter arrived saying that the paper had been accepted, I felt only existential dread that would have choked Kierkegaard. Presenting the paper at the APA would pretty well guarantee my tenure. I had friends from grad school who were still flitting from one temporary teaching position to another and would give a gonad to be in my brogans (which I actually wear sometimes for the sake of durability and cost, but which my ethnicity-crazed colleagues think make me "authentic," whatever that could mean). Did I really not want tenure? Did I think my failure to secure a permanent teaching position would lead to the dissolution of my desolate marriage? Did I want my marriage to end? Should not I, of all people, know the answers, with a Ph. goddamn D.?

I was not even sure why I decided at the last minute to go. This was my sorry state: If I did not go, tenure was somehow out of my spineless hands, and I would just play the cards dealt me by fate. Grossman had long ago reserved a hotel room at the Charles Towne Convention

Center I could share if I changed my mind. I had seen him earlier in the week sniffing three-dollar mangoes at the grocery store, and told him I was still not going. When I called to say that now I was, he *cooed*.

※

"You haven't told me why you changed your mind." Through his thick glasses, Grossman squinted at the exit sign and arched his upper lip to reveal incisors that looked especially white in contrast to his dark beard.

"This is it," I said, "I-4 East. I'll tell you what. Don't ask me to explain why I decided to go, and I'll let you know when we hit the South."

"Am I going to meet your family?"

I thought my plate wound, my new annoyance indicator, would explode. "Goddammit, Grossman, between college, grad school, and St. Pete, I've been home, what, four times in sixteen years—"

"Five."

"—and only the last two were *almost* tolerable, because everyone's attention was on Tally, whom they all just love to death. Me, they seem to share a basic distrust of. Without her there to run interference, somebody's liable to end up getting shot. And it might be you."

I told him about my most recent visit. My sister Willie (from Willa Jean) threw herself a divorce party, which she planned far more carefully than her elopement seven years earlier. She asked me to sing "Free Bird" for her, and I did not know how to play any Lynyrd Skynyrd songs, especially not an acoustic version of one famous for its extended electric guitar duet. But I practiced it, and from my makeshift stage—the back of somebody's '72 El Camino—I played the guitar and sang as two dozen of her drunken friends cheered her on. Willie never looked more beautiful, twirling a dance with her two-year-old on her hip. On the bookshelf in my office sits a picture of her in newly divorced glory, her head thrown back, winking at the camera, looking like a weary but joyous Tuesday Weld, and offering the whole world a long neck Budweiser toast and an invitation to kiss her ass.

"I've seen that picture, Greazy," Grossman said. "Your sister is very beautiful. I'd like to meet her."

"Jesus, Grossman. Stick to logic—don't try to be funny." I felt like a jerk again. He was obtuse, but his feelings could get hurt on occasion. I once told him he needed to bathe before his date—a colleague, also single, was escorting him to the Founders' Day banquet—and he started crying. I apologized, and he shook my hand, which was as intimate as I had ever seen him with anyone, and, for the first time, called me "Greazy" (the nickname I prefer to my given name Legare, pronounced in South Carolina Huguenot style L*egree*), although he had to practice pronouncing it with the "z" instead of the Yankeed "Grea*s*y."

"Stop up here at a station, and I'll buy you a Co-Cola and peanuts to put in it," I said. "That'll be your culinary introduction to the South."

He grinned his childlike grin and put on his blinker a quarter mile too soon.

༄

Inside the Long Haul truck stop was a diner/souvenir shop combo where you could have French fries with gravy—whether sausage, chicken, or unspecified—and then buy naked woman silver silhouettes to stick to your mud flaps and wonder why you never actually had a naked woman in the vehicle with you. The bathroom smelled a little like Irish Spring and piss, and some other odor that struck me as lonely and reminded me of a tobacco barn. It had three showers for truckers and, in addition to the machine that dispensed hotel-sized bars of soap and squirts of Old Spice for 50 cents, four machines sporting all manner of technicolored, ribbed "for HER pleasure" rubbers, French ticklers (I cannot imagine purchased by anyone but high school sophomores to wave in front of freshmen in the gym locker room and ask, "Hey, numbnuts, know what this is?"), and Stay Hard ointments for 75 cents. I have always believed that a portion of truckers' union dues went to pay for the installation of these machines just to announce to the gullible rest of us that truckers might have the world's most boring jobs, but they sure as hell get laid a lot.

Grossman and I leaned against the outside of the Long Haul and watched the big rigs pull in and out. The air was laced with diesel fuel and burnt rubber. We could see a huge sign saying "America World Theme Park and University—Exit Now" out on the highway. I popped a couple of Goody's powders while showing Grossman the proper way of building-leaning: one foot on the wall so that the knee sticks out in front. In his brown cardigan sweater and deep-welled, gray corduroys, he was not quite ready for squatting.

"Should one eat the peanuts as they pour out with the soda?" Grossman asked.

I suppressed a "Jesus." "Yeah, but some'll stay on the bottom. You'll have to shake them out."

We walked around to the back and saw two picnic tables. The nicer, fiberglass one, chained to the fence around the propane tank, was occupied by Spanish-booted and Stetsoned truckers. The other was wooden, grayed by rain, and missing a slat, and was sat and leaned upon by drivers with lace-up work boots and ball caps. Grossman watched my slow nods to the cowboy wannabees and listened to my "Wha ya say, bo?"s to whites and "A'ight, a'ight"s to blacks in work boots who walked by.

"Is this a special language?" Grossman asked. He scribbled in his little notebook.

"You bet it is. You're witnessing a complex social dynamic here."

"Should I try to speak it?"

"No way in hell."

A truck left the highway, circled around the station past the fuel tanks, and pulled onto the grass just behind the picnic tables. On the pentimento sides of the tractor-trailer, I could just see the outlines of palm trees beneath a new coat of white and the clumsily hand-painted "'Hume Shipping'" with quotation marks. The lace-up work boot truckers moved from their table as if they were used to the routine. Two white men in guayaberra shirts and military-style fatigue pants climbed down from the cab and walked around to the back of the tractor-trailer. The back of one man's square-cut shirttail bulged with what had to be a pistol stuck into his belt at the small of his back. They opened the back doors, and eight black men walked out of the trailer very slowly in single file and to the picnic table, where they scrunched together in silence.

"Who are they, Greazy?" Grossman asked.

"It looks almost like a prison work crew, but I don't think it is. I've got no idea what it means."

"Meaning is a property of propositions, not objects or events," Grossman said, exactly as someone trained in Anglo-American analytic philosophy is supposed to. "Is your family in the shipping business?" He was referring to "Hume," my last name, on the side of the truck.

"My family has never been *in* any business, and surely not shipping people across Florida." A guayaberra'ed man placed sandwiches in front of the black men at the table. One of the pseudo chain-gangers looked over in my direction, expressionless, with half-closed eyes.

"Let's get back on the road, Saul." I threw my empty Coke bottle into the trashcan a few feet away. Grossman tried the same, but missed by a yard. "Way you drive, it'll be midnight before we reach Charleston. You did put a hold on your room with a credit card, right?"

"What?"

"Nothing," I said. "I just hope it's not a problem."

We got on the road to South Carolina—the road I thought would bring us back to Florida.

TWO
The Hermeneutic Circle

Levels of meaning lie covered and dark. I do not mean just the obvious examples: a poem, a painting, a painting on top of another, a loan officer's raised eyebrow, a whiff of familiar perfume when no one is there, a touch on the shoulder by the junkyard owner who snatches back his hand and says he thought you said something. Our every experience is fraught with pre-thematic revelation about our basic situatedness in the world. The phenomenologist tries to peel back the layers of worldly encounter to disclose the existential structures, the meaning-making fundamentals that make possible the experiences themselves.

The frustration is that this reflective enterprise is always outside the experience being examined, yet is itself an experience. So, paradox one: looking beneath requires rising above. Paradox two (which may be the same as one): this transcending attempts to be part of what is being transcended. You want to read the textures of your life like a story, but you cannot step outside yourself to get a view of the page. Even if you could, might you find that the meaning of your life has been written between the lines, and you can't quite see it?

The meaning of that sometimes silent drive in the night on that dismal stretch of I-95 through Georgia was transparent and thereby seemed an exception to my levels view. I was on my way to a tedious philosophy conference—no more, no less. But I was not so much occupied with the content of my thoughts as I was with a quality of them I was not used to—a quality of feeling free to think whatever I wanted, and not just how I could hope to finish grading the heap of papers on the floor by my desk (half of them beginning with, "Since the beginning of time, man has asked themselves..."). Or how to slip out of the apartment without incurring Tally's wrath so I could go wade-fishing, or pick guitar with the banjo player I had met at the music store while scheming to smuggle a CD past my wife, a sentinel who keeps a mental inventory of every object in my possession. The knot on my head had not hurt since Orlando.

I initiated most of the conversation during the trip—mostly shop stuff, like our spring teaching schedules, our incompetent dean, our bombardment with the AmWorld vision statement, and reminders in every communiqué from the provost to uphold the image. Even Grossman noticed, and was irked by this pressure to represent AmWorld first and to educate second. But Grossman could not maintain conversational stamina in such trivial matters. He was interested in very particular philosophical problems and hardly anything else. So, somewhere around Jacksonville, I brought up the topic of the paper he was giving at the conference, and he talked nonstop—I think he was presenting the paper verbatim—getting increasingly excited for about thirty minutes. It had something to do with Tarski's being wrong about truth not being definable within a formal, syntactic system, and so Gödel's Incompleteness Theorem does not need to rely on the concept of provability. I kept up with him for a few minutes, and then just nodded along. His only pause had come when his attention was caught by a dungareed leg and its bare foot sticking out the front passenger's window of a passing car. I gave him a brief explanation of the epithet "trash."

He rarely talked philosophy this long with anyone. He knew that only a handful of philosophers in the country could or would try to follow—a select group that did not include me. Was talking with me at length about philosophy his way of telling me I was his friend? Was sharing his most cherished ideas his only way of connecting with me?

We crossed the Savannah River into South "We Don't Need Your Constitution Except the Second Amendment" Carolina. Sandlappers have their own version of U.S. history. Ask them who won the Revolutionary War, and the answer invariably will be Francis Marion. (Marion skirted the Redcoats through Hell Hole Swamp, which was practically my backyard. I am among the few South Carolinians not claiming direct descent from Marion.) Ask who was the first President of the

U.S., and you are no more likely to be told George Washington than a choice of Henry Middleton and Henry Laurens of the Continental Congress. The little pie-shaped state gave the nation John C. "Nullification" Calhoun, otherwise known as the "Grandfather of the Civil War." It achieved a brand new bag of redemption by producing James Brown, the "Godfather of Soul."

Grossman jerked forward in his seat. "Where do I turn? Where do I turn?"

"Relax. We've got a ways to go before we get to Highway 17, or as they say here in the Low Country, sayumteeyun. That'll take us right into Chall-ston."

"I'm hungry again."

We had stopped at Hardee's only an hour before. "Let's wait until we get onto 17. The Interstate is culturally uniform the whole length. You know who owns the stations and restaurants on it? The same people who Yankeed Florida. Soon as we get off it, you'll be in the South." I slipped into hillbilly drawl. "You just a hoot 'n' a holler away."

"What's the Low Country?"

"Coastal region, two or three counties inland. Then you hit the Piedmont, the Up Country. There're some slight differences in lifestyle, diet, accent."

"Like the boroughs?"

This seemed to me a breakthrough. Had "Mr. Socially Unattuned" noticed that Manhattanites and Brooklynites were not the same sort of New Yorkers?

"Yeah," I answered. "Something like that." Was it possible he harbored some opinions about his neighbors? "Say, those Bronx people can be pretty annoying, can't they?"

"I haven't noticed," he said.

Well, it was worth a try. For the next few minutes, I attempted to imagine what Grossman's experience of the world must be like. Missing so much about people's inclinations and irritations would be odd enough, but if his genius lay, as I suspected, in a nearly autistic ability to focus so that he was perpetually "lost in thought," he might not have an ordinary sense of spatial presence, a concept of *here alongside other things*. Perhaps his temporal experience was peculiar, too. He was not only the proverbial absent-minded professor, usually late for and sometimes even forgetting class altogether. Maybe he did not experience events in the ordinary sense of time. He never said anything to indicate he considered the drive *long*. He never consulted my watch—he did not have one. He never said things like "I know we *just* ate, but I'm already hungry again" or "How much longer do you think it'll take?" Perhaps memory functioned for him in some way radically different than for the rest of us. He was not forgetful in general—in fact, he had an amazing memory. But he did not seem to experience his memories as temporally distant.

At least as far back as John Locke (who, by the way, as secretary to Lord Anthony Ashley Cooper, Earl of Shaftesbury, a Lord Proprietor of the colony of Carolina, wrote the Fundamental Constitution of Carolina, whose liberal position on religious tolerance made the colony a refuge for the religiously unsettled, like Huguenots), philosophers have recognized the importance of memory to our concept of self. To be the same self through time, said Locke, is to be the same consciousness, and your memories are the marks, the knots in the threads of that consciousness as you look to the past. Your memories do not constitute your selfhood, but they are how you know you're the same person as twenty years ago. If you were told that you could wake up tomorrow morning the best-looking, smartest, richest, and (fill in your favorite superlative) person in the world, but would have no memories of anything before then, Locke challenged, would you do it? Would it be any different from dying tonight? Grossman seemed so fully within an extended present that I wondered if he did not continuously die and resurrect himself.

Willie often accused me of memory loss. "You can move away as far as you want," she said in one of our monthly phone conversations, "but family's still family. You don't shed them like a locust hull." The cicada, which we called locust, outgrows itself after years underground and emerges winged and triangular, almost all head, to hook to a tree or fence post and split its stiff, parchment skin, fly up to light on a high limb, and buzz its lonely twilight song. Except for its translucence and the slit along its back, the toast-colored hull looks like a complete and substantial insect whose bristled legs cling to anything. Many's the time Willie found that one had been quietly placed on her shoulder, and after years of discovering them there, she shrieked no less. Did the cicada take along with him those subterranean nymph years as he sat far above his previous, underworld home? Was his a song of liberation from darkness and a grotesque, cramped shell, or a song of memories, insuring a Lockean continuity of identity?

Just before the 17 turnoff, I realized this was one of the first times I had gone any distance from home without Tally and not felt as if I would face an ass-cutting when I got home. Getting tenure or not, or wanting it or not, did not seem to matter. The out-from-under-Tally's-thumb feeling was good. A day removed from the plate incident, I was convinced I had been liberated to take some new direction in my life.

We crossed over the Coosawhatchie and saw the sign for US 17. I reassured Grossman three times, and he finally took the exit.

"Here you are, Saul—the South."

"I want to try some of that," he said, pointing at my bulging lip and then my Hardee's cup into which I had been spitting my Copenhagen.

"Not while you're driving," I said.

෴

A few miles off I-95, near Pocotaligo, we saw a sign for "Hog Heaven—*24 Hours!—Our Barbeque is Devine.*" I remembered when I was about nine or ten going to Pocotaligo with my friend Lawton Villeponteaux. His truck driver father, Josh, had to pick up his rig, which had broken down or something, and they invited me along for the three-hour roundtrip ride. Lawton's mother and his older brother Parson drove their Impala back to Cordesville while Lawton and I rode in the back of the Peterbilt with his father. Before we left the two-crossroads town, Lawton's father, who was the only white man in the county who wore a bracelet and was thereby trusted by few, pulled into the Miss Cue pool hall for the cup of coffee he said he could not drive the big rig without. Lawton and I sat in the cab of the truck, and through the window with the Falstaff neon sign, could see him sitting at the bar talking to a waitress. Through the gray twilight, we watched her climb onto the stool beside Josh and cross her legs, revealing fishnet stockings with the black seam running up her calves like shrimps' backs that most people call a vein but is really their intestines. I thought about how seeing someone in a restaurant de-veining shrimp was a sure sign of Up Country-ness. But Lawton read something else going on at the bar. His father returned to the truck with his coffee in a paper cup with the little folding handles and told dirty jokes on the ride back that had me howling. Lawton was silent the whole way home.

Hog Heaven was empty except for the waitress smoking on a stool at the kitchen's serving window and the fat-jowled cook on the other side. The dining area was one big room filled with alternating aromas: slightly burnt french fry grease, a sweet-tart scent that was probably the barbeque sauce, oil-cloth table covers, and something fruity, peachy even, that gave me the feeling you have when you hear a corny punch line. Through the little speakers on the shelves that also held all manner of porcelain pigs and bottles of Hog Heaven BBQ Sauce, Regular and High Test Fiery!, came Don Williams singing "Amanda." The cook smiled, waved a fat hand, and gave us an "Evening, boys" as the waitress set her cigarette in the ashtray and came to greet us.

She hiked up her checkered, tablecloth-matching skirt with her right elbow while reaching behind her ear with her left hand to pull out a pencil. I caught the scent of her hairspray—sparkly and sad. "Good evening," she said. Her teeth bucked a little, so I could not be sure if she was smiling. "Y'all having a late—?"

"Do you have pork cooked with mustard sauce and hickory wood?" Grossman blurted as he struggled out of his parka. The question was an example of his amazing memory. About three years before, he had overheard an argument I had with the Texan historian in which I defended the virtues of cooking a hog over coals from the mighty hickory as opposed to a cow over the scrawny mesquite. I also praised South Carolina mustard-based barbeque sauce over what is indistinguishable from ketchup everywhere else. My argument put me in an odd position: For ethical reasons, I had long since given up meat-eating (mammals, that is; I still ate fowl and fish), but I could not shake the need to defend this regional accomplishment, which was as sensible as having pride that the Civil War had started in your state. This contradiction was not lost on the Texan, who won the argument in one fell swoop: "What does a vegetarian know about barbeque?"

"Is there any other kind, sugar?" the waitress asked. "Skeeter," her name tag read, had a lazy left eye that might have been glass and looked as if it were winking. She was probably in her early thirties—about my age—but she had no doubt lived harder, been up more nights, and looked a decade older.

Grossman, not used to such familiar address, blushed and jotted something in his little notebook. Skeeter led us to the table nearest the serving window, where she could hand us our plates with a mere pivot on the stool, and verbally ran down Hog Heaven's specialized fare instead of offering menus.

"The plate comes with rice and hash, cole slaw, light bread, and tea. Or you could have the sandwich with onion rings or French fried potatoes." She seemed to look at both of us at once.

"Don't forget that beefalo," came the cook's nasal voice from the back.

"Oh, yeah, it's new," Skeeter said. "Plate or sandwich."

I ordered a pork plate for Grossman and a side of onion rings for me. I saved Grossman the usual Northerner's surprise at receiving iced tea when thinking that "tea" means hot tea. Skeeter went back to her cigarette and chatted with the cook, whom I guessed to be the owner, about someone named Etch, who, as best I could tell, could not get *into* jail. Alan Jackson was singing "Here in the Real World." Skeeter gave us an across-the-shoulder "Be up in a minute." Her bad eye floundered over. Grossman blushed.

"What's with you?" I said.

"Greazy," he said, "she's *looking* at me." This was a first—Grossman showing some sort of sexual, though misdirected, awareness.

"For Godsake, Saul, she wasn't giving you the eye. She has something wrong with it. But the important question is, are you attracted to her?" I felt like a teenager about to give nookie advice to a hapless, pimply-faced kid brother. Grossman was not ugly, as best I could judge such things. He looked to me like a sawed-off Charlie Callas but for that ridiculous beard—the one vestige of his ultra-Orthodox boyhood.

"Here you go," Skeeter said, setting the plates and glasses down in front of us with a stylish ease that at once spoke professional confidence as well as impoverishment of aspiration. The barbeque had a powerful vinegar and pepper—red and black—smell. Skeeter must have sensed Grossman's lack of table manners.

"Now don't be spilling that on that your shirt, sweetie. Hard to wash out." She wrist-popped open a cloth napkin and stuffed it into his collar. "There you go, sugar."

Grossman could hardly hold his fork.

"Easy," I said. "She was just being nice." He ate with his usual carelessness, although it was a bit more pronounced due to his tremors.

"How y'all this evening?" said the cook/owner, now standing by the table. He smelled lemony as he pulled up a chair from the next table, turned it around backwards, straddled it with massive thighs, and crossed his fleshy forearms on the back. "Monroe Little. Glad y'all stopped in. But I tell you, you made a mistake not trying that beefalo." He wiped his forehead with a paper towel.

Grossman gave me a desperate look for help.

"Pleased to meet you, Monroe Little," I said, shaking his hand. "I'm Legare Hume, and this is Saul Grossman. You make a good onion ring." He did—the fat kind, no more than four or five fitting into the paper basket they came in. "Saul here has never had *good* barbeque before. I think we're putting some hair on his chest tonight."

Monroe reared back and guffawed. "It'll do that now! Ain't nothing in this *world* like good barbeque. Folks said I was crazy to try and improve on it, but I think this beefalo thing is going to be the trick."

"What's beefalo?" Grossman asked.

"Cross of a cow and a buffalo. They's a fellow over around Moncks Corner supplies it to me. It ain't nothin' but good."

This could mean only that Monroe Little had made a bad investment in the beefalo industry. He could recoup some loss with each plate of the misbegotten meat.

"Is that Blease Wright?" I said. I had not thought of him in over twenty years, but I remembered my father pointing out the bison each time we rode by Wright's farm on the way to visit my cousins on the other side of Lake Moultrie in Cross.

"That's him. Made him a millionaire. Ships it all over the world. Them Japanese eats it on spaghetti. Y'all boys from around there, knowing Blease Wright and all?"

"That's where I grew up. Saul's from New York."

"No joke?" He turned to Grossman. "I been up that way. Dadblame *big*-ass city! Had to go to my son's wedding when he married a Jew girl from up yonder. In the Navy together. Ain't that the beatingest thing? Sailed around the *world* to come back and marry a Jew girl from New York City. She turnt *him* Jew—wears one of them little hats and grew him a beard, just like yourn. Like to kilt his mother. The church says a prayer for him every Sunday morning, but it ain't done no good so far."

Grossman's obtuseness paid off this time. He had no idea that everyone else would have expected him to be offended. He finished up his food and began his usual teeth-picking. He labored at a molar, extracted a speck of food, pulled his glasses a couple of inches from his face, and squinted as if examining a diamond for flaws.

"I'm here to tell you," Little said, "you never know what to think. Who in this world woulda thought to breed a cow and a buffalo? And I never in my life woulda thought that I would get me a Jew daughter-in-law and, hey, a Jew son even. They ain't but one thing I know is true—people's got to eat. That's how I've been right chere for eighteen year now."

Grossman wiped the morsel onto his sweater and cleared his throat. I could tell his attention had been caught by Little's unwitting epistemological dictate about only one true thing. I had to jump in before Grossman got started.

"You got that right, Monroe," I said with exaggerated head-nodding. "You can't be sure of nothing."

Skeeter returned to the table. "How about some pecan pie?"

I smiled to hear the proper pronunciation of *pee*-can, but Grossman went into his swoon again. Just as a customer entered, I answered "no thanks" for both of us, and Monroe Little had to take his leave.

"Y'all boys come and see us again," he said, puffing as he rose from the chair.

I paid for the meal, left a respectable tip, and went into the bathroom to check the bandage on my head. Conway Twitty was singing "You've Never Been This Far Before" when I returned to find Skeeter standing at the table and handing Grossman something on a small paper dish wrapped in a napkin.

"Why don't you take some pie, sugar? You look like you could use a piece."

I stood agape. She smiled at me as she turned away, knowing that later I would have to explain the encounter to my "slow on the uptake" friend. So the little bugger was right—she *had* been giving him the eye! I had never seen, or at least never noticed, any woman paying sexual attention to Grossman—all 5'5", 140 pounds of him. When we unwrapped the pie—I smelled the Kayro syrup—in the car, we found a telephone number on the napkin.

"Saul, we don't have to get to Charleston right this minute."

"What do you mean?"

"Godamighty. I *mean* we could go have a beer and shoot some pool for a while, and then you could call that number." Was that old pool hall Miss Cue still around?

"Why would I do that?"

"*Je*sus, Saul. What did she have to do, write that on a plate, too? Listen to me. God knows I thought you were imagining it, but that woman in there—Skeeter—was in fact giving you the eye just as you suspected. That woman—Skeeter—very possibly wants to screw you. I'm saying we can hang around at a bar tonight while you occasionally call that phone number the woman in question wrote on that napkin for you. Sooner or later, said woman will get home from work and answer the phone, and then we can go to her, Skeeter's, house, where I'll sit on the couch and watch TV while you get some pussy. Now, how does that sound to you?"

"But we need to get to Charleston, Greazy. It's late." He cranked the car.

"Jesus Harold cabinet-maker Christ on a rubber-fucking *crutch*!" That was my older brother Lucian's favorite way of cussing. We were churchy kids, but while I never cussed, I delighted in his creative oath-making. Sitting there in the Volvo with a twenty-some-year-old virgin savant, the oath seemed appropriate. My forehead was pounding. I took a few deep breaths as I dug my Goody's powders from my pocket. "You're right. Let's hit the road. Philosophy calls."

Grossman smiled. "That barbeque was delicious. Let's stop here again on the way back."

I knew I might never uncover my original motives for taking this trip, but I had been presented with one that was at least as noble—to get Saul Grossman laid, if I did not kill him first.

༄

We pulled out of the gravel parking lot back onto US 17. I needed something to wash down the Goody's powders, and just across the road was a Citgo station with a sign in the window announcing Blenheim's—pronounced blen-ums—Ginger Ale. I had not seen that peppery stuff in years. When I was a kid, the ability to slug a bottle's worth of the impossible drink was a test of manhood attempted only after you had braved the 180-proof stumphole liquor from a Mason jar trial. I directed Grossman to the station. He pointed and said, "Isn't that your truck?"

The Hume Shipping truck hauling the human cargo we had seen earlier in the day sat by the diesel pump. How was it that its pace along the Interstate had been as slow as ours? One of the white guys was pumping gas while the other, the one whose pistol I had noticed, walked towards the station. He looked about 6' 2", two-fifty with a textbook heart-attack-by-fifty gut, and wore a wide-brimmed state trooper-style hat. As he passed the Volvo, he squinted through the windshield and hesitated for a heartbeat. He suggested a nod and continued inside.

"Forget it," I said to Grossman. "Let's just get the hell on." I took two Goody's powders without aid of liquid.

About two miles later, we passed the Miss Cue.

"Is that the place you told me about earlier?" Grossman asked.

"Yeah. Want to stop?"

"Why?"

"Forget it."

Highway 17, though changed over the years, had fairly well resisted the overdevelopment that had swallowed up so much of the Low Country. The stretch between I-95 and the first clear signs of Charleston's urban sprawl at John's Island was marked more by the Catawba-named rivers we crossed—Combahee, Ashepoo, Edisto—than by the towns we passed through. I thought of the ubiquitous waters of my childhood: crappy hooked in the Santee River, bass in the Big Pee Dee, shad (we cooked their roe with scrambled hen eggs) in Lynches; swimming in the Wando, skiing on Lake Moultrie (which I could not do in a jon boat), camping out by the Cooper to shoot ducks the next morning. A high percentage of those few memories worth keeping from my youth involved fresh water. Moving to St. Petersburg, I had made a trade in ablutive substance. I still fished and swam, but the salt sea demands a different comportment in the world, a different mode of being.

We crossed the Ashley River and onto the Charleston peninsula. The local joke is that the Ashley and Cooper Rivers meet here to form the Atlantic Ocean. (Spend an hour with an SOB—*South Of Broad* Street, the border between old and earned money—Charlestonian, and you'll find that this joke hardly begins to scale the heights of the native self-image.) The salty Charleston Harbor to the south, the fresh waters of the Ashley to the west and the Cooper to the east—perhaps my being here was a crossroads, or cross currents, of sorts. Maybe things really were coming together for me. Then again, maybe my head wound was more serious than I would admit.

Directing Grossman through Charleston to the Convention Center downtown was a trial indeed. By the time we arrived at midnight, the throbbing had spread from just above to my left eye to inside my left eye, which had become blurry and begun to water. I had not had a beer, and I had that mock diarrhea, either from riding all day or from eating greasy food, that never quite leads to a satisfactory purgation. We spiraled up to the sixth floor of the parking deck before finding a spot. Grossman hit the brakes each time he heard the echoes of his squealing tie rods.

The Convention Center was packed, and had a strange smell of stone, of the holly from the Christmas wreaths, mixed with some sort of fabric, maybe Herculon. A large banner hung across the lobby: "Elixir—Racing, Wrestling, Gettin' REAL!" I puzzled over it for a moment, figuring that Elixir, the trendy soft drink that claimed to be all natural, whatever that meant, must have made the inevitable move to sponsoring sports events.

I went to the bathroom to change my bandage and left Grossman to wait in line to check in. He was confused about the process, but I insisted he do this alone.

The bathroom smelled soapy and piney, the black and white checkerboard-tiled floor undoubtedly having been recently mopped. Two men at the wall urinals agreed that something was better than Darlington ever was, while a guy with a mullet haircut at the sink informed a friend that the caged matches were "pureteen stupid."

I came out and scanned the lobby and bar next door and saw some familiar faces. At the "Local Attractions" kiosk, peering at a brochure of Manigault Plantation (where for two-hundred bucks a night, you could sleep in the restored slave quarters) was Kirk Biro, University of Florida, who had just published his second book on indexicals. His first was devoted entirely to the use of the word "that." The second, which was causing much discussion, was on "this."

Sprawled on a couch and listening intensely to a big-tittied young woman as she traced something in the air with a swizzle stick was Ernest Leavengood of Stanford, a past president of the APA, who seemed to have built a reputation on power of personality alone. I had never met anyone who was altogether sure what Leavengood's specialty was or what his major publications had been.

A group of forty or more people in the bar surrounded a raised table with high stools. David McDavid and Donald Donaldson, a.k.a. the Big-Timers, the most famous living philosophers in the country, were playing tic-tac-toe. McDavid of Berkeley held a view he called unrealism, in which he claimed that reality is created by language and that literally no world existed until language appeared. His first book, *In the Beginning Was the Word*, was widely considered the culmination of the dominant philosophical approach since the analytic tradition took the "linguistic turn" in the 1920s. Donaldson of the University of Virginia propounded anti-unrealism, which he first presented in *Unspeakable Worlds*, charging that McDavid's view left us with no stable world at all, or with as many worlds as there are natural and artificial languages, each in flux. McDavid parried that, with Donaldson's theory, we float hopelessly out of touch with an unapproachable reality. The flamboyant McDavid appeared on the jacket of one of his books in medieval armor brandishing a sword and shield to slay the mythic dragon of absolute reality. In turn, Donaldson's next book featured him cowboy-clad, six-shootered, astride a Palomino, and wearing a towering hat that would have embarrassed Tom Mix.

American philosophers were split into three camps: the McDavidites, the Donaldsonians, and a remaining ten percent, which included me, and which neither tweedle-dummed nor tweedle-deed between what seemed merely flat, old beer in new philosophical cans. I found myself making the same evaluation I did as a kid handling the Chevy or Ford dispute: nothing was really at stake in the squabble. As a fourth-grader, I told a fifth-grader that there was no difference, and he beat my ass until Lucian showed up and beat his.

The rivalry did not prevent a friendship between the Big-Timers, who had taught together somewhere at the start of their careers. They met at several conferences a year, and would play hundreds of mindless games of tic-tac-toe. Every game ended in a draw, and this very algorithmic, idiot's delightfulness fascinated the Big-Timers. Their series of inconclusive matches had been the second biggest draw of the APA conferences for the past six years; the biggest was the Big-Timers' squaring off on the final afternoon of the conference. They alternated each year: one would read a paper, the other would respond. The first would rebut, the other would reply, etc. The previous year, eight hundred philosophers crammed into a five-hundred-capacity auditorium to hear the bull geese spar for two hours. The next issue of the *Proceedings of the APA* was devoted entirely to that "thrilling, historic event," with its frequent interruptions of cheers and boos from the audience and a near scuffle that resulted in a warning from the hotel management. With the possible exceptions of a professional wrestling match, in which grown men delight in watching other grown men in a homoerotic simulation of violence, I could not imagine a more despairing way to spend an afternoon.

The APA Executive Committee voted to hold this year's conference at a site with an auditorium large enough to hold the crowd and with adequate security. By contrast, the tic-tac-toe competition was conducted with the solemnity of a chess match. After each game, the onlookers would applaud softly amid "Good show"s and "Dazzling strategy"s. I watched a game, convinced that something wonderful had to be happening beneath the surface to so capture the attention of these great minds. I could not find it, but I did notice that Donaldson wore a polo shirt with the Elixir logo embroidered on the chest.

Waving from the far side of the spectator group was Sue Meierson, an acquaintance from grad school. I pointed to the front desk, indicating I would see her after I checked in. I had just walked in and already had to worry about avoiding somebody for the next three days. Meierson fancied herself a feminist aesthetician, and, in an odd sort of intellectual seduction, she delighted in luring others into showing any sort of preference for a matter of taste: favorite singer, automobile design, Plato or Aristotle, Oswald alone or patsy? Then she would proceed to show how that preference reflected male bias for "phalliform," her proud coinage.

She was still wearing her pendant necklace that looked something like a swollen coquina shell. She called it a "vulvish," another of her coinages, this one from "vulva" and "fetish." She explained that it was "a talis*wo*man radiating vaginal energy." Its magic had worked on me and, I later found out, on every other male philosophy grad student and three of the faculty members at Rutgers. Sue might have hated the phallus, but she loved a dick. She was not particularly attractive and even claimed that her plainness was a rejection of phalliformal notions of beauty. We were once hanging around after class, talking about a phenomenological theory of art, when I made a remark about penetrating through obfuscating layers of something or other, and she gave me a lecture on how men phallicize truth as penetration, while women vaginalize wisdom as opening up and taking in. She had me drooling, and we were in her apartment within minutes. If she knew anything, it was that a man can listen to a woman say "vagina" only so long before he has to see one.

I vaguely recognized more faces from other conferences—some just exuded academia and were certainly there for the APA. But I saw others who surely were not. Six huge body builders in black leather jackets and sweatpants, carrying duffel bags instead of suitcases, stood near the elevators and listened to a designer-suited, briefcased man sketching something on a clipboard. A man with "Dale Earnhardt #3 Forever" on the back of his jacket and "NASCAR" on his webbed cap shuffled up to the giants and appeared to get autographs. The racing fan returned to a table in the lounge, where his companions scrutinized the document, which looked like a menu, with great and drunken interest.

I looked towards Grossman to signal him I was going to get a beer (at the opposite end of the bar from Meierson) and saw him motioning frantically for me to come to the desk.

"No reservation."

"They lost it?"

The little desk clerk's jerky eyes darted towards me and back to his computer screen. "We had to give it away, sir—no hold on it."

"Grossman, you didn't hold it with your credit card?"

"I don't have a credit card."

I should have guessed. I turned back to the desk clerk. "You don't have another room?"

"I'm sorry, sir. We're capacitied."

Capacitied? I had never heard the word. "Can you call another hotel for us?"

"Ordinarily I would be happy to, sir, but there's a line of people *with* reservations waiting behind you, and I need to check them in." He heard my snarl and darted his eyes at me again. "Here, you can use my phone, and here's my list of numbers for all the hotels in town."

I took the list from him and picked up the telephone receiver.

"The first page is all downtown hotels," he said, "but there's no use calling them, what with Armageddon and the race and all."

"Armageddon?"

He raised an eyebrow at me. "The big wrestling tournament—world championships."

Through my tear-blurred left eye, I could see Grossman smiling.

"What the hell is so funny?"

"We *could* stay with your family."

The urge to smash the receiver into Grossman's grin—I had even tensed my shoulder in an infinitesimal start of a back swing—was just slightly weaker than the pain in my forehead. I leaned against the desk, rubbed my head, and glanced up to see another bodybuilder, this one with the kind of flattened nose that comes only from having been broken several times, standing in line beside me. His wink immediately conveyed eager anticipation to see me deck Grossman and a promise to do the same to me if I did. A greater fear at that instant was that he would discover the true and pissant origin of my head wound. He would inform everyone else within earshot, with his considerable baritone, that a woman had plated me in the head. I realized that he and the other mesomorphs were professional wrestlers attending the match the desk clerk had mentioned. But I had to do something about toothy Grossman.

"Shut up," I told him.

Despite repeated rejections, I dialed all the numbers with Sisyphusean resolve. No, that was not it. Camus's hero does not rebel in hopes of changing his state; his nobility, his self-created meaning, comes from the rebellion itself. I was just desperate for a hotel room. *Camus*: Accept the fundamental absurdity of life and make it your own. *Me*: Bitch and whine every minute of your life. Dread set in. *Kierkegaard*: Only in dread can a truly authentic and self-creating choice be made. *Me*: I don't need this shit. It seems like everything is against me. *Sartre*: Affirming facticity at the expense of transcendence constitutes bad faith. *Me*: Slam down the receiver, give up, and cuss myself for expecting anything more.

I pulled Grossman to a nearby couch.

"We are going to stay with my family, but you must abide by rules." He hugged me. "What the hell's wrong with you?"

"I'm happy, Greazy."

"Rule number one: *Never* hug me again. Rule number two: Tell my folks any lie I instruct you to tell, beginning with this one. We planned to stay with them all along. Got it? My mother will see it as a Christmas surprise. You go along with it, OK?"

"OK. A surprise." He wrote in his notebook.

"Next, Tally is sick and could not come."

"What does she have?"

"Good, you're catching on. Strep throat—very contagious."

"This is fun." In his giddiness, he bounced his legs up and down so fast I thought he would pee in his corduroys.

"Finally, as for my bandage, I slipped in the bathroom and hit my head on the sink."

"But that's not a lie, Greazy. That's what you told me this

morning."

"I know. I just wanted to make sure you remembered. We'll go there now, spend the night, then drive back here in the morning. As soon as we've presented our papers, we'll head back to St. Pete."

"But Christmas is the twenty-fifth. Our papers are both the day after tomorrow—the twenty-first. If you're here for a Christmas surprise, then we'll be leaving too early—"

"All right, goddamnit! I'll think of shomething." I had slurred the "s" in "something" and figured it was from being tired, and from praying my forehead would fall off. I tore open three Goody's powders, swallowed them without water, and glanced toward Old Flat Nose. Was he man enough to do the same?

"One last thing," I said. "Don't tell them you're Jewish. Just shay you're Orthodox. At most, shomebody may have heard of Greek Orthodox and think that's what you are."

Earnhardt and his NASCAR buddies walked by us and to the elevators. They were four men in their thirties or forties, wearing shiny nylon, elastic-waist jackets embroidered with cars and checkered flags and names of their favorite drivers. They threw their red-faced heads back when they laughed their deep, cleansing laughs. They called each other "Hoss" and "Bo" and "Peckerhead." They were men away from home without their women, to whom they would soon return to hear how much they were missed. They ate and drank too much. They laughed too loudly. They worked hard during the day. They watched the sports channel at night. They loved their children. They were exactly as they appeared to be. They could be my cousins, uncles, or brothers, and I was as foreign to them as the Buddha.

Grossman giggled all the way to the Volvo as I tried to make sense of this convergence of professional wrestlers, stock car drivers, and philosophers. The near-solstice air was warm even for Charleston, and carried the spongy fragrance of pluff mud—oysters, green and weedy, and a touch of hog pen. At the top of the parking deck, I got that feeling of remembering where you put something you'd forgotten you'd lost.

The Hydra constellation was stretching up from the horizon. Down below glowed St. Michael's steeple and the soft lights of the beautiful, historic city.

I thought I would vomit.

THREE
Rationalism v. Empiricism

Whether or not God exists would make no difference to my sorry life. At least that had been the most recent of my theological positions until that day. Before college, the only challenge I had ever had to my Pentecostal militancy was my Uncle Rembert's declaration that he had never thought about God "one way or t'other."

"But don't you care about your soul?" I had asked.

"I don't know nothing about no soul," he said between swallows of Brass Monkey on a back porch that shaded twelve bad dogs. I would ride my bicycle to his place during the summer to make a few dollars cropping tobacco, and then have to wait at the gate of the seven-foot chain link fence while he called off the hellhounds.

I tried another tactic. "How do you think it all got here, then? Something had to create the world."

"I wa'n't around when it happent, so I don't know. And you sho as hell wa'n't neither."

My Pentecostal training had prepared me for a world filled with Satan's helpers—atheists, false prophets, would-be messiahs, pope-worshipping Catholics, Christ-killing Jews, communists, rich people—not indifference. But Rembert did not exactly lack concern; he was the ultimate empiricist, calling them, like an umpire (umpiricist!), as he saw them. Could he really be content with a reality that extended no farther than the range of his sensory experience? Of course, neither I nor anyone else had ever seen God, but reason could establish his existence, right?

As an undergraduate, I came to understand that my belief in God had nothing to do with reason. After two philosophy courses, one sociology, and most damagingly, one on the history of Christianity, I was convinced I had simply been spoon-fed theological pabulum from the plates of pew-jumpers, foot-washers, snake-handlers, and demon out-casters. I decided to purge myself of that divine diet and became a vengeful atheist, but I was a living ironic freak, a Hazel Motes in the flesh, more haunted by the ghost of the dead God than ever possessed by a living one.

In grad school, I abandoned my efforts to shoo the God-fly from bothering my intellectual abode. He no longer stalked me, no longer spooked me in the dark corners of my mind. I dismissed my religious obsession as quaint, as did my professors and fellow grad students. I focused instead on phenomenology, Heidegger, Merleau-Ponty, and William James, trading interest in the ground of being for excavation of the structures of experience. The existence of God became supremely uninteresting to me; to say that God did not exist was no more and no less meaningful than to say the rascal did.

Then came the ontological argument. I first encountered Hartley's version in a textbook I'd considered using in my philosophy of religion class. The argument had lurked in the dusty halls of the history of philosophy for nearly a thousand years and would not vacate. I was intrigued with what seemed a puzzle, like the old story about the bellhop who has to split a five dollar refund from a thirty dollar charge among three guests but pockets two bucks so that the guests seem to have paid nine dollars each. But their twenty-seven plus the bellhop's two makes only twenty-nine, so, where is the other dollar? You are hoodwinked, until you see that the two should be included in the twenty-seven that the guests have already paid, to which you add the three in *their* pockets. Hartley had not revived the old ruse but had pinned its eyes open and propped it up in the chair to look alive and well. In time, someone would discover the gimmick.

Immediately prior to the flying plate attack, however, the argument seemed sound to me. I had maintained, as most philosophers did, that even if the argument worked logically, that would say something only about the *argument* and its formal properties but nothing at all about God, existence or otherwise. But I was almost willing to change my mind, and that contributed to my decision to go to the conference and talk this over with some other philosophers. Maybe somebody could straighten me out.

That I was later in a raggy Volvo with a savant who does not own a credit card and thereby cannot reserve his hotel room, riding through the Hell Hole Swamp region of the Francis Marion National Forest to my parent's house at one a.m., seemed to be about as much evidence against the existence of God—a minimally benevolent one at any rate—as anyone could muster.

We took the "back way" through Mount Pleasant to SC 41—my revenge on Grossman. I figured that going over the Cooper River Bridge would give him a conniption. It did. I regretted this little scheme about halfway up when he threatened to turn around and go back against traffic. I coaxed him through it, and he hummed a monotone to himself for the next five minutes. Forty-one from Wando to Huger (another Huguenotism, pronounced hew-jee) and 402 to Cordesville are dark, lightly-driven roads that induced Grossman to ask me twice what we would do if the car "malfunctioned." Still feeling vengeful, I told him we would have to walk, trying not to draw the suspicion of ever-vigilant-for-revenuers, inbred moonshiners who, despite being my kin, would be apt to shoot us and deposit our bodies in the swamp with no hope of recovery.

Grossman worried even more, but the possibility was not that far-fetched. My great-uncle Vander had been a moonshiner, and his brother-in-law, a Metts, revived an old feud. Generations earlier, either a Hume or a Metts, depending upon who told the story, had killed the other's mule, and a judge ruled that the mule-killer's *family* had to compensate the killed-mule family. A dispute over who had paid whom lasted a few decades but was virtually forgotten until Vander and his brother-in-law fought over a dog swap. The Metts guy accused Vander of typical Hume crookedness and, by the way, where was that money for the mule? Vander whipped Metts down the road with a leather cow leader, and for revenge, Metts informed the Treasury Department about Vander's liquor-making business. The feds busted up the still, and Vander was sentenced to a year and a day in jail. When he was released four months later, he went home to get a shotgun and then drove his wagon to the Metts guy's house and shot him dead.

"Was he convicted of murder?" Grossman asked.

"The story always ends there, with no explanation of how Uncle Vander avoided arrest. I reckon a moonshiner killing an informant is simply understood as fit and proper."

I had no instructions from Circe on my way to Erebus, no sheep to bleed into a votive pit for the ghosts, no Tiresias getting the first gulp in return for a vision of what awaited me. I had Grossman. Memories buzzed me like gnats or flitting shades eager for a sanguine swallow, and I figured the best way to swat them off or appease them was to speak them, like demons that flee a body when their names are called. So we drove deeper into the swamp, and I told Grossman stories about the landmarks, interspersing the bios of family members he would soon meet.

The last time I traveled that route was when I took my fraternity brothers camping for Brother Mann Night, the final initiation rite for our pledges. Adam Mann was a fictional frat member. Having broken his oath and told our secrets to civilians, he had to be murdered by his frat brothers. Hapless pledges, after hours of blindfolded humiliation, were told that their initiation would be consummated by eating a morsel of Mann's preserved flesh—in fact, a pickled chicken liver made rank with asafetida. Every member of our chapter for fifty years had swallowed this lie and gladly opted for cannibalism rather than risk blackballing. To amplify the indignity, the brothers removed the pledge's blindfold, and instead of heaping upon him the congratulations he expected, told him that moments before, all the other pledges had refused the human flesh and thereby proven themselves, unlike him, men of dignity and worthy of membership. Like every member before him, he would fall to his knees and cry. His brothers would begin to laugh, and after a few seconds of bewilderment, he would recognize the subterfuge and leap up to tell them how he loved them to death.

We camped near Bullhead Chapel, claiming that its tiny graveyard once had held Adam Mann's body. We cleaned the beer cans out of an open, ground-level tomb, stripped the pledges to their drawers, and crammed them inside with the instruction to be silent. Leaving them to sit for four dark hours anticipating unspeakable torture while the rest of us slipped back to camp to drink beer was the cruelest and therefore best initiation we could imagine.

When we returned with the jar of chicken livers, the pledges were gone. We got to camp, only to be met by Mutt Furman, the magistrate who lived nearby and attended Sunday services at Bullhead Chapel. He took us to the county jail to join the pledges, who sat bug-eyed, wondering if this was part of the initiation. The next morning, Sheriff Gamewell Umphlett took us back to the chapel. (At the age of 16, I had taken his daughter to the county fair once. She wanted to go to the hooch show, and the ticket guy barred me, but let Martha in. She emerged fifteen minutes later with her blue-black hair un-pony-tailed with a boy I recognized as having dropped out from my high school the year before, and she told me she would see me later. I thought she meant later that night. She did not.) In return for not informing our parents, Umphlett sentenced us to sling-blading weeds, raking leaves, piling brush and fallen limbs onto the back of the flatbed truck we had just ridden on, dusting the oak pews, and sweeping the pine floors of the chapel. Harley Tanner even knelt at the little altar and whispered a prayer.

Umphlett gave us some ice water from his cooler and told us to study hard and keep out of trouble. We thanked him; we were not sure for what. We stood together, looked at our work, and sang the fraternity song. We had been pulled together in some more complete way than chicken livers could ever do.

A week later, I quit the fraternity.

Like other newcomers to rural Berkeley County, Grossman was surprised to pass a monastery in the middle of peckerwood habitat.

"Is that how the town got its name?" he asked.

"No. There's a 'c' in Moncks Corner, named for a Thomash Monck who owned a trading post there in the colonial days."

"It seems highly coincidental."

"Shome things you just can't help."

Cainhoy Abbey, once a rice plantation on the reverse curve of a Wadboo Branch that emptied into the Cooper River, was donated to the Cistercians in the 1930s. A dozen or so monks lived on the three thousand acres that included an egg farm and flower gardens, which they perpetually weeded and trimmed. The only contact most locals had with the hooded men was the gray-bearded liaison abbot who sold you the freshest, brownest eggs around. The public was invited to sunrise masses each Sunday, and the county's three or four Catholic families, who usually went to Charleston for church, sometimes took them up on it.

I was familiar with the abbey because the Old Man, Lucian, and I belonged to the Cainhoy Huntsmen's Club, where we spent every Saturday and holiday from August to January. Methodical precision was the hunter's advantage: We encircled an area, released two or three packs of hounds, and waited at our stands for the dogs to "jump" a deer and chase it out. The hunt ended when (1) someone killed a buck, (2) someone shot at but missed a buck, costing the hunter his shirt-tail and some manhood, (3) the dogs jumped an illegal-to-shoot doe, or (4) the dogs gave up from lack of quarry. In cases (2) and (3), the hunters would try to catch the dogs so the chase would not spill out of the designated area, but sometimes the dogs would evade catchers and cross Wadboo Road into the abbey. Somehow, the monks would catch the dogs and tie them to the bell post by the time a hunter arrived to retrieve them.

I once determined to find out what sort of power the woolen-cloaked and silence-vowed celibates held over deer dogs. A pack ran a doe towards Wadboo Road, and I jumped into the Old Man's pickup (at thirteen, the dirt roads of the hunting club were all I was allowed to drive) and went to where I could have cut them off. Instead, I let them get by while I snuck into the abbey's woods. Squatting behind a thick cypress near the store, hearing the dogs get closer, and hoping to glimpse the monks in action, I felt a hand on my shoulder, gasped, and jumped up to see a young monk with a long, sad face. I ran, so frightened that I left my sixteen gauge Browning.

Shorty Cumbee brought back the dogs and my gun, which had been unloaded and leaned against the bell post. I offered no explanation. Lucian teased me for years about letting the candy-ass monks take my gun from me. I never found out how they caught the dogs, but the next morning, I rode my bike through the gray October dawn seven miles to the abbey for their mass. The long-faced monk nodded at me as I went in to sip the wine from the goblet and eat the little white host cracker, which was odd to someone used to the Pentecostals' once-a-year Dixie cupful of grape juice and a thumb-sized hunk of light bread. I got home before I was missed and in time to get ready for church.

I never went back to Cainhoy Abbey, but even now I can't scramble an egg without seeing the serene countenance of that speechless young monk who spooked me in the cypresses.

༶

We came to the railroad tracks two miles from my parents' house, and I had Grossman stop.

"Pull up onto the tracks, cut off the lights, and turn off the engine."

"Why?"

"The Cordesville Light." I rolled down the window and smelled the creosote in the railroad ties and something metallic—the rails?—that seemed wistful, like hearing strangers tell each other goodbye. "Local legend says a woman went out one night with a lantern looking for her husband. A train hit her, but her ghost still walks the tracks. Shometimes you can see the lantern."

"Where had her husband gone?"

"The legend doesn't say. Probably with another woman."

"Superstition."

Versions of this story abound across the country, but nearly everyone swears to have seen it. Rational types say it's swamp gas—whatever that is, maybe like St. Elmo's Fire. Others say it's moonlight reflecting off the rails. Some maintain that no one ever saw anything—that all were victims of self-deception. Whatever the real explanation, the ghost story proved a great way to lure a date out onto a dark road. The girls always displayed the proper terror, throwing their arms around you with an "Oh, Lordy!" or else they were quicker than we thought and welcomed their roles in the stratagem.

As a child, I would lie in bed and listen to the rumble of the Seaboard Coast Line. One still night, without cricket chirp or whippoorwill hoot, I heard the whistle approaching, but this time it blew continuously. I heard the crash. An hour later, we were in the hospital praying for Lucian to survive. The Old Man, typically stoic, sat smoking while Mama sobbed into her ever-present tissues. Willie held Mama's hand and kept asking, "What was that dumbass *doing* on the railroad track?" to which Mama would respond, "Willa Jean, don't talk so ugly."

The girl who had been in the truck with Lucian died. He survived with a limp, loss of hearing in his right ear, and brain damage that left him with a peculiar speech deficit. He got his prepositions and pronouns mixed up so that "He placed the snake into my hand" might come out "It placed the snake out of your hand." But he could write perfectly normally. The worst result was not quite depression but better described as a loss of ambition. He drifted from job to job, taking a few college courses, mostly literature, and writing thirty-nine long letters of apology to his dead girlfriend's family.

Years after the accident, when I was at the College of (now University of) Charleston, he sent me a letter explaining that his brush with death had finally made sense to him. He had come to understand "life's arbitrariness, its ultimate contingency. Knowing that I do not <u>have</u> to be alive and therefore have nothing to lose has been the most liberating event of my life." He telephoned to make sure I got the letter and made me swear never to mention it to Mama. Though we spoke for only a minute, he told me about his new lease on life and sounded happier than I had heard him in years.

Later that night, he parked his truck beside the road near the railroad crossing, walked out onto the tracks, and waited for the train.

At the graveside service where we buried what was found of Lucian, I brought my guitar intending to sing "I Am Bound For the Promised Land" as Mama wanted. But at the last second, I decided to do "Mystery Train." Lucian loved the Band's version of it, but only Willie agreed with me on its appropriateness. The Old Man stared vise-jawed at me while Mama wailed like a banshee. She would not speak the rest of the day.

"Greazy, look over there." Grossman pointed down his side of the tracks.

"Shon of a bitch, a light." Then we heard the train whistle. "Crank up and get on out of here, Saul." I opened the car door. "I'll shtay here on the tracks and you go on."

"What? Greazy, the train—"

"I'm just shitting you." I closed the door. "Let's go."

༄

The gnat-naming exorcism did not work. Rather than scare them off, calling out those memories seemed to pump them up to the size of blowflies swarming swollen roadkill along any given half mile of the highway shoulder. Speaking of them did, however, dull them some, like beekeeper's smoke, and temper my dread as we neared the underworld.

As we turned off 402, I figured that neither Grossman nor his Volvo had ever been on a dirt road. This one was barely wide enough for two vehicles to pass without sliding into the ditches that, during summer and fall, were lined with wild grapes that I suppose are muscadines or scuppernongs—we called them bullaces—blackberries that we called briarberries, and passionflower vines with fruit we called maypops. The grapes had thick, bitter skins you could mash between your fingers, causing the sweet pulp inside to pop out into your mouth to be swallowed, seeds and all, without chewing. Mama made grape pies from them, but she believed that snakes fed on the briarberries and forbade our picking them. We did not obey, and when purple fingers and lips betrayed us, she would whip us with her favored instrument, the wire end of the fly swatter. The maypops had leathery skin like turtle eggs, into which we pushed toothpicks for arms and legs, making little maypop people. With their skinny limbs radiating from turgid torsos, they looked like most of my tick-shaped aunts. Even better were the slightly sour flesh sacs enveloping their many slippery black seeds. I found nothing else that tasted quite like them until I moved to Florida, had my first mango, and became hooked on tropical fruit.

The road serpentined unlit through the sweetgums and cypresses for about two miles until it dead-ended at Drowned ("drowneded" to locals) Horse Creek. Everyone called the road, despite the county's not planting a sign to mark it, Drowned(ed) Horse Cut, and three hundred yards off Highway 402 was my parents' limestone gravel driveway, a hundred yards long and one vehicle wide. Halfway down the drive, the blueticks and walkers in the dog pens out back announced our intrusion. The mercury vapor lamp on the service pole near the pump house cast a dull, bluish light across the side yard. I could see the outline of the old dog pens, out of use since the Old Man built his more efficient above-ground versions twenty years before. The rickety old pens standing in the darkness seemed to host vague, balloon-like shapes—the guineas. I was glad to see that descendants of the original two given me still roosted there.

As a teen, I squirrel-hunted often, and partly out of charity but more because I hated cleaning the damn rodents, I would take my kill to Mr. Altoon, an old black man whose last name I never knew. He lived with his common-law wife in the woods off a path you more sensed than saw. We had a deal: in return for cleaning them, he kept half of the eight or ten I brought. The first time I delivered the squirrels, Miss

Plasenda (she told Mama that, when she was born, her mother heard the doctor say "Let me have a look at that Plasenda") asked if I wanted the heads on them, and I answered that I did not. Just as I thought my answer might cause them extra work, she announced, "We'll mush 'em for you, too." Decorum seemed to demand that I not ask her to explain the procedure, and when I returned a couple of hours later not knowing what to expect, they gave me the perfectly cleaned and, I supposed, mushed squirrels. As I left with my half, they grinned, apparently convinced they had got the better end of the deal.

I once took them eight squirrels and two rabbits. Mr. Altoon and Miss Plasenda were so grateful and probably sick of squirrel that they repaid me with two guinea fowl in a plastic laundry basket with a sheet of cardboard on top. I put them into the old dog pens, and after I later removed the doors from the hinges so that the guineas could come and go as they pleased, they and their offspring continued to live there.

A fyce wandered into the pen and deposited her puppies. I took my cousins DeWayne and Purvis to see them, and the bitch snapped the tip off Purvis's left ear lobe. Purvis was a bona fide shitass, and he cracked her on the head with his stainless steel flashlight ordered from the Old Man's store catalogue, and the dog crumbled up dead. I nursed the puppies with a baby bottle, and seven out of eight survived. But the remarkable thing was that the guineas adopted them. The puppies followed the birds around, and when they got bigger, would scramble up the pen posts to sleep on top with the roosting guineas. The Old Man finally told me I had to get rid of the sooners or he would knock them in the head with a *ball peen hammer*, and I believe more out of sympathy for me than anything else, Rembert took them. All seven slept off the ground—on a fuel drum, tractor, or truck bed—until they were too old and had to join the other curs under the porch.

My parents' house was a façade, a palimpsest that veiled a doublewide trailer beneath. I grew up in a singlewide, where Lucian and I slept on bunk beds in one room and Willie had her own in another. The year I went to college, the Old Man bought the double. He and Uncle Spessard bricked around the bottom to hide the undergirdings and ductwork. For years, the Old Man would not remove the tires from underneath, despite repeated offers from Pooky Peagler, owner of Moncks Corner Tire & Brake. He stressed that the property tax increased with a "permanent dwelling structure," which a wheeled mobile home was not. By the time he gave in to Mama's nagging and pulled them off, Peagler no longer wanted the tires, so the Old Man cut them in half, painted them white, and stuck them in the raked and swept yard in front of the house as walkway borders. Two he somehow turned inside out and scalloped to become planters for Mama's bougainvillea and hen-and-bitty. He also built a screened-in porch that stretched across the front, added vinyl siding, and stuck a satellite dish on the roof on the opposite end of the lightning rod he was so proud of locating, since "you can't hardly find nobody what even makes 'em no more."

We stepped from the car, and the porch light flicked on. In the dry night air, a hint of freshly cut pine mingled with the dog from the pens and something else that smelled like snakes. The screen door opened, and the Old Man, in his boxer shorts, squinted into the night.

"Well, I'll be John Brown," he said.

Mama stuck her head out the door. She began to cry. "He's come home for Christmas."

༶

I hoped I had properly briefed Grossman about whom he would likely meet on this bastard leg of the trip. I had told him about the Old Man, born Phillip Pledger Hume in Macedonia, nine miles away from his present home in Cordesville, the sixth of eight—or seven, depending on whether you counted Chalmers—children born to Beulah Burbage and Talmadge Kyper Hume. I recall little of Grandma Beulah, but I remember her fondness for sitting on the porch sucking on a spoonful of snuff, the tiny spoon included in what looked like a miniature coffee can. Chewing tobacco for men tended towards masculine names: Bull of the Woods, Red Man, Brown Mule. A precursor to Virginia Slims, women's snuff was branded Rosebud, Taste of Honey, or Mammy's Best. Grandma favored Pink Lily, which gave her a perpetual sweet-sour smell and a stern look from the lump in her bottom lip. She spat into a baby food jar, which, with the label removed, was transparent, clearly revealing its contents. Since she had "the palsy," her tremors caused the jar to shake, swirling the juice that threatened to overflow and douse the unfortunate grandchild occupying her lap. Her legacy to me came from the occasional taste of the brown powder—I being the only one of the grandkids who did not, on the first sample, turn pale and fall to the floor.

While most of his siblings opted for the linthead life in the textile mill, or anything else over one of bending in the tobacco field pulling horn worms and breaking leaves, the Old Man got his Uncle Vander to co-sign a loan to buy a gun shop, thereby making the Old Man the first non-farmer and non-mill worker in the family. When he was not in his shop, he hunted, fished, tended the dozen or so hogs he kept at the far back of the property, and taught Lucian how to fiddle.

Raylene Bodiford was the oldest child of Hoke and Evangelene DuPree Bodiford of Huger. She probably would have married anyone when the Old Man asked her, if only to escape the siblings she was forced to raise while Evangelene spent her final years sinking into dementia. The following year, Mama's sister Arlene ran off at fourteen to marry Spessard Driggers, who worked at the mill for thirty-five years, then retired to spend his time carving gaunt, macabre lawn jockeys from cypress knees.

The one family member I thought Grossman would find the most inscrutable was the Old Man's brother Rembert. Despite his shady side, he was my favorite uncle, and certainly the easiest to put up with. His profanity and irreverence made him a perfect foil for the saturnine Old Man. Rembert's unlawful tendencies began in the 1960s when he heard he could avoid the draft by enrolling in college—something no one in the family had ever done. He indeed enrolled but did not attend. To Rembert's mind, the matter had been settled, but the draft board disagreed and had him arrested and sent to boot camp. He served in

Vietnam for several years until discharged, perhaps dishonorably. The Old Man said it had something to do with contraband.

Rembert was married twice and widowed at least once. The first wife drowned in Wadboo Branch when, Rembert claims, she fell from their boat while crappy fishing. Rembert met his second wife in Ocala, Florida, when he went there to buy a horse from her father. He said she left him a year later and returned, he assumed, to Ocala. Her family, however, never saw her. They had connections with the South Carolina State Law Enforcement Division (SLED), and the agents stayed on Rembert's back for years.

Rembert traveled for weeks at a time "on business," which made little sense for a tobacco farmer. When he was gone, I fed his dogs with a twenty-five pound bag of Field Trial dumped onto a sheet of tin every other day. Somehow, the sooners recognized me as their meal ticket and turned as gentle as puppies. My secondary job was to check in on Uncle Chalmers, the family retard. Half the family was unsure of, and the other half would not speak about, Chalmers's origin. What was suspected by Granddaddy Talmadge's grandchildren, yet denied by his children, was that Chalmers was Talmadge's outside child, deposited at about age three on his doorstep by a mother who refused to raise him alone when his retardation became manifest. According to rumor, the woman was Talmadge's cousin, which was believed to explain Chalmers's condition.

Chalmers was a little older than Rembert and, on every weekday of his adult life, hitched a ride into Moncks Corner to make his rounds. Some of the Cordesville residents who worked in town would pick him up in the morning and drop him off at Powell Murphy's Shell Station, where he would sit on a Coca Cola crate and have a Yoohoo and a pack of nabs before moving on to Hill's Feed and Supply to watch the farmers back their trucks up the ramp and get loaded down with heavy sacks of sweet feed and cracked corn. The other storeowners on his circuit considered Chalmers's comings and goings even more reliable a chronometer than the whistle that blew from the top of the old mill on the hour from eight to five, and they would all graciously bid him good morning as he took his long-claimed seat or lean at his favored spot, saying only his "Hey"s and "A'ight"s. After the length of time he allotted each stop, he moved on, eating his grilled cheese sandwich at precisely twelve-thirty at the Twin Pines restaurant and making it back home to Rembert's at five. But on Wednesday, he would get home hours earlier, since the town stores all closed up that day at noon, when a triply long blast from the whistle signaled mid-week. It was the only time Chalmers needed to hear it.

We also had the rumor that Chalmers had been castrated. Supposedly, he had tried to rape Grandma Beulah and was taken to a special state hospital for the procedure. The state apparently had enough twelve-year-old retarded rapists to warrant funding an institution just for their emasculation.

The best evidence I had that Chalmers's outside origin was true came at Rembert's annual Christmastime barbeque, when someone mentioned our cousin Shelia, who had disappeared for a few months to "go to another school" but returned with a three-month-old baby. Lucian, who was only about fifteen then, remarked that the family was no stranger to fooling around and its unwanted results. The Old Man's arm darted out like a snake, delivering a backhand across the mouth that knocked Lucian and his chair over and into the bed of coals Rembert was nursing to put into the barbeque pit. Lucian, who got up with his flannel shirttail smoking and his lip bleeding, went inside for a can of Miller High Life, returned right back where he had been, and drank the entire can in one gulp. I was certain Lucian had taken his last breath, but the Old Man, whose lack of expression had not altered the entire time, took another sip of his tea and asked Rembert how the coals were looking. Rembert replied that he wished he could freeze some of them to save for next year. Everyone laughed, the incident was forgotten, and Lucian took his place in the ranks of men.

Years later, after Lucian's death, Willie told me on the phone that there was more to the Old Man's reaction to Lucian's remark. At the time, she said, something was going on between Mama and the Old Man; in fact, she had reason to think the Old Man had just discovered

49

that Mama had had an affair sometime in the past, and his popping Lucian across the mouth had to do with his thinking that the remark was more an oblique reference to Mama's past than it was to Chalmers's parentage. I told Willie I would believe nearly anything about our muddied and shallow gene pool but not that Mama had seen another man. Willie said there was much more that I would not believe. I hung up on her.

Not long after wife number two's disappearance, Rembert vanished for two weeks in defiance of SLED's order not to leave the state. I was at his house when he returned, and he took me inside to show me "something what you can't be*lie*ve." He slapped down upon the kitchen table a recent issue of *National Geographic* with a cover photo of a highly adorned member of the Wodaabe tribe in Niger. "That there's a man—look at him. Would you *ever* a-thought that was nothing but a womern? Bunch of damn jungle bunnies." I read the cover story and found that Wodaabe men, as part of an elaborate courtship ritual, make themselves up to look like women. Rembert had scanned the article enough to find out where to buy his plane ticket to, but not enough to discover who his date would be. The SLED agents scrutinized Rembert's passport and hotel receipts and such. He had indeed gone to Niger, I suppose to woo a woman like the one he found so beautiful on the cover of the magazine. Swindled by makeup and beads, Rembert never again looked twice at another woman, I believe.

To these people, anything Grossman uttered was apt to be misunderstood. If he could remember to speak only when interrogated and to reply minimally, perhaps we could preclude as much as possible of the Old Man's cold-shoulder (his sense of hospitality would prevent him from shooting Grossman) and Mama's sobbing over hurt feelings. The stay would take more energy than I could work up. If Willie and her kids show up, I thought, they could provide some misdirection. They might also diffuse the tension from my collision with what Marx called the idiocy of rural life. Grossman and I would be on our way back to Florida in a couple of days.

"Legare." The Old Man offered his right hand for me to shake and patted my shoulder with his left. He had not hugged me since the day he dropped me off at the college dorm when I was a freshman, and there was an unspoken agreement between us that we did not want to face that awkwardness again. Compact and sinewy, he looked like Robert Duvall with a shock of white hair. His hand felt thin. My head was pounding.

Mama put her arms around me, and I felt the tears seep through the neck of my shirt, and smelled the Oil of Olay face cream she always applied just before bed. "You gained weight," she said, which was her way of saying that Tally was feeding me fattening and thereby healthy foods. She simply would not acknowledge that I did most of the cooking, any more than she would acknowledge that I had given up meat for ethical reasons, preferring to think it was due to the crazy notions that educated people get about what is good for them.

"Hello there, young feller," I heard the Old Man saying. His voice felt like an ice pick in my ear. He was shaking Grossman's hand as Grossman smiled nervously.

"Thish is my friend Saul Grossman. He teaches at the college, too."

"Well, come on in outen the cold," said Mama. It wasn't cold at all. "Where's Tally?"

"She has strep throat," Grossman said. "Very contagious." He looked at me, grinning like a Cheshire cat but without disappearing.

"The poor thing. She gets sick a lot, don't she?" Mama said. "Y'all want some coffee?"

"No, Ma'am," I said. "We've been on the road all day and got a philosophy conference in Charleston to get to early in the morning. So we got to hit the shack. We'll attend the conference for the next two days, then I thought we'd shtay through Christmas ... if that's all right." Nice added touch, I thought.

"What are you talking about? Sho it's all right." The Old Man smiled and pushed Grossman onto the couch and sat with him. "Don't you want some coffee, Mr. Grosser? How 'bout some pecan pie?"

Saul looked at me in horror. Maybe he was afraid he would say something that would overstep our rehearsal or feared that any offer of pecan pie carried with it a sexual invitation.

"We really have to go to shleep," I said. I looked away from the Old Man and his idiot smile. "We left early this morning, and we're wore out."

"Early this morning? It's only about eight or nine hours, ain't it?"

"Not my route," Grossman said. "If you travel—"

"We shtopped a lot." What the hell was he doing? "Shaul has colon problems." That would teach him.

"My friend Mildred Huff has the spastic colon," Mama said. Here we go. Her speciality—ailments. "She can't hardly go nowhere. Mmm, *mmm*." She looked at the floor and shook her head. She looked up again. "Legare, honey, what happent to your head?"

"He slipped in the bathroom and hit it on the sink." Grossman grinned again and even tried to wink at me. The Old Man may have noticed.

"Ish nothing, Mama. I figured Shaul could take Willie's old room." I felt short of breath, like I was struggling to remove a thick, wool sweater. I wiped my eye with the heel of my palm. A mistake.

"You talking funny," said Mama, her expertise kicking in. "Did you go to the doctor? You might be caught a concussion. Rebecca Bowers got one getting out of her car to take some peach cobbler into the fellowship hall for prayer meeting, and it knocked her plum out. Laid up for two weeks. You better get the doctor to look it."

"I'm fine. Just tired."

"All right. Let me get him a extry blanket," Mama said and went to the hall closet.

"We'll have time to visit over breakfast in the morning," the Old Man said to Grossman. "If you need anything, just holler. Make yourself at home."

"Thank you, Mr. Hume." Grossman glanced at me to make sure this comment was acceptable. He and I brought in our suitcases, then I showed him the bathroom, the towels, and such.

"I'm setting my clock for seven," I told him. "My folks will already be awake by then, but they'll let us sleep. If you wake up before me, just lie there until I come and get you."

"OK, Greazy, but I don't understand your concern. Your parents seem quite pleasant to me."

"Yes, they're very pleasant. Now brush your teeth and go to bed."

Grossman finished in the bathroom, and I was about to turn off my light when I heard Mama whispering. "Legare?"

I opened the door. She was plump and almost dwarfishly short-limbed, somewhat like Ethel Merman. Her always sagging eyebrows had drooped to give her a look of perpetual pleading. "I wanted to tell you how happy I am you came to see me." This was not easy for her to say. "I just wish Tally coulda come. I know it's long distance and all, but I'll get in touch with her tomorrow on the telephone and tell her I'm thinking of her."

"No—we dropped her off at her shister's in Lakeland. The doctor shaid she needed to spend at least a week in bed. She knew how much coming here meant to me, so she insisted I come without her. She said to tell you she loved you."

Mama smiled and shuffled off. Her bedroom scuffs scraped against the vinyl flooring as she cut through the kitchen. Not so bad, I thought. I had survived the initial encounter. I would get some sleep and make an escape as soon as possible in the morning.

※

I woke up to, or maybe was awakened by, the sharp smell of buttsmeat frying. *Another battle*: me, a non-mammal eater, in a culture in which string beans cannot even be boiled without a chunk of fatback thrown in, where squash is sliced, breaded, and fried in bacon grease, and even biscuits are made with lard. The grits might be safe, but chances are some pork grease has been dripped into them for flavor.

I glanced over at the clock—8:10. The alarm had not worked. As

I jumped up and fished a pair of sweat pants from my suitcase, I heard talking: Grossman's voice! He was alone in the kitchen with my parents. I threw on a T-shirt, then heard laughter and a number of other voices. Someone else was here.

I ran to the kitchen to find a bizarre tableau: my parents, my sister, and her two children were sitting at the table listening, and Saul Grossman was *talking*. I felt nauseated.

"So I got out of the cab and said, 'Mayor Koch, next time the coffee is on me!'" Grossman's New Yorkese rendered "coffee" as "kwah-fee," yet they all understood this punch line and reared back and haw-hawed. Even four-year-old Wynonna chirped with glee.

Willie saw me and leaped up. "Hey, Bubba!" She ran over and threw her arms around my neck and hugged me for a long time. Her hair smelled like wheat germ shampoo, like rain was coming. "Unitas and Wynonna—y'all come say 'hello' to your Uncle Greazy."

Unitas, her nine-year-old son, grinned and stuck out his hand. He could probably remember seeing my face only once or twice, but I had sent him gifts over the years and talked with him each time I, the mysterious jokester uncle from an exotic land, made my monthly phone calls to Willie. For the past couple of years, he had sent me birthday cards he had made himself. He was an exceptionally smart kid who loved puns. He liked it when I called him "U" and did a variant of the Abbott and Costello "Who's on first?" routine, confusing "U" and "you."

Rupert, Willie's ex, a grand instance of Uncle Spessard's maxim that "They's good and bad in no matter what color and no matter where you go; but they ain't nothing like Yankee trash," was from Pittsburgh, also the hometown of Johnny Unitas, whom Rupert idolized, even though Unitas had retired in 1972 when Rupert was a toddler. Rupert moved with his family to Baltimore when he was ten or eleven—a move he likened to Unitas's from the Pittsburgh Steelers to the Baltimore Colts in the '50s, "the darkest day," he said, "in the history of the Keystone State." He had Colts memorabilia all over their rented bungalow in Myrtle Beach, where he was assistant manager (his shirt said so) of one of those T-shirt shops where you select the shirt and the decal for a Rupert to iron on. Before I met Rupert, I considered Johnny Unitas the greatest quarterback of all time.

Upon first hearing that the baby had been named Unitas, Uncle Spessard had responded, "What kinda goddamn name starts with a 'u'?"

"Sheriff Umphlett's name has a 'u'," Mama said.

"Did Gamewell Umphlett or his daddy or his granddaddy pick that name? You don't pick a last name." He had her there.

"What I can't figure out is why the boy's daddy," the Old Man, who could never bring himself to call Rupert by his name, said, "keeps that iguaner setting up on his shoulder like that." But Rupert had been out of their lives for almost three years, leaving only a "u" as a legacy.

I poked a finger into Unitas's belly and called him "booger breath." He doubled over laughing and feigning pain, then cupped his hand around his mouth and said, "Listen." I bent over and he whispered, "Mr. Saul's last name is Gross Man," giggling.

I transformed into avuncular comedian. "Hello, I'm gross, man," I said, imitating Grossman's voice. "Well, I'm greazy, man," I said, answering myself, "but I don't go around bragging about it."

Unitas fell on the floor, holding his sides in hysterics.

"You two cut it out," Willie said. "Wynonna, give Uncle Greazy some sugar."

Wynonna buried her face in her mother's lap.

"You better say 'hey' to me, you little monster," I said and tickled her side.

"Nuh uh!" she hollered.

I felt good: my head ached a little, but my eye was mostly clear, and I was no longer slurring. The air smelled, even felt, buttery, black peppery, and dark blue.

"Sit down, Legare, and let me fix you a plate," Mama said. "Saul was telling us some funny stories about New York City."

"Oh, he's a regular card," I said. *Saul*-no-longer-"Mr. Grossman," looking at me sheepishly, was telling stories.

Mama turned to Grossman, "What else you need, shug?" *Shug?*

"I'd like more of that bacon, if you please." *If you please.* He was laying it on thick.

"Buttsmeat," the Old Man said. "I was raised on it. That and cornbread. They say it's all bad for your heart, but it ain't hurt me nair bit." Why was he not out deer-hunting? That's where he would usually be this time of year.

"You do indeed appear fit, Mr. Hume," Grossman said. Jesus, was he moving in?

"Hurt everybody else in the family," Willie said. "You're the only one in our family—what's Uncle Rembert, sixty-two?—to make it past sixty-five. Most of them died from heart disease in their fifties. They'd probably all still be around if they hadn't filled up on salt and fat every meal."

"Never hurt me none," said the Old Man.

"I don't eat none of it no more," said Mama, returning with my plate. Her hands looked like water oak leaves pressed between the pages of an unread book. "I've been buying oatmeal in the little packages and have me one of them in the mornings. And I don't add no kind of grease to my vegetables. Now I will fry me a piece of fish when we get some. Purvis brought us a mess of shellcracker right after Thanksgiving. I just can't eat fish but it's been fried."

"She don't even fix fried chicken no more," the Old Man said.

My plate was heaped with grits, wheat toast, and bacon.

"That's turkey bacon," Mama said. "And I cooked it before I fried the buttsmeat in the pan, because I knew you wouldn't want the pork grease to get on it. Do you want some margarine on your grits?"

I sat stunned. Was I still asleep? "Ah, no, ma'am. This is fine."

Wynonna was on Willie's lap, staring at Grossman, now crunching a piece of skin from the salt pork. "She can't get over that beard," Willie said.

"Hit's a whopper all right," the Old Man said. "My daddy used to have a beard." He pronounced it "byaird" and pointed to a photograph on the wall. "His'n wa'n't as thick or as long as yourn, but hit was white as snow all his life."

This again?

"Daddy," Willie said, "you're going to scare the children."

"No he won't," Unitas said.

"His mama," the Old Man said, "who'd been two year dead, come to him one night when he was sleeping." Willie huffed and took Wynonna from the room. "She sot right down on the side of the bed and told him that the girl he'd been courting wa'n't no good, but he ought to marry him another'n what lived down the road. She told him that she'd leave him a sign for proof. He got up the next morning thinking he'd dreamt it, but his hair had turnt white as snow, and him just nineteen year old. So he courted that other girl, and she ended up my mama. That first girl married some other feller, and he come home early from work one day and caught her in the bed with another man and kilt all two of 'em."

"Pledger!" Mama hollered. "You didn't have to put that ugly part in."

Unitas squealed and looked at me to share in his joy.

"If my grandma ha'n't a come to my daddy, I wouldn't be hyere," the Old Man said. "So, don't you never doubt no ghosts."

"I'm done," I said, feeling haunted enough. Grossman was about to speak, undoubtedly about the Old Man's triple negative. "Saul, we need to get going. The conference is about to start."

"But we don't have to be there right away."

I felt a tinge of pain in my forehead and saw my face reflected in the china cabinet behind Grossman. It was the same pursed-lip, terrifying face Mama made when I acted up in church.

"Oh, yeah," he said. "You're right."

I quickly showered and shaved, put on a bandage, and threw on some clothes. I re-emerged to find the Old Man showing Grossman the mounted deer head from my first kill at age nine. Grossman glanced at me with a half smile, as if he knew a secret. I struggled to push us out through the "so glad you're staying with us" and "goodbye"s. Mama was talking about what she would fix for supper, but I told her the conference went long into the night and not to wait up. She said she would make a big pot of purlieu anyway. Unitas saluted me out, Wynonna uncovered her face long enough for a perfunctory "bye-bye," and Willie hugged me again.

"You can tell me about Tally later," she whispered.

I convinced Grossman to let me drive. The accelerator, clutch, and brake on the Volvo had no pedals, just metal rods with flattened tabs at the end. I had to depress the clutch all the way to the floor, and my foot kept sliding off just when I changed gears, so the grinding transmission would sound like a skill saw hitting a knot. The accelerator rod was too high for me to rest my foot on the floor and still reach.

"How come there're no foot pedals on this thing, Saul?"

"Foot pedals?"

We made it out and back onto 402, and I rolled down the window for my first full breath of the morning. Through the side mirror, I could see a cloud of exhaust belching from the tailpipe. The car was burning oil.

"Looks like we're working for the county, Saul."

"I don't understand."

"A common joke around here. See all that smoke coming out the back?"

Grossman looked in the back seat. "No."

"The back of the *car*. Looks like we're spraying for mosquitoes."

"I don't get it."

"Never mind. Relies upon too many assumptions."

A pocket-size green book lay in the corner of dashboard. When I pulled it out, it made a cracking sound coming unstuck from the windshield—Gideon's New Testament with Psalms and Proverbs. Why would he have this? I put it to better use, wedging it under my heel to prop up my foot just enough to reach the gas.

"So, what did you think of the Hume clan, Saul?"

"Your sister is very beautiful," he said and stared straight ahead.

FOUR
The Mind-Body Problem

Every "Introduction to Philosophy" course taught in the Western world tells you that René Descartes was the father of modern philosophy. You learn how he shuffled off the last flakes of dead Medieval-style-thinking skin and built his entire epistemological system on an untried foundation: the individual thinking subject. Unlike anyone before, the old French boy started fresh, assuming nothing, questioning everything. After all, he said, hardly a day went by when he did not discover that something he had always believed to be true turned out to be false. We make mistakes of judgment, we are victims of optical illusions, the reports of others turn out to be inaccurate, and we can err even trying our hardest at precise calculations like arithmetic and geometry. What's a nice seventeenth-century philosopher to do?

You learn that Descartes, who had a habit of lying in bed thinking all morning while everyone else was out making a living on their mistaken judgments, sought anything at all he could not doubt—one self-evident truth sturdy enough to support the whole weight of the structure of all possible knowledge. He found it in his famous cornerstone slogan: *I think, therefore I am*, which is about all anyone remembers from Philosophy 101. As long as there is thought, Descartes informed us, something is thinking. Tucking his indubitable truth into his pouch like a smooth stone, off went the brave René to sling it at, and redirect the history of, philosophy.

What you do not learn in "Intro to Philosophy," and perhaps miss even in grad school, is how Descartes thoroughly FUBARed it.

One world was not enough for old René. He had to have two—one for his mind, one for his body. This thinking thing at the heart of his approach could not be material, and the body to which the thinker is related cannot think. So you got your mental world of non-spatial, invisible minds and their immaterial ideas, and you got your physical world of extended bodies with their perceivable shapes and sizes and other qualities. But Descartes, *mon ami*, you left us with one rancid, hairy, floating, dead dog of a problem: how do you get the two things together? Of course the mind and body interact, Descartes assured us, but when pushed by his contemporaries on just what sort of influence a thing can have upon another thing with which it has *no* characteristic in common—one takes up space, one does not; one can be perceived, one cannot—Descartes replied with the philosophical equivalent of mooning them and leaving the room.

Thanks to Descartes, the mind-body problem, as we affectionately refer to it, has loomed like a specter over philosophy for four centuries now. Few philosophers these days believe in non-corporeal minds separate from, but somehow magically comporting with, brains. But just how consciousness emerges from a cauliflower-looking hunk of jelly in our skulls is anybody's guess. Mind you, this does not mean there's a shortage of publications in the field of "philosophy of mind." Six-hundred-page tomes abound, all promising to have the definitive theory. But what you actually find inside are entries in cleverest puzzle contests, each claiming to illustrate the most incorrigible mind-related problem. I have to hand it to those guys, though: some make for amusing reading with notoriously horror-show-like thought experiments. For instance, if your brain were in a vat sending and receiving radio signals to and from your body, would you be able to tell? If all the memories, preferences, and other information from that brain were placed onto a computer program so someone could flip a switch and have the computer "run" your body instead of your brain, could you tell? Which one would really be you?

Or try this one: is it possible for there to be a zombie whose brain still worked so that he could talk, eat, and appear to do everything else we take to be the hallmarks of consciousness, but who would nevertheless be completely *un*conscious? Or, would a brain, by virtue of causing those behaviors, *be* conscious, so there could be no such things as zombies?

Regardless of the nature of consciousness, and whatever we figure out about it, there is no such thing as a non-physical mind. I am sure of that.

Except when I go fishing.

Since moving to St. Pete, I've traded casting for crappie from a jonboat for wading out into the ocean nearly every weekend and hooking a few speckled trout, redfish, and sheepsheads around the piers, or, if I'm really lucky, the king of all inshore sport fish, the wily snook. Standing up to my waist in the green waters of Tampa Bay, scooting along in the dimpled sand in my beachcomber shoes to avoid stomping the stingrays, watching an osprey plunge down to snag a ladyfish, spotting dolphins bump up through the waves like shiny rolling inner tubes, sighting the occasional manatee rise up to snort like a water horse through stubby whiskers, you might think I would be so fully integrated with wild nature, so un-self-consciously immersed in my surroundings, that the concept of the aloof Cartesian mind, removed from the palpable world, would never enter my mind.

But it does. Nowhere else do I feel so utterly separated from the thickness or the weight of the world. I become a spectator of a universe out there, metaphysically cordoned off, partitioned, impenetrable. At best, the very flesh on my bones feels like my property—stuff that is mine—but not me. My hands and arms still put shrimp on the hook, flick the rod and cast the line, and wind the reel. They continue to cup slimy bellies and risk slipping fingers into sharp gills—but they do all this on their own. I am just there for the show, safely peering out from a box seat in my skull, enjoying a *Mutual of Omaha's Wild Kingdom* special on "that heavy bear that goes with me," as the poet said. Having this experience is not my reason for fishing. It just happens, daring me to ignore it, defying thematization, flying in the face of ordinary immersion in the mundane, our being-in-the-world.

I am the Cartesian Angler. I found T-shirts in a tackle shop imprinted with "I fish, therefore I am" and bought three.

Maybe I have been too hard on Descartes. He may have given

philosophical articulation to this view, but he did not create it. Most people, after all, try to keep their minds or souls or selves (as if "mind" is not a confused enough concept) safely quarantined from the transgressions of the flesh, right? Religions all agree that we keep out of trouble when mental faculties—reason, wisdom, prudence—control the relentless urges of the body, which all reduce to one: lust.

This is one of the few things I think religions have gotten right, and it has been one of the few comforting thoughts of my adult life. When I am not sure why I do what I do, which is most of the time, and try desperately to peer beneath the surface to identify my own motive creeping along the sea floor (is it a ray? snook? shark?), moving too fast to make out the outline, I can say to myself, "Probably just lust," and have a fair idea whether to bait up and cast towards it, stand still until it passes, or get out of the water. At least that is the reassurance I have ahead of time. The follow-through is what I can never quite manage.

As I stood with Grossman at the APA registration table at the Conference Center, I had a good look at one motive. I wanted nothing more at that moment than to jump on Jacqueline Armstrong and sink my face into the hollow of her neck and shoulder and inhale the scent of that glorious flesh. My sense of smell seemed heightened acutely. Not only were scents far more powerful than they had ever been for me, but I was able to distinguish multiple fragrances when I entered a room or was approached by someone. Stranger still was that I experienced sensory cross currents: an odor would have a certain color or mood. But every other man within sight (or smell) of Jacqueline Armstrong wanted to do the same.

Armstrong, a medievalist at the University of Chicago, was known for her work on Arab philosophy. Her most famous claim had been published about ten years earlier in *Finding Aristotle*, in which she argued that Ibn Rushd, a.k.a Averroës, a twelfth-century Cordoban Moor who wrote several commentaries on Aristotle, must have been familiar with some of the "lost" works of the great Macedonian. All scholars agree that Aristotle, and every other ancient writer, wrote more than is now extant. Ancient sources name a number of pieces by Aristotle that were either lost in the shuffle of the centuries or burned up when Julius Caesar torched the library in Alexandria in the first century BCE. Armstrong argued that Ibn Rushd attributed certain ideas to Aristotle, and implied others, none of which can be found in existing books, but we can reconstruct much of the lost Aristotle by a thorough reading. She also claimed that Ibn Rushd wrote dozens of commentaries that, in turn, are lost to us.

Some of those ideas, if they really were Aristotle's, would spackle up some gaps and solve age-old problems in Aristotelian scholarship. So, she gave ancient philosophy a shot in the arm, revived interest in Ibn Rushd and other medieval Arab philosophers, and got awards and offers to speak at several universities in the Middle East, the first time some of those institutions had made such invitations to a woman.

But these intellectual accomplishments were no rivals to her true fame: being the most beautiful woman in philosophy. Few in the audience ever listened to a word she said, but her talks at conferences were always over-attended, almost entirely by men, who would show up for a seat long before she was scheduled to speak. The feminists hated her. It was not that she was not a feminist. One of the very few feminists specializing in medieval thought, she was something of a pioneer. Nor was it exactly petty jealousy. It was more the fact that Armstrong wore sexy dresses showing lots of luscious leg, carefully applied her make-up, and, while reading papers, caressed her elegant neck with her fingers, stroked that luxurious red hair, shifted her weight from foot to perfect foot, and hypnotically swayed her fine hips. In the world of philosophy where mind reigns supreme, Jackie Armstrong dared to flaunt body in the worst way.

Just after the terrorist attacks on the World Trade Center and the Pentagon, she wrote an op-ed piece that appeared in both the *Chicago Sun-Times* and the *Chicago Tribune* cautioning readers against a witch hunt and war, reminding them of the unparalleled achievements of Arabs and Persians, during the Middle Ages, in mathematics, science, and medicine while Christian Europe languished in the Dark Ages. The backlash was vicious. Dozens of letters to the editors of both papers and endless voices on the radio talk shows demanded that the university fire her. When she appeared on Larry King's TV show, however, and the nation got a look at her matchless face, every call praised her wisdom.

At this conference, you might see one of the few really famous philosophers approached by the occasional, trembling grad student asking the author to autograph a book. Armstrong got those requests, too, but she alone in the world of philosophy gave out signed photos like a rock star. I watched her sit at a table signing books and pictures, flashing her luminous smile while her agent/bodyguard tended the line of hard-on-ed fans. Probably fifty but appearing twenty years younger, she looked to all the world like Ava Gardner in her prime, and spoke in a Kathleen Turner growl. As each admirer tried to express his adoration in some respectable way but inevitably babbled like a pimply-faced, first-time-at-the-whorehouse kid with forty bucks from his uncle, she would graciously laugh her smoky laugh, twirl a finger in her thick, dark red hair, and say flirty things like, "Here you are, handsome," or, "Haven't we conferenced together before, love?"

"Greazy," Grossman said, breaking my trance. He had just finished registering and was perusing the agenda. "Look at this. 'Mimetic Engulfment.' Sounds like your sort of phenomenological stuff, doesn't it?"

"Yeah. Maybe I'll check it out." I had not yet comprehended his bizarre personality transformation. He had entertained my family earlier that morning, but it had been temporary, because in the car on the way to the conference, he had reverted to his old weirdo self. He was quieter than usual and sat smiling slightly. So I talked—about Charleston, about maybe taking him on a short tour of downtown, and a bit about my student days at what used to be the College of Charleston. I reminded him that there was usually a mixer on the first evening of the conference and asked if he wished to stay for it or to drive around town.

"But we need to go back to your house," he said, almost pleading. "Your mother is making that parlay for us."

"Purlieu," I said. "It's just chicken and rice, and you heard me tell her we probably wouldn't make it back in time." He looked at the floor. "Saul, do you *want* to go back there for supper?" No reply. "Saul, what's going on?" Still no answer. I decided to let it ride for the moment. Maybe I could put a couple of beers into him later and get something out of him.

I wrote out a check to the woman at the registration table, and she gave me a program, a name tag, and a ticket for the open bar mixer that evening. I opened up the program to the next day's schedule to find my session. Sometimes they rearrange things at the last minute without telling you.

"Saul, my darling!" a woman shouted nearby. I looked up to see Jackie Armstrong throwing her arms around Grossman's neck.

"Hi," the little dickweed said, glancing at me, embarrassed. This was the Grossman I knew, not the one who had been playing Shelley Berman at breakfast.

"Saul, it's been *years*," Armstrong said. My God, had they been lovers? "I heard you were teaching down South somewhere, you poor boy. Are you OK?"

"Sure," he answered. The most desirable woman on the planet had her fingers interlaced behind his neck and was staring into his eyes, and all he could manage were monosyllabic responses.

She turned to me. "Hello, I'm Jackie Armstrong," and smiled and stuck out her beautiful hand, which I instinctively clasped in both of mine and almost bent to kiss it but figured that would be uncouth. I did squeeze it a little too hard and too long, though. Her perfume smelled like pale pink azaleas and was *chewy* like a bagel.

"Yes, I know," I said like an idiot. "I'm very pleased to meet you. I'm Legare Hume, Saul's colleague." Keep talking, I thought. Say anything.

"Hume?" she asked. "Good taste in names." She was referring to the eighteenth-century Scottish thinker David Hume, generally considered the greatest philosopher in the English language. To be a philosopher of my caliber today named Hume is about as much of a blessing as being a white guy named Sammy Davis, Jr. who insists on calling guys "cats." I was used to people trying to say something clever about it. At that moment, Armstrong could have said that both David Hume and I were pig-fucking dipshits, and I would have knelt and thanked her.

"I do my best," I said and finally released her hand. I still had my jacket on, so I didn't worry about concealing my erection. "How do you know Saul? He hasn't mentioned you."

"He hardly mentions anything except logic," she turned to him, "do you, love?" Then back to me. "I'll bet he never mentioned that he's fluent in Arabic, either. And Russian and German and Hebrew and, of course, Yiddish. I was a visiting scholar at Columbia for a year when Saul was a graduate student there. He attended a talk I gave for the faculty and questioned my translation of a passage from Al-Ghazali. He was wrong, which is rare, but I was impressed with his knowledge of Islamic thought."

Did she notice my struggle to keep from staring straight at her tits, which were not very large, but so round, so firm?

I just knew the bandage on my head made me look like a freak and wished I could say something in Arabic besides "hashish." Just beyond her shoulder, I saw an old buddy from grad school, Gary Winters, pointing at me and laughing at my expense. He knew exactly the torture I was going through.

"He's damn impressive, all right," I said. Grossman stared at his program.

"Are you on the program, dear Hume?" she asked.

"Yes, tomorrow. I was just looking for it."

"No, you're not, Greazy," Grossman said. "See?" He held his program too close to my face. "You've been re-scheduled to the next day."

"Christ, they could have told me." My forehead began to ache.

"That means we'll need to stay another day," Grossman said, grinning. One quick punch would crush his larynx.

"Then we have even more time together, darlings," Armstrong said. "Can you two lunch with me tomorrow?"

"Sure!" I said. I would have declined anyone else who verbed "lunch," but the dark night of my soul was brightening.

"What is the topic of your paper, dear Hume?"

"The ontological argument."

"Fascinating. I *must* come to hear you. You know, I've argued that Ibn Sina offered a version of it. He didn't articulate it explicitly, but—"

"Jackie!" Her agent grabbed her by the arm. "Jackie, there's a line for you." As she was being dragged away, Armstrong said something like, "Got to go, look for me at the mixer," and tipped her head towards and gave a pseudo-kiss to Grossman, who was writing something in his little notebook. I did not want her to go, yet I felt an enormous relief.

"Say, who was that nobody schmoozing with Legare Hume?" Gary Winters said.

"Just another groupie trying to blow me. How you been, you old bastard?" We shook hands. I had not seen him since he had interviewed at the University of Tampa three years before, and I had driven over the Bay for a couple of drinks. The UT opening later fell through when the small, private university dissolved the philosophy department, which at the time had only two members. Several of the other humanities disciplines were also axed in favor of becoming a business school almost entirely. He did get a job at a community college in Louisiana, but suffered horribly from battling the "hermaphrodites," as he called his administrators. Gary's favored psychological theory for why anyone would seek public attention and power—actors, rock stars, business tycoons, and especially politicians—was to compensate for a small penis. Overachieving women, he believed, were obsessed with their dicklessness. He wrote me about his "educratic" administrators, the myriad VPs (9), assistant VPs (12), provosts (4), deans (11), associate deans (8), directors (17), coordinators (15), plus a president with two assistants, all of whom had Ed.D.s and thus *know*—despite no college teaching experience, no degree in an actual specialty, and no dissertation—what is best for faculty.

"The mini-dicked strut around campus," Gary wrote, "leaving clouds of Marxist mystification and insisting on being addressed as 'Dr.' but call all of us 'instructor.' They spit the word out like a hair and give it all the mock respect one might give an 'environmental engineer'—the guy who runs the leafblower past my classroom every day. They don't give a damn about scholarship, but they'll make me start the semester four days before classes begin so I can attend Professional Development seminars on, I swear to God, the 'New Learning Paradigm' or how to administer personality tests to students (would you describe yourself as {a} a squirrel or {b} a nut?). They haven't a clue about the monstrous caesura between their paper stack world of administrivia and ours. Then I have to teach five classes a semester and hope to be awarded tenure—no, make that a 'continuing contract'—based solely on good student evals."

What stuck in his craw most were the universitied types who assumed, when they found out Gary taught at a community college, that he was not a real philosopher. He had in fact published quite a bit—ten or twelve articles, two monographs, a book-length translation—and had read papers at several conferences in Europe. The trouble was that his specialty was 18th- and 19th-century German Idealism, which was acceptable if your focus was Immanuel Kant, and marginally so if G. W. F. Hegel, but not Gary's Arthur Schopenhauer, long out of fashion in the chauvinistic English-speaking philosophical world. Even worse, Gary's publications were all in European journals.

"How's Tally?" His name tag did not read "North East Louisiana Community College" but "N E Louisiana."

"Fine, but she's got strep and couldn't come." Had I added that too quickly?

"That's too bad. Give her my love. So, how's Florida?"

"They tell me it's nice, but I wouldn't know. Now if you want to buy some year-round passes to America World's Wonderful World of Virtual Water Cyber-Fun Family Park and Resort World, I'm your man."

Gary laughed, Saul didn't get it or didn't notice, and then I introduced the two. "Oh, right," Gary said. "I read a piece of yours in *Fichte Studien* a year or so ago. That was a good paper."

Did everybody know Saul Grossman?

"Thanks." Grossman turned away. "I have to go." And he did.

"Talkative fellow," Gary said, but Gary, as it turned out, was no better, rushing off to a job interview in his latest attempt to escape the confines of community college. "Michigan needs someone in nineteenth century," he said. "Well, they didn't exactly put it that way in the *JFP*, but maybe I can convince them." The APA's fall issue of *JFP*, *Jobs for Philosophers*, is the big one, listing all the expected openings for the next academic year. Most of those positions are filled through cattle-call interviews at the December conference. If you're on the market but have no interviews scheduled beforehand at the APA, you are pretty well shit out of luck for the next academic year.

I could tell Gary was not very hopeful about the interview, but he did, at least, have something to go back to. Good for him.

❦

Twenty audience members sat thumbing through their programs as the speakers at the front of the room exchanged introductions. The room reeked of the detergent, more leafy than soapy, that was probably used on the carpet earlier, and coffee with lots of sugar. The audience sported tweeds and black turtlenecks, a few khakis and Bass Weejuns, and a couple of bulky parkas on weather-overestimating Northerners. A woman wore hiking boots and mittens, for Godsake. One of the speakers settling in at the front table was a gigantic black man, taller even than Bartholomew Gilbert, my 6' 4" grad school mentor, and this session's chair. The giant, who must have weighed at least 280, wore dungarees and an Emory sweatshirt cut at the front for his bizarrely massive neck, which spread out onto his shoulders like a wind-eroded pyramid. We used to call deer looking like that a "staggy," so I christened him "Staggy Man."

"Good morning, ladies and gentlemen," Gilbert began. "I'm Bart Gilbert and proud to chair this session, one of two, if you can believe it, on phenomenology this year."

Chuckles and smirks rippled through the room. It was a subtle little dig at the establishment—one that couldn't have surprised anyone who knew Bart Gilbert. He was a kind and gentle man whom you would not have guessed had swum fiercely against the ruthless philosophical stream his entire career. He denounced Anglo-American analytic philosophy as narrow, intolerant, ignorant of history, and anti-humanistic. We say that philosophy is about the big questions, about living the "examined life," as Socrates put it. When asked "What is the meaning of life?," Gilbert complained that "professional philosophers" (and that label says it all) filibuster about the meaning of "meaning" and well-formed formulae until the bewildered and belittled asker of the question throws up his metaphysical hands and leaves. He established a maverick group called the Fagots, from the French phrase *Il sent le fagot*, "he smells of the fagot." In other words, he sounds like a heretic. The Fagots were specialists in continental European thought and American pragmatism, disciplines considered soft by the hardened analysts and represented, at most, by one faculty member in any American philosophy department. They succeeded in getting some of their membership elected as officers in the APA in the sixties and seventies, but their subordination in philosophy departments remained unchanged.

"I'll ask our two speakers to follow our customary rules of engagement by not exceeding twenty minutes each. After their presentations, we shall hear from our respondent, who will comment upon both papers. I ask that you graciously hold your questions and remarks until we have heard from all three." He looked about the room as if giving any dissenters the opportunity to protest. He spotted me by the center aisle and nodded. Like others of his academic minority status, Gilbert was thrilled to have graduate students work with him, and he had been protective of me. He coached me through my dissertation and loaded my committee with sympathetic members of other graduate programs at other universities. The rest of the Rutgers philosophy department threw me and Gilbert's few other protégés a few bones to keep him quiet. He was on the verge of retirement when I was his student, so none of the analysts showed up at my dissertation defense to cause any trouble. But since his connections at other universities were the pariahs of their own divisions, he could be of little help in my job search. I had not heard this from him directly, but I was sure Gilbert thought megacorporations like America World were part of the same tyrannical, culture-monopolizing force as analytic philosophy. I worried he would accuse me of collaborating with the fascists.

"Our first speaker is Peter Boykin of Emory, on 'Mimetic Engulfment: Sport as Theater.'"

Staggy Man stood up and took his place behind the lectern. He was about thirty and bald, and had a nose that must have been broken a few times and a forehead with peculiar cross-hatched scars. His voice was gruff but soft as he began to distinguish the concept of play from that of other human activities. He made the claim that all forms of play—whether staged dramas, board games like chess, competitive sports, or even individual activities like solitaire—require a sort of meaning-making activity that carve out their own little worlds of rules and roles that are inapplicable to other forms. He drew nicely upon a range of sources, from Aristotle's work on tragedy, the *Poetics*, to Sartre on roleplaying. He even mentioned Gilbert's book on theater.

Then came the kicker: his primary example, which took up the bulk of his paper, was professional wrestling. More than any other sport/theater, he said, professional wrestling involves the audience in the meaning-making process so that, properly speaking, there are no spectators at all. Its world *is* its mimetic engulfment. What a prize this guy was. I imagined he'd been a football lineman in college, and released after a couple years in the pros. Maybe he didn't have the speed or couldn't keep off the injured list, so he fell back on pro wrestling. But Boykin was neither handsome enough nor menacing enough to be either loved or hated by the fans. So he reached into the hopper and pulled out grad school. Now here he was, reading a paper at the APA, while his ex-colleagues were working on their scripts for that night's opening bouts of Armageddon. He was an ex-athlete academic. A black philosopher, and a black philosopher doing something other than social/political philosophy. How many stereotypes could this guy single-handedly explode?

When Staggy Man was about ten minutes into his paper, a fuss started in the back of the room. Six more giants had come in and were rearranging chairs and arguing over who was sitting where. Staggy Man stopped reading. He lifted his head to face the intruders. "Hey!" Half the audience ducked.

The giants froze and mumbled a few "Sorry, Pete"s and sat in a line with their feet up on the row of chairs in front of them. I was right: he *was* an ex-wrestler, and his old buddies who happened to be in town had come to hear him "philosophize." This had to be a first. Talk about mind and body. What could his ring name have been? The Metaphysician. The Cogitator. Leviathan, from Hobbes's book. The Geist, from Hegel's.

When he finished and the audience began its polite applause, the wrestlers stood up and cheered like they were at a rock concert. "Yeah!" "Fuckin' A!" Three of them "roo, roo, roo"ed and waved their fists in little circles. The rest of the audience either stared in utter shock or slunk down sheepishly into their seats. Gilbert reared back and laughed.

"I doubt that Aristotle himself enjoyed such an enthusiastic response at the Lyceum," he quipped. Everyone laughed nervously, and the wrestlers finally took their seats.

The next guy, who was from Purdue, read a paper entitled "Guts and Glory: Jaspers on Boundary Situations and Heidegger on *Augenblick*" that really said nothing new, except for an interesting attempt to formulate a notion that he called a "whole-life moment." He argued that, despite the standard existentialist principle that one's life is never finished or complete like a story (Heidegger wrote that we do not ripen like fruit), one can achieve wholeness in one's life through a decision or action that becomes a focal point providing a "quasi-narrative" structure. If so, was it possible to have such an experience without knowing it? Could your life be defined by something you have done or decided, yet you *think* your life is all about something else? This seemed somehow relevant and I planned to ask him about it later.

The wrestlers, politely silent throughout the paper, clapped delicately like everyone else when the speaker was done. Then came the respondent, a young woman from somewhere in California who must have still been in grad school but lucky enough now to put an APA program on her c.v. She bent close to her paper and began reading in a near whisper. "Can't hear," someone said, and she raised her voice a bit without starting over.

". . . not altogether different from Wittgenstein's theory of language games. While Boykin claims that role-playing is the central and world-making feature of his notion of play, role-playing is less definitive than metaphorical in his scheme. By his own account, the linguistic and nomothetic nature of the structure . . ."

In her youthful exuberance, she was attacking the presenter instead of engaging in a dialogue. That approach is always a big risk: either (1) you produce a serious and memorable critique, which makes sense for your career only if leveled at a well-known philosopher's work, or (2) you look like an ass, which is far more likely and just what she was doing, and hope everyone forgets it. The critique was sadly superficial. Staggy Man was furiously writing down notes. Several audience members exchanged uncomfortable glances. The wrestlers began to murmur. Even they had caught on.

"Bullshit!" one of them yelled and jumped from his chair. "That's fucking bullshit!"

California Woman was stunned. She stared, terrified at the wrestler, then turned to Gilbert, who rose to his feet.

"Sir, please show respect to our speaker and exhibit some decorum."

But another wrestler was up and standing on his chair. "She's a liar! Pete didn't say nothing like that!"

"Yeah!" another yelled. "Don't take any shit from that little bitch, Pete!"

Staggy Man bared his teeth and rolled his eyes. He stood up and slammed both palms onto the table with a *tunk* so hard the lectern bounced up a half a foot, the woman's papers flew up, she squealed a little "ike!," jumped back, and put her hands on her chest.

"Out!" Staggy Man yelled as he pointed towards the door with one hand, placing the other on the table and leaping over it. He stomped towards them, kicking over two chairs on the way. "Out, you fucking yahoos!" The wrestlers held out their open palms like supplicants.

"Come on, Pete," one said. "We thought we were helping out," said another. "We're sorry," they all repeated.

He pushed them out into the hall, mumbling something about being mortified, being an idiot for inviting them, etc. The room was silent except for Respondent Woman's sobbing into Gilbert's shoulder.

So I had to laugh. I threw my head back, my arms fell limply to my sides, and I flopped my knees apart like T.S. Eliot's "Apeneck" (was that his name?) Sweeney, together again in a seated Charleston. A good country laugh, as if some old boy named Coot had told a good 'urn. The joke was on us, and I was the first to get it. Staggy Man, the Andy Kaufman of philosophy, had put one over on us—having mimetically engulfed us all, so fully co-creating this piece of theater that we did not even realize it. One by one, the other suckers began to laugh, too. Gilbert tilted his head back and guffawed loudest of all. Respondent Woman, who had probably been in on it, too, yukked it up.

Any second, Staggy Man and his accomplices would come back into the room and take a few bows.

They did not. We all left the room chuckling, exchanging knowing glances, no one daring to whisper, "It was a joke, right?"

※

"So, Legare Hume, our paths have crossed again." Gilbert, a head taller than I, placed a hand on my shoulder as we walked through the hall. He smelled like Darjeeling tea, somewhat waxy but brittle.

"It's good to see you again," I said. "You look fit." Actually, he looked terribly thin.

"I thank you, but I wish I felt fit. I've had some medical complications of late that have taken quite a toll on me."

That was where any decent person would have inquired about the nature of his ailment. Me, I never ask people about their health.

I always fear they're going to say something like "I have cancer—two months to live," and what can you say then? People want to hear something inspirational and hopeful, but that's not my style.

"Well, it hasn't diminished your character," I said, whatever that meant. "That was some performance in there, eh?"

"Yes, I suppose it was a performance, but then we are always performing, are we not?" He squinted an eye at me. Was that some kind of loaded question? Was he on to something about me?

"Absolutely," I said and chuckled as if we shared an inside joke. This was just like grad school. He was always a step ahead of me but seemed to think I was keeping up. Sometimes he even convinced me I knew a lot more than I thought I did. At the moment, it was not that I did not want to speak with Gilbert. Instead, I felt pressure to live up to being his student. "Heading to another session?"

"No. I'm going up to my room to stretch out for an hour. The chemotherapy that's supposed to keep me alive is unfortunately severely enervating. I take several naps a day, and much of the rest of the time I feel I'm somnambulating."

"Tell me about it." What a sorry sack of shit I was—I couldn't even let the man relate his misery to me without equating my self-pitying, whiny ass to his probably terminal condition. Gilbert raised an eyebrow and waited for me to elaborate. "My father was on chemotherapy for over a year before deciding he couldn't live that way any longer, so, he just stopped taking his medication." I had promised myself many times that I would develop the habit of *planning* my lies instead of simply blurting out what seemed convenient. I had broken that promise, like every other promise I had ever made to anyone.

"How has he fared?"

"He's fine. No recurrence at all in over three years."

"Good for him. That's encouraging. Most encouraging." He pressed the elevator button. "What sort of cancer did he have?"

That one was easy. "Lung. He'd been a shmoker all his life." My shibbolething had started again. "Had half a lung removed, but shays now he can breathe more fully than he ever could." Am I going to ask about his type of cancer? Maybe he appreciates my not prying. It was agonizing. "What about you?" There—I'd done it.

"Prostate. Had it removed ten and a half months ago."

Jesus H. Christ—why did he say it like that? What could that mean but that he has counted the days since his last erection ten *and a half* months ago? Can I just let that slide in a conversation? Does etiquette demand that I ask if he has tried Viagra? Or one of those pump implant things?

The beautiful *ding* of the elevator sounded. As he got on, he turned to say, "Joyce is here, too. She would love to see you. You'll attend the mixer?"

"You bet," I said, and the doors closed. Not so bad. For no apparent reason, I had lied to, and all the while wished to get away from, a good man who had for years offered me only aid and kindness. On the other hand, I think my story had given him some, albeit false, hope, but what harm could come from that?

※

I went to the bathroom to examine my head and get a dip of snuff. The room was nicer than the one in the lobby; the floor looked like real marble with greenish black veins running its length. I could smell lilac-scented soap, paper towels, and something else, pinkish-yellow and whispery—maybe the complimentary eau de water in the atomizer by the black, scalloped sinks. It was a far cry from the Long Haul truck stop. I removed the bandage, pressed a damp paper towel to my forehead, put on a fresh bandage, took a pinch of Copenhagen, rinsed my hands, and returned to the hall. I stared at my program for a while, hoping that something among the ridiculous titles would miraculously look interesting. The history of early modern philosophy session featured "Descartes on Second-Order Epistemic Disintentionals," "Leibniz's Law and the Indexicality of the Identity of Future Indiscernibles," and "Locke on Reclaimed Memory and the Narrative Self," the last of which looked good. Environmental ethics had "Rawlsian Contractarianism and Agentive Assertion Rules" and "Nature, the Naturalistic Fallacy, and Non-Supererogation." Epistemology offered "Neo-Defeasibility Theory and Kline's Skepticism" and "Two Dogmas of Rationalism: A Conjunctivist Defense." I thought I had left hell.

The philosophy of mind session boasted the audaciously titled "Case Closed: How the Brain Creates Consciousness," and the speaker was MIT's Samuel Sennet, the leader in the field. This promised to be one of the conference's premier events, probably second only to the Big-Timers' showdown, and was being held in a 500-seat auditorium. According to rumor, Sennet had made the breakthrough he'd been laboring at for thirty years. At least his talk should be fun, and the discussion afterwards lively, maybe even contentious, though perhaps not in the league of jeers from wrestlers-turned-philosophy fans. And Sennet was to hold forth in the room next door. I walked over to the coffee and Danish tables to get an empty Styrofoam cup to spit into.

Or, I could call Tally, see if she had dumped all my clothes with Goodwill, hocked my guitar, and chucked my fishing rods into Tampa Bay. Maybe she had been lying in bed crying since I had left, contrite over the attempt to kill her own husband, not knowing if I had even made it safely to South Carolina, what with the nut driving, and knowing that the trip was necessary to my continued career at AmWorld. Yeah, maybe I should call.

Sennet was already reading his paper as I slipped in and made my way to the back for one of the few empty seats in the room. It smelled a little like rotting bananas, but pleasant and relaxing. People were laughing; the famous Sennet wit was at work. I scanned the auditorium and saw anti-computationalist John Darrell of UCLA, another philosophy of mind luminary. He was laughing, too, but would surely fire things up when question time came around. Perry Fowler, of my old alma mater Rutgers, the leading proponent of the functionalist model of mind, was sitting three seats away from me, looking as sullen as ever. The gang was all there, but no one in the room, not even Sennet, could really believe that the origin of consciousness from brain matter was a closed case.

I got lost in all the talk about neural networks and alternating recursive connectionism and something called the modality problem that Sennet said he had also solved. I started to wonder if Sennet's notion of consciousness as a multitude of activities the subject dimly notices, and of ego as an emergent, second-order activity, was only a highfallootin' version of Kant's take on the transcendental ego. But before long, even I could see that just wasn't the case.

Then a murmur, of the something-remarkable-is-taking-place as opposed to the what-a-piece-of-shit sort, slowly swelled through the audience. There should have been anguished cries of disbelief, but the argument left no holes, no questions, nothing to disbelieve. Darrell shifted about in his chair like a guilty kid in church, and Fowler's jaw was jutting forward so far that his bottom lip almost touched his nose. Others nodded, rubbed their temples, glanced pig-eyed at colleagues, or rolled up their programs like Sunday school bulletins.

Sennet was solving the unsolvable mind-body problem.

This, simply, could not be happening.

He spoke for over an hour, during which time I, out of general pissantness, tried to find some flaw to amuse myself. But I couldn't and surrendered. The bigger brains, the biggest, kept up the struggle—I could see it on their faces—but by the time Sennet was done, they'd given up, too, and given in. It was perfect. When he finished, a most extraordinary thing happened (at least for academic conferences): nearly everyone in the audience stood and applauded for a good minute, while the few who didn't, maybe couldn't, sat shaking their heads.

The avuncular old guy chairing the session allowed the commotion to subside on its own, and then introduced the respondent, Paulette Templeton from Northwestern, another famous thinker in the field and Sennet's severest critic. Reviewing one of his books, she once said that you "would have to be brainless to defend such a theory of mind," and that Sennet did "not know his mind from a hole in his head."

She took her place behind the lectern, held out her empty, upturned hands, and said, "Samuel Sennet is right. Case closed." She sat down.

That was just too much. For about five seconds, there was absolute, thick silence. And then the crowd roared, applause as thunderous and complete as the argument. People hugged each other and hopped as if their high school football team had won the state championship. One man fainted and was dragged from the room. We had all been freed from those heavy metaphysical chains that had bound us for the past four centuries. Who said philosophers only ask questions but never answer them? History had been made. We were now in the post-mind-body-problem era.

The smiling, slightly bewildered chair waited for several minutes before holding up his hand and pleading for order, which finally came. Another seventy or eighty people had wedged into the auditorium to find out what all the ruckus was about. The chair made a brief comment on how remarkable and historic the session had been, and then asked for questions. He recognized someone at the side of the room—Gary Winters—who asked something about Kant's transcendental ego. Maybe I had been onto something after all. I wondered how Gary's interview had gone and if his question was really meant to impress one of the interviewers whom he hoped was present. But Sennet that his notion had nothing in common with Kant's, and Templeton nodded. Sennet's response was only slightly short of dismissive.

The moderator looked around for further questions, but no hands rose. Sennet quipped that he was not used to leaving one of his sessions so early. Then someone stood up in the front row and began talking in a soft, measured voice: Saul Grossman, of all people. I couldn't quite make out what he was saying, and probably couldn't have followed it anyway, but I could see him working himself up, speaking louder and faster. For fifteen minutes, he rattled on, more frenzied than I'd ever seen him, long after the chair of the session ordinarily would have cut him off. But the chair, like everyone else in the room, recognized that Grossman was poking a hole in, in fact boring a mineshaft through, Sennet's argument. No one stirred as Grossman, pacing back and forth in front of the room as if talking aloud to himself, constructed an elegant, irrefutable counterargument based on Gödel's Incompleteness Theorem.

Kurt Gödel was perhaps the greatest logician of all time, and, no surprise, a nut. Believing he was being poisoned, he starved himself to death, but that was long after he had had perhaps the most profound thought of the twentieth century: in any formal system, such as math or logic or a computer language, true statements can be expressed by the rules of formulation for that system, but they cannot be proven. In other words, no system can be both consistent and complete—if it implies no contradictions, it cannot produce all its truths; if it produces all its truths, it will also contain contradictions. In my ordinary level of intellectual agility, I was left far behind as Grossman got rolling, but I could at least understand the approach: Sennet's new theory was doomed by its very comprehensiveness. It crumbled under its own weight.

Sennet and Templeton both looked as if a jury were reading a verdict against them. Jaws dropped in ripples as listeners realized how far Grossman's criticism ranged. Gödel's Incompleteness Theorem-style approaches to other theories of mind had been offered before, but they were used as criticisms of models of the nature of thinking, not as theories about how mental events arise from brain processes. Grossman had crystallized a Gödelian critique in a spontaneous *tour de force*, so powerful that not only was Sennet's theory demolished, but it seemed that Grossman had just shown once and for all, to a roomful of astonished philosophers, that the mind-body problem was utterly irresolvable. And then, in truest Grossman style, he suddenly stopped talking and left the room.

This time the silence was massive—I do not think we could have moved from our chairs as that soundlessness squatted on us like a huge toad. And in what seemed to have become truest Legare Hume style of late, I laughed, a regular Democritus the Abderite. I held my sides, I rolled on the floor, I kicked my feet like a child being tickled, and I pissed a few drops in my drawers. I heard someone else laughing, and I blinked the tears from my eyes to see Perry Fowler *hawn hawn hawn*-ing like an adenoidal mule.

Unlike the session earlier that day, however, the laughter did not spread any further. I climbed back up into my chair to see how the others were taking it. Nearly everyone in the room continued to sit in silence. Some were looking to others for a sign. Sennet wrote something on a piece of paper, shook his head, scratched it out, wrote something else, and repeated this exercise six or eight times until Templeton patted him gingerly on the arm and *shhh*ed him. John Darrell was making a *ts*king sound out the side of his wrinkled mouth and jerking as if he had tasted something salty and foul. Finally, seventy or eighty people hurried from the room, I suspected, to track down Grossman and interrogate him.

I knew I should go to his rescue, but I was still laughing from having another big joke pulled on me. At one moment, I had feared that the mind-body problem had been solved right in front of me, but I was not swift enough to follow. In the next moment, it appeared that the problem had been proven unsolvable, and I could not keep up with that proof either. It was like the whole world was showing me its ass.

I was reminded of the first deer I killed. I was nine years old at the deer stand, eating seeds from the little whirlybirds that fell from the loblolly pine cones and spitting onto the dirt road when the resin taste got too strong. Beside me, the Old Man squatted on the ball of one foot, which, as opposed to the catcher-style both-balls-of-feet squatting that looked somehow Asian to me, always struck me as manly. The other foot flat, its shin perpendicular to the ground, and forearms across the knees, the Old Man could hold that pose for hours, at most rotating ninety degrees to place his weight on the other foot's ball. It seemed conducive to smoking, and I never felt myself an accomplished squatter—or *allowed* to be, by my imagined Manhood Authority—until I was seventeen, when I started smoking.

The dogs had not jumped, and it was getting time to call them in and try another area of the hunting club. Out of nowhere, a buck was standing not ten yards (or "steps" in deer hunter lingo) from us. The Old Man whispered, "Looka yonder, son."

I looked. "What?"

"A buck."

I saw only trees. "Where?"

"Right in front of you. Shoot him."

"Where?"

"Shoot him!"

I saw the Old Man raise his twelve gauge. He must have feared that the buck would get away before I shot. I shouldered my .410 (the Old Man had taken .410 shells, removed the small shot, and stuffed in a few single-ought buckshot) and shot straight ahead at the trees. Something fell, like a part of the woods broken off, and crumpled to the ferns and pine straw. I had hit the eight-pointer I had not seen—square in the face.

Back at the camp, the men gathered to necropsy the buck as Frampton Timmons, the designated or elected or self-ordained cleaner, and the Old Man hung the deer up by its Achilles tendons on a pole and crossbar. I knew what was coming—the first-kill baptism of the deer's blood sloshed over me. Timmons made a show of having to hold me, and as I pretended to try to escape while the Old Man rubbed his bloodied hands over my face and through my hair, I could not help laughing.

As we rode home that evening with my occasional gagging (I smelled like hell, since the custom was to leave the blood and guts on until you got home), it seemed to me that, even though the Old Man never mentioned my blind-luck shooting to anyone, it was not the other hunters who had been deceived, but somehow me. The Old Man had his own take on it. "I reckon you got to be pretty good to be able to kill something you can't see."

༄

Grossman was backed against the wall looking terrified as the curious, the confused, and the admiring mobbed him. Some wanted an encore to reaffirm that they had indeed witnessed what they thought they had. Some were overwhelmed and horrified that their half-finished dissertations or one-chapter-to-go book manuscripts were now superfluous and they might be out of their jobs. Others had become instant disciples, trying to be made whole by touching the hem of his garment. "Do you mean that the problem of consciousness, the hard problem, is in principle unanswerable, or only that Sennet's and similar models of consciousness necessarily fail?"

"I have a new version of the private language argument—would you read my paper on it?"

"Could you please repeat what you said about supervenience?"

"May I buy you a cup of coffee?"

I pushed through the crowd, grabbed Grossman by the arm, and led him down the hall as the groupies tailed us. I pushed him into an elevator and hopped in behind him just as the doors closed and the elevator started upward.

"Thanks, Greazy." He had tears in his eyes.

"It's all right. It's time to go get something to eat anyway."

"I'm sorry."

"Sorry? You beat all, Grossman."

"I didn't mean to anger everyone. I'm, well, you know, somewhat naïve about the propriety of these affairs."

"No shit. Listen, you really don't know what you just did there, do you? Saul, I've never seen anything like it. First of all, you confounded one of the most famous philosophers in the country by demolishing his theory. Nothing that significant ever happens at these conferences." Except, of course, for the wrestlers that morning. The elevator stopped at the fourth floor, and somebody got off. Grossman thought he was supposed to leave too and started to step out. I grabbed his coat sleeve and pulled him back.

"Second, I'm no expert here, but you may have just put the quietus on one of the hairiest philosophical problems of all time."

"You mean the mind-body problem?"

"What the hell else? Yes. Saul, nobody was angry at you—they were awestruck. And this was all off the top of your pointy damn head. You need to write up what you said in there, send it to the *Journal of Philosophy* or the *Review of Metaphysics*, and become a celebrity."

"But I'm not interested in philosophy of mind, Greazy." The elevator stopped at the sixth floor.

"Let's get off here." I sat him down on a bench in the hallway. "Look, you don't have to do anything right away, but you might want to consider whether you have an obligation to philosophy to publish this." I handed him a handkerchief, and he wiped his eyes. "Right now, let's go get some food and a beer."

We took the stairs down to the underground parking garage and then back up to the street. It was fun, like I was smuggling Elvis out of the building. As we stepped onto King Street, I saw Sue Meierson at the corner staring at a map. I 180'd and led Grossman towards Market Street, ducking people. How pissant can you get?

༄

On the way to Cap'n Henry's Big Fish Lounge for a couple of its famous marlin burgers and some onion rings, we walked through the Old Slave Market. The steps in front of the long building served as the auction block where most of the African slaves brought to the colonies were sold. Now you can walk inside to find the mall where you can buy "Charleston—the Holy City" tank-tops for nine dollars, "Charleston—Where It All Began" framed prints of Fort Sumter for twenty-five, and "Charleston's Own Hoppin' John" eight-ounce burlap sacks tied up in twine and containing thirty-nine cents' worth of rice and dried field peas for six bucks a pop. I imagined Frederick Douglass taking all this in for a few minutes and finally being able to say only, "Typical."

The Slave Market runs along the middle of Market Street with a lane of east-bound traffic on one side and west-bound on the other. On either side are arrays of specialty shops, where you can purchase authentic, antebellum, good ol' days horseshoes, single tracers, stirrups, and plow handles in the tack-and-tool antique shop, or get authentic, antebellum, idyllic life, olden-times Sunday dresses, button-up shoes, heirloom brooches, and hand-painted folding fans from the ladies' apparel antique shop. You can acquire your very own authentic, in-bellum era (when men were men, by God, and everybody knew his place) powder horn, deer-antler-handled knife, and Confederate soldier hat, complete with hole from mini-ball that doubtless killed poor Johnny Reb the day before the War of Northern Aggression ended, from the war and weapons shop. You can dine at the famous Smythe's, featuring Continental cuisine "prepared in authentic Charleston fashion" and offering a monstrosity called a burgundy grits soufflé, which I hoped no self-respecting peckerwood had ever tasted. And you cannot miss the horse-drawn carriage tours featuring history lessons from authentic Charlestonians who will assure you that no traditions have been lost in the Holy City. They'll also tell you where to find the best she-crab soup and whether the "eye-sters" are in season.

I was walking with perhaps the only out-of-towner unimpressed by all these scenes. In his usual, non-localized state of unawareness, nothing struck him as either charming or chintzy, so I decided we should cross State Street to the open-air flea market portion of the Market, where things are harder to ignore, and where Frederick Douglass would have been left gagging. Here the local blacks will hawk their vegetables and "authentic" folk arts. A little boy will run up and tug your pants leg, imploring, "Gimme a chance, sir. Gimme a chance!" He won't be begging, as he may have three-hundred years ago, that you stop the sale of his mother—just that you buy *his* cucumbers over those of the other three cucumber sellers. If a local turns the child away with a "Get on from hyere, son," the child might return a, "Oh, you one of we." You will find tables filled with "precious" African-American collectibles: cast-iron pickaninny banks that flip coins into their mouths; 45 rpm "race records" from the '30s with titles like "Jiggle That Jelly" and "Tight and Right"; tin signs that used to adorn grocery stores painted with tremendously lipped, nappy-headed, expert watermelon eaters pronouncing, "Dey sho is sweet!"; even guide books for *How to Speak Gullah*.

From her upturned washtub seat, a Hattie McDaniel look-alike, complete with bandana-wrapped head and apron covering her Tommy Hilfiger T-shirt, will flag you down with her sawgrass basket, and when you ask the price, will inform you she hand-wove it just as her grammammy did. And when you ask again how much it costs, she will tell you that she *earrr*ly in the morning hunts up the sweetest grass to be found on Jim (James) Island, and when you finally acquiesce and place a twenty dollar bill into her broad hand and expect change returned for the saucer-sized, bowl-shaped "basket," will not move that hand until you bless it with an additional ten dollar bill, whereupon she will signify that you have closed the deal with an "I thank you, sir."

I expected Grossman to be a shaken by these mild accostings, but he appeared only somewhat annoyed. I had forgotten that he had faced panhandlers nearly every day on the streets of New York and had to develop survival tactics. But then a gray, smoky smell cut through the sawgrass—leather and cardboard—and I heard a familiar voice. Grossman stared ahead with a look of wonder towards the source of the sound: the unmistakable, trademark call of the Peanut Man, who had walked these aisles at least as far back as when I was an undergraduate. He looked eighty back then, and I was astonished that he was still alive and still pulling behind him the *same* cart stacked with bags of peanuts. His marketing trick was to deftly insert a peanut into your hand as he passed by, and you would probably hail him back for a bag. He was still singing his signature song in his rough baritone:

Stick out yo' haaand,
Here come the Peanut Maaan.
I got 'em boil, I got 'em roas',
I got 'em parch, I got 'em toas'.
What kind you wanted?

Grossman accepted the peanut sample like a three-year old given a shiny quarter. He looked at me, as if awaiting permission, so I told him, "Go ahead," and he ate, handing me the shells.

"What kind was that?" he asked.

"Boiled."

"Bald?"

"Boy-uld."

Clicking away in his wingtips, he caught up with the Peanut Man and returned with a damp paper sack of boiled peanuts, then turned and watched as the old hawker continued on his circuit.

"What is it, Saul?"

"He reminds me of my grandfather."

"How's that?"

"He used to sell things from a pushcart and sing like that."

"I thought your grandfather was the *rebbe*."

"He was."

This was the same guy who may have made philosophical history in an articulate, sophisticated act of brilliance just twenty minutes earlier, but I felt like I was trying to drag something from an autist. "What did he sell?"

"Flawed diamonds and other second-rate stones that my uncle wouldn't sell in his jewelry store." He offered me a peanut, ate one, and handed me the shells again.

"He was the *rebbe*, and he hawked discounted jewels on the street? I didn't think they did that sort of thing."

"He was somewhat unorthodox." He tried to hide his smirk by squinching up the side of his mouth, but he was proud of his pun and could not contain a sneezy grunt of a laugh.

"Good one, Saul. Let's go eat some big fish."

Cap'n Henry's still looked like a big garage with mismatched chairs around cheap, Formica-top tables. It smelled like grease, starched white cotton, and straw brooms. The Tams's "What Kind of Fool?" was seeping through the speakers. A hand-drawn poster near the bandstand in the same old corner announced the appearance that night of the Half Rubbers, the most popular local band back when I used to haunt the place as a college kid. (Their name came from a game like baseball, originating on the South Carolina beaches. Two-man teams played with a broomstick, and with a rubber ball cut in half that curves wildly when pitched.) Another poster was signed by members of Bill Pinckney's Original Drifters who had performed there the previous September. No doubt the KA frat boys, their Tri Delt counterparts, and a few unaffiliated preppies had thronged the place in their flat-front, heavy-starch khaki pants, button-down, oxford-cloth, pastel shirts, and sockless deck shoes to do the shag, the official dance of South Carolina Republicans and the sexually frustrated.

Still behind the bar was Cap'n Henry himself, looking and sounding and filling up the room like John Huston, referring to himself in the third person, calling everybody Bubba and Sister as if he had always known them. The only noticeable difference, besides Cap'n Henry now having gray hair, was the doubled price of a marlin burger, still meaty and good and a bargain at twice the doubled price.

Grossman had loosened up and was, for him, in a talkative mood. He asked about the phenomenology session. I told him, and tried to explain professional wrestling. He told me about a philosophy of language paper he had heard but walked out on when he realized that its premise rested upon a logical error. He finished his sandwich and ordered—well, had me order for him—more fat onion rings and another round of beer.

For a few moments, we were both relaxed and ordinary, sitting there in my favorite bar as if Grossman were an old college buddy (he even almost tried one of my raw oysters; perhaps he clung to some kosher principles). And yet nothing had changed, which was the despairing part. Most people would have savored the moment, rolled the nostalgia around on the tongue, relished its flowery bouquet, appreciated the woody undertones of this fine vintage. I had to spew it out—a lardy wad of foul memories, a phlegmy hocker of a literary cliché. I was about to make my existential statement by paying the bill and leaving, but the waitress set a fresh pitcher on the table. The same damn place, the same laughing Cap'n Henry, the same people sitting up in the trailer at home, and the same sorry me returning like Lot to pat the woman-sized salt lick, survey the ruins, and *Mm-mm* at the dead suckers without the sense to flee but finding instead that it all is still here and hunky-dory. But the beer was cold, and angst slid down as smooth as an oyster. O lost Thomas Wolfe! O dark angel! How I wish you were here right now so I could kick your big Tarheel ass.

I saw no chance of getting Grossman back to the conference that afternoon and started to worry he might also refuse to go to the mixer, where we would have free drinks—paid for by our registration fees—and I could scope out a few acquaintances I wanted to run into. I also felt guilty about how I had treated Gilbert, and figured I could make it up to him by seeking him out and listening a little more sympathetically. And I would like to see Joyce. They had fed me supper at their house many times, and Joyce, an Alabaman and so another Southerner aliened in a strange land, sensed my culture shock and treated me like a son. At the very least, I could, with Grossman as my ticket, spend an hour at the mixer staring at Jackie Armstrong.

"Can't wait for that mixer tonight," I said. "Free drinks, finger sandwiches, stuffed mushrooms, and what do they call them? Crudités? No pressure to sound brilliant, just friendly chit-chat. Ought to be fun, eh?"

"I can't go, Greazy," he said, carefully splitting open an onion ring lengthwise with his greasy fingers as if he might be surprised by what he would discover inside.

"Aw come on, Saul. Those people aren't going to hurt you. They are in *awe* of you. You're their hero now. Do you realize how many people would kill to be in your place?"

"I don't want to be anybody's hero. I just want to do logic." He pulled the onion circle out of the split breading. I think he *was* surprised.

"Look, if you're scared they'll bother you, I'll take care of them. Remember, I'm a redneck." I smiled, winked, and punched him in the shoulder. "I can kick some ass when I need to."

"I'm not scared of them." He rubbed his bony shoulder.

"Then let's just go for one beer. If you get nervous or bored, we'll leave. Hell, we can come back here. There's a damn good band playing here tonight."

"I'm going back to your house for prelow."

"*Pur*lieu. That again? Saul, you're being very sweet, worrying about hurting my mother's feelings, but believe me, she's not expecting us. I told you, she knows the conference goes late."

"The conference doesn't go late. The mixer does. It's optional."

"The whole motherfucker is optional!" The conversation had taken quite a turn from two-good-buddies-having-a-beer a minute earlier. I had to take a chance. "Don't you want to see Jackie Armstrong? She was all over you at the registration table this morning." That would get him there, or backfire and scare him shitless, or I would finally learn he was gay.

"I'm not interested in her that way."

"Saul, are you gay?"

"No," he said and dipped an onion ring into his beer and studied the bubbles collecting on the breading.

"Then there's *some*thing you're not telling me. Either you have some reason for not going to the mixer, or some reason for going to my folks' place. Come on now. Time to 'fess up."

He bit the beer-soaked onion ring, chewed, swallowed, and had a sip of beer. He looked straight into my eyes, glanced towards the bandstand, then looked back, blushing. "Your sister is very beautiful. Just like that picture in your office."

"Oh my fucking God," I said. "You hard-peckered little bastard. Is that what this is all about?" He stared at his hands, palms up on the table and pressed together like a book. "You wanted to stay with my family all along, didn't you? Did you even *make* the hotel reservation?" He rocked and mumbled. I finished my beer in one long pull. "Saul Grossman, looks like there's only one thing for me to do." He looked up at me, terrified.

"Waitress," I called. "More beer."

FIVE
Hume's Fork

Maybe we will never see beneath the surface of the world's appearances, never peek behind the edge of the ontological veil. No amount of begging will get that skirt of Being hiked up so we can snatch a blushing glimpse of substance, succulent and raw. Even so, what if we found infinite layers of slips, petticoats, bloomers, and pantyhose, making for a tantalizing but endless phenomenological striptease that resulted in nothing more enlightening than a solipsistic jerking-off? What if there is no veil at all, no underneath? What if what we see is what we get—a big false promise, a fake palimpsest? Looking for more may be, as my namesake wrote two and a half centuries ago, just so much epistemological piss aimed into a skeptical wind.

The loveable David taught us there are only two ways of knowing. If certainty is what we want, we got our relations of ideas: tautologies, math, and logic. "Red things are red," "Triangles have three sides," and "Two and two are four" are necessarily true each time they are uttered. These are the sorts of things we can know with certainty without relying upon experience; we know them just by figuring them out. As soon as we see that "triangle" and "three-sidedness" are necessarily connected concepts, we know that we do not have to look at each newborn triangle to make sure it has the correct number of sides and is not a premie with only two. The drawback is that, in modern philosophical argot, assertions that are analytically true are only trivially true. Philosophers like to say that true statements are necessarily true in all possible worlds, which means they do not have anything to do with the actual world. "Psychologically well-adjusted logicians are psychologically well-adjusted" is necessarily true though no such people exist in the real world.

Now, if you want to say something true about the actual world, you've got your "matters of fact," as the elder Hume called them. The good thing is that they are non-trivial—that is, truly about reality. The bad thing is that they are at best contingently—just happen to be, do not *have* to be—true. The frustrating part, said the chubby old Scot, is that when I say "A chair is in the room" is true, all I can really be sure of is that I am having sensations of the sort I call a chair and a room. I can never know whether my description of what I see matches up to what is really out there. Like Uncle Rembert—a Hume and, unbeknownst to him, a Humean—we can only call them as we see them.

Thus the famous Hume's Fork: knowledge is either (1) necessarily true, not known through experience, but trivial, or (2) non-trivial, dependent upon experience, but contingently true. In other words, if you cannot see, smell, feel, hear, or taste it but think you know it, then it cannot have any material effect on your life. If you can see or smell it, you cannot know a whole lot about it. These are the only two tines to the empirical fork, and passels of tasty looking morsels fall onto the floor. Dear David said you would not want to eat that shit anyway. Let the dog have it.

No philosopher has slept well since. Gentle David said we cannot really know that one event causes another, or how. To slaughter just a few metaphysical sacred calves, we cannot know what substance—the stuff of things—really is; what the self, the "I," whatever makes me me and not you, is; whether or not God exists. If the old boy was right, then the ontological argument is shot all to hell. Even Immanuel Kant, whose massive philosophical enterprise was a response to Hume and undertaken simply to save us from complete skepticism, agreed with the good doctor that the old anything-goes metaphysics was, if not graveyard dead, at least in a persistent vegetative state. And even Kant, who tried to resuscitate as much as he could, pushed a pillow into the bony face of the ontological argument just to be sure.

So why did this thousand-year-old argument, this metaphysical relic, this ghost, this zombie, so haunt me? Was I truly convinced by Hartley's reincarnation of Anselm's baby, or was I like the desperate son consulting the charlatan psychic, who assures me of the dead father's continued love and protection? How could I not know whether or not I was convinced by the argument? Any sad sack in the street could be out of touch with his feelings, but it takes an accomplished, double-barrel dumbass not to know his own thoughts.

Of all the things you could say about squirrelly Saul Grossman, you could not accuse him of philosophical indecision. Ask away: "Grossman, is Descartes's argument for the existence of God in book three of the *Meditations* circular?" *Yes.* "Is Kant's categorical imperative binding upon all rational beings?" *No.* "Can unconscious zombies exist?" *Yes.* "Is Hume's Fork an accurate description of the limits of human knowledge?" *Yes.* "Does the ontological argument work?" *No.* "How will you mend your broken heart when my sister breaks it?" (No answer.) "Do you understand the question?" (No answer.)

༶

I drove the Volvo around Charleston to show Grossman the Dock Street Theater, Rainbow Row, the old Customs House, and the sideways-turned houses along the pinched streets, all of which failed to impress him about as much as they had always failed to impress me. We went to the Battery and looked at one hugely columned house after another. When I was a student here, I had imagined the residents of these obscenely-priced homes the descendants of the genteel plotucrats who had orchestrated a war, which the conscripted, co-opted, consumed crackers actually died for. Their sorry seed was still paying for it, breaking backs in the field or bony-fingering in the mill. The spawn of the high caste were, as always, sitting up in the cool of the big house. We stood by the concrete railings, and I pointed out across the harbor.

"Yonder's Fort Sumter."

"That island?"

"Yeah, where the war started. It accomplished exactly what it was intended to—the rich came out still rich and the poor peckerwoods who survived it were poorer than ever." The Marxism of my undergraduate days had long overslept, but the sight of those SOB palaces and the emblematic fort startle-effected it.

"You're talking about the Civil War, right?" Grossman broke the filter off a Winston. He must have run out of Chesterfields.

"I'm talking about switching my major from English to philosophy my senior year when I finally saw that Plato was right about how art covers up reality and pushes us another step down the dark passageway from truth instead of switching on the hall light. My interest in literature was mostly due to an early love of metaphor. I was about five when I figured out that when Johnny Cash sang about falling into a burning ring of fire, it was just a graphic image illustrating the emotional danger of love. And Leiber and Stoller, who wrote the song, would probably tell me I'm wrong, but I'm still convinced the Coasters were singing about a woman named Poison Ivy and not warning us about an allergenic plant you're likely to encounter in the woods."

Grossman lost three matches against the sea breeze. I snatched the truncated cigarette from his mouth and put it into mine, took the book of matches from his hand, and lit up on the first strike. The smoke smelled violet and crispy and tasted like being hit in the mouth by a raggy baseball. God, it was good, but I handed it back to him.

"The problem was, I began to think that everything was a metaphor for something else more true or more real. I reckon looking too hard for metaphors is not nearly as bad as not being able to see them at all, or not seeing them for what they are and mistaking them for the real thing, which is the problem religious people have." I leaned over the concrete railing and spat into the water.

"Anyway, later in grad school, I didn't know what to think when I found Aristotle stating the Platonic truth that the forms at work behind the scenes was a scam—a con to drum up enrollment for the Academy." Grossman looked at me as if waiting for a question. A gull flew near our heads, and Grossman winced, trying not to look too scared.

"In a Southern Lit seminar my senior year, the professor told us that somebody once asked Walker Percy why the South had produced so many great writers. Supposedly, he answered, 'Because we lost the war.' There was the obligatory hush, and I swear the professor teared up. I felt like the only Snopes in a roomful of Compsons, and I had to say, '*He* didn't lose any war. He was born sucking a silver tit.' Well, that was blasphemy, and in her notion of penance, she made me write my term paper on the importance of socio-economic class in Percy's novels. Mind you, I never said I didn't like his writing. In fact, he was one of my favorites—still is, too."

Grossman stared at me, probably awaiting some clue as to what sort of response I expected.

"Saul, have these stories I've been telling you the past couple of days been just farting in the dark? Do you have any idea what I've been saying? Hell, I'm not even sure I do."

He turned to look out across the harbor. "Do you remember that newspaper article the *St. Petersburg Times* did about us when we were hired?" he said.

"Sure. 'The New Faces of AmWorld U.,' or something like that—mostly about you, the boy genius. I thought it was pretty good."

"The interviewer's name was Rebecca Rosenberg," he said. "She knew nothing about philosophy, so it seemed to me we had little to discuss. But she asked me lots of questions. What do you think of Benjamin Netanyahu? Interfaith marriages? Is America ready for a Jewish president? I told her repeatedly I had no opinion on those matters. She got upset and said, 'What kind of Jew are you?' and left." He took off his glasses and wiped them with his fingers.

"It continues to trouble me," he said. "Even though, as you well know, Greazy, I'm often unaware of other people's views, it underscores the fact that they have expectations about me that I rarely fulfill. I can't control their estimations of me, so it's useless to worry. Nevertheless, knowing that I disappoint people, and knowing I lack a remedy, it hurts."

We were deep into December, but the breeze flowing across the harbor from Fort Sumter was not cold at all. The evening sun was darkening over our right shoulders. We watched a barge pass. The exhaust from the cars on the street behind us blended with the salt, birds, and coquina shell-based concrete to smell like spoons, like someone refusing a gift.

"Let's hit the road, Saul. Maybe I could use a big plate of Mama's purlieu."

✺

The underworld may be approached from any direction. Since Grossman had pitched a fit that morning when he realized we had to cross over the Cooper River Bridge again to get back into Charleston, I took the other route through the peninsula and North Charleston. It was the reverse of the route the Old Man would usually take when we had to make the journey to our Unreal City when I was a child. Traveling beyond the county line was an epic deed for us—one we would talk about for weeks preceding. "Don't forget now," Mama would say. "We're going up to Round O to see Uncle Noble and Aunt Pearl Saturday week."

"Are you naming gnats again?" Grossman asked.

"Yes," I said.

North Charleston, a nest of strip malls, tattoo parlors, a Super Slide that you could toboggan down on a square yard of felt for a dollar (which was a dollar too much for us), and Yankees who had descended to take jobs at the shipyard, was only a half hour away, but our jaunt there was torturous. Highway 52 turned four-lane at Goose Creek, where we changed counties, and the Old Man would place his left elbow against the car door and press thumb to temple. "I got my Challston headache a-coming," he would grumble.

To Mama, the four lanes meant big city traffic, and she would ride the rest of the way half-covering her eyes. The Old Man insisted on driving in the left lane because "They put the extry lane there so's you'd use it," and each time a vehicle would pass on Mama's side, she would whoop, "Hoo! They getting close!" Lucian found the ordeal hilarious and would aggravate Mama's fear with "Lord, what a big Mack truck coming now!" The Old Man would be too busy nursing his headache to say anything to Lucian, Willie would color and ignore everything else, and I would sit there wishing we would wreck.

Fortunately, these trips were rare. We would go to J. M. Fields department store in early August for school clothes (my brogans!) and then again in late October for some winter items. I usually got Lucian's coat from the previous year. Once, when I was eleven or twelve, I read the writing on the wall that I was about to inherit Lucian's Atlanta Falcons jacket, which he in turn had inherited from our cousin Pudge, who had actually been to Georgia when he worked with a fair (it left him in Augusta after he was caught passed-out drunk riding the Tilt-A-Whirl he was supposed to be running). I was a Miami Dolphins fan (probably because the quarterback was Bob *Griese*; it was close enough to "Greazy" for me) and was not about to betray them, so I took my Barlow knife and jabbed eleven gashes in the jacket.

"I don't know what Lucian's been up to," I said to Mama as I examined the damage, "but it's shameful how he rurnt that coat." Mama, saying not an impatient word, got out her sewing box and removed eleven spools of thread in different colors: a lime green, a scarlet, a powder blue, two shades each of yellow and orange, three pinks (two hots and a cool), and some color I still cannot name, maybe mauve or magenta. The only other time I have ever seen it was six or seven years later on a stripper's boa in a joint not far from J. M. Fields. Then she gave *me* the needle.

"Why can't I use the same color?"

"Might as well make it pretty," she replied. She made me wear the jacket that year, jagged little sutures and all. Dolly Parton herself would have been mortified by that many-colored monstrosity with the salmonish-orangish scar running across the falcon's head.

The rare drive to Charleston proper required a serious disease demanding the scrutiny of a *specialist*—the very word, uttered by Mama to her friends, propped her up with nonpareil pride—or the purchase of some item from Sears & Roebuck downtown on King Street that the Old Man believed could be bought legally nowhere else. Our first clue would be either Mama's setting everyone down in the living room to announce the appointment with the specialist for a condition she would never divulge, because "you would worry yourselves sick if you knew how bad off your mama is," or the map-staring the Old Man would begin about a week before and continue nightly despite repeated past trips and a total of three turns off Highway 52 to arrive in the Sears parking lot. If the trip to the specialist was serious enough to engage the entire family as well as an extra aunt as some sort of spare, we would even stay out of school.

Lucian once petitioned to be released from going to Mama's doctor's appointment, because, according to a rumor, it was the day the fabled sex education film was to be screened in gym class. There was no such film, of course, but all post-sixth-grade boys claimed to have seen it in gym class in the sixth grade. Lucian said he was assigned a book report on *The Deerslayer*—thinking the title would impress the Old Man, who would absolve him from the trip—and he was working *so* hard on it. To Mama, this meant only that her first-born was unconcerned with her grave malady, and she sobbed all night, which caused the Old Man to go out at *ten p.m.* to Flippo's Landing, the only place he believed to be open that late despite our assuring him that several gas stations in town, the Rexall, and probably the Piggly Wiggly were still open, but he could not risk having to backtrack, to get Mama some Kleenex. All Flippo had in his baitshop/pool hall (if one table constitutes a hall) were the individual purse-size packs, and the Old Man came home grumbling about how much he had to pay for six of those, admonishing her to "get three or four good blows out of each sheet."

Lucian pouted all the way to Charleston that day, but when the Old Man shocked us on the way home by stopping at Hampton Park to "see some monkeys," Lucian had to smile. He was probably more amused thinking the Old Man had made a wrong turn, ended up at the zoo, and saved face by pretending he had planned it than he was at the prospect of viewing the menagerie. Willie, only three or four, was spooked by the bigger animals, but not as much as Mama. She had been in a good mood following the doctor's referral to yet another specialist (the phone lines in Cordesville would overheat for the next couple of days). But all she could do at the park was cringe and whoop each time a bear, anteater, or sloth, all of which she called "boogers," would move or, worse, look her way.

The Old Man was mesmerized by the array of monkeys: rhesus, macaque, lemur, and spider. Ignoring the warning signs, he handed the macaques kernels of popcorn through the bars. A big male finally got annoyed, or jealous of the attention, and hurled himself at the bars like lightning and bit the Old Man's thumb. Lucian fell to the ground laughing, and the Old Man laughed, too, trying to act as if he wasn't hurt, but he went through an entire pack of Mama's Kleenex making little tourniquets. Lucian loved to tell the story, saying he couldn't tell which noise was louder, "that monkey slamming against the bars or the Old Man's asshole puckering."

By the next day, the thumb looked like a fig, but the Old Man swore it was due to his hurting it in the shop. Mama begged him to go to the doctor before "you catch the rabies," but he refused, and even after the swelling subsided in a few days, she continued to castigate him.

"Pledger, you like to got kilt from worrying them monkeys," she said.

"Ain't nothing worth doing," he said, "that don't nearly 'bout kills you."

In the meantime, Mama basked in the limelight at church, since she, because of her approaching, second-order specialist appointment, and the Old Man, with his monkey bite, needed prayers. After the laying on of hands—on her and then on me, proxy for the Old Man *in absentia* as usual—and the church let out, Lucian's teacher, Miss Turpin, told Mama how sorry she was, and in turn Mama told her how much Lucian hated missing school and not giving his "*Deerkiller* program." The next day, Miss Turpin told Lucian how happy she was that he wished to give a book report to the class and that he could do so the following day. He only "Yes'm"ed and went by the house of his friend, Sonny Cumbee, that afternoon to search through Sonny's closet of comic books until he found the Classic Comics version of *The Deer-*

slayer. He gave his book report and brought home a note from Miss Turpin expressing her surprise and delight that he had developed a love for great literature.

Grossman showed real interest in my recollections, asking for details like how old Lucian, Willie, and I were in each episode, whether each was a happy or bitter memory, and if the family discussed the event afterwards. Perhaps he was getting more from this memory exorcism than I was. He really perked up when we got to Moncks Corner and asked me to show him the school and kids' hangouts. All the while he wrote in his breast pocket notebooks, finishing one and starting a second. We passed Berkeley Elementary, whose blue metal-roofed, green vinyl-sided structures hardly resembled the collection of brick buildings I had attended. I pointed out the Center for Well Being, a narrow, two-story building, home to acupuncturists, chiropractors, and assorted other quacks and charlatans, which used to be Berkeley County Hospital where Lucian and I were born. Grossman asked where Willie had been born, and I explained that it was Tri-County Regional, which opened in Goose Creek a year or so after I was born, making the old hospital in Moncks Corner redundant. Lucian and I would make Willie cry by saying that Mama, out of shame, had gone to another county to have her.

When I announced that we were approaching Berkeley High, Grossman let out, "Home of the Stags!"

"How did you know that?" I asked.

"You told me."

"When?"

"In May, three years ago. It was the AmWorld commencement ceremony, and you told me how you and some of your friends had attached deer antlers to your mortarboards when you graduated. You did not attend your college commencement, nor your master's or Ph.D."

"How do you remember all the crap you do?"

"I thought it was important to you."

I was not sure what he meant, but just a few blocks past Berkeley High, I changed the subject by pointing out Moultrie Academy, the private school founded when South Carolina, a decade behind the rest of the nation and Berkeley County a year behind the rest of the state, integrated its public schools. R. A. Purify, which had been one of two black schools in the county, became the middle school for fifth through eighth grades, and the buildings that had been Berkeley Junior High and High, across the street from each other, combined to form an enlarged Berkeley High. Daily fights pitted the races against one another. At first the altercations occurred only at the high school. But after a couple of weeks, the middle school kids began emulating their older brothers. The trouble trickled down to the elementary school, and I led things off.

Our bus driver, a black woman named Zenobia Major, renowned in Cordesville for her homemade wine, arranged passengers according to age: twelfth grade in the back, first grade up front, which is probably how they would have sifted out on their own. The school board had instructed all the bus drivers to place white and black middle and grammar school kids in the seats together to promote "fellowship."

The Board wisely did not submit the high school kids to this seating scheme. Mrs. Major placed me between her son, Lyndon Johnson Major, and another black boy, Poitier Prioleau, son of the local root doctor, Poinset Prioleau, an albino whom everyone called Forty-Four. I had seen Poitier fishing the other side of the creek from me two or three times and remembered an occasion in which he laughed after catching a respectable redbreast while I had caught none. I couldn't forget how he howled when he pulled in a sizeable warmouth to my still nothing, and hopped around in a mud-slapping buck dance when he yanked up the biggest bluegill I had ever seen as my bobber remained half dry. I hurled a rock that did not make it across the creek, then went home.

Some time later, the Old Man dropped Lucian and me off at the canal to fish for catfish, and I saw Poitier and a couple of older girls, probably his sisters, fishing down the bank from us. Everyone was catching, and I lost track of who was leading. Lucian caught a leviathan of a flathead cat that must have been thirty pounds. I saw Poitier and the girls staring at the monster, and I grabbed its lower jaw in both hands, lifted it as high as I could, and hollered, "It's your little brother!," not knowing whether they were familiar with the local whites' epithet "nigger baby" for an overgrown catfish. Lucian told me to shut up.

The two girls turned away from us, bent over, flipped their skirts over their backs to expose their drawers, and chanted, "Lick it to the red, lick it to the bone. If you can't find the bone, just stand there and moan." Then one of the girls called us "ignorant crackers."

I knew that "cracker" was the blacks' slur for whites, but I had never heard it actually slung at anyone. I felt more embarrassed than hurt or angry, because even at that age, I recognized that a white being slurred by a black did not carry the same weight, the same threat. Nevertheless, I will never get used to Florida's dirt-diggers' acceptance of the term as equivalent to white native Floridians (by which they mean, as best as I can gather, that at least one parent, and at least one grandparent, were born in Florida, the other ninety-five percent of the population transforming the state into Jersey South) swearing no racial content to the term and claiming it originated as an onomatopoeia for the *crack* of the whips used by cow men herding scrawny cattle through the sandy scrub, earlier entries in the *OED* notwithstanding.

We rode the bus together in silence for the first four weeks. Lyndon Johnson slept to and from school, and Poitier, who gave no sign of recognizing me, stared out the window. Then one afternoon, on the way home, Poitier turned to me and said, "Been catching any?" and in my eight-year-old way of thinking, I needed no further provocation. I popped him in the mouth, and his head slammed against the window. For the other kids, the powder keg had been touched off, and a free-for-all ensued. The girls cried, and the boys took swings at each other. Lyndon Johnson, who then woke up, must have thought we had wrecked and started screaming. The reactions were so fast, and confusion so abundant, that Poitier had no chance to retaliate, though I suppose he tried. Mrs. Major, muscular and about thirty, stopped the bus in the middle of the road, leaped to her full height—close to six feet—and started swinging the leather strap she kept under the seat, with every lash leaving welts on fighters and the innocent alike. Six or eight high school boys of both colors tumbled out the emergency door and rolled around the road and into the ditch.

Calhoun Funderburk, who had retired a few years earlier after being sheriff for a decade and had graduated to bully of most of the county (a position that relied on no votes, not that Funderburk ever fretted over them as sheriff), stopped and helped Mrs. Major get everything settled down. Funderburk crammed all the white kids in the back of his flatbed truck and took us to our homes. For me, it was practically a ticker-tape parade, with the other kids—the boys at least—singing my praises. Lucian dubbed me "Smoking Joe" after fellow Low Countryman Joe Frazier, who had, as the Old Man said, "put a hurting on that loud-mouth Muhammet Lee." Funderburk, who had built a fearsome reputation on KO'ing drunks and backtalkers instead of using a billy stick and handcuffs, said to me as he dropped us off at the trailer, "Looks like you tagged that boy pretty good, sport. Pledger'll be proud of you."

He was not. After hearing Lucian's excited recounting of the episode, which I did not deny, the Old Man took me first to Mrs. Major's house and had me apologize to her *and* to Lyndon Johnson (I was tempted to ask, "For what, waking him up?" but wisely did not). Mrs. Major and her five children, of which Lyndon Johnson looked to be about the middle one, all ran out onto the porch as we drove up. She crossed her arms and listened to me. Then she said she appreciated my coming to her like a young gentleman and understood that the tension coming from the parents of "all two" colors was the real cause of my outburst. Nevertheless, she would make her report to the principal the next day, and one more incident from me would put me off the bus. Some sort of mutual respect sprung up between her and the Old Man. She gave him a bottle of scuppernong wine, and he asked if she liked venison. She said she and the whole family "loves some deer meat," but since she ran her husband off, she had not had any. The Old Man promised to bring her some soon.

We then went to the Prioleau home, a two-story, unpainted, splintery clapboard building with a rusted tin roof. You could not see the house from the paved road, but everyone knew the root doctor resided down that barely discernible, grassed-over lane, which ran about fifty yards in front of the house. The Old Man parked his International truck behind Forty-Four's old Nomad station wagon—with the back part of the roof cut off and the trunk dug out to form something like a pick-up—and walked through the muddy yard across springy one-by-six planks to the porch.

Forty-Four was rumored to have had thirty children by nearly as many women charmed by his hoodoo. None of the women lived with him in this house, but various, overlapping combinations of the children did. During the years I rode the bus to school, it was anybody's guess as to how many—usually four to eleven—would be at the bus stop that week. His progeny was explained by another rumor that he had three testicles and thereby an insatiable desire for poon-tang as well as extra-potent jism. Any woman dropping by to ask that a haint be placed on an enemy, or requesting some herbal remedy for the woman's miseries, was liable to leave seeded.

The Old Man rapped on one of the square posts holding up the porch roof. Heads peeked out through the windows, but no one answered. Chickens scratched in the mud, and something—we presumed a dog or two—bumped around under the house. He rapped again. Nothing.

"Mr. Prioleau? Pledger Hume, the gunsmith from over on Drowneded Horse Cut. I fixed your old double-barrel Fox a few years back."

"I know you, Mr. Hume," said Forty-Four, who emerged from the house. "That old gun still shoots good."

I had never seen him up close, and despite his bizarrely white skin, he did not appear as frightful as I had expected. He was thin, and his resemblance to Chuck Berry was reinforced by his curling-iron-straightened hair, which was also white. He appeared to be older than the Old Man, but that could have been due in part to the limp from his wooden left leg. The standard tale was that a jealous husband had shot him in the kneecap when he was a teen. He hid in the swamp for several days and came out with a gangrenous leg that had to be amputated. Still fearing the murderous cuckold, he left the county for several years, but supposedly returned immediately after the man died from a fever while frantically calling from his deathbed, "Poinset Prioleau! I sorry 'bout your leg!" The story served as proof that Prioleau, while on hiatus, had been trained in the hoodoo arts, and, as the gun that took his leg was reported to be a .44, it explained his *nom de guerre* as well.

"My boy Legare has something to say to your boy."

"Which one?"

The Old Man turned to me. "Which one?"

"Poitier."

"Well, tell Mr. Prioleau."

"Poitier, Mr. Prioleau."

Poitier, who had surely been peeking out the window, eased through the door and came to the top of the steps. His top lip was swollen, with a bright red split running through the fleshy part. He stuck his hands into his pockets and looked at me, but something more was in his gaze. It sounds like a cliché, almost like the bar fight in the old Western movie that ends in friendship between the lead and his rival, but Poitier and I came to an understanding, and I sensed that he too resented the adult meddling in something that should have remained between us.

"Tell Poitier what you came to tell him, son," the Old Man said.

"Poitier, I'm sorry I hit you."

"OK," he replied.

"Now go shake his hand," the Old Man said.

As little boys would, we did an exaggerated up-down pump. The Old Man sent me back to the truck while he and Forty-Four talked for a few minutes. I saw Poitier beside the house throwing a stick at wasps or dirt daubers under the eave. He glanced my way a couple of times. The Old Man came back with a rusty .410.

"Forty . . . Mr. Prioleau asked me to re-blue it for him," he said. "Probably for your buddy to shoot squirrels with."

The Old Man and I had to attend a conference with Rev. Sinclair T. Vanish, former R. A. Purify principal who had become the new assistant principal of Berkeley Elementary. County council member and tireless voter registration canvasser, he was a decent man who had worked hard but in vain the previous months to quell the fears of white and black parents and make the school integration as smooth as possible. Even in his ministerial regalia—three-piece, dark purple pinstripe suit (I developed the habit, from this experience, of addressing any black man in a suit as "Reverend"); lapel pins: Lions Club, VFW, some sort of fraternity; gold watch chain stretched from one vest pocket to the other and threaded through a button hole with a gold cross with "STV" on the crossbeam hanging from it; gold South Carolina State ring ('56?); gigantic, cube-like, gold pinky ring with what looked like the Greek letter psi on an opal; gold cross on a necklace over a yellow necktie propped up on a gold collar pin; round, gold cufflinks with little Bibles etched onto them—he looked less resplendent than exhausted. He spoke for fifteen minutes—sometimes to himself, it seemed—about how he had dreamed for years of equal access to education for every child, and had all but given up on seeing it in his home state in his lifetime when finally the good Lord answered his prayers. He surely must have seen my eyes welling up when he said, "Do you understand me, Mister Man?" calling me by his favored term of endearment for black and white boy alike. I did and answered, "Yes, sir. I'm sorry I hurt you," and he understood me and sent the Old Man and me on our way.

Grossman looked puzzled. "I don't understand the purpose of all the fighting."

"I'm glad you don't, Saul."

"Another thing," he said. "What's their relation to the dish your mother is preparing?"

"Jesus. The name is *Pre*-low. The dish is *per*-low."

꿈

At the edge of Cordesville is a region some of the old folks still call Gough. Marked by the ruins of Tabeau Church to the West—a foundation and a pile of bricks that used to be a chimney, only too burnt to be swiped and reused—with Hard Pinch Road to the east is the limestone road that leads to Rembert's place. I wanted to see him but was not sure how to fit in a visit. Besides, I would surely have to ditch Grossman somewhere. He was not ready for Rembert, who was not exactly Mr. Warmth and Hospitality when it came to strangers on his turf. As we passed the road, a truck was pulling out.

"There's your truck again," Grossman said.

"What truck?"

"Hume Shipping."

I looked into the rear-view mirror and saw a big white truck. "The one we saw on the way up here? Are you sure?"

"Yes. Quite a coincidence."

"That's no coincidence. That's my Uncle Rembert's road. Wonder what that old bastard's up to." Chances were that nobody else in the family would be able to tell me. They did not fear Rembert, but they all knew he was involved in shady dealings, and marveled at his ability to keep out of jail.

When we got to the folks' trailer, a red Oldsmobile sat in the yard.

"Now, who the hell is that?" I asked.

"I don't know, Greazy," Grossman answered.

"I *know* you don't. Could be Uncle Spessard and Aunt Arlene." He always drove red cars.

Mama came to the door in a jogging suit, beaming and wiping her hands on a dishtowel. She turned and said something into the house. By the time Grossman and I got to the porch, Spessard and Arlene were standing in the door, with Unitas between them.

"We was hoping y'all'd be here to eat," Mama said and hugged me.

"Great dow, Slick! You still ugly!" It was Spessard's standard greeting, which he seemed convinced was a riot. Arlene, who smelled inexplicably like green cinnamon apples, put her arms around my neck while Mama patted Grossman on the shoulder and said she hoped he was hungry. Spessard shook my hand. He looked so old, grinning and smelling like Mennen Skin Bracer and suede.

"Uncle Spessard, Aunt Arlene, this is my friend Saul Grossman." I turned to Saul. "Spessard and Arlene—"

"Driggers," Grossman said.

"Greazy musta warned you already, eh?" Spessard said.

"He said you were a card," Grossman said.

"The ace of *spades*, Bubba," Spessard said (another time-worn joke he still expected to be funny) and slapped Grossman on the back. Grossman coughed.

I held out my hand for Unitas to give me five as we assembled in the living room. The house was full of cooking smells: chicken (that should be crisper; she must have removed the skin first) and onions browned in the aluminum pot (the water and rice had not yet been added), pepper, cornbread with (imitation?) bacon bits, and something faint, maybe pole beans with a spoonful of olive (!) oil. It all smelled like the greenish yellow color and texture of a papaya.

Spessard, long and gangly and looking something like the actor Sterling Holloway but taller and about thirty pounds heavier, wore carpenter's dungarees as always, but instead of work boots, he had on deck shoes. His Duxback chamois shirt was pricier than I expected to see on him, but the CAT bulldozers cap was more true to character. Arlene's hair, which she used to dye black but had let go to brownish gray, was cut short and, my God, not teased. She wore a red sweatshirt with "Feliz Navidad" embroidered over a Christmas tree appliqué, a green polo shirt collar sticking out of the sweatshirt, Guess jeans, and Reebok tennis shoes. Wynonna, who hid behind Mama, followed her into the kitchen.

Unitas jumped up onto the couch beside me. "Uncle Spessard and Aunt Arlene came over to have supper with us. Then we're all going to watch the first night of Armageddon."

"Yeah, man!" Spessard said. "They's going to be some whomping up on this one! All the big boys are there. The Scourge, Beelzebub, the Texas Rangers, Jeb Stuart, Triple Six—"

"Azrael—" Unitas said.

"Mr. Wrestling Three—"

"Behemoth Hogan—"

"The Four Horsemen—"

"The Wrath of God—"

"Most of those guys have Biblical names," I said.

"I don't like it either, Legare," Arlene said. "They shouldn't blaspheme the Lord's Word like that."

"He's another one, 'The Word,'" Spessard said.

"And Gyges," Unitas added.

"Gyges?" Grossman sat up straight.

"He's my favorite," Unitas said. "He's got a magic ring that makes him invisible. He's a good guy wrestler until he gets real mad when the bad guy starts cheating, then he turns invisible and does all the dirty stuff to the other wrestler while they can't see him."

Grossman and I looked at each other. Gyges was a character in Plato's *Republic* whose ring—actually, I seem to remember it belonged to Gyges's ancestor—when turned around on the finger, made the wearer invisible. The character who tells the story suggests that any possessor of such a ring, even the most morally straight-laced, would have no reason not to rape and steal and kill as he pleased, since he had no fear of punishment. So, we had ourselves a philosophically literate wrestler.

"Aren't those contests fake? They follow a script, don't they, Greazy?" Grossman may have just committed a faux pas. I narrowed my eyes and gritted my jaw at him.

"Hell yeah it's fake," Spessard said. "Just like all that boxing, man on the moon, electing the President. It's all the same thing—just the gubment trying to cornhole us all."

"Spessard!" Arlene said.

"They probably fix racing, too," Spessard said. He turned to Unitas. "Hey, knothead, we're going to the race tomorrow, ain't we?"

"Yes*iree*!" Unitas said and jerked his chin to the side. He had picked up the mannerisms of old men.

"But they know who's going win it," Spessard continued, after interrupting himself. "*We* don't know, but them what runs it does."

"Doesn't that spoil it for you—knowing it's determined?" Grossman said.

"It would if I knowed who's going to win it, but I don't."

"But the result is no less pre-ordained." Only Grossman would try to make a philosophical discussion out of professional wrestling and stock car racing.

"It's kinda like watching a movie," Unitas said. "The movie's already been made, but you like watching it. I watch some movies over and over."

Even Grossman looked impressed by Unitas's precocity. Mama peeked her head out from the kitchen. "He sure does. He's watched the one with that singing bear about a hundred times."

"*The Jungle Book*," Unitas said.

"Who's that feller what does the bear?" Mama asked. "I always liked him in movies and things."

"Phil Harris," I said.

"That's him," she said. "He was funny."

"He was a drunk," Spessard said. "I seen him on the Merv Griffith show one time, drunk as a damn coot. Couldn't remember what the song he was singing was."

"Anyway," Mama said, "that's why your daddy bought that new TV and the tape player, because Unitas and Wynonna are over here so much. They love them movies."

I had not even noticed that the old RCA console was gone and a new thirty-six-inch Hitachi was in its place. A VCR sat on top with a stack of VHS tapes on the shelf behind it. A DVD player sat beside the VCR.

"Y'all want some tea?" Mama asked from the kitchen.

I looked at Grossman. He smiled and nodded. I wondered if the iced tea from Hog Heaven had been his first. Spessard and Unitas both said "yes," so I called to Mama, "A round for the house."

"Y'all been getting much rain down there in Floridie?" Spessard asked.

Jesus God, here we go with the weather obsession. Mama and the Old Man were even worse. I spoke with them on the phone so rarely you would think they would have something else to ask me about. Mama would assure me that the Low Country had recently been hotter or colder, drier or wetter than whatever I had reported about Florida. Then the Old Man would get on the phone, and I would go through the same routine with him about their meteorological hell.

"It's been sort of dry down there."

"Talk about dry," said Spessard, who took off his cap and hung it on the toe of his right shoe that was crossed over his left knee. "We been having the worst drought ever. Hard on the farmers this year, and the gubment won't give 'em nair *bit* of hep."

Arlene looked at the floor and shook her head. "The Bible says there'll be famines in the last days. Mmm."

I looked to Arlene. "Say, where's the Old Man?"

"He's gone to the grocery store, sugar," Arlene said. She looked somewhat like Alice Ghostley, and sat in her usual mousy posture with her hands folded in her lap. She loved *Reader's Digest*, and in an attempt, I always supposed, to make up for quitting school, she tried, rarely successfully, to memorize its "Increase Your Word Power" section "Your mama needed some ingredients for her . . . festive comesticles, what with Christmas and all. How did you hurt your head, shug?"

"He—" Grossman began, then caught himself when he saw my gritted teeth.

"I slipped in the bathroom just before we left yesterday morning." The subject badly needed changing. "Where did you get that pretty sweatshirt, Aunt Arlene?"

She grinned and brushed as if crumbs were on the shirt. "Lily Kirby brought it back to me from Mexico. You remember her from the beauty shop? She and Merle—that's her husband—took them a little jolt down there a month ago." She pulled at the sides of the sweatshirt to display the writing. "It says 'Merry Christmas' in Mexican." *Mexican.*

"Merle said they had the shits the whole time, too," Spessard said.

"Spessard! Don't be so ugly," said Arlene.

"Them doctors put something in that water down there that gives you the galloping trots," he continued. "That's the only way they can get anybody to go to them. Ain't nair one of 'em got no real doctor degree."

"That ain't so," Arlene said. Unitas giggled at the fight. "Legare, hon, your mama said Tally was sick."

"Yes'm. Strep throat. She's staying with her mama."

"Mmm, mmm," Arlene pursed her lips and shook her head. "That can be a real bad affaliction. Let me help Raylene with that tea." She went to the kitchen.

Grossman fidgeted in his seat, as if he was trying to work up to saying something. I had a good idea what it was.

"What is it, Saul?" I asked.

"I was just wondering," he said, and his eyes darted around to the others in the room. "Um, where's Willie?" I'd been right.

"She went with Papa to the store," Unitas said.

Wynonna peeked around the corner. I stuck my tongue out at her, and she smiled before disappearing back into the kitchen. Her mother was like that as a child: feigning shyness, not letting anyone have a full view of her. When she hit her teens and a hormonal flood washed through her, she transformed into anything but coy. She started sneaking out at night at thirteen, and none of the Old Man's whippings at first or groundings and threats later slowed her down. Mama found birth control pills not well hidden in Willie's dresser when she was fourteen. She had a bigger chip on her shoulder than Lucian or I ever did and seemed to invite confrontation with the old folks.

"Me and Lucian are not any more goody-two-shoes-er than you," I said to her once. "We just don't brag about what we might be up to."

"I do as I please," she said.

"I ain't telling you not to. I just can't figure out why you make it so hard on yourself, like that stunt with your pills."

"What?"

"You put them right there for Mama to find them."

"I did not!" She threw an Adidas tennis shoe at me. I caught it and tossed it to the floor.

"I'm trying to help you!"

She continued her tantrum, punctuating her words with a barrage of apparel and cosmetics. "I don't need *your* or *Lucian's* or *Aunt Arlene's* or any goddamn body else's *god*damn help! God*damn* it!"

By the end of the tirade, I had managed to dodge her other shoe and her blow dryer, but her compact frisbeed directly into my forehead, spraying rouge all over my hair. I didn't realize then that my forehead was a magnet for female-hurled discs.

Within a week, a similar manifesto of independence was declared in varying degrees of goddamnness to everyone close to Willie. She wanted minimal contact with the family, and since Lucian had already moved out, and I started college only a few months afterward, Mama and the Old Man were the primary targets of her avoidance. Mama had the church congregation pray for her and for Willie every week. The Old Man stayed late at the shop every day, unable to bear the silence and emotional absence of his daughter.

Unknown to the rest of us, she was taking extra courses so she could graduate from high school a year early. Immediately after that, she moved out of the trailer and in with an older friend named Trixie ("A trash name," the Old Man said) in town who had just divorced and opened a gift shop. Willie was Trixie's sole employee and babysitter, saving every penny all the while. When Trixie re-married a guy from the shipyard who took her back to his home up north, Willie used her savings and a small loan co-signed by Spessard to buy the shop and convert it into a dress boutique.

The shop did pretty well, and she took business courses at night at Tech and then at the College of Charleston until she completed a bachelor's in business administration and even took a few grad courses toward an MBA. She was truly independent and felt safe enough, I suppose, to reconnect with the family. She never exactly apologized, which no one expected or would have believed anyway, but in her own way made it clear that her rash days were behind her, she was mature, and using her favorite word for a while, was "centered."

Then she surprised us all—and probably herself—by marrying Rupert and moving to Myrtle Beach, but she remained proprietor of the boutique, consulting daily by phone with the manager. When she left Iron-on Boy, she returned to Moncks Corner with the kids and picked up right where she had left off, except happier than ever. Within a year, she had opened a second dress shop in Jamestown.

"Mommy!" Wynonna squealed, scampering out of the kitchen toward the front door as Willie and the Old Man entered. She jumped into Willie's arms and looked back at me, then just as quickly hid her face.

"Has mean old uncle Gweazy been bovering you?" Willie said.

"Well, look who's here." The Old Man took off his Carhart coat. "How was your big philosophy sashay?"

"It was OK," I said. "Nothing exciting."

"It was good," said Grossman, standing to shake the Old Man's hand. He shifted from foot to foot. "How are you, Willie?"

"Fine, Saul. I thought y'all weren't going to make it back in time for supper. Let me set these bags in the kitchen."

"Allow me," Gentleman Grossman offered.

༄

I had never seen Grossman eat so much. For his third plateful, he did not even wait to be asked, feeling at home enough to reach across the table and mound it up himself. In the exuberance of this extended helping, he kept the serving spoon to shovel the rice up to his mouth. He shined two thigh bones, gnawed a back, and held a parson's nose up to the light, making sure no sinew escaped.

"He does pretty good for a little feller," the Old Man said.

"Y'all remember the Goat Man?" Spessard asked, pointing at Grossman. "I be dog if don't look like the Goat Man."

"Who's the Goat Man?" Unitas asked.

"Here we go," Willie said. Wynonna had crawled up onto her lap, still playing coy.

I had heard tales of the apocryphal Goat Man who came to town periodically in a wagon with a string of goats following. He sold various goods depending upon whom you asked—some said pots and pans, others said work clothes, some swore it was Feel-Good Tonic.

"He *do*," the Old Man said in his archaic emphatic subjunctive, a vestige of Elizabethan English or just backwoodsese, "with that beard and him so skinny and all." He washed down a last bite of cornbread with his tea. "Good thing he don't smell like the Goat Man. Lord *God*, you could tell he was coming the day before he got there."

"I bought a knife from him one time," Spessard said. "One of them camping kind with a fork and spoon on it. Had a corkscrew. Now what in hell would you do with a corkscrew out in the woods? Wine bottles got the screw caps, anyhow. It just don't make no sense."

"Go on," Arlene said. "He didn't sell no camping knives and such. He carried kitchen apparatusments like frying pans."

"He was really a preacher," Mama said. "He preached from the back of his wagon, and it would turn into a revival. My Uncle Drayton got saved one night at one of the Goat Man's preachings."

"I don't remember no preaching," the Old Man said.

"You sure don't," Mama said.

I could not remember whether, as a kid, I had actually witnessed the Goat Man and his caprine entourage. I had heard the stories so often I had probably constructed false memories, but I did know that the fuss about the exact nature of the goat procession—a modern-day Dionysian triumph—would keep them occupied for at least another twenty minutes, and Grossman was thoroughly engulfed in stripping every crevice of a chicken neck. So, it seemed a good (or opportune—none was exactly good) time to slip out and call Tally. I went to the folks' bedroom for privacy; the one other phone was in the kitchen. I had no idea what I would say, but by Tally's reckoning, I could say nothing as insulting as not calling.

"Hello?"

"Hey." Long pause. I knew she would wait for me to continue.

"How are you?"

"Fine."

"Everybody's doing pretty good here. We're staying with the folks instead of the hotel. Uncle Spessard and Aunt Arlene and Willie and the kids are all here having purlieu. I snuck off to give you a call."

"Hm." I thought I heard Jason Alexander in the background. She must have been sitting in her chenille gown watching a *Seinfeld* rerun.

"What are you doing?"

"I'm sitting here by myself having a Lean Cuisine teriyaki chicken with almonds." Well, it *was* a sentence.

"I really wish you were here with us."

"Jesus."

"I told them you were sick and couldn't come. I couldn't tell them, you know—"

"Oh, for Godsake!"

"They really love you, Tally. Could I tell them you didn't want me to come see them so much that you pegged me with a plate?"

"Could you tell them I was not invited—that you just up and left? What happened? Did the hotel lose your reservation? You didn't tell them you were not there to see *them*, now did you?" OK, she was ready to talk.

My head started to ache for the first time in hours. "No. And yes, the hotel lost the reservation, but that's beside the point. Look, you know it's important I read this paper—"

"Don't tell me what's important. You have no idea."

The door opened, and Mama came in. "Is that Tally? Let me talk to her."

"Mama, she's not feeling—" She took the phone from my hand.

"Tally? How are you, shug?" She waved me away. "Oh yeah. I know he is. That's right." She waved again and said to me, "You go on out. I'll get you back when I'm done with her."

I went into the bathroom and removed my bandage. There was no blood, so I didn't replace it. The bump around the quarter-inch scab was about an inch in diameter and purple with orange around the edges. I found some Extra Strength Tylenol in the medicine cabinet, took four of them, then returned to the kitchen. Willie, Arlene, and Grossman were removing the plates from the table. Unitas was listening to the Old Man and Spessard say something about the race the next day. Wynonna was sticking her tongue through a napkin.

"We're fixing to have some grape pie," Willie said. "Want some?"

"No thanks, I'm full." I was about to throw up.

"Looks like he's got a daub of it stuck to his head," the Old Man said. "That's a pretty nasty-looking knot. It still hurt?"

"Not nearly as bad."

"They say you ought to put frozen peas and carrots on a bruise," Arlene said. "They supposed to stop the swelling."

"It don't got to be peas and carrots," Spessard said. "Just so's it's cold."

"The magazine in the *doctor's* office said peas and carrots." Arlene set down her tea glass a little too hard. Unitas giggled.

I looked at Willie. Sensing that my tolerance was nearly sapped and that I was about to bolt, she made a blowing sigh and gave me a look that said it really was not that bad.

"Maybe the frozen peas," I said, "since they're little, could mold around a wound pretty well." If you can't beat 'em, join 'em. Willie raised an eyebrow at me.

"Well, I sure as hell wouldn't eat 'em after that," said Spessard.

"You don't take them outen the bag, Spessard," Arlene said. "I swanee, sometimes you exaspergate me so!" Unitas laughed and snorted tea out of his nose.

Willie and Grossman set the plates with pie slices onto the table. Wynonna stuck her fingers into the purple goo seeping out from between the layers of crust.

"Where's Mama?" Willie asked, wiping Wynonna's hand on a dish towel.

"She's on the phone," I told her. "With Tally."

Willie widened her eyes and smirked at me. "You might be wanting a slice of that crow pie on the stove over there." I made a nyah-

nyah-very-funny face at her.

"Unitas laughed. "Crow pie! That's a good one, Mama.""

Did *every*body suspect the strep throat story?

"How's she feeling?" Arlene asked.

"A little better. She said to tell you all she loves you." It was time to divert attention. "What's old Uncle Rembert up to these days?" I asked.

"Still running around with that white nigger," Spessard said.

"Spessard!" Arlene said, popping his shoulder with the back of her hand.

"Honestly," Willie said and clanged her fork onto her pie plate. She got up and took the tea pitcher back to the refrigerator.

"Well, I can't call him 'colored,' now can I?" He looked at me and turned up his palms in a who-understands-women gesture. Grossman had already finished one slice of pie, and Willie got him a second.

"Him and Forty-Four been up to some kind of dealings for the past year or two," the Old Man said. "We don't hardly see him—him gone so much. Says he does international trade."

Unitas asked to be excused and ran into the living room to turn on the TV.

"Past year or two? Hell, Rembert and Forty-Four been asshole buddies since goat was calf." Spessard turned to me. "They started running off to South America or somewhere back when you was still living here, Greazy. They go down that way about every year."

"What for?" I asked.

"Who the hell knows?" Spessard said. "But one thing's for sho. Hanging around Forty-Four don't improve his rel*ation*ship none with old Calhoun Funderburk."

"What do you mean?"

"Bubba," Willie said, "do you *really* want to hear this?"

"He ast me," Spessard said. "See, Funderburk don't like Rembert nair bit, but he can't stand Forty-Four, ever since that thing with his wife."

"You don't know that," Arlene said.

"Everbody knows it. How it started was . . . you know how Forty-Four's got them three balls?"

Grossman leaned towards me and whispered, "B*oi*ls?"

"No," I sighed, "this time it's balls."

"So, he was always sniffing up the leg of ever woman who come in his sight," Spessard said.

"I got to go to the bathroom," said the Old Man. His jaw was set at an odd angle, and he mumbled something as he lurched down the hall. I looked at Willie, who glanced at me and then at Arlene.

Spessard continued. "Hatch Tillman, the deputy, was riding by Funderburk's house one day and seen Forty-Four going in it. Hatch pulled side the road and radioed Funderburk, which was a big mistake 'cause it got Hatch's ass chewed out, because everbody in the county—the ambulance, the game wardens, the road crew—used that same band, and Funderburk woulda just as well kept the whole thing to hisself. Then—"

"Mr. Driggers," Grossman said. He picked something from his teeth—probably a grape seed—and held it up an inch from his eye. "I don't think we can meaningfully attribute motives to others. The problem of other minds—"

"What Saul is saying," I said, "is, who told you this? Funderburk?"

"Hit don't matter who told me. Everbody knows," Spessard said.

"Third and fourth hand, Legare," Arlene said, "and all come from Hatch Tillman to start with. I believe he fabricatered the whole thing."

"Can I go on now?" Spessard pointed his fork at Arlene. "So Funderburk got home and clumb out of his sheriff's car with his shotgun, told Hatch to stay right where he was. His old lady, Ginny—that was one good-looking womern—come a-running out in just her house coat, and hit already leb'm in the morning, a-hollering 'What you doing home? You ain't supposed to be home' and Funderburk just walked on past her and into the bedroom, but he didn't see nothing. Not at first." He took a forkful of pie and chewed. Grossman stared wide-eyed at Spessard and clinched a handful of oilcloth.

"Then he looked down, and sticking out from under the bed was Forty-Four's foot. So ol' Funderburk unloaded that twelve-gauge pump ... no he didn't. The last shell jammed, because he brought it to your Daddy to fix right after that, and Pledger said Funderburk just ha'n't took good care of it. You know a pump is pretty simple and don't hardly never hang up, especially a Browning, unless you don't keep it oiled up good."

Grossman whispered, "*Oi*led?"

"You're catching on," I whispered back.

"Well, he got off four shots, and Ginny was screaming, and Hatch come running in, and Funderburk had blowed the bed and the floor all to hell. But there wa'n't no Forty-Four there." He had a long swallow of tea.

"Where was he?" Grossman said. He shifted his eyes toward me. I made no sign.

"Hit was just his wooden leg! Ha ha!" Spessard said and punched Grossman in the shoulder. Grossman winced and tried to smile. "He'd pulled it off for a decoy while he slipped out the back door and hopped through the woods and made it out of there with just one asshole."

"Spessard, don't be ugly," Arlene said. She took her dish to the sink.

"Why didn't Funderburk ever get him later on?" I asked. "Nobody could have stopped him."

"Because he's scared shitless of Forty-Four," Spessard said. "Funderburk believes in all that hoodoo. He went off for a couple of weeks after that—said it was to a big sheriff's convention in Savanner. Everbody knowed he was just afraid of some haint Forty-Four'd throw on him. When he got home, his old lady'd left him, and he ain't heard from her since."

Grossman looked amazed. "That's a fascinating story, Mr. Driggers."

"He ain't done, honey," Arlene said.

"Forty-Four come to me a few days later with a big old cypress knee. That was even before I got serious about carving. He seen a couple things I'd carved and set out in the yard, so he ast me to make him a new leg. I traced his left foot—"

"*Which* one?" Grossman asked.

"His onliest one, and he told me about the old leg—how the top was cupped out and had a leather pad on it and straps hooked to it and all. Then he drew some little shapes and words, Spanish or something, on a piece of paper and told me to carve them in the leg, too. Some kind of root doctor pictures, I reckon. Hell, what did I give a damn? He said it worked just fine, and I didn't charge him anything for it, because I didn't really know what I was doing anyway. That cypress foot turned out to be pretty good advertising, because wa'n't long after that people started asking me to carve things for them. I ain't seen him in a while, but Poitier says hit's still the one he's got on."

"Poitier? You see him?" I was curious as to what he was up to.

"I take a dog in ever now and then," Spessard said. "You didn't know he was the vet now? Has been for about five or six years. Went to a regular vet school and everything."

"There's only one kind," Willie said, also knowing his "regular" meant white. "I swear."

Spessard ignored her. "And you know what else? He don't charge me a dime, because of that foot I made his daddy for free."

Willie cut her eyes at me, acknowledging the double irony of (1) the root doctor's son studying bona fide medicine, and (2) the boy who scammed half the hunters, including Spessard, years ago by mysteriously finding their lost hunting dogs for a few bucks after the hunters had given up, was now healing their dogs.

As a kid, Poitier would ride the country roads on his bicycle, find a lost hunting dog, loop a rope through its collar, take it home, feed it a couple of days, and then show up at the hunter's (whose name would be etched onto a small brass tag on the collar) house and offer his finding services. Believing in the mystical abilities of black folk, especially the son of a root doctor, the hunter would hand him three or four dollars, and the next day Poitier would deliver the animal. He got a bit too greedy ("long-eyed" in the local blacks' lingo) and stopped dealing in errant dogs, instead kidnapping them from their pens.

Poitier's mistake came when he tried to get one of Jeremiah Bunch's redbones from a pen newly encircled with electric wire. The jolt was strong enough to burn Poitier's hands and melt one of his shoe soles. Bunch, who had no idea how powerful the charge was, heard the pop and went outside to find Poitier sitting on the ground stunned and mumbling something that Bunch, who recognized the root doctor's son, took to be a black magic curse. He rubbed butter on Poitier's hands, gave him a pair of his own son's shoes, stuffed a five dollar bill into his pocket, and took him home to Forty-Four. After that, when someone would ask him to find something, Poitier would say he had lost his power.

Spessard's story may have finally run its course, so I tried to get back into the conversation. "Does Uncle Rembert have a big white truck?"

"Hume Shipping," Grossman said.

"That's his'n," said the Old Man as he returned from the hall. "He runs it up and down the Interstate to Floridie for something or other. Y'all shoulda hitched a ride with 'em."

"Is he still planting tobacco?"

"Wacky tobacky," Spessard said and poked Grossman in the ribs. Grossman choked on his tea.

"He does not," Arlene said. She patted Grossman on the back.

"No. He does mostly corn now," the Old Man said. "Some special breed that grows up way high and gets these big old tossles on it. You can't hardly see the swamp from his house when the stalks get up."

Mama returned and took her seat at the table. "Tally says Merry Christmas and to tell you all she loves you." She looked at me. "Her throat was bothering her, so she had to hang up. She said for you to call her tomorrow if you had time for her."

Not if I had time, but if I had time *for her*. Was that a clue she had spilled her guts to Mama? My head was drumming between my eye and ear as if a red cockaded woodpecker was trying to peck his way out of my skull.

"The pie was terrific, Mrs. Hume," Grossman said.

"Well, thank you, shug," Mama said. "Here." She raked another slice onto his saucer. He took a bite.

"It's a shame you and Tally can't be together on Christmas," Arlene said to me.

"How's Uncle Chalmers?" I asked, ignoring Arlene.

"Chalmers's the same as he's always been—still walking the road," the Old Man said.

"Purvis works with Rembert some," Arlene said.

That was Arlene's way of saying her feelings were on the verge of being hurt for my failure to inquire about my cousins. I asked, "How are DeWayne and Purvis doing, Aunt Arlene?"

"Fine," she said. She looked away and pulled at the hair behind her ear.

"Purvis don't turn a lick," Spessard said. His bottom lip stuck out in a scowl.

"He does so," Arlene said. "He bushhogs."

"How many times? Twice? He loads up *my* tractor and *Thaydo's* bushhog and cleared a couple of pieces of land for Judge Villeponteaux," Spessard said. Thaydo—that is, Theodore—was Arlene's and Mama's brother. "That ain't hardly working."

"Not everybody likes to work," Arlene said.

"Nobody *likes* to work," Spessard said. "You know Purvis married him a brass ankle last year, eh?"

"She is not," Arlene said. "She's half Chinaman."

I never knew its origin, but I'd heard the term "brass ankle" all my life. A population of curly-haired, brown-skinned people lived towards the southern end of the county. Most looked as if they might have been Hispanic, while others looked like Anglos with kinky hair. About six or seven surnames covered them all, two of which were Filipino. One popular theory was that a couple of Filipino families ended up there and intermarried with some of the locals, producing a cur strain unique to the region. Others considered the Filipino presence accidental and unrelated to the brass ankles proper who composed an aboriginal breed *sui generis.*

Lucian speculated that "brass ankles" referred to leg shackles and argued that they were the descendents of runaway slaves, sixty-fourth-aroons at least by then. However their origins were explained, the local white bigot scale usually placed them below Hispanics (of whom there may have been one or two in the county) and just above blacks. For my generation, thankfully, the term was nearly completely descriptive, and almost entirely wrung of any residual connotation of moral difference.

"What's DeWayne up to?" I asked, rubbing my temple with the heel of my hand.

"He works at a tittie bar in Charleston," Spessard said.

"He does *not!*" Arlene said, backhanding him again. "He's the manager at a lounge. DeWayne says its just businessmen stopping off for a ree-spite after work."

Unitas ran into the kitchen. "It's Armageddon!"

SIX
The Ring of Gyges

Jackie Armstrong would be holding court. The Big-Timers and their kibitzers would be dominating one portion of the room with their mindless game. The sorry souls on the job market would be cutting their drinking off to prevent hangovers at their morning interviews and thinking about hitting the sack early, while holding out hope that weaving one more networking fiber would be useful. Sue Meierson would surely be giving some dickhead an earful of vaginalalia. Gary Winters's interview might have gone so well that he could be having a celebratory round with his soon-to-be new colleagues; more likely, he was on his fourth scotch and hoping his plane would crash on the way back to Louisiana.

Instead of symposing it up with the floating clabber of America's philosophical crop, I was sitting in a trailer in Hell Hole Swamp with people whom just the day before I had schemed to avoid, about to watch on TV the world's grandest professional wrestling tournament. There were disquieting companions on either trail I walked—for some of us, Siddhartha, there is no middle path.

The wrestling tournament began with a dazzling spectacle: Huge screens projected images of wrestlers' menacing faces with a backdrop of assorted U.S. state and wrestling league flags, along with sordid scenes of destruction with fiery buildings, mushroom clouds, Dantesque piles of writhing and tormented bodies, and batlike demons winging through dark gates made of skulls.

A tremendous stage had been erected with stringily-clad dancers gyrating on top and trapeze flippers swinging beneath. Acrobats hovered over the screaming heads of the fans, lasers zipped and pulsed through the arena, and playing in the background, barely recognizable over the blasting bass, came the Talking Heads's "Burning Down the House."

Circling outside was a blimp whose electronic billboard sides scrolled "Elixir—Racing, Wrestling, Gettin' Real!" and alternately flashed "Merry Christmas" and "Armageddon."

The cheery hosts roamed ringside, gushing over a parade of celebrities: a former U.S. senator turned CEO of Elixir, three athletes turned actors, two rock stars turned authors, the People's Party's former presidential candidate turned comedian, former Miss America turned NRA President, Miss South Carolina, Ms. South Carolina, a TV chef, two televangelists with lacquered pompadours of black and white, respectively, and the official inaugurator of the tournament—legendary racecar driver Cale Yarborough. Cale was also set to announce "Boys, start your engines" at the Elixir 600 the next day.

Reporters stalked the dressing rooms interviewing the growling, taunting, already sweating wrestlers. Most promised it would be "judgment day" for one of the others, while some called for a "day of atonement."

"Hey, it's Yom Kippur," I said to Grossman, who did not seem to hear me.

One wrestler even assured another, Jesse-Jacksonly, that it was too late to propitiate. That one, despite elaborate make up and a hooded cloak, looked familiar.

"There's Gyges," Unitas said. "Man, he looks pumped!"

"That's Gyges? I believe I know that guy," I said. "I think he gave a paper at the conference today." The camera panned across the huge crowd, isolating an unsuspecting face here and there. "Saul, look!" He was lying on the floor beside Unitas and writing something in his notebook.

"Who wants some coffee?" Mama called from the kitchen, where she and Arlene were piddling.

"I do, please," Grossman said.

"Me, too," the Old Man said, and Spessard right after.

"Saul, in the stands," I said. "I think I just saw McDavid and Donaldson."

"I didn't see, Greazy."

"This is bizarre," I said to Grossman, who did not seem to agree. "I noticed an Elixir logo on McDavid's, or was it Donaldson's, shirt last night. Worlds in collision."

"Legare, honey, did you want some?" Mama called.

"No, ma'am." My headache had tapered off, and I was afraid caffeine might bring it on again.

"Them fellers they just showed in them neckties is philosophers?" Spessard asked.

"Not just philosophers," I said. "They're about the most famous philosophers in the country, in the world even."

"You see what I been saying?" Spessard's top lip pulled up as if he smelled something foul. "You can't hold onto a damn thing. They took country music from the po' man. Half them singers with their four-hundred-dollar cowboy hats is from New York City." He glanced quickly at Grossman, who seemed to be paying no attention. "People in all the big cities is driving eight-cylinder trucks and calling them SUVs. And it ain't enough to put all them fancy lights in the wrestling arenas and run them burley-cue girls around the ring and dress up the wrestlers with they shiny suits like Porter Wagoner. Now the big college puh*fess*ors got to get in on it, too."

He was certainly right about this much: professional wrestling had changed considerably since my childhood days, when I watched the Missouri Mauler, George Becker, Johnny Weaver, and Chief Wahoo McDaniels. The days of thick-waisted, middle-aged men on Mid-Atlantic Wresting Sunday afternoons from Charlotte seemed to have passed. Back then, Lucian and I pulled for the bad guys, half-ridiculing the whole bunch, while the Old Man would defend them with, "I'll tell you this, them fellers are in shape."

The coffee was brewing—rich and cool (that's how it smelled, cool) and oval—not instant.

One of the announcers climbed into the ring. The bell rang, he welcomed the crowd and thanked Elixir, whose CEO stood up and threw a kiss to the crowd. Then the announcer promised "a battle of cosmic proportions between the forces of good and evil." Every sentence he spoke brought cheers or boos from the audience. One of the wrestlers—the Wrath of God, who claimed also to be a minister—offered a prayer, asking that "God's will be done in the ring as it is in heaven." Cale Yarborough invited everyone to join him in an Elixir toast to christen the event. Then a guy dressed like an angel came out and played the national anthem on a trumpet, and the wrestling started.

Most of the bouts ended inconclusively, with bad guys pulling stunts undetected by the tunnel-visioned refs. Fans held up signs with Biblical citations: Matthew 24:21, Luke 13:34-35, but most from Revelation. A couple of times, the wrestling looked more like a mob scene, at which point the announcer would gleefully declare, "There's pandemonium in the ring!" Even Grossman seemed to enjoy this modern-day passion play, and we all whooped it up, applauding the good guys and condemning the dirty deeds.

The women joined us and brought coffee and another round of pie. More weather talk commenced, along with commiseration about various afflictions appearing in people whose names I somewhat recognized, news about children who had been arrested, and several polite questions to Grossman about life in the big city. He gave short answers and turned his attention back to wrestling. Occasionally, Unitas would make an impatient grunt and turn up the volume over the adults' voices, and Willie would make him turn it back down and threaten to take him home.

The halftime show promised analyses of the matches we had just seen, but first a heavy metal band called the Beast did a song about locusts, pits, and horns, and choosing something before it is too late, followed by a rap group encouraging listeners to do something with or to a booty. Mama turned the volume down.

"Legare," Arlene said, "I wish you'd sing us a song—a pretty Christmas song."

"I'm sorry, Aunt Arlene. I didn't bring my guitar."

"I wish we'da knowed that," Spessard said, snapping his fingers.

"We coulda brought DeWayne's. It's just sitting up at the house."

I had forgotten about DeWayne's attempt at music. A girl he was interested in told him he resembled Jerry Reed, which he did, and that she really liked Jerry Reed, so DeWayne bought a copy of the Jerry Reed album with "When You're Hot, You're Hot" on it, memorized the song, which Reed more talked than sang, and subjected us all to countless recitations of it. He quoted Reed's lines from *Smokey and the Bandit* and called everyone "son," or "sawn," as Reed said it. He then said he would get a guitar and learn to "pick like old Jerry," ignoring my advice that he set his sights a bit lower, since Reed was an extraordinarily gifted guitarist despite his good-timing movie persona. Regardless, he went to a pawnshop in North Charleston and picked up a guitar (not a bad one, a Guild) and, like most other hopeful beginners, took two months of lessons before leaning the instrument in the closet.

"I'll bring it by tomorrow," Spessard continued. "You might have to tune it." He turned to Unitas. "What's Santy Claus gonna bring you, sport?"

"Well, what I *really* want is a four wheeler." He glanced at Willie, who raised an eyebrow at him. "But Mom says they're too dangerous. I also want a Mega-Dimension. It's a virtual reality game."

"It's mega-dollars, too," Willie said. "Come on, sweetheart, let's get you a quick bath during intermission." She and Unitas left for the back bathroom.

Arlene turned to me. "Baby, I'm *so* sorry you and Tally won't be spending Christmas together."

I knew she would not be satisfied until I supplied her with a tearful, pitiful answer so she could go "Mmm, mmm" and pat my hand. Better to give her one now than put up with her expectations later. "Actually, Aunt Arlene, I think Saul and I are going to have to leave the day after tomorrow. I hate thinking about Tally being sick and me not being with her."

"But that's the day you're reading your paper, Greazy," said Grossman.

"We're going to leave right *after* my paper."

"Saul, honey," Arlene turned to Grossman, "are you going to spend Christmas with your family?"

"I'm Orthodox," Grossman said and smiled at me.

Willie came back, leaving Unitas to bathe himself. "Saul is Jewish, Aunt Arlene," she said.

"He is not," Arlene said, turning to Saul. "You're probably not used to how they joke around here."

The throbbing in my head returned and was picking up speed.

"Y'all remember old Cleave Newsome? Used to own the hardware store?" the Old Man asked. "He was Jewish. Wouldn't drink Co-Colers."

My head felt like a homunculus with a grubbing hoe inside trying to chip a hole through my temple.

"He was a Mormon, Pledger," Mama said.

"He was a Jew. Had a different Bible and everything." The Old Man's jaw jutted out to one side.

"The Mormons have a different Bible," Mama said.

"And they love Jesus," Arlene said.

"Saul is Jewish," Willie said. "You should all respect that."

"Well, I don't think there's nothing wrong with it. It ain't his fault," Arlene said. "Saul, does your family put up one of them madeiras at Christmastime? Manny Solomon used to put one up in the store window right beside the Christmas tree. It was so pretty with them little candle-looking light bulbs and all."

"That's a menorah, Aunt Arlene," Willie said, "and it's used during Hanukkah, which just happens to come around Christmas time. Manny Solomon and his family were the only Jews in town, but he put up a Christmas tree in the store window, too, because he knew all his customers expected it."

I rubbed my head with both hands. I felt nauseated and trapped. "Can we please change the shubject?"

Unitas returned in pajamas with a wrestler on the front and "Elixir" written to look like dripping blood on the back. "It's almost Armageddon again," he said.

"You never mind them, shug," Mama said to Grossman, patting his arm. "You're just as welcome here as anybody. They musta all forgot that the Jews is the Lord's chosen people."

"Oh, God," I mumbled. The room looked blurry, and I felt dizzy. I had to get out.

"It's quite all right, Mrs. Hume," Grossman said. "I'm not a practicing Jew. I'm . . ."

"Shaul!" I said.

". . . an atheist."

༄

The stadium was tremendous—a dome with a ceiling painted to look like sky and clouds so that the screens, scoreboards, and speakers seemed to float over the heads of the tens of thousands of screaming spectators. They were dressed in period costumes: ancient Greek robes and Roman tunics; monastics' hooded cloaks; Medieval Arab turbans and pointed Persian shoes; stockings, flowing coats, and wigs of seventeenth-century noblemen; heavy nineteenth-century suits with vests and high collars; a few more recent but decidedly old-fashioned and upper class.

Each side yelled "Sophist sons of bitches!" and "Traitor bastards!" and "Monk fuckers!" at the other across the ring. Just as often, they squabbled among themselves and pointed fingers alternately at neighbors and the combatants in the ring. Fans got up and tried to enter the ring and were knocked out again, while others seem to appear from nowhere to address the crowd to boos and yeahs in various languages, all of which, inexplicably, I could understand.

Faces gradually became distinct, and I began to recognize the contestants and spectators. In one corner of the ring, dressed in wrestling tights with "Anal." stenciled across the back and pacing around in a circle, were Moritz Schlick, Rudolph Carnap, and Ludwig Wittgenstein. Their managers just outside the ropes were G. E. Moore, continuously waving to the crowd, and Bertrand Russell, wearing a ridiculously tall hat and drinking tea. In the opposite corner, looking at each other rather suspiciously, and labeled "Soft" were William James, about half the size of all the others, Martin Heidegger, stern-faced and marching stiff-kneedly in place, and Alfred North Whitehead, mostly keeping to himself and occasionally glancing across the ring at Russell. Their managers, who would not speak to each other, were Søren Kierkegaard, hopping off and on the ring apron, and Friedrich Nietzsche, wearing a CAT cap.

Every once in a while, someone from the Schlick-Carnap-Wittgenstein gang would yell a few words at the other team, and their side, which included Gottlob Frege, A. J. Ayer, Carl Hempel, and Gilbert Ryle, would stand together, cheer in unison, and moon the other side. Then someone from the James-Heidegger-Whitehead axis would speak for several minutes, and their fans, among whom I could see Edmund Husserl, John Dewey, Jean-Paul Sartre, Maurice Merleau-Ponty, and Karl Jaspers, would huddle up, mumble, and bicker at length, then finally do an Electric Slide sort of dance, culminating in a crotch grab.

I recognized some others who were in a section on a third side of the arena that looked neutral, sometimes cheering for one side and sometimes the other, sometimes looking confused, but more often indifferent. One set of bleachers was taken up by ancient Greeks: a bedraggled Thales; Pythagoras, confounded by a pocket calculator; Heraclitus, shifting around uncomfortably; a rotund Parmenides lecturing to a motionless Zeno; the other Zeno, nearly as static as the former; Diogenes barking insults at contestants and spectators alike; Carneades shaking his head in disbelief; and Democritus laughing at the whole bunch.

In the center section, David Hume, muttering to himself, "I can't believe this bullshit," sat beside a nodding-off Kant. Just behind Kant were Schopenhauer, humming a tune, and Hegel, looking pale. Schopenhauer would thump Hegel's ear, and Hegel would look around and whine "Quit it" at Marx, who would say, "I ain't done a *damn* thing, Georgie boy!" and wink at Ludwig Feuerbach while Schopenhauer pretended not to notice. Aquinas shoveled down hot dogs. Ibn Rushd, a little plump but somehow snaky, hovered at the side of the stands smoking a hookah. Spinoza stretched out supine along a bleacher, staring up like a backed turtle, while a grinning Descartes sat at the top, fading in and out of view.

Dancing around the outside of the ring in top hat and tails and twirling a cane was Kurt Gödel singing "Bei Mir Bist du Schön."

From two sets of special box seats, the occupants looked down on the arena. In one, Plato and Aristotle sat together drunk, throwing their empty Old English 800 cans at the ring, but nobody seemed to notice. In another were Jesus and the Buddha, looking like twins and staring at their ticket stubs as if they doubted they were in the right place. Someone, maybe Jaspers, kept trying to climb into the ring, but Heidegger would jam a black boot into his face, yelling up to them, "Hey, how about a little help down here," and J. C. and the Buddha giggled.

Someone hopped over the ropes and into the ring, and the others cowered in their corners.

"He stole the predicates!" said Moore, pointing at the intruder—Anselm. Skinny and saggy-eyed like Frank Gorshin, he ran across the ring, bounced from the ropes, hollered "Raven!", and was propelled to the other side, where he bounced off that set of ropes and hollered, "Writing desk!"

Hume elbowed Kant in the ribs and yelled, "Wake up!"

Kant jumped up and shouted, "Off with his goddamn head!"

Wittgenstein snatched Gödel's cane and broke it over Anselm's head. Heidegger kicked Schlick in the balls. Russell threw his tea into Whitehead's face. James jumped onto Carnap's back, and the two spun. The bleachers emptied, and there was pandemonium in the ring.

And the Buddha, laughing, said, "Yeah, you damn zombies, wake up!"

J. C. went into a fit of wheezy laughter, gave the Buddha a high five, said, "Good one, Sid," and then leaned out of his seat and shouted down, hee-heeing so uncontrollably he could hardly get it out, "Lazarus, you dead ass, wake up!"

Then the two of them lost all composure and nearly fell from the balcony.

※

"Wake up, Uncle Greazy," Unitas was saying.

Something covered my eyes. I reached up and peeled back a damp towel to see Unitas and Willie bent over me. I lay on the couch. I peered around to see Mama in the straightback chair wiping her eyes with a tissue and Aunt Arlene sitting on the floor with her forehead pressed to her knees. Both were praying. Grossman paced and mumbled and wrote in his notebook. The Old Man and Spessard came in through the front door.

"OK," the Old Man began. "Let's get him—"

"He woke up!" Unitas said.

"Are you OK, Bubba?" Willie asked, stroking my cheek.

"What happened?" I asked. Grossman was suddenly above me, looking into my face.

"You fainted!" Unitas said. He lingered on the "f," perhaps indicating his disbelief or disgust that a man—and a relative at that—had swooned like a woman.

"How long was I out?"

"A couple of minutes," Willie said. "We're taking you to the hospital."

I sat up. "Oh no, I feel fine."

I heard Mama whisper, "Blessed Jesus."

"Just because you feel fine doesn't mean you are," Willie said, clenching my shoulders. "We're still taking you."

Grossman sat down beside me. "I'm sorry I upset you, Greazy."

"No, it wasn't you, Saul. I'm just tired. We were on the road all day yesterday, and I didn't get much sleep last night. It's all just catching up with me." I really felt good—perhaps it was like the calm epileptics feel after a fit.

"He'll be all right," Spessard said. "He just got a little light-headed. Hell, it happens to me sometimes."

"You're twice his age, Spessard, and on blood-pressure medicine,"

Mama said. "Son, I think you ought to go to the doctor."

"Hit was probably just one of them things, Raylene," the Old Man said. "You sho you all right, son?"

"I'm fine, really. I just need to take it easy."

"Don't be an idiot, Greazy," said Willie. "I'm wondering if that bump on your head is more serious than it looks. It wouldn't hurt to get a CAT scan."

I laughed, thinking of Spessard's CAT cap.

"Arlene had one of them one time," Spessard said. "The doctor said, 'I got good news. We looked inside her head and didn't see a thing.' Ha! Ha!" He pinched Unitas.

"Didn't see a thing," Unitas said and rolled his eyes. "That's so old, Uncle Spessard." Someone else was laughing, but a second late—Grossman. I was not sure if I had ever heard him laugh.

"Didn't see a thing," Grossman said, pacing again and writing in his notebook. "I like that one, Mr. Driggers."

"I'm going to check your blood pressure," said Willie. "Then I'll check it again in a few minutes, and if it's still too low or too high, you're going to the hospital if I have to drag you myself. Mama, where's your sphygmomanometer?" Mama was already proudly coming from her bedroom with the blood pressure device and a box of tissues.

"Sphygnomotomer," Unitas said to himself. "Who were you talking to, Uncle Greazy?"

"Talking? I must have been dreaming. Don't even remember it."

Willie strapped the sphygmomanometer's band around my arm. "Now keep still," she said.

I felt my pulse pop against the band as she stared at the dial and then wrote down the reading. Though we talked on the phone regularly, I could not remember our even saying "I love you" to each other. I squeezed her hand.

"Have a swaller of this here," the Old Man said. He held out a glass with about an ounce of clear liquid in it. "That'll pep you up."

"Pledger!" Mama said. "The children."

"I know what this is," I said, "and it'll probably knock me back out again." I swirled the glass around and watched the moonshine bead up on the sides of the glass, which was the test of the real thing. I took it all in one gulp and tensed my throat and chest as it burned on the way down. It was good.

"Give it a try, buddy roe," the Old Man said, handing a glass to Grossman.

"I'm not believing this," Willie said. She got up and went to the kitchen.

Grossman, as I had, swirled it around and gulped it. He closed his eyes and gritted his teeth and pulled back his lips. The tendons in his neck spread out like guy wires.

"Fire in the hole!" Spessard hollered and slapped Grossman on the back, almost knocking him over.

Grossman coughed and gagged and bent over and stomped his foot and stood up and repeated the series before finally catching his breath. Unitas fell over laughing, lost his breath himself, and suddenly jumped up and said, "I got to pee!" and ran giggling down the hall. Grossman wiped his eyes and took deep "whew"ing breaths.

"How was that?" the Old Man asked as he let loose a quacking laugh from the sides of his mouth.

Grossman turned to me. "You were right, Greazy. That Blenheim's Ginger Ale really is strong."

The laughter was deafening. The Old Man put his hands on his knees, bunked over, shook his head, and whooped. Spessard leaned against the wall, looked up towards the ceiling, and "whaa haa"ed as if he were being tortured. I rolled off the couch into a fetal position on the floor and cackled until I cried. Even Mama and Arlene covered their mouths and laughed, though half afraid they would hurt Grossman's feelings. But he was laughing—a hoo-hoo—too, probably not sure at what, but enjoying the mirth nevertheless.

Unitas, pulling up his pants, ran back into the room fearing he had missed the best joke of the night. "What happened? What? Tell me!"

"Mr. Grossman just choked on some homemade . . ." Spessard said, ". . . ginger ale!" The old men heed and hawed all over again.

Willie returned with a glass of ice water. "Come on, Bubba. Let's go out on the porch for some fresh air."

I stood up slowly, feeling a little unsteady but trying not to show it. I could not abide the thought of two old men helping me to the door. "You want to come out with us, Saul?"

"Maybe later," he said. He knew from my disapproving look I did not want to leave him unattended.

"Don't forget y'all's coats," Mama said and wiped her nose with a tissue.

"It ain't cold out there," the Old Man said.

"The Bible says that, in the last days, you won't be able to tell the summer from the winter," Mama said.

"Mmm, mm," Arlene chimed in.

Willie and I rolled our eyes in tandem. We knew that if the weather turned the next day, Mama would quote some other supposed scripture that said the summers will get hotter and the winters will get colder.

༄

Outside was only a few degrees cooler than inside, and the air did seem to strengthen me. Someone was burning oak in a fireplace—there was a trace of kerosene—and after a moment, I decided that another scent was guinea feathers, smooth and like a shoebox with the corners bent in. The porch swing we sat in was not there the last time I had visited.

"You see how the Old Man marched out of the kitchen when Spessard told his Forty-Four and Funderburk story?" I asked. "What stuck the bur up his ass?"

"Well, well, after all these years, you finally noticed something," Willie said. "Think you're a big enough boy to handle all the family's dirty laundry now?" She laughed a little to herself. "If you aren't, you'd better be getting there."

"What's that supposed to mean?"

"Nothing. But, Greazy, you shouldn't let them get to you so

much."

"I know." The swing creaked at the forward pitch. The chain looked too light to me.

"They're annoying as hell," Willie said, "and God knows I'm always straightening out the kids from some ridiculous thing they heard from them. But they're not as bad as you make out." She paused, probably expecting me to object. "Mama asks me about you all the time. She wants to think that moving away turned you a little strange and cold, but you know how she is—convinced she's done something to make you so distant."

"What do you tell her?"

"I tell her to ask you. The problem in this damn family has always been that we don't really talk. Lucian'd still be with us if we'd listened to him."

"Can't we have one conversation without you saying that same shit?"

She folded her legs up under her and lay her head back. My pushing the swing alone gave it a wobble.

"Look at Mama and Daddy," she said. "They're probably as happy with each other as they've ever been, as they can be, with who they are. But have you heard them exchange a sentence between each other?"

"They never did."

"I know that, but you could try a little harder. Here you are with a Ph.D., for Godsake, and you're about the most inarticulate person here. Something happens to you when you come home, like you have some deep resentment towards them."

"You're exaggerating," I said, rubbing my palms together. They used to be calloused.

"You're doing it to me, too. You can talk nonstop for an hour on the phone, but you've hardly said twenty words to me since you got here."

"I've got some stuff on my mind."

"Like what? Tally?" She flicked a finger in the hair on the nape of my neck. "What's going on with you two?" My skin crawled on my neck and I hiked up my shoulder. She moved her hand away.

Willie was always more straightforward than I ever was. When she was married to Rupert, I never asked her what she saw in him. She knew that, like everyone else, I thought he was a cipher, and she even asked me why I thought so. When I denied it, I think I angered her more than anything I could have said about him.

"She didn't want me to come, so she's mad."

"Why wouldn't she want you to come? She gets along fine with everybody. Wait a minute—you didn't ask her to come with you. Is that it?"

I picked up a musky odor coming from the edge of the yard. It felt or looked like a sphere with a dent in the top. I told Willie about the APA, about Grossman, about Tally's hurling the plate, and my pissantness when I telephoned her earlier. (I skipped the part where I hadn't intended to visit at all.)

"You're a pissant all right. Tally's a good woman—the best thing that ever happened to you. If you don't get on the stick, you're going to end up like Purvis."

"What do you mean?" I saw something moving low to the ground in the direction of the odor.

"You remember Derma, his first wife? You know I set them up just after he got out of jail. She was really good to him, and Purvis seemed to do some growing up, but he started running with Rembert from hell to breakfast and not telling her when he was leaving or when he'd be back. So she left. She told me it wasn't him being gone. It was him not showing her any respect—just doing what he pleased and treating her like shit in the road."

"What was he up to?" I stretched my neck up to look towards the scent. I could hear Grossman's voice inside and the others laughing.

"That's beside the point, but he begged me to help him get her back. I finally convinced him she was gone for good. Anyway, it took me forever to piece things together about him and Rembert. You know how stupid Purvis is. It seems Rembert's been buying and selling stuff on the black market for years—mostly European medicine that the FDA hadn't OK'd yet and a bunch of stuff from China and Korea, like tiger's claws or something people believed were miracle cures. Then some old army buddy of his who trained guerillas somewhere in Central America for the CIA asked Rembert to help him bargain for some weapons from . . ." She paused. "I think Purvis said Russia, but who the hell knows? Rembert found out he could sell guns and soldiers to both sides at the same time."

I shifted on the swing, and something seemed to give where a bolt holding the chain went through the two-by-four that held it. Once, when I was about six, Lucian and I were on the porch swing at Spessard's and Arlene's when Purvis jumped onto it. He was a fat kid, and the swing was old, and both chains gave way and the swing crashed to the floor. The others laughed and were unhurt, but my legs were bent back under the seat. The Old Man came out and thought at first I was laughing, too. He realized I was screaming from pain and snatched the others up and pulled me away from the swing, fearing I had broken both legs. I could move them, so they weren't broken, but my knees ached, probably from torn cartilage, and I had blackish-blue bruises on my calves for weeks.

"I don't trust this swing," I said and got up.

"Next thing you know, Rembert's some kind of agent for soldiers of fortune. Problem was, he had to fly all around the world, and, you know, he's not a kid any more. He needed somebody to take up some of the slack. Purvis was perfect, because he didn't have enough sense to know what he was getting into. Plus, he's not blood kin to Rembert, so Rembert wouldn't feel too guilty if something happened to him."

"Jesus, this is too much, even for Rembert. I never would've thought he was involved in something that serious."

"There's a whole lot you never thought."

Whatever I was smelling had moved closer to the house. I eased towards the screen door, and the odor hit me like a gust, pungent and changing shape to wavy and rough like a cat's tongue—a possum. The guineas must be accustomed to the local night vermin, or they would be raising a fuss.

Willie walked up beside me. "What *are* you looking at?"

"A possum. But I'm not really looking."

"Lord. You don't have possums in Florida? Are you listening to me?"

"Yes. So is that the international trade Rembert's doing now?"

"Kind of. Purvis said he stopped with the guns and soldiers, and now he's more in cahoots with Forty-Four. They'd done some local stuff for years, I reckon with those medicines Rembert was bringing in. Purvis wouldn't say exactly what it is, because they had some kind of falling out. I think he's afraid that if word gets out, Rembert'll think he tried to undermine whatever the operation is, and he's scared to death of Rembert."

Another round of laughs came from inside.

"I'm going to check your blood pressure again. You don't need to be standing up yet." Willie went inside, and as she opened the door, I could hear someone making some kind of animal sounds. When Willie came back out, she was chuckling and shaking her head.

"That Saul's a bird."

"What's he up to?" I eased down beside her on the swing again, making sure my legs weren't hooked under the seat.

"Telling wild stories and pretending to be the Goat Man. Unitas was so tickled he could hardly catch his breath. Wynonna's asleep, or she'd be having a ball, too."

Saul Goatman—I pictured him as a satyr, blowing the Pan pipes, gamboling in the night forest in some Orphic rite. "I think I'm coming to like Saul," I said. "You know, he might actually be the most brilliant logician in the country, but he's pretty naïve about most things, especially when it comes to dealing with people."

"Pot!" she said, slapping me on the shoulder. "What color was that kettle again? Greazy, he's as sweet as he can be, and he's trying hard to please you. He looks to you for approval before he opens his mouth."

"Good. He needs somebody to watch out for him. You saw him eat. And you heard him announcing he's an atheist. Mama's probably on the phone to her preacher now. What's his name? Mercer? Getting him over here for a laying on of hands. Grossman doesn't know how to keep the academic world, where you can get away with all kinds of shit, and the real world apart."

"I'll grant you he's a little uncouth. But even if he is in some ways like a child, you can't treat him like one."

"Look," I said, reaching over and squeezing her arm, "there's something else I have to tell you."

"Wait a minute," she said. "Let me get this on you." She wrapped the band around my arm and pumped it up. I suspected this was her way of wriggling out of my holding her arm. Whatever we were, we were not a touchy family. "Hold still."

For a moment, I thought I was about to make a huge mistake. By telling Willie, I was certifying it a problem. Perhaps I should keep my mouth shut and make it through the next couple of days, and then Grossman and I would be back in Florida, and he would forget all about his infatuation. But would that be fair to Willie? We always say we have a right to know anything that might affect us or be about us, good or bad, but too often we find out and wish we hadn't. I recalled a passage from *All the King's Men*. Old Red used the metaphor of getting a letter that might have bad news, but we just have to open it, because, he wrote, the end of man is to know. Probably I could make a case that the need to tell was equally terminal.

"All right," she said, removing the band. "You look OK for now. Now what was it?"

"Grossman's in love with you."

She threw her head back and laughed. "Oh, get out! Did he tell you that?"

"In his way. I'm just afraid this'll turn into a comedy of Eros, with him getting hurt."

"There you go again. He's a big boy."

Unitas burst through the door. "The wrestling's back on! Hurry!" He zipped back in.

I stood up. "Just be careful what you say to him, OK?" I said.

Willie smiled at me. "Don't worry. You go on inside. I'm going to stay out here a minute."

"You want your coat?" I asked. "It's starting to get cool."
"No. I'm all right."
"Yes," I said. "You are."

༄

The wrestling hosts were announcing the next match: the Scourge versus Gyges.

"There he is!" Unitas said, and hopping up into the couch beside me.

Gyges came down a ramp to great fanfare, high-fiving fans along the way. When he got to the ring and removed his cloak, the camera zoomed in on his face, and there was no mistaking him: Staggy Man, who had read the "Mimetic Engulfment" paper earlier.

"Saul," I said, "that's the guy that—" But he wasn't there. I looked around and realized he'd slipped out of the room without my noticing.

"He said he was going outside to smoke a cigarette," the Old Man said.

Gyges and the Scourge exchanged slams and grimaces for a few minutes until the Scourge's accomplice, a gorgeous, tremendously-tittied blonde named Baby Lon, came out in a black negligee looking like a muscled Mamie Van Doren. She flashed the referee, who was no less stunned than had he gazed upon Medusa. The Scourge took advantage of the unmonitored moment to bend a folding chair over Gyges's bald pate. The Scourge commenced to choke, eye-gouge, and humiliate Gyges in unspeakable ways, and even Baby Lon got in a couple of stilettoed stomps. The ref regained consciousness and scolded the Scourge long enough for Gyges to recover. He raised his left hand, pointed to his bejeweled finger, and looked to the crowd for advice. The fans roared, "Ring! Ring!" He gave the ring a twist, and a cloud of green smoke filled the ring. The Scourge looked around in confusion and suddenly flipped in the air and crashed to the mat. He flipped and crashed again, jumped/was thrown over the ropes, climbed/was dragged back into the ring, and finally lay limp on his back. Baby Lon ran up and down the apron, looking from side to side, her mouth wide open.

Gyges emerged from the cloud of smoke to pin the Scourge. To the crowd's thunderous approval, the ref held up Gyges's hand to signify victory, and then Gyges, smirking, walked towards Baby Lon, who backed away warily. He smiled, held his left hand overhead, turned the ring with his right, and disappeared again in the green vapor. Something unseen yanked at Baby Lon's arm, and despite her resistance, she was spirited from the ring by the invisible, irrepressible force and hauled up the ramp that Gyges had descended a few minutes earlier. The abduction drew the longest and most clamorous ovation of the evening.

The phone rang. The Old Man, Mama, Arlene, and Spessard exchanged worried looks. A call after ten p.m. could only mean bad news. Mama went into the kitchen to get the phone while the others sat in silence. I heard Grossman's and Willie's voices coming from the porch. Were they having a date out there? Mama came back into the room, looking grave.

"That was Rembert," she said, her voice cracking. "They found Chalmers dead side the road."

Grossman, Unitas, and I continued to watch Armageddon while Wynonna slept in the folks' bed and the others went to join Rembert at the funeral home. I thought about all the other family deaths that had occurred when I was young. Upon hearing of the death, you were required to go somewhere—the hospital, the funeral home, the deceased's residence—dragging children along to watch the women sob and the men shake their heads and hear them all pronounce it a shame and God's will in the same breath. I was heartened that Willie refused to take her children on the pointless drive—after all, Rembert was making the arrangements—and besides, my babysitting absolved me from having to go.

I had not attended a funeral since Lucian's. I had taken the philosophical position that twenty-first century humans should have long ago grown out of their necrophiliac tendencies, particularly because funerals only perpetuate religious myths about afterlife, reunion with loved ones, and heavenly rewards. I knew, however, that funeral rites, perhaps more than any other religious ceremonies, provide a tribal sense of kinship and belonging necessary for the survival of our hunter-gatherer ancestors. Religious belief for rank-and-file religious people has nothing at all to do with intellectual decisions and philosophical considerations like the ontological argument, but is a genetic inheritance that sustained our forebears for ninety-nine percent of the time *Homo sapiens* has occupied the planet. Anything that bound the tribe securely helped to guarantee survival. A tendency, like mine, to rebel against those ancient patterns meant early death and thus no broadcasting a genetic legacy. We all have been endowed with a powerful yearning to replicate those social forms our ancestors practiced, and it might take a few hundred thousand more years to drain them from the gene pool. As Nietzsche and Russell and the grand old boy David all knew, despite the futility of kicking against the religious pricks, I expressed my defiance through non-attendance. The good thing was that when relatives died during those years, I had been too far away for anyone to expect me to show up.

Willie, Mama, and the Old Man returned (Spessard and Arlene went home) just after the first night's installment of Armageddon was over to find Unitas asleep on the couch. Willie left him there—she planned to bring him and Wynonna back in the morning for Mama to watch while she ran the shop. She took Wynonna, who did not stir as she was put into the car, and told us all goodbye. Grossman walked out with her, came back in, told the Old Man he was sorry about his brother's death, and went to bed.

Mama sat by me on the couch with her tissue wadded in her hand. The coffee, brewed hours earlier, had just been microwaved. It smelled bitter but still oval, although more elongated, like recognizing a road you wish you had not turned down. The Old Man sat frowning in his recliner. He never showed a hint of worry while awaiting a diagnosis of ailment, injury (the coolest man imaginable when sitting outside the emergency room), or threat of financial ruin ("It ain't like I got much to lose no way," he would say). But death of kin penetrated his thick pelt and dislodged something that worked its way up from deep in his breast.

"They don't know who hit him," he said. "Whoever it was just drove on off—probably didn't even stop." He pressed his bottom lip up into his top and shook his head. "Rembert said he was bloodied up pretty bad."

"Why was he walking?" Mama asked. "Why wa'n't he riding with Merle or somebody? That's what I can't figure out."

"The funeral's day after tomorrow," the Old Man said. "Rembert's gonna move his barbeque up to tomorrow night, and that'll be the setting up. The hog won't be done till that next morning, so we'll eat it after the funeral."

What the rest of the English-speaking world called a "wake" we called a "setting up." I had harbored the vain hope that my family no longer followed the open coffin practice in the home of the deceased but had joined civilization and now held wakes at the funeral home, but the Old Man had just busted that bier bubble. Chalmers would be laid out in the big room at Rembert's house, where the women would mill about, wait on the men, and rearrange dishes of mourner-brought food: a couple of hams (one with pineapples and fated to untouchedness), several versions of fried chicken (the primary differences being the amount of black pepper used, although some imaginative gourmet might throw in an exotic herb, like oregano), endless deviled eggs (the only occasion in these parts when paprika was used, so a can would last a cook's lifetime), three or four pots of peas and rice (half with snaps, all with fatback), a dozen sweet potato pies (half fluffed and moussey and a couple of those made even more dreadful with miniature marshmallows melted into flat, tan disks on top, the other half thankfully pone, thin and gummy and well worth the whole trip).

As they had for the past thirty years, Aunts Lula Mae and Bernice, both with their fanciest hankerchiefs and teased-up hair and smelling like powder, would be there first to prop themselves up on the moaning couch. Family protocol held that you file past and console them before offering condolences to the immediate family of the dead person. The men would sit around the fire outside smoking, spitting tobacco, and perhaps sharing a bottle of liquor, which, since this one would be a setting up/annual barbeque combination and thus the affair of the decade, would warrant not Brass Monkey or Old Grandad bourbon, but the good stuff: Crown Royal in the blue velvet bag. Most would leave around ten, others by midnight. But three or four of the men, reenacting some ancient rite, would actually "set up" all night long. Other than a dead body for all to see and avoid dropping biscuit crumbs on, and the higher grade liquor, it would hardly differ from Rembert's ordinary, annual Christmas barbeque.

"Chalmers always loved you, shug," Mama said. "He used to say, 'That Greazy's a pretty boy.'"

I remembered Mama once challenging that aesthetic assessment and said to Chalmers he thought everyone was pretty. He said, "Yeah, I do. E'body's pretty."

"Sometimes he'd have whoever'd picked him up drop him off at the head of the road out chonder," the Old Man said, "so he could walk up here and give you a treat—a squirrel nut or one of them suckers with the doubled-up string han'le like they give young'uns at the doctor's office." He looked at me for a sign indicating my unlikely promise to attend the funeral or probable excuse for absentia.

I was surprised that, despite the look, nothing had started pummeling my skull.

"Then I'd drive him on over to Rembert's," the Old Man continued. "He loved to ride in the back of the truck instead of up front, and he'd wave at the vehicles going the other direction after they'd passed." He tilted his head toward me in a semi-wink. "And your brother—he'd get to cutting the fool and Chalmers would get tickled . . . Lucian was sweet to him."

"Everybody'll be at the setting up and the funeral," Mama said, wiping her nose. "My people, too. I know they all want to see you."

That did it. My breath began to get rapid and shallow. It was as if a succubus, squatting on my chest, was flattening my lungs, intent on squeezing out and snuffing up my sorry soul. My mouth was dry. The top of my throat felt swollen and narrow. This must be the way my obese great-uncle Rotknocker lived every day, bending to the side as he sat on the edge of his chair to wedge on his slip-on, dime store skips, pellets of sweat covering his tomato-red face. My actuarial calculations, based on family history, however, put me at least ten years away from my first heart attack.

"Can I get another snort of that stump-hole?" I said.

This appeared to cheer the Old Man some. "Sho you can, Bud," and he was up and on his way to the kitchen.

"It would mean a lot to your father if you went to Rembert's tomorrow night," said Mama when he was out of sight. "Maybe you don't have to go to the funeral." She squinted at me. "Are you all right?"

I took two deep breaths. The Old Man came back with the home brew in a juice glass. "You can take the whole jug back down to Floridie if you want to. I don't hardly ever touch it 'cept I got a cough."

I gulped it down. It did the trick. "Where do you get this stuff?"

"Calhoun Funderburk. They say Al Capone used to send his men down here to buy liquor from Patrick Funderburk, Calhoun's granddaddy. He got rich selling liquor and bought up half the county. That's who Rembert bought his place from, and that's why Rembert and Calhoun don't get along, 'cause Calhoun thought that land shoulda gone to him. The whole time he was sheriff, he kept worrying Rembert and even sicced SLED on him a time or two."

"Why would anybody want to make moonshine nowadays? It's got to be way too much trouble, especially when there's a liquor store on every corner."

"They's people what'll still buy it—say it's better than store-bought. I think for Calhoun it's his way of showing he can do what he pleases and ain't got to be the sheriff to break the law in broad daylight and get away with it." He breathed deeply through his nose, quasi-snorted an exhalation, and stared at the floor. "Yeah, old Calhoun might be crooked, and he don't truck with Rembert, but he'd give Chalmers a ride every now and then and woulda done anything in this world for him."

"Jesus Christ, OK," I said, like a broken prisoner of war, ready to say whatever the interrogators wanted to hear. I saw Mama wince at my Lord's name-in-vain taking. "There's a big deal at the conference tomorrow night—the presidential address—but I reckon Saul and I can drop by Rembert's in time to see everybody."

The demon had climbed around to perch on my shoulder, like a grotesque on a cathedral roof, and giggle into my ear.

"You don't have to, now," the Old Man said. "We know you're busy with your meeting and all."

Did he have to push it? "No, I want to come."

My gargoyle laughed and said, "Whoa ho! That's a good 'urn!" and slapped a clawy hand on a boney knee and almost lost his talony footing.

༄

I got up at 6:30, hopped into and out of the shower, rustled up Grossman, and was ready to leave by 7:05. The Old Man was already in the woods, having told Mama he would hunt until noon and then help Rembert get set up for the barbeque. We told Mama goodbye, and as I was backing the Volvo out of the yard, saw Unitas waving a groggy hand at us through the window.

"Why only one anus?" Grossman asked as we pulled onto 402.

"What?"

"Your Uncle Spessard said that Forty-Four survived with only one anus."

"Oh, another joke with too many assumptions. It's the idea of a man and a woman having an adulterous affair and being caught by the woman's husband. The adulterer flees out the back door with the enraged husband shooting at his shiny ass."

"I see," Saul said, although I'm still not sure he got the joke. "In any case, I enjoyed last night, Greazy. They're entertaining people."

"Yeah, you were enjoying yourself, all right. You and Willie spent a little time alone out on the porch, eh?"

"Oh, she's terrific." He took a long drag from his cigarette. The smoke smelled pinkish-red and was the shape of the twisted frills on a chenille bedspread. He blushed a tiny bit. "That reminds me. Do you suppose we could go by her boutique as we pass through Moncks Corner?"

"What for? She won't be there for a couple of hours."

"I'd—I'd just like to see it."

His paper was coming up, and he was probably terrified. I had planned on taking the bypass to save a few minutes, but it wouldn't hurt to indulge him a little. I drove around to the far side of Main Street and slowed down as I approached the unremarkable looking little shop with "Moncks Corner Ladies Shop" in cursive on the window.

"There it is," I said.

"Pull over," he said.

"Why?"

"Please?" His hand was already on the door handle, as if he was going to open the door and bolt.

I stopped the car on the other side of the street. Grossman hopped out and scampered across. He cupped his hand over his eyes to see through the door window, looked back at me, scooted a few inches so his back was towards me, and appeared to drop something through the mail slot. He ran back to the car, smirking like a pranksterish kid who had just rung the doorbell and run. He jumped into the seat, his eyes shifting, and lit another cigarette.

"Let's go!" he said.

"I'm going, Jesus." I pulled back onto the street. "What was that all about?"

"Nothing." He stared out the window, away from me, and threw his burnt match onto the floorboard. "I just wanted to see it."

"What the hell is going on with you?"

He ignored me. I think I heard him giggle.

We were out of town in a couple of minutes. "What time's your paper again? One-thirty?"

He grabbed the dash and swung around and looked at me. "Oh. I'd forgotten about that."

"Relax, Saul. You've got the whole thing memorized. You're gonna knock 'em out."

"Greazy, um, I'd like to ask you a favor."

I knew what it was, and I could have made him sweat it out and fumble around for a minute. I pretended not to hear him. "Say, you don't mind if I drop in to hear your paper, do you?" I asked.

"No, of course not! I was—" He smiled in a way I'd never seen him—he had caught on. "Thank you, Greazy. Thank you." He thumped his cigarette out the window. "Can I try some of that Amsterdam snuff of yours?"

"Not today, buddy roe."

SEVEN
Qualia

Synaesthesia: cross-wired sensations, spliced perceptions, mix-breed impressions, multi-textured experiential content arising from singly sensuous stimulation. I had read of some famous synaesthetes: Vladimir Nabakov, when a child, supposedly told his mother that all the letters on his blocks were in the wrong colors, and a curious number of composers—Beethoven, Sibelius, Liszt, Scriabin—reported seeing notes or keys in colors or as dancing geometric shapes. Could those guys have been sniffing along the right trail?

Our tendency in the Western epistemological tradition—thanks are due, again, largely to old René—is to analyze, to divide and conquer. Reason breaks opaque substance down into its component parts, decomposes the too, too solid (or sullied, if you are one of those) flesh of the object of knowledge, cuts from the booming, buzzing herd of wild nature a solitary specimen to tame and call understood.

I began to think that this severing activity might slice even deeper, perhaps to our originative, pre-reflective bone of experience. Suppose the phenomenal data of the world are given to us all in a piece—a chunk of undifferentiated, noematic material available as pre-thematic, pure experience, and any isolated visual, aural, tactile, gustatory, or olfactory perception is only an abstraction. If so, then my manifold impressions were not mongrels at all but purebred originals.

Maybe our brains evolved to do logic and calculus, to speak, or to flake off slivers of one rock with another to make a knife only by building cerebral structures that pushed the primordial perceptors out of the neural neighborhood. Tally's plate might have jostled something in my head, redirected and reconnected some pathways running through my olfactory center and other sensory nodes so that I was having tiny tastes—whiffs of the world as it really is, integrated, unitary, whole. Maybe my search for levels of meanings enfolded within worldly encounter had led me to look in the wrong places, and in the wrong ways. Or perhaps I should not have been *looking* at all, a victim of the Cartesian reason-as-analysis prejudice that not only rends and compartmentalizes the several senses but privileges sight and quarantines it off from the others for fear of contamination from earthier touches and smells.

Obsessed with reason, that bureaucratic paper-pusher of the mind, we align it with seeing, a prejudice reflected in the language: we *see* the answer, we have in*sight*, he is a man of *vision*, open your *eyes* to the truth, broaden your *view*, take a fresh *look* at the issue. Rubbing, sniffing, nibbling, even listening are carnal, intimate, and dank-grimy crevice-entering, while looking is reflective, safe, and clean. We gaze at our beautiful lovers, but we close our eyes to kiss, and we make love in the dark. So if sight is the most distancing sense, yet deemed paradigmatic, is it any wonder that for four hundred years, philosophers have struggled in certifying the reality of a world *out there*? If we could dislodge this reason/sight centrality, maybe we could better explore the other, more emotive ways in which we are embedded in the world.

Could my new synaesthetic experiences, then, be philosophical blessings? Phenomenologists are fond of talking about getting at the essence of things. Is it an accident that scents are also called essences? Maybe I had been so thoroughly hoodwinked by the knowing subject-as-spectator approach of philosophy that I had wasted many dollars stuffed into reality's belt trying to buy a peek under the layers of her skirts, while meanings all along were free for the asking by the noseful. Those years of reading James, Dewey, and Whitehead had paid off by preparing me to make some sense of my new synaesthetic perspective on our overlapping matrices of relations to the things of the world. If there is any meaning in the world at all, it is something that courses through the experiencer, who forms a nexus of those movements—an anchor to the webbed tissue of sights, sounds, touches, tastes, and smells that is the throbbing organism we call the world.

In my first year of grad school, when I enrolled in an aesthetics seminar with Gilbert, I was taken by Dewey's theory of art as providing an integrative experience—an opportunity for the observer to get a sense of wholeness absent in our mundane moments. Dewey described art's unifying ability as relying upon synaesthesia, by which he meant calling upon all the senses to contribute to and participate in the aesthetic experience. I made a class presentation on the paper I was writing on Dewey, and the discussion veered off in the direction of the other sense of synaesthesia as mixed perceptions. One of the seminar participants said she sometimes experienced sounds tactically—a melody crawling across her stomach like a millipede, a voice rapping like fingers on the nape of her neck, a birdsong pressing her inner wrist as if taking her pulse. She and I continued this conversation after class—my first sniff of Sue Meierson.

She now sat on the opposite side of the room from Grossman and me. I was listening to a paper entitled "Skepticism East and West: Buddhist versus Indo-European Thought," read by a guy named Parathpanamnda from the University of Hawaii. It was lucky I had remembered to bring my program along and not left it at home like Grossman did, because he did not want to go by the registration table earlier when I suggested we get new name tags—he wanted to lay low—and otherwise we would not have known where anything was to take place. I knew a little about Buddhism, and thought this session would be as interesting as anything else. Grossman was there, fidgeting, scribbling in his notebook, because he was too nervous to let me out of his sight, and Meierson was there, I figured, because she hoped that a paper on Buddhism would include some discussion of tantric sexual practices (which, she would be disappointed to find, were related to the Tibetan, not Theravada, tradition).

Only about twenty people (including two women in saris, a man who looked Indian but in ordinary Western clothes, and two men whom I guessed to be Japanese, both wearing T-shirts sporting pictures of professional wrestlers holding bottles of Elixir) sat in the room that could hold four times that many, and five of them were at the table: two reading papers, two commenting, and one chair. Meierson saw me, shot me a big smiling O, pointed to the hall, and mouthed, "After." This time I actually wanted to speak with her.

Parathpanamnda claimed that the Indo-European, by which he meant Hindu and Euro-American, intellectual tradition had inherited from the Indo-European root language—from which Sanskrit, Hindi, Greek, Latin, and lots of others descended—the tendency to equate "sight" words with knowledge. For instance, the central Hindu texts are the *Vedas*, whose name is from a Sanskrit word for knowledge or wisdom that in turn came from the same Indo-European root that gave us the Latin *video*, "I see." So, in the Indo-European tradition(s), to know something is to see it, but because sight is the distancing sense, according to Parathpanamnda, this way of thinking lends itself to the skeptical view that reality may not match up to what we see "out there."

In contrast, Buddhism's founding texts are the *Tipitaka*, the canon of the Theravada tradition originally written in Pali, another ancient Indian language that, although derived from Sanskrit, minimized the sight-as-knowledge association. Parathpanamnda explained that a virile skeptical tradition arose within Theravada philosophy, but it issued from the general Buddhist notion of the impermanence and groundlessness of reality itself, not in the attempt to mate our impressions to the things themselves.

When the paper was done, I jumped up first with a question, something I had never done at a conference. "Does Buddhism replace the sight-as-knowledge metaphor with another? Say, smell?"

Parathpanamnda, whom I guessed was Indian or Sri Lankan, smiled graciously, or perhaps patiently. Asians' smiles always strike me initially as friendly, but then I wonder if they are not more for the smilers' benefit, a way to remind themselves, "Be nice to this obtuse white guy. He can't help it."

He nodded, too, as if he had expected my question. "I should not say 'replace,' but perhaps 'makes extended use of,' and metaphors not so much for knowledge as for moral traits. In some passages in the *Dhammapada*, flower fragrances are equated with virtue. One line, by the way, about a flower losing its fragrance has always struck me as uncannily similar to Jesus' remark about salt losing its flavor. However, you find this theme more pronounced in the Mahayana literature. The *Avatamsaka Sutra*, for example, is filled-filled-filled with images of beautiful aromas as signs of good character. The *Nirvana Sutra* uses taste, and classifies the Buddha's teachings into five flavors of dairy products. But you must remember, for Buddhism the entire epistemological enterprise is directed not towards the phenomenal world, but away-away-away from it and instead towards the inner person—the lotus in the heart."

What gives me the red ass so about religions is their relentless and cowardly renunciation of the world. Christians will tell you that the experienced world does not really count, but the unseen/unsmelled one to come does. They accept being in the world, at least for now, but reject being *of* it.

Buddhists go even further, and try to deny both prepositions. They will tell you all about being reincarnated into the world countless times, but turn right around and deny that the world really exists. At least the Buddhists do not have a God or Son-o-God or a Holy Ghoul looming over their heads and threatening to pounce. But neither offers any phenomenological help making sense of our worldliness, our existential situatedness. And if that was not hairless-ballsed enough, just when you turn away to take your ruminations elsewhere, a smartass like Anselm pops you with the ultimate rabbit punch, the Ontological Argument, and says "chew on that cud a while."

Grossman and I left as the next paper on Eastern thought was being introduced. In a few seconds, Meierson emerged from the room and scampered over to hug me. She was dressed like Diane Keaton in *Annie Hall* but without a hat, so her bristly hair could announce her anti-phallocratic unkemptness. She smelled like sandalwood and a green, coiled rope. "Legare, you slippery devil, I would almost suspect you've been avoiding me. How are you? You look wonderful!"

We went through the abbreviated catching up: "I'm fine, nothing much, she's OK, happy to hear that, haven't seen him in years."

"This is my colleague, Saul Grossman."

They shook hands, then she stared at him as he crossed his arms and rocked as if he were at the yeshiva learning Talmud. His paper was up in two hours, and he was in a rare anxious moment.

"Sue," I said, "I'd like to discuss something with you. We're on our way to lunch." I saw Grossman shoot a glance at me. He was probably nauseated and could not eat. "Can I treat you?"

"You bet," she said and rubbed my shoulder.

We turned towards the elevators, when a voice called from behind.

"Saul, darling! There you are!" Jackie Armstrong strode towards us. The slit in her tight, purple skirt came just above her left knee, but when she turned sideways to me to hug Grossman, it revealed a bivalve calf that would have made Michelangelo cuss his chisel. Grossman hardly changed his posture, barely tolerating Armstrong as she caressed his back and patted his hair.

"I looked for you at the mixer last night," Armstrong said. "Did you forget our lunch date, hm? Ah, young Hume. Are you conferencing well?" She offered me her hand, which I again held too long.

Armstrong smelled like a freshly snapped crape myrtle twig, crimson and Möbius-stripped. "Jackie Armstrong, this is Sue Meierson."

"Nice to meet you," Meierson said.

"A pleasure." Armstrong said. "You will join us, won't you? The hotel restaurant has a splendid buffet." She pronounced it "boo-fay."

✺

Grossman had coffee and rocked, I had she-crab soup and a salmon Caesar salad, and Armstrong peeled and ate a tremendous mound of boiled shrimp while listening enrapt as Meierson, eating eggy potato salad with a tablespoon and chicken wings with knife and fork all in the same bowl, explained the significance of her vulvish and the phalloformal dimensions of silverware. Armstrong gave up on the nearly catatonic Grossman and asked me about our evening plans. I told her that Saul and I were getting together with my family. Other than that, Armstrong spent the meal regarding Meierson with the same apparent endearment she granted Grossman. Meierson said something about how the male tendency to penetrate and ultimately dismember was reflected in Western cuisine, and I saw that as my cue.

"Sue, that's what I wanted to talk to you about. I remember your telling me one time about your synaethesia experiences."

"I remember, too," she said. "Our first real conversation." She turned to Armstrong. "I was explaining something to Legare about art theory, and I illustrated by telling him of my inter-sensory experiences. Certain sounds would elicit tactile sensations on the surface of my skin. But he wasn't really interested—it was just a seduction ploy. After talking for about an hour, he dragged me off to bed!"

I choked on a crouton. Grossman noticed nothing, Armstrong stretched up her exquisite neck and laughed, and Meierson brushed back her wiry hair and winked at me.

"Hold on!" I managed before I began coughing again.

Armstrong rapped me on the back with the heel of one hand and held my upper arm with the other. "Oh, don't be embarrassed now, young Hume," she said. "Who could blame you?"

She could have said something flirty, like "Lucky Sue," which would have given me an instant hard-on. But "Who could blame you?" What the hell did *that* mean?

I could not stop coughing, and went to the bathroom to regain some control. I splashed water on my face beside two other men at the sink, one in a suit with an APA nametag, the other in jeans, a cap, and a NASCAR jacket.

"How you reckon he does it?" the NASCAR Guy asked.

"Magicians do that sort of thing all the time," said APA Guy. "I suspect—*aarnk!*—he conceals himself beneath the ring while the spectators are distracted by the cloud of smoke. *Shit!*"

"Probly. Well, I got to get on to the race. You coming to the match tonight?"

"*Rink!* I hope so." His right shoulder shot up towards his ear. Must be Tourette syndrome.

"I'll look for you." NASCAR Guy turned to me. I was still gagging a little. "You a'ight there, buddy?"

"Yeah. Something just went down the wrong pipe," I said.

"Got to keep your plumbing straight," he said, leaving with the APA guy right behind him. APA Guy let out a grunted—as if he were trying to suppress it—"*Fuck!*" as he stepped through the door.

I paper-toweled off and returned to the dining room. NASCAR Guy's mentioning the race reminded me that Spessard and Unitas were going. Spessard and Chalmers were not even exactly in-laws, so Chalmers's death would not require Spessard to arrive at Rembert's place early. Besides, he and Unitas would be back in plenty of time for the wake. I heard my name called and turned to see Gilbert waving from a table. Joyce and two people whom I did not recognize were sitting with him.

"Legare, my dear," Joyce said as she got up to hug me. She smelled like orange blossoms and the bottom half of a bagel. She had always been sweet to me, and I felt a pang of guilt for not keeping in touch with them. She introduced me to the couple. I did not catch their names, but the woman taught at the University of Miami, and I thought I had seen her at the Florida Philosophical Association conference two years before in Gainesville. She may have been there, she said.

"Legare, honey, we were just telling them about you," Joyce said. "Tell him, Bart."

"Joyce and I have come to a decision, Legare," Gilbert said. "And we have you to thank for it." He jerked his head up firm-jawedly as a gesture of resolution. "I have stopped my medication. Only three doses so far, but the effects have been immediate. I awoke afresh this morning, and look, I'm eating real food at this very moment." Some chicken bones had been carefully arranged on his plate. "And more significantly and, shall I say, happily, I feel, ah, lively, if you get my meaning. I'm accustomed to spending the afternoon in bed, but today I don't plan to nap."

Joyce blushed and poked his shoulder, and the other two people laughed and clapped. Was talking so openly about sex suddenly acceptable? Was it customary APA practice? I had to get away.

"That's great," I said, worried that I had been caught involuntarily grimacing at the image of the naked Gilberts. I looked in the direction of my table and pretended to respond to a sign. "Looks like my companions are fixing to leave. Are you going to the Presidential Address?"

"Yes, we are," Gilbert said. "Then we're thinking of attending the wrestling competition." But they're at the same time, I thought.

"I think it's called a tournament," the other man said.

"No, match," Miami Woman said.

"Then I'll look for you," I said.

Back at the table, Meierson was talking continuously to rocking Grossman. I heard "cleft" and "labia." Armstrong was not there.

Grossman stopped rocking and beamed at me. "Greazy! I was afraid you had left."

"No, just needed to straighten out my plumbing. Where's Jackie?"

"Her agent came for her," Meierson said. "Said there was a long line at the book table. She left a fifty for lunch. Legare, I think she was hitting on me. She made me promise to meet her at the bar at four. Is she a lesbian?"

"How would I know?" I said, though I almost said, "She sure as hell didn't *look* like a dyke, and if she were, any argument for the existence of God was shot all to hell." But I knew Meierson would never let me get away with that one. "Saul, is Jackie a lesbian?"

He finished what must have been his fifth cup of coffee. "I never asked."

"Well, I'll just have to ask her this afternoon," Meierson said. "You're not jealous, are you, Legare?" She laughed at her little tease. I figured she meant I should be jealous because she was meeting Armstrong at the bar instead of meeting me, but then I thought she may have meant *she* was meeting Armstrong at the bar instead of my doing so.

"Listen, Sue, did you say earlier that you *used* to have synaesthesia?"

She sighed, probably not because of her loss of synaesthetic experience, but because I had changed the subject. "Yes. It stopped a few months after I took the job in Denver. I think it was the altitude—the thin air."

"Did you ever get a medical explanation for it?"

"No, why should I? It wasn't causing me any problems. Actually, it was rather enjoyable. Why, is it happening to you?"

"With smells. They're not only heightened, but I smell colors and shapes, sometimes even textures."

"What do I smell like?" She put her cheek up to mine.

"Sandalwood and green, in a coil."

"Oh." She looked down at her bowl.

"Sue, I was hoping you would have some insight—help me understand what it means—or if it's something I should worry about."

"No need to worry, except that some of your prejudices may be dismantled. I think Parathpanamnda was right in talking about the Western, male tendency to privilege the gaze that confines the Other over different modes of knowing. I never knew the Buddha was a feminist!"

"I'm not sure he was saying exactly that—"

"Think of your hypersensitive smelling ability as actually something more basic, and enjoy it while it lasts. After all, mine worked on you, didn't it?"

"Yes! That's exactly what I've been thinking—I mean, the part about something more basic."

"Saul Grossman?" Someone else stood by the table. "I'm Paulette Templeton. I've been looking everywhere for you. In fact, the entire APA Executive Committee has been." Grossman looked at me for help.

"Professor Templeton," I said. "Saul has a paper coming up. We were just about to leave." I waived for the waiter and made the check sign in the air.

"That's what I want to speak to you about." She sat down beside

Grossman. "Your achievement at the Sennet session yesterday has been the talk of the conference. Many of us who were present think you've done nothing less than alter the course of philosophy. As you probably know, the Presidential Address tonight has been moved up from eight p.m. to five because of all the interest in the wrestling event."

Grossman rocked faster than ever.

"No, we didn't know that," I said.

"We were talking about it earlier," Meierson said. "What do you mean you didn't know?"

I looked at her as if she had pinched me.

"Oh, you must have missed the notices at the registration table," said Templeton, "and we asked all the session chairs to make the announcement. You see, one of the APA members arranged last night for free admission to the tournament for all conference attendees, and many people skipped the mixer to attend. The reaction was so positive that the Executive Committee voted to reschedule things so that the Presidential Address would not conflict with Armageddon."

So that explains how I saw McDavid and Donaldson in the audience last night. Had Gyges arranged for the free admission of APA members?

"Professor Grossman," she continued, "because a number of sessions had to be shifted around, it turns out that the auditorium is free during the time you're scheduled to read your paper this afternoon. The Executive Committee requests that you forego your logic paper and instead run through the argument you presented yesterday. Sennet, John Darrell, Perry Fowler, Orin Feigelman, and I will be on a panel with you to discuss the significance of your theory. CNN is going to be there, too. What do you say?"

Grossman stared at me. His eyes looked like bleached hog nuts.

"I know this is short notice," Templeton said, "but you're not registered at the hotel, and we couldn't find you at the mixer last night."

"Look, Paulette," I said, "Saul is a little shy. I'm not sure he'd be up to it."

"Well," boomed a new voice, "you've tracked down our boy,

have you? Now don't make him a job offer before I do! Sam Sennet, young fellow. Magnificent show yesterday. Magnificent. So, Paulette's explained the change in the agenda, I trust."

"I asked him," she said without looking up at Sennet, who seemed to have recovered nicely from the shock of having his life's work totally dismantled before his eyes.

"Asked? It's all been arranged," Sennet said, smiling broadly. "Notices are posted all over the halls. People are already jockeying for seats in the auditorium. Not often a philosopher makes the news. You're big, young man—very big."

Grossman lit a cigarette. The waiter was about to remind us that we were in the no-smoking section, but I bared my canines at him, and he backed off.

"Give us a few minutes," I said. "We'll be in the hall."

I told Meierson I would see her later. Promising to attend my paper the next day, she told me she was staying in room 1066 ("Like Hastings," she said. "Make haste!") if I wanted to get together in the meantime. I took Grossman by the arm, led him out of the restaurant, and shuffled him down the hall in the direction of the largest of the several bars in the convention center.

"Saul, you can do this. There's nothing to be afraid of."

"I really don't want to, Greazy. It's not my specialty, and I may not remember what I said yesterday, and—"

"And all those big shots, right?"

He looked at me as if he had broken something and I was about to scold him. We went into Belle Alley, which was much larger than I expected, and leaned against one of those tall tables for standing drinkers. A crowd of sixty or more packed into one side of the bar just yards away from us, under a banner that read, "Try a Russian Revolution: Elixir and Vodka." There was silence for a moment, and then chattering and light applause. Grossman rubbernecked, trying to see what the hoopla was about. I heard "Nice move" and "Brilliant" and "Good show"—it was McDavid and Donaldson and their tic-tac-toe game. A guy stood beside them copying their moves onto a chalkboard so the mass of sycophants could get a better view.

"Saul, you're way smarter than all those guys. If you're worried about them embarrassing you, then forget it."

"It's not that," he said, standing up on the foot-rest rail that ran around the table.

"Is it the people watching? Saul?"

"Yes, they're watching and blocking my view. Oh, you mean . . . yes," he said and looked at me. "I don't like people watching me." He turned back towards the tic-tac-toe game again.

"Maybe you should take off your glasses."

"But then I couldn't see the game."

"Not now, goddammit," I said, "in the auditorium. It's an old public speaker's trick. You're nearsighted, right? If you can't see them, it's like they're not there. Just talk to the people at the table."

I heard more light applause and praise of strategy—another game must have ended.

"Say," he said, almost to himself, "that'll work." But I couldn't tell if he was talking about the glasses or the game, because he immediately stepped down and made his way through the tic-tac-toe crowd. I stood up on a chair from a nearby table to see what the hell he was up to. I could barely hear him as he approached the Big-Timers.

"May I try?" he said.

McDavid and Donaldson stared across the table at each other as if each was waiting for the other to do something. Such an audacious request had probably never happened, much less in public, so the Big-Timers had no standard rebuff for the upstart. The crowd was equally stunned, and Grossman had eyes upon eyes focused squarely on him. But for all his anxieties about being the center of attention, for all the fears he'd just been consumed by, when Grossman focused on something like he did yesterday, he noticed nothing else.

"Certainly, young fellow," McDavid finally said. Then to Donaldson, "You or me?"

"Please," Donaldson said, bowing in mock pageantry, "do the honors."

He backed away from the table and Grossman stepped up. The onlookers at first whispered excitedly, but then their shocked expressions changed to smirks, and I heard "fool," "murder," "tell me when it's over." Donaldson said, "Show some mercy, old chap," and others cackled. I elbowed my way through the mob and stood near Grossman.

"What's your name, young contender?" McDavid asked.

"Saul Grossman."

McDavid leaned back and made of show of examining the full five and a half feet of Grossman. "Are you the Saul Grossman I've been hearing about who made such a stir at the Sennet symposium yesterday?"

Grossman looked back towards the table where we had been. I tapped his shoulder and said, "Here." He smiled and turned back to face McDavid.

"Yes," he answered.

"Well, let's just see if you'll prove a Jacobin or Jacobite," McDavid said to snickers all around. "You may be X and go first."

The moves went quickly. I could not quite make out what they did on the paper, and I was nearly against the chalkboard, so could not see that either. The chalk guy froze, his face ashen, his hand squeezing the chalk as if trying to break it.

"Write it!" Donaldson said.

I heard two scrapes on the board, then the gasps, and I knew Grossman had won.

"Let's try that again," McDavid said, downing a glass of wine.

There were murmurs of disbelief, and I heard someone whisper, "No, no, that's *got* to be illegal." The second game started. Several people rushed away, no doubt to spread the news throughout the APA membership that a coup of sorts might be in the making. I detected a gray, dusty scent like when rain is coming.

The chalk guy was crying as he made those two, slow scrapes again. This time the crowd uttered a collective "What the *fuck*?" Donaldson's face was blood red, and he grabbed McDavid by his tweed lapels and yanked him from the table.

"OK, you insolent little bastard," Donaldson said to Grossman, "let's see what you've got. I'll go first."

Grossman's response to Donaldson's first move was quick, but Donaldson's response took thirty seconds. I had seen Grossman look this focused only when working out a logical proof or disproof of something, and he responded to Donaldson immediately. Donaldson took three minutes for this third move. Grossman answered with his third even before the weeping chalk boy posted Donaldson's. Donaldson got up and walked to the bar, ordered a jigger of something, slugged it, walked over to a ficas to throw up in its pot, went back to the bar for another jigger, and returned to the table. He looked at McDavid, who was perched on a stool and breathing into a paper bag, and winked. Donaldson, grinning while he made his fourth move, hardly had time to remove his pen before Grossman recorded his retort.

The chalker stared at the paper, turned to the board, his lip twitching, dropped the chalk, said, "I can't do it!" and fled the room.

McDavid descended from his stool, retrieved the chalk from where it had rolled under the gaming table, drew a circle in a corner square, traced the circle around and around, spiraling outward until he filled nearly the entire board, finally whipped a diagonal slash across the board, and announced, muted by the paper bag as if he were speaking through a trumpet, "Circle wins."

Then there was pandemonium in the ring.

The sudden uproar rattled Grossman, who looked around dazed like a bhikku jolted from vipassana meditation, and I grabbed him before he could become frightened and before the parasites surrounding us transformed into a herd of disciples clutching at the hem of his garment. I shoved our way out, even punched one guy in the stomach and elbowed another in the jaw. They both dropped like sacks of rice, and Godalmighty it felt good.

When we made it into the hall, we saw Paulette Templeton scurrying towards us with her arms outstretched. She stumbled, stopped to pick up a dropped shoe but left the broken-off heel, and said, "There you are! Hurry! You *are* coming, aren't you?"

I glanced at my watch and saw we were ten minutes late. I turned to Grossman. "So, are you up for this, champ?"

He turned to Templeton. Eyes arched, with a too-toothy smile as if she was about to brush her teeth, she bent to put on her heelless pump, and looked frantic. He turned back to me. "Will you come with me?"

"Of course, Saul. I promised you that this morning."

"No, I mean, up on the dais. I'd like you . . . I'd like for—"

I looked at Templeton. "That OK?"

"Fine, fine! Let's go!" she said.

I looked back at Grossman. "Come on, Robespierre—you've got more heads to roll."

※

Only every few centuries do you get to view the body of a philosophical problem—they usually regenerate into something more ferocious, like Heracles's many-headed hydra. So the mood of the five hundred or more philosophers in the auditorium was celebratory yet reverential. At the table where he and the others sat, Sam Sennet was checking out the microphones on the stage. Two video cameras perched on tripods at the side aisles. A reporter with a cameraman was interviewing Fowler. As we strolled down the inclined center aisle, Templeton bobbing up and down in her broken shoe, heads turned, necks strained, fingers pointed, and the sacred name "Grossman" was whispered as if invoked for some ancient ritual. Grossman would probably become APA President by acclamation, and he could hitch himself up to any philosophy faculty in the country, name his salary, teach one class a year, and get a Nastassja Kinski-looking grad student to bunk over the desk and do his grading.

By the time we reached the steps to the stage, the happy chatter had changed to a low moan. Sennet noticed us, pointed an open hand towards Grossman, and the other panelists stood and clapped. In the audience, I saw Biro, Leavengood, the Big-Timers, some faces I recognized from the Sennet symposium, Armstrong and, beside her,

Meierson, all waving and joining the applause. So did Grossman, not realizing it was for him. I pulled his glasses off and placed them in his breast pocket. He smiled.

Templeton whispered something to Sennet, who left the stage during the ovation and returned in a moment with a chair for me. She then asked politely for order, got it, introduced herself, and described the structure of what she called the "emergency session": Grossman would reconstruct his remarks from the day before or simply speak for an unlimited time, then the panelists would offer comments. Grossman would reply to those remarks as he saw fit. She introduced Sennet, Darrell, Fowler, and Feigelman, who, as his name was mentioned, went "*Hernk!*"—he was the Tourette guy from lunch. I then remembered that in the preface to one of his books I had read years before (well, actually I didn't get much farther than the preface), he mentioned that his Tourette syndrome had led him to study neurosurgery, but an interest in consciousness sidetracked him. He completed his medical degree but opted for a career in philosophy. Maybe he would have some insight into my synaesthesia.

"And this is . . ." Templeton said. She paused, then bent over and whispered into Sennet's ear. Sennet whispered into Darrell's, Darrell into Fowler's, and Fowler into Feigelman's. He leaned over to Grossman. Grossman whispered something back to Feigelman, who whispered, along with a "*Vvvvrrt!*" to Fowler and so on back to Templeton, who then said, "And Professor Grossman's companion, Kwasi Hume."

Kwasi? Did I look African? Or was I *Quasi*-Hume? And *companion?* Did I look gay, too?

"*Shit!*" Feigelman said.

Grossman appeared calm as Templeton turned the show over to him. He spoke into the microphone clearly and deliberately, oblivious to Feigelman's occasional "*Hrrroon!*" and "*Fffth!*" But I had to laugh: the congruence of Charlie Callas lookalike Grossman beside Charlie Callas soundalike Feigelman was too much for me. I feared that somebody might think I was laughing at Feigelman, so I covered my mouth, coughed, bit my tongue, and like a kid who hears a fart in church, tried every trick to conceal how tickled I was.

Soon Grossman began to pick up speed and get more animated. I realized he was now repeating verbatim what he had said the day before. As he got to the part where I got lost, he got excited and stood up. The reporter tried to motion him back to the microphone, but he was alone in Saul Grossman world and took a few steps away. I grabbed a mike and walked along with him as he paced near the front of the stage. Cameras flashed. Still laughing, I soon became aware that my mirth was being amplified through the microphone.

Just as it had happened the day before, Grossman was suddenly done, and would have left the stage had I not, chuckling, led him back to the table. I sat down by him and hung my head in a desperate attempt to hide, but then Templeton said that the first comments would be from Feigelman, who immediately went "*Rrrrroot*!" I fell to the floor, laughing louder than I think I ever had. I heard a "*Hawn, hawn*" coming from Perry Fowler, who must have thought I was just reacting as I had the day before and was joining in as he had then. Templeton's voice came through the speakers, "Hume! Quasi Hume, please!" Voices were all around, and suddenly I was lifted from the floor. I paused in my high-spiritedness long enough to see who was hauling me from the stage by my right arm: Peter Boykin/Staggy Man/Gyges. I burst into guffawing again and tried to say, "Twist that ring and get me out of here," but I could not get the words out.

Then somebody was tugging in the other direction on my left arm, and I was furculaed into a wishbone: Grossman! I wished I could say, "Sometimes I thinks I wants to go, sometimes I thinks I wants to stay" (which I thought was from Stepin Fetchit, or maybe Jimmy Durante), but could only laugh again. Then about a dozen folks rushed the stage to aid the tug-o-war while the rest in the audience swayed and moaned in that odd embarrassment you feel when witnessing a spectacle.

"Gentlemen, please! I have an announcement! Please! Gentlemen!" Sennet's baritone came in over the confusion. Gyges turned me loose, and Grossman and I and everyone else on my left toppled into a pile of knees and elbows and linen and tweed. Whatever was pinned to the floor beneath my solar plexus knocked the wind from me. I heard a muffled "*Prrrut*" and rolled over to find Feigelman's head under me. Gyges grabbed my arm again and helped me to my feet, and I hooked my elbow into the elbow of Feigelman, who was lifted in the same motion.

"You OK, man?" Gyges asked. I nodded. "No harm meant. Just trying to help."

My breath came back in a big gasp. "No problem, hoss. Thanks."

"Here," he said, and pressed something into my hand: two tickets to Armageddon.

I turned to Feigelman. "Are you all right?"

"Yes, thank you. *Asshole!*"

Templeton was kneeling by Grossman, rubbing her hand across his hair. He was trying to put on his glasses, which were broken at the bridge.

"If we can take our places, ladies and gentlemen, please," Sennet continued. The noise died down and most were seated again. "For those of you who haven't heard, Saul Grossman, who not only has shown the mind-body problem once and for all to be irresolvable and thus not a problem. I presume we are in agreement, are we not, panelists?" They all nodded. "Also, not half an hour ago, Dr. Grossman defeated both David McDavid and Donald Donaldson at tic-tac-toe."

Half of the audience gasped, while the other half broke into "*yeah!*"s and "*wooo!*"s. Then the first half, over the blow, hollered, too. By that time, another three hundred people had wedged themselves into the auditorium.

"The Executive Committee of the American Philosophical Association," Sennet said, "has voted to cancel the Presidential Address and has declared that the rest of the afternoon be spent in celebration of this historic occasion. Free drinks in Belle Alley bar down the hall, compliments of the APA!"

Gyges lifted Grossman onto his shoulder and left the stage with him. Grossman looked back, bewildered, but I followed and yelled, "It's OK, Saul!" and he smiled. Gyges carried Grossman up the center aisle.

Falling into line were hundreds of philosophers, like so many satyrs and maenads in a bacchanal procession behind the Goat Man.

※

Belle Alley was a cauldron of *olla podrida*—to me, it smelled peppery, slightly fruity (mangoes?), orangish brown, oily, and lumpy, but amorphous—of two parts hotel staff, three parts wrestler, and fifteen parts wrestling fan, and saturated with eighty parts philosopher, all overflowing the hall. No diehard racing fans were in the mixture, for they were already at the racetrack. But the primarily wrestling, secondarily racing fan audience had just settled in to watch the Elixir 600 on the big-screen TV. Unhappily, they found their view blocked by a wave of metaphysical jubilation producing an indecipherable din from which could be heard the occasional "Gödel," "eliminative," or "mysterians win."

The protestors soon welcomed the intrusion as the bartenders, per instructions from the APA execs, handed out bottles of imported beer, assorted shots of spirits, carafes of wine, and fruity and sour and salty cocktails of blues and pinks. Within minutes, glasses were dispensed with altogether, and any manner of bottle, along with "Elixir"-embossed corkscrews and church key-openers, were passed indiscriminately from hand to hand, rippling out from those nearest the bar—the hall spillage yelling, "Back here!"—so each ingredient in the melange got libations *gratis*.

I (the *companion*! Silenus?) was singing to myself a Merle Haggard song, "Rainbow Stew," and leaning against the bar's one pool table, which Grossman was now sitting atop. A stool, set on the felt, was serving as throne, and King Grossman was now autographing APA programs and napkins for a ring of supplicants and actually enjoying the adoration when a triple-voiced, stentorian "Hey!" hushed the revelry.

Everyone turned in the direction of the yell to see Gyges and two other wrestlers towering above the crowd, standing on a table. Ernest Leavengood, who must have put them up to hollering for attention, then made a toast I could not quite hear—something about "not since Aristotle passed through the sacred gates of the Academy"—but was funny enough to elicit hails of laughter. Then a woman on the other side of the room offered a mock eulogy to the mind-body problem, segueing into a limerick praising Grossman. This also produced wide laughter. Then one toast from a guy by the bar turned serious and got "Hear! Hear!"s and even a couple of "Amen"s.

The salmagundi simmered for a moment, until the unequivocal opening of the Talking Heads's "Take Me to the River" throbbed from the hefty speakers, greeted by whoops all around, and bringing the soup to a boil again. Half the churning, frothing mass started singing along at exactly the right instant when David Byrne's chirpy voice spread over the room, and by the time the chorus, with its plea to be dipped in the river, came around, the rest became choir as well, with those who did not know the lyrics singing nonsense words, the spirit possessing and moving through them not to be denied. Grossman was one of the inspired babblers, but he and the others so unselfconsciously mouthed their glossalalia in perfect rhythm to the music that it made some primitive *Sinn*, untranslatable—not further analyzable, and no possibility of interchangeability *salva veritate*.

Then the Goat Man stood, and with his eyes closed and his arms raised high, danced a gyrating, thrusting, enthused hoochie-coochie that drew from the celebrants a low moan, which grew in volume and pitch and erupted into an ecstatic scream of sheer, orgiastic abandon. Two women (both of whom I remembered seeing in the auditorium) were hurled onto the pool table on either side of the Goat Man and began to bump and grind. They whirled their lanky necks about, darted their tongues (brightly stained from tropical-style drinks), tossed clothes to the crowd, and twirled imagined nipple tassels as a relentless, extended disco version of the song pounded on. I looked around at the swirling St. Vitusing mass, with currents and eddies that swept those outside in and back out again so no one remained in the same spot for long. It seemed to transform into one heaving organism, its unifying pulse jolting through every part, the twitches of the individual components manifestations of the feelings of the composite leviathan feeling itself in an undifferentiated ur-sense, neither sight nor smell nor sound nor taste nor touch, yet all at once.

The song finally ended, and the writhing beast released a roar that was also a sigh and, like a rapidly dividing amoeba, disassembled into discrete cells, although continuing in the celebration. The table-mounted women remained where they were—one with shirttail exposed and shoeless (early on flung across the room), the other down to bra, high-waisted panties, wool socks, and Birkenstocks—but stripped no further. The intensity subsided, but most in the crowd continued to dance, sing, make-out, and grab-ass for a couple more hours. A line shuffled past the dancing Grossman who, grinning as I had never seen him before, reached down, never missing a beat to the music, to touch each extended hand. He seemed to be taking care of himself just fine, so I slipped off to try to find Feigelman.

I passed the hundred or so partiers who had turned their attention to the TV (a banner hanging above it read "Try a Transformation: Elixer and Bourbon") to watch the beginning of the race (I saw Cale Yarlborough on the screen). After a briefing from the non-philosophers on the nature of the contest (go fast for six-hundred miles, try to come in first, try not to get killed), the philosophers were soon rednecking with the seasoned old boys, choosing favorite drivers and shouting commentaries like "That dirty-driving sumbitch bumped him!" and "Lookoutlookout! God*damm*it, you let that suckfish get around you!" The wrestlers mugged for photos, indulged biceps fondlers, and demonstrated chokeholds. Gilbert, his head sticking above the crowd, held high a bottle of something, maybe Absolut, as if toasting everyone. In a dark corner of this garden of earthly delights, just beyond the video games, I swear a couple was humping.

Someone stuck a Heineken beer into my hand, and I realized I had not had a beer during the entire festivity. I sucked it down in one delicious draught, maneuvered through the crowd toward the door, stepped into the hall, and paused for my pupils to adjust to the light. To one side, just outside the door, was a five-foot high pile of jackets and sport coats, and I noticed that everyone, including me, was sopping wet. I heard a *"Yank!"* and turned to see Feigelman leaning against the wall with a half-empty bottle of Bushmills in his hand. He looked like Soupy Sales with male pattern baldness, and he stood up straight when he saw me approach him.

"Been quite a day, hasn't it?" I said.

"Well, if isn't Democritus, or perhaps Momus incarnate. Mother*fuck*!" A spasm ran through his shoulder as if he were shaking a lizard off it.

"Look, I'm sorry. I know how it must have seemed to you."

"Forget it. No one laughs at me more than I do myself."

"No, it really wasn't *at* you," I said, trying too hard to sound sincere. "You see, Grossman looks so much like Charlie Callas, the comedian, and—"

"You noticed that, too, huh? *Vrrrut*! I love Charlie Callas." He chicken-winged his arm against his side. "Is he still around?"

"I don't know. I haven't seen him in years."

Feigelman poked the Bushmills towards me. "Have a snort?"

"Thanks." I turned up and pulled at the bottle. It burnt exactly enough, and smelled like cones of suede leather being crowded to the edge of the bed. "Listen, do you know anything about synaesthesia?"

"Some—*Rrroot*!—which is about as much as anybody knows."

I described my experiences, related my plate-forehead convergence, and asked if they could be related.

"Fascinating," he said. "But first, nearly all synaesthetes have cross-ups in sight and hearing. Letters or words are experienced as—*Shit*!—colored, or music produces something visual, usually geometrical shapes or, again, colors. But synaesthesia produced by smell is extremely rare. I recall only a case or two as complexly detailed as yours"—he shoulder-jerked again. "Second, the olfactory sense is associated with the temporal lobe." He indicated the area by putting his hand to the side of his head. "And the—*Cunt*!—limbic system, particularly the hippocampus. Now, A, the cases I'm familiar with were not accident victims. In fact, they usually report having their experiences from as far back as they can remember. B, it's unlikely, though not impossible, that a blow to the—*Prick!*—forehead would cause damage to those areas. C, brain damage ordinarily causes impairment to the senses, not what could be described, in your case, as enhancement. *Rrrink!*"

The Police and a couple hundred philosophers were singing "Spirits in the Material World" with the bass turned up to the max.

"I've been toying with the notion," I said, "that something might have been triggered in my brain so my experiences are—and I know this sounds nuts, instead of deviant—more accurately representative of reality. I just don't know whom to discuss this with."

"Sounds Eastern. There's a Buddhist tradition of equating nirvana with—*Shit!*—some sort of holistic experience, and if the Hindus are right with their pantheistic idea about everything being Brahman, well maybe you're on the right track." He reached up and scratched his ear furiously. "But mysticism aside, I think it would be a good idea to get an MRI or a PET scan. What's disturbing is that these experiences have come on all of a sudden. I don't want to—*Fuck!*—alarm you, but that may indicate some sort of anomaly that needs immediate attention."

Not only do I ordinarily resist asking other people about their health, but I can't stand it when somebody tells me to see a doctor, have that mole looked at, or not let that cough drag on too long. You would think a pissant as lacking in direction as I would latch onto any advice coming my way, but I take a certain pride staying alive despite all the untreated maladies others attribute to me.

But I thanked Feigelman for his advice and offered him the tickets Gyges had given me, which he happily accepted. Grossman could deal a little longer with the twitching beast in the bar. I had my own monster to try to pacify.

༄

"Hello?"
"Hey. It's me. I'm at the conference."
"Hm," Tally said.

"Grossman's the big hero here. He dissolved the mind-body problem."

"That's nice."

"You don't understand. He's famous. He made history."

"*I* don't understand?"

A woman on the phone next to me, probably a grad student in her twenties, was giggling and telling someone about the "end of Cartesian tyranny."

"Look. You know I didn't want to stay with my folks. And Saul needed me—"

"*Saul* needed you."

"Yes. He would never have made it without me. And we both know you couldn't abide him a whole day in the car. So, if I hadn't come, none of this would have happened for him."

"For him?"

"Jesus, Tally, I've got to give my paper tomorrow. I don't need this on my mind."

"That's what's important? What's on *your* mind."

I turned towards the woman beside me. Her nametag, on a blouse that was untucked and unbuttoned to reveal most of the left cup of her bra, read "T. A. Gallagher, Clemson." She held a half empty bottle of Jack Daniel's, and when she looked up and saw my face, she broke into a big, open-mouth smile and swelled her beautiful, green eyes in a look of recognition. She reached over and took my hand.

"His companion," she said into her phone, "is right here beside me," and handed me the bottle. I took a swallow and turned back around.

"OK," I said into the phone. "Tell me what I need to do."

"I don't believe this. No, I do believe it."

A hand tugged at my shoulder. "Hey."

I turned to see T. A. Gallagher still smiling. She held the receiver toward me.

"Hey, tell my friend about the Grossman solution." She put the receiver back against her face. "Here, his name is Quasi *Hume*. Isn't that cool?" Or did she say "Kwasi"?

She pointed the receiver in my direction. I pushed it away, set the bottle down beside the phone, and turned back around. "I have to go check on Saul. But before—"

"Sounds like you have to go, all right." Tally hung up.

I turned back to T. A. Gallagher and took the phone from her. Another young woman was at the other end, and I told her that indeed the entire APA was celebrating the death of the mind-body problem. T. A. Gallagher continued to smile at me. She touched my hand, and I snatched it back as if from a snake. I told the other woman goodbye, gave the phone back to T. A. Gallagher, and started to walk away.

She grabbed my arm. "Come on, Quasi, this might be the most philosophically significant day of our lives, *ein Wendepunkt der Geschichte*," she said, holding up the bottle of bourbon. "Let's celebrate together." She stretched her face up towards mine and licked her top lip.

If only Tally could see this. I have put up with her shit for too long. I do not have to. I am a goddamn good-looking man. I could have as many T. A. Gallaghers as I wanted.

"I'm sorry," I said. "I'm with someone," and pulled away.

Pissant.

※

Inside the bar, the bulk of the inhabitants still danced, now undulating to Culture Club's "Karma Chameleon" (whoever was in charge of the music must have brought in his record collection from high school), although a larger crowd than earlier was packed in front of the TV watching the race car drivers go round and round. I shouldered my way to the pool table upon which the Goat Man, whom someone crowned with several napkins plaited together into a ring, was still cavorting with four or five new women.

I am a cynical, sardonic, frequently contumelious, bitter son of a bitch. The feeling with which I am most rarely acquainted is sympathetic joy for the accomplishments of others. But on that afternoon, amid that surging hash of philosopher and non-, I was happy for Saul

Grossman. A grand day it was in the history of philosophy, but it was *the* day in the life of Saul Grossman. I had been visited a few times by such vicarious gladness for Lucian, and perhaps most for Willie at her divorce party. Watching Saul cut loose like that, I felt like big brother Greazy who had arranged for his little bubba to lose his virginity.

I cut into the adoration line, pulled out the round can of Copenhagen, and offered it up to Grossman. He squinted, then recognizing the gleaming, silver top with its "It Satisfies" motto, accepted the gift tenderly. He carefully scooped out a pinch and placed it behind his lower lip, as he had seen me do so many times. He tried to hand the can back to me, but I motioned him off and gave him an Elixir logo-ed plastic cup to spit into. He slipped the can correctly into the hip pocket of his wide-well corduroys and smiled. A trail of brown-speckled saliva meandered down his beard and a tear down his cheek.

If the world was not revolving around Saul Grossman, then it would be as soon as he got a swallow of that snuff.

EIGHT
The Immortality of the Soul

I have no fear of death. I took my first step towards developing this distinctive trait just after Wednesday night supper and prayer meeting as the forty or so attendees milled about the fellowship hall—a fifteen by thirty-foot cinder block addition to the little A-frame, asbestos-shingled church—as I was fixing to go home. I asked Rev. Pearson, in the presence of the two deacons, how we get to heaven. He pressed a spiced (as the Old Man would say, *sparsed*) ham hand on my shoulder and said he was surprised at the question, for surely I knew that when someone accepts Jesus Christ as his Lord and Savior and follows the path of righteousness, the Blessed Lamb-o-God takes care of the rest.

That was not what I meant, I said. How is it that someone can be dead for many years (it could not be too many more, because the Second Coming was on the way) and the body moldered away and yet that person, who, in the formula I had heard so often, was an amalgam of body, mind, and spirit, could be the same thing in heaven? His red face pealed into a grin that pushed his jowls down into his neck, and he told me I should not concern myself with such questions but simply be assured that God can do anything. "That was no answer," I mumbled.

"What? What did you say, son?" He reached into the patch pocket of his burgundy sports coat. His other hand tightened so hard on my shoulder that I felt a charley horse coming on.

Out the corner of my eye, I saw Mama gazing proudly at me from across the room. Her precocious son was conversing with the church scholars like young Jesus at the Temple.

"Well, not *any*thing, I don't reckon," I said. "He can't make two plus two equal five, can he?"

Rev. Pearson, a Pentecostal Holiness preacher whose expertise included pew-jumping and foot-washing but not questions of personhood, had already retrieved a little vial from his pocket, unscrewed its top, and eyebrowed a signal to the deacons, who waved the ranks to come rally around. In a flash, my forehead was anointed and hands lay all over my head and shoulders. People prayed aloud individually, beckoning the Holy Ghost to descend and something else to get hence, until Sister Doris was filled with the Spirit—she held the church record for inhabitations—and began speaking in tongues. Brother Winston, a deacon who was missing two fingers from his left hand from amputations following a popular church festivity involving reptiles, interpreted the Comforter's message that the demon had been run off and that the young man, despite a near loss to the other side and thanks to a fully saved, sanctified, Holy-Ghost-got, and to a well-armed congregation, was destined to be a great Man-o-God.

Mama, overcome by the gravity of the event or, more likely, embarrassment, threw her arms around me and said, "Thank you, Jesus. I been so worried about this one. Blessed Jesus."

Fat-breasted, powder-smelling, conical-haired Sister Doris waddled to a chair to recover from serving as vessel for the Ghost. Attendants cooled her with paddle fans that had a picture of a skyward-looking Jesus on one side and Brother Hargus's Woodmen of the World address and telephone number on the back. Others, awestruck by the miracle they had helped bring about by the laying on of their unctuous hands, continued to wail or mumble prayers. Mama sobbed through a pack of tissues.

To take full advantage of the presence of the Holy Ghost, Rev. Pearson declared the need for an impromptu communion, and the deacons scrounged up the nearest things they could find to body and blood: a box of Chicken-in-a-Biscuit and some instant coffee, a radical departure from the usual hunk of light bread and sip of grape juice, but an omnipotent God who could make twice two equal five could surely transform even these meager materials. (For years, I believed I had been imbibing genuine wine at church until Lucian broke into the Old Man's stash when I was eleven and poured us up two glasses of Zenobia

Major's homemade brew. I took a gulp, tasted the difference right away, and knew I had to be wary of other lies by the church.)

The preacher and deacons then huddled up to determine: (a) whole or half cracker per mouth, and (b) black or with-milk-and-sugar coffee. They settled on half crackers (God, of course, would ensure that they not run short, but why try Him?) and, finding no milk, decided on coffee with sugar (otherwise some child might spew it back at them). Rev. Pearson assured Brother Dozier that the salty crackers would not raise his high blood pressure. Further, he said, Sister Dottie need not worry about the sweetened coffee's effect upon her sugar diabetes. When the paper plate with the bisected Chickens-in-a-Biscuit came around, my two mistakes were (i) taking four chunks of Jesus (we never got these at home, because Mama insisted that they, like fruit, were too expensive) and (ii) eating the little stack immediately, not waiting for the preacher's sign. He gave me an eat shit look and probably entertained the notion that I had invited Asmodeus, whom he had just called out. The coffee was cold by the time it arrived in Dixie cups, and I hated sugar in my coffee, so I took only a tiny sip.

"Drink it all," Mama whispered through sphinctered lips, "or it won't take."

"It's nasty."

"It's Jesus' blood."

"I drunk his blood before."

I had already caused one spectacle, and Mama could not take another. (The next morning, she went to the doctor's office to have Opal, the nurse and the *de facto* physician for most women's complaints, write out a prescription for some more nerve pills.) She pinched me. I forced the stuff down.

When it was all over, as everyone else filed out, Rev. Pearson, Mama, and I stood in the fellowship hall doorway. She hugged me and said, "God bless you, Legare," or "Don't forget, son, the Lord's called you." Katie Peagler, a year older than I and the one good-looking girl amongst the church's corn-fed members, squeezed me and kissed my cheek, winking as she pulled away, fully aware of how she had just transformed my body and blood. I thought of asking the preacher how lust compared to prick-teasing on the sin scale. Instead, though I continued to go to church until I left home just to keep Mama happy, I took the first step that night on a slow walk along my own road to Damascus by realizing that neither he nor any other preacher had anything sensible to tell me about self-identity, death, or God; that the rest of the congregation was composed of full-grown men and women no longer unaccountable for their gullibility and passing their private hells on to their children—I could hardly abide them for an hour-and-a-half church service, much less an eternity in the afterlife; that death, or the fear of it, was the best friend all the Rev. Pearsons of the world ever had; and that nothing in religion seemed satisfying, even if true—at best it offered mythology (a barely dressed-up Zeus tyrannos, possession by demons neé Furies), at worst produced boredom.

Through my teens, I became increasingly adept at identifying various forms of mythology and dismissing them along with the accompanying fears they manufactured, but boredom was more resilient. I admit that my initial attraction to philosophy had much to do with my loss of religion, not trying to replace a dead God with an equally obsessive idol or something to compensate for eternal life in paradise. It was more to find some satisfactory relief from a pervasive ennui whose symptoms religion could only mask.

Major movements in the history of philosophy struck me as promising attempts at a cure. The Epicureans' entreaty to avoid "disquietude"—their fancy word, as I took it, for boredom—by seeking pleasure sounds good initially, but only certain pleasures are worth pursuing: the "necessary" ones, like (not over-) eating and resting, and the mental ones, like pleasant conversation. The Stoics, like the Buddhists, seemed to say that we should embrace boredom by alleviating desires. I could not see the point of that, nor of Spinoza's version, which he described as acquiescing to the determining forces of the universe/nature/substance/God. So, as I saw it, he sold out. Besides, I could not deny, like Spinoza did, the freedom of the will; yet, I could not go to Schopenhauer's polar extreme of attributing everything to the blind striving of an uncontrollable, irrational will. He thought that all you could do was find some occasional, fleeting respite in music, and that part I found agreeable, except that by music, he did not mean Hank Williams. Had he read Izaak Walton and got inspired to go wet a line, he would have added fishing, too.

When I discovered the existentialists, I thought I had found the guys who had straddled the boredom boar and held his ears while somebody at the other end clipped his dangling *angsts*. But they all carried on about despair, dread, nausea, self-deception, finitude, nothingness, and death, death, death so much that methought they didth protest too much. It was not that they were depressing; it was that just when it looked like they were the violent ones who could bear the Godless kitchen's heat away, they slipped—even leaped, as did Kierkegaard, dragging Marcel and Tillich and some other promising young bucks with him—out the back door.

Heidegger got off to a hell of a start with *Being and Time*, then abandoned the project and turned his attention instead to writing stacks of gibberish that half the philosophical world could not suck up fast enough and that I remain convinced was an elaborate joke that will not be caught until the next century.

Sartre too seemed to nail it in *Being and Nothingness*, where he said that we humans are useless passions. Then I read that when asked why his work seemed so pessimistic, the wall-eyed little troll replied that he had never had an unhappy day in his life. I could not put up with that bullshit.

Even Nietzsche, the big game hunter with God's mounted head hanging in his Hall of Dead Absolutes, scared himself into his Eternal Recurrence of the Same, the stupidest idea any philosopher ever had. Old Fred reasoned that since the universe is made of a finite amount of stuff, then that stuff may configure in a large, yet finite, number of ways. After this one fizzles out or implodes or however it happens, it will reconfigure into another form. But since time is infinite, the universe will be able to reform itself into every possible configuration. When it runs out of patterns, it will have to run through the old ones, and we will all live exactly these same lives an infinite number of times. So, you better live a life you would happily repeat endlessly.

I mentioned this to Lucian, long after his accident. "Damn. That'd be just his luck—get reincarnated but come back as itself." What he meant was, *That'd be just* my *luck—get reincarnated but come back as* my*self*.

"But my professor insists that Nietzsche's physics was all wrong," I said. "There's no reason why the series has to run out, and no *particular* combination would have to repeat."

"Don't matter. He's a metaphor." *It's a metaphor.* "What matters is that they should live a life she would want by repeat." *One should live a life one would want to repeat.* He was rolling a joint, and I told him once again that pot makes people stupid. His standard line was that he had nothing to lose then.

"I just think Nietzsche, like everybody else, was afraid to die," I said, "and this was the lie he told himself for comfort."

"We ain't afraid for die." *I ain't afraid to die.* "Sure as hell beats living forever. Why do everyone, if they have eternity to do you?" *Why do anything, if one has eternity to do it?* "What *is* scary is the thought of dying and not being done, we know, incomplete. People just live and die throughout the chance to wrap it all around." *Without the chance to wrap it all up.* "If people really did live exactly three-score years and ten and just keeled over, then they could plan our lives in." *Plan their lives out.* "If she knew that," *if one knew that,* "but was still afraid to die, then *this* seems like it would be saying that where he did while alive was meaningless." *What one did while alive was meaningless.*

"Do you believe in God?"

"Well, yeah, but what the hell's She got to do with it?" He lit the joint with a Zippo that had a deer head on one side and "Marlboro" on the other that I had given him for his eighteenth birthday and got from months of collecting proofs of purchases from the Old Man's smokes and other R. J. Reynolds-brand packages I dug out of trash cans. He took a long toke from the joint and offered it to me. I waved him off.

"It just seems strange. You say all the sorts of things that atheists usually say."

"You proved it for him, remember?" *Proved it to me.* "The ontological argument."

"Wait a minute. I never said I thought it works. I was just telling you about it."

He finished off the doobie. "For a college boy, they," *you,* "don't know shit."

I have often wondered if Lucian was already considering suicide when we had this conversation. Sitting on the train track, waiting to be mangled, may have been his twisted way of taking charge of his death and wrapping up his life in some way he found satisfying. Camus said he had never seen anyone die for the ontological argument.

Maybe I had.

꩜

Turning the Volvo onto Rembert's road, I already felt a little guilty, occupied with thoughts of Lucian when I should have been thinking of Chalmers. Grossman was reserved, not interrupting at all during my monologue on the history of the philosophy of boredom. Perhaps he was still reeling from the adoration heaped upon him earlier that day. He had bent over from atop the pool table to say into my ear, "I'm nauseous." I did not tell him that the term was one I had never heard until my stint in New Jersey and one that I had immediately found to be foul, for reasons I do not understand. I would ask the Northmen, "Why can't you say *nauseated*?" At least he had not said "noxious" as I had sometimes heard.

I helped him down from the pool table and smuggled him into the bathroom, where he threw up, said he was too dizzy to walk, and stretched out on the chaise lounge or whatever you call those little couches with one arm. At that point, I realized we were in the women's bathroom. For the next ten minutes, as we rode out Grossman's vertigo, women came in, said smiley "hello"s, peed or barfed, and left as if it were a unisex world, like at a college dorm. Some even offered to fetch us drinks.

Grossman knew a little about Chalmers and what would occur at the wake. I gave him no instructions concerning whom or what topics to avoid. Willie would be proud of me.

The big fence around Rembert's house was gone, and the front yard already had about ten cars parked in it. As we got out of the car, I could hear the curs raising a ruckus, but the sound came from far behind the house. Perhaps he had shut them up in the tobacco barn for the evening. I veered around to the side of the house for a look out over the field. Beside a raked-out area was a stack of wood from a hickory Rembert had felled a year ago and allowed to season for just this annual event. It's where he would build the fire and let it burn for a couple of hours until the violet hues of the coals met his approval and which he would then transfer, a selective shovelful at a time, to the pit over which the peppered and vinegared pig would roast slowly through the night.

Grossman studied the architecture of the pit over by the chinaberry tree as I tried to make out what had been added across the stubbled field beyond the barn. The building looked like a huge warehouse secured by a chain-link fence. I saw the dogs inside. A couple of them jumped against the fence, under a sloping tin roof nailed to creosote posts that must have become, as opposed to the yard around the house for their ancestors, their permanent home. "Freeze," came a voice from behind me. I raised my arms above my head.

"Now turn around, real slow-like."

Rembert stood on the little back porch with his right index finger pointing like a pistol barrel and his thumb cocked like an exaggerated hammer. Taller and no grayer in his dark brown, never-combed hair, Rembert hardly resembled his brother, the Old Man. He looked somewhat like Warren Oates and as if he had just crawled out from under a leaky diesel engine. The green briarbuster fronts of his camouflage britches were nearly worn through at the knees, but the red chamois shirt with the glasses case in the pocket looked new.

"Come'ere, you sorry little suckfish," Rembert said.

I walked up the cinderblock steps, and we gave each other a handshake and half hug. He had a warm, khaki smell that was nevertheless splintery, like an old floor sill. I looked back to see Grossman peeking out from behind the chinaberry tree.

"Come on out, Saul. It's OK."

"Kinda skiddish, eh?" Rembert said. We stood side by side, his hand on my shoulder squeezing my trapezius. The old boy still had a grip on him. "I ain't really gonna shoot you," he said to Grossman. "Yet." We both laughed, and Grossman slinked out and approached the porch.

"This is my Uncle Rembert, Saul," I said, turning to Rembert. "Saul Grossman teaches with me down at the university."

"Glad to have you here, son."

"Pleased to meet you, Mr. Hume."

"I hear you're from New York City, eh?"

"Yes, sir."

"Well, don't you worry," Rembert said and squeezed Grossman's shoulder, which elicited a wince from Grossman. "There's a cure for 'bout everthing." We laughed, Grossman, too, who had changed the timbre of his nasal *hyan, hyan* to a throatier *heh, heh* followed by a falsetto *hee, hee*. "Maybe I can learn you how to do barbeque the *right* way, and you'll forget all 'bout New York *and* Floridie and be wanting to move in hyere."

Grossman smiled and shuffled his feet. He crossed his arms, uncrossed them, put his hands into his pockets, and giggled, as if he had been invited to join some prestigious conclave like the Vienna Circle or the Rat Pack. He had enjoyed the worship he had received earlier, but the invitation to apprentice with a master flesh roaster seemed to overwhelm him.

"I'd be honored, Mr. Hume," he said. "I'd be very honored."

Rembert chuckled and slapped us both on the back too hard. "Let's go on in, boys."

The back door led into the kitchen, where Mama, Arlene, Willie, and the Old Man's sister, Miriam, who must have been about seventy-five, were arranging pots and platters, as they would do for hours to come as more sympathizers delivered food. All the usual smells were there: chicken, rice, and string beans, mostly yellow-green with a little blue around the edges of a many-pointed and swaying star. Miriam wiped her hands on her apron and threw her flabby arms around me, half in welcome and half, it seemed, in comfort for our loss. She then did the same to Grossman before anyone told her who he was, even telling him she was glad to see him. Like her older sisters, Lula Mae and Bernice, who surely were in the big room already with Chalmers, Miriam was about 5' 2", overweight (most of her mass settled into her deep hips for a low center of gravity that provided both stability and a waddle), and widowed. All three had bunned hair that had never been cut, were slightly buck-toothed, and wore large, white beads with matching clip-on ear bobs and nondescript dresses that would have looked like housecoats on younger women.

"Y'all go back out and come in the front," Willie said.

"Hello, Willie," Grossman said.

"What for?" I asked.

"Hey, Saul," she said. Then to me, "Aunt Lula and Aunt Bernice—you got to go around and see them. You know that."

"Y'all go around and see everybody and then come back in hyere for something to eat," Mama said.

I fished around the kitchen drawers until I found some duct tape for a temporary mending of Grossman's glasses, then we went out and back to the front porch, where the Old Man and Merle Kirby, a long-time family friend who often chauffeured Chalmers, had claimed the rocking chairs.

"Dog if it ain't Greazy," Merle said. "Ain't you a beaut."

We shook hands, and I introduced Grossman, whom Merle wished a pleasant visit. The Old Man asked how the conference went. I told him that Grossman was the hottest thing in the philosophical world, and the Old Man said, "Well, good."

We went inside. The lower floor of Rembert's house comprised a bathroom, a kitchen/dining room, and an awkwardly large room that should have been divided into a living room plus a den and perhaps even a third room. Two couches, two recliners, and a number of straightback, cane-seat chairs were all pushed against the walls, leaving an open space of about twenty by forty feet that looked like a dance hall. On that night, however, a coffin occupied the center of the room. The front door was off-center so that you entered with a wall a few feet to your right, along which ran a couch where Lula Mae, senior and therefore nearest the door and to be addressed first, and Bernice were planted and would be found until they left at about midnight. I knew the routine. It had been bludgeoned into my head all my life.

"Aunt Lula Mae," I said. "It's Legare, Pledger's son. I'm so sorry." I bent down and hugged her.

"Thank you, sugar," she said. "Thank you for coming. God bless you."

"This is my friend, Saul." Grossman hugged her without a prompt.

"Saul, King of Israel," Lula Mae said. "God bless you, son."

We repeated the entry rite with Bernice. She was almost entirely deaf, so I had to shout into her ear.

"Paul?" she asked.

"No, ma'am. *Saul!*"

"King of Israel," Lula Mae said.

About twenty other people were there—only a portion of those who would drift in and out through the night. Most were the children, with their husbands and wives, of the Old Man's two dead older brothers and his three sisters. Some of these cousins were so much older that I grew up calling them "Aunt" or "Uncle." With them and many others whom I had not seen in so long, I felt for the first time that night that they were speaking to me as a peer. Lily Kirby was reading a book to Wynonna. I looked around and realized what seemed amiss—Unitas and Spessard were not present. They must have been on their way back from the race.

We shook hands and hugged around the room as the others tried to find places to set their plates of food or glasses of tea. I knew the names of only one in-law cousin and a few of my first cousins once removed, a couple of whom were my age. I did not bother to explain why Grossman was there. A couple of them said "thank you" to Grossman—perhaps it was an incomplete "Thank you *for coming*," or else they thought he was connected to the funeral home.

At the end of the circuit sat Purvis and his wife.

"Look outside, Markley," Purvis said to another of my cousins, "and see if it's hailing, 'cause when Legare Hume blesses us with a visit, it is *some* kind of sign."

A couple of people chuckled, but several were sure to have thought it inappropriate to make a joke in the room with the deceased. Purvis handed his plate to his avian wife and stood up to shake my hand. I could smell liquor on him—Crown Royal—like a leaning stack of pennies, but deep blue like the little velvet bags the bottles come in.

"This is my wife, Marie."

"How do you do," she said in an accent I did not recognize as she held out her tiny hand. She was Asian and could not have been more than twenty-two or -three and thus twelve or thirteen years younger than Purvis. She was sitting, but I could tell she was hardly five feet tall and could not have weighed ninety pounds. She wore four-inch heels on her bony feet. We small-talked for a minute or two. I realized that no one asked me about Tally. Perhaps they had been briefed.

It could no longer be put off—the time had come to view the body. If I waited any longer, Lula Mae would instruct her son, Cecil, to lead me to the open casket. From where we stood, I could see the top of Chalmers's head, which few had ever seen, since he always wore a striped, almost bill-less welder's cap, even to church. He had a bald spot, and at just that instant, as I turned back and tugged Grossman by the sleeve to get him away from Marie, with whom he was conversing in French, I saw for the first time that Grossman had a bald spot, too. How could I have never noticed that before? We walked to the casket and stared down at a face so heavily made up that he looked like a mannequin. A pinkish layer had peeled back a tiny bit from just in front of his ear. I was feeling irritated on the insistence for this abominable open-casket routine.

Then Grossman spoke.

"What was his full name?"

"Chalmers Rance Hume."

Grossman reached down, took one of Chalmers's hands into his own, and then began speaking, in Hebrew. He was reciting the kaddish.

"Saul, don't," I said, trying not to let anyone hear me. Instead, he got louder.

Everyone else—a few more had come in while Grossman and I had made our circumambulation of the room—hushed. The women in the kitchen and the men on the porch, looking puzzled, came in. Someone said "Praise God," and somebody else, "Blessed Jesus." They gathered around the coffin. Mama and Arlene each assumed the Holiness posture: face turned upwards, eyes closed, one hand on the breast and the other raised high overhead as if flagging down the Holy Ghost.

To them, Grossman was filled with the Spirit and was speaking in tongues.

Willie stood in the kitchen door shaking her head. I backed out of the crowd until I bumped into Purvis. Marie, her head bowed, was beside him, and mumbling in another strange tongue, maybe Tagalog.

"They can do what they want," Purvis said to me, "but Chalmers ain't getting up."

۞

Rembert's fire was squeezing out beautiful coals, the pig had been roasting for a couple of hours, and visitors had dropped in and left by the dozen. Sitting around the fire along with Grossman and me on folding tripod hunting stools, wooden crates, and a couple of five-gallon paint buckets was a collection of family I hadn't been a part of in years. The Old Man was next to Spessard, who was still talking about how the race had ended in a massive wreck without a winner; Unitas, who was in and out of the house, torn between the mysterious world of men and the plethora of desserts inside; Purvis, who had hardly said a word, I suspected because of the feud that Willie had told me he was having with Rembert; DeWayne, who said the guy who was supposed to fill in for him at the lounge had shown up an hour late, waiting out the summons officer whose car he recognized in the lounge parking lot; Cecil, who went inside every few minutes to check on his mother; my cousin Pudge; my cousin Strom Thurman, whose nickname was Booger, a tag he accepted until high school, when he realized that a nickname thought cool by pre-adolescent boys was not necessarily regarded with the same affection by teenage girls (still no one ever got into the habit of calling him Strom); a cousin Markley, whom we called Anchorhead as a child because of his talent for crushing or breaking anything from cans of peas to hickory nuts on his adamantine forehead, and who obviously missed his calling to be a circus geek; Mama's brother Baron (pronounced Bay-ern), who had her sagging eyes, giving him a resemblance to Harry Dean Stanton; and her other brother, Thaydo, neé Theodore. His first wife had shot off his left arm with a shotgun in an argument. She left him, taking the gun with her as a memento. When she returned a year later, and they were having another fight, he expressed his rage by shooting off the stump of the arm himself with the same gun. But what I found creepy about him was that he looked exactly like Dan Duryea, except for the number of arms; so, I always suspected he was scheming up something.

While Rembert arranged the coals, he would tell a joke, make a comment designed to get somebody's goat, or sing a verse of a song he had made up: *Went to shoot a peckerwood, a hat full of eggs, / you kiss a dog's ass, and I'll hold his legs.* As if that were not entertainment enough, we watched the second night of Armageddon on a seventeen-inch TV sitting on a card table and powered by a long orange extension cord running to the house. In the clean night air of the solstice, the rabbit ears picked up the signal perfectly.

The aroma of the burning hickory, the roasting animal, and another, woody and slick, that I took to be exuded by the chinaberry tree from the heat of the fire beside it, was thick and slippery and moving like an eel. I wondered if the subtle changes in the ashy scent of the coals were what guided Rembert, whose every move Grossman, making notes in his little book, was studying, speaking only to inquire about the proper temperature of the coals at transfer from fire to pit, the texture of the flesh indicating that the carcass needed turning, and the exact proportions of mustard, pepper, and vinegar in the sauce. The questions demanded a precision that Rembert, who applied his craft by instinct cultivated over years of practice, could not meet.

Newly arriving couples would part at the front porch steps, the men finding their way around back to the fire to shake some hands, comment on how good the pig looked, promise to come get a plate of it the next day after the funeral, and have a smoke and perhaps a swallow of Crown Royal before joining their wives inside for a peek at dead Chalmers. Unrelated neighbors and acquaintances from his daily course through town came with covered dishes and lingered for only a few minutes. Powell Murphy came, though he no longer owned the gas station and may not have spoken directly to Chalmers in years. Roosevelt Inabinet, who managed the Piggly Wiggly and was one of six or eight black visitors, brought a huge fruit basket and a turkey. Booger was irked by their presence, and each time one arrived, he would say, "They got to get in on everything," or, "Well, damn if there ain't anothern prissing up here."

A black man in a dark suit and homburg hat, and adorned with watch chain, lapel pins, and sundry other decorations, came to the fire and spoke to the Old Man and Rembert—it was Rev. Vanish. I did not expect him to remember me, but I got up and shook his free hand—the other balanced a plate of ham and plastic cup of tea. He greeted me with his universal familiar "Mr. Man," safely presuming I was a former student.

"Well damn," Booger said when Vanish left. "I was just fixing to get me some of that pig ass, but I don't reckon I will now that Reverend Jig's been in there rubbing up on it."

By that time, Markley had had enough of Booger and told him to shut up. When Markley half rose from his seat, we all thought they were going to hook up, which would not have ended well for Booger.

"Hyere, hyere!" the Old Man said, like he was calling his deer dogs.

"Markley set down, and let's watch us some wrestling."

"Yeah," Spessard said. "The Wrath of God's fixing to cut some ass."

Most of those related to Chalmers only by marriage also stayed just long enough to spread their condolences, like Mama's and Arlene's sister Flolene, who was widowed, as were most women on both sides of my family over sixty, and, who, like most of them, could not drive. She depended on her son J. B.—whose given name was John the Baptist and whom Lucian called John the Bastard—to haul her around, which was not a problem for the chronically unemployed J. B., by family consensus the sorriest person in the county. He used these driving duties as explanation for why he had no time to secure a job. Besides, each drive provided an opportunity to convince his mother to buy him a six-pack of beer for his troubles. He sat in the car until Foghat's too loud "Free Ride" was over, then blew the horn for DeWayne, Purvis, and, when he realized I was there, me to come to the car and talk.

"What's that drunkass sumbitch wanting?" DeWayne said.

"Let him sit there and blow," Purvis said, "if he can't drag hisself out the car."

"Is that Greazy yonder?" J. B. yelled out the car window. "Gotawmighty, Slick, come'ere and let me talk atcha."

"Don't go over there," DeWayne said. "We're just as far from him as he is from us."

Flolene emerged from the house and stood akimbo at the top of the steps. She stomped down to the car wagging her finger at J. B. and fussing her way into the back seat. She must have thought he had blown the horn for her to hurry. He cranked up.

"A'ight, then." J. B. hung his head from the window as he backed the car out. "Y'all ain't got time for me. That's a'ight. That's a'ight."

"What happent to his grill?" DeWayne asked.

As J. B. turned the Skylark to get back onto the driveway, the car swung around to show a badly dented front end and a hood tied down by a piece of yellow boat rope looped around the bumper.

"Probably drunk and hit another'n them cows," Markley said.

"Funny how that pasture looked just like a road to him."

"He's gonna end up in jail if he don't watch it," Baron said.

"Be the best thing ever happent to his sorry ass," DeWayne said.

On TV, Triple Six was battling the Word. Commercials came on—Elixir! The taste of a new life! Rembert again ran through the story about how he went out looking for Chalmers and found him crumpled in a ditch.

"How come nobody give him a ride?" Booger asked.

"They was working on the whistle, so hit didn't blow that long blast like it usually do on Wednesday at noon. Chalmers didn't know his days of the week and depended on that whistle to let him know hit was Wednesday so he could catch a ride back home on account of everbody knocking off work early. I reckon he got confused and wandered for awhile and couldn't find nobody and tried to walk the whole way home." He took a pull off one of the Crown Royal bottles. "They coulda told somebody the whistle was going to be turnt off."

"It said it in the paper the other morning," Purvis said. He finished his beer and crushed the can in his hand.

"Some people work instead of reading the paper," Rembert said.

He returned to the story of how he found Chalmers. I remembered my Uncle Ransom's funeral from when I was seven or eight. The men retold the story all night of how Ransom had suffered a heart attack while plowing and had died trying to stumble back to his house. The Old Man and his other older brother, J. W., who died a year after Ransom, pieced together how Ransom must have lost consciousness. The big Massey-Ferguson tractor had turned sharply mid-row, run over the hog wire fence, and stopped against a pine, waking him up. Then he fell from the tractor, leaving knee prints just in front of the back tire, and scrambled towards and fell over the fence, ripping his shirt on the barbed wire running along top the fence. He managed ten steps in the freshly plowed field, fell again, covering himself in dirt, and stumbled back to the fence, leaving a second set of footprints. There he sat down and leaned against the fence, probably hoping to catch his breath and try for the house again, but his breath never returned.

Ransom had several times gone broke trying to get something—tobacco, corn, millet—to grow in those acres of clods he called a field, a pasture to scrawny cows a couple of years earlier. Ransom had even rented it out once to a midget evangelist for a revival. The diminutive preacher shouted from atop two salt licks, then led the gathering down the hill and into the swamp to the creek for a baptism he said was "guaranteed to take." No one had told him that the creek had been dry for several weeks because of the drought, so the disappointed revivalists left and did not return the next night. He demanded his money back from Ransom, who yanked his belt from his breeches and chased the midget out of his house, lashing him until he found refuge in his LTD. Ransom died readying his field for a crop of soybeans, which years before he called a communist crop and swore he would never plant. His wife, my Aunt Eller, insisted on burying him in that field. Rembert said that maybe Eller thought it would bring Ransom back, believing sooner or later *something* had to come up from that dry dirt.

On TV, half of a four-man tag team called the Gospels was clashing with Azrael and the Serpent, and something came up about snakes, a topic bound to be discussed when a meeting of country men lasts long enough. Rembert told of his uncle Wilbur's baptism in Wadboo Creek and how he jumped up immediately after the preacher had dunked him, screaming, "A moccasin done bit me!"

"That ain't so," the Old Man said. "He was hollering, 'Pilate, a pilate got me.'"

An alternative local name for copperheads was "rattlesnake pilate." For years, I had heard people described as "mean as a pilate" but had heard "pilot" and wondered why flying airplanes had such a negative effect upon one's temperament.

"Same difference," Rembert said. "Anyhow—"

"Hit *do* make a difference," the Old Man insisted. "A pilate don't stay underwater, but a moccasin'll make his nest there. That's how we knowed they wa'n't no pilate a-biting him."

Rembert took a swallow of Crown Royal. "Point is, most everbody got scairt and was running out the water, and the preacher—"

A warbling sound came from Rembert's direction. "Hold on," he said, pulling his cell phone from his belt. "What?" He spoke in "yeah"s and "huh-uh"s for a few seconds, then ended the conversation with "Tell 'em I said, 'Hell no.'" He picked up the pilate story. "What was that damn preacher's name, Pledger?"

"He was a Wright, I believe."

"Preacher Wright stuck his head underwater, then came up saying, 'Hold on! I seen it! Hit weren't nothing but a pretty little cuda!'"

Other Southerners call turtles "cooters," rhyming it with *scooters*, but in the Low Country, the word rhymes with *good-a*. However pronounced, it is inexplicably also an epithet for vagina, nothing about which I would describe as turtle-ish. Whether at the deer-hunting club, in the fishing boat, or in any other setting, local men of the Old Man's generation preferred the term, just a few votes ahead of *poon-tang*, to *pussy*, which I had never heard any of them say; similarly, their euphemism of choice instead of *dick* or *cock* was *pecker*. I once saw Pudge's father, from whose mouth cuss words flowed with a frequency and volume matched only by his son's, slap Pudge nearly unconscious upon hearing the boy say *cunt*. Pudge's reply of "You go to hell, you goddamn sumbitch" was hardly noticed.

As a kid, I had heard Rembert's baptism/false snake story a dozen times, and it never failed to get a clamorous reception, I had always thought, simply because of the confusion of reptiles. But on that night, it finally dawned on me that I had missed the importance of the congregation's hearing the preacher utter a sexual term. I wondered how many other jokes had been hidden from me over the years due to my arrested development.

Baron related an incident of some uncle or great-uncle who had a heart attack in the hog lot and "the hogs eat him before Aunt Kit found what was left of him that evening." This story I knew to be apocryphal—a rural legend, given that a version appeared in an Erskine Caldwell story as well as a Stanley Brothers's bluegrass song. It was agreed that "you can't trust no hog," and further, Rembert added, that anything can turn on you. Purvis shot Rembert a go-to-hell look, but

Rembert was pointing out something about the coals to Grossman.

Thaydo asked me if I was still teaching school. Cecil, who spoke up for me and explained that I taught at a university, asked if I had ever read a book called *Night* about the concentration camps by a "feller named Weasel."

"Sure," I said. "It's a classic. You read it?"

"Last week. I read a lot. Last month I read one called *Nightwood*."

"By Djuna Barnes?"

"That's him," he said. "Da-juner Barn-ess."

"Did you like that one?"

"Not hardly. I couldn't make nair bit of sense of it, except something about lisbans."

"So why did you read it?"

"It's a night book."

"A night book?"

"I like books with 'night' in the title. Like *Night Rider* by a feller named Warner."

"Robert Penn Warren," I said. "Now that's a really good one. Could you make sense of hit?" I heard the *hit* for *it* slip out as if someone else had said it.

"Yeah. It was about, sort of like a Klan for tobacker, but I'm not exactly sure what happent at the end. I believe they got him. But, I tell you, one of my favorites is *Nights Behind the Curtain*. It's a bunch of times better'n them other'ns."

"I don't believe I know that one."

"Oh man, you got to read it, Greazy. This womern loves this man and hides behind the curtain in his bedroom and fools him into thinking she's his real wife sleeping in another room of the castle, but he knows it's her but don't tell her. Then she slips in ever night to make love to him until he can't stand it no more and kills his real wife. But then the womern gets all scairt about the murder, and . . . well, I don't want to ruirn it for you."

Ears cocked up and eyes squinted at Cecil when he said "make love." Some necks stretched around, suspecting that Cecil had noticed a woman approaching and tempered his language. I was more concerned with his indiscriminate reading of good literature alongside cheap romance novels. But at least he was reading, and actually trying to make some kind of connection with me—taking a baby-step into my world instead of dragging me down into his.

Unitas enticed Spessard to describe for the rest of us the pile-up at the race again. Spessard began but suddenly paused and said, "Well, I be dog if *he* ain't got balls like anvils."

We all turned to see a tall, gray-haired man with a wide-brimmed hat climb down from his V-8 dualie.

"He come to see Chalmers," the Old Man said. "Nothing wrong with that."

After a moment, I recognized the long, measured stride of Calhoun Funderburk. Everyone grew silent as he came around to our side of the house, raised his hand, and touching the brim of his hat, said, "Evening, gentlemen." Most mumbled something back.

"Pledger," he said, "I'm sorry about your brother. I'll miss him."

"I appreciate that, Calhoun," the Old Man said.

"Well, I hope y'all have a good service," he said, and turned as if to leave when he caught my eye, stared a moment, tipped his hat again, and then returned to the front and went inside.

Rembert poked at the coals as if Funderburk had not been there. Grossman asked how he calculated the amount of wood needed, and Rembert snatched Grossman's little notebook out of his hand and threw it into the fire. All the men whooped it up, probably wondering what took Rembert so long. In a few seconds, Grossman was laughing along with them.

"Since when you and old Funderburk buddies?" DeWayne asked me.

I did not answer. Purvis got up and said he had to "go take a dookey," gave me a head-jerking sign, and walked around to the far side of the house. No use putting it off until he's drunker.

"I got to wiz," I said, and as I was walking away, I heard Pudge say something about one of his deer dogs that died from worms because he did not "use them."

"What the hell you mean?" Spessard asked. "Didn't *use* 'em?"

"A dog's got to use them worms, or they'll kill the dog sho as shit."

"I believe you the one with worms," Spessard said, "and they in your head."

※

"You can't believe what Rembert's into, Greazy," Purvis said. He was leaning against the outside of the house, smoking, which I had not seen him do so far that evening. He must have told his wife he had quit and was sneaking. No mercury vapor lights shone on this side of the house, and I could see Purvis's face and that ragged right earlobe only when he took a drag from the cigarette. The shirt under his Members Only jacket was open one button too many and revealed a gold chain necklace with a lightning bolt or fang pendant.

"Purvis, it really doesn't mean anything to me. He's always been into something."

"Not like this. You ought to take a look out in that *garage*, as he calls it back yonder. Ain't no tractors in it."

I told him I knew that he and Rembert had been fighting, that he just needed to get something off his chest, and that, for some reason, I looked like a sympathetic ear. But it was not my affair.

"But I can't tell nobody else, Greazy."

"Why not?"

"Because, you're—" he peeked around the edge of the house and then thumped his cigarette away. "You ain't one of us no more, Greazy. I mean, you've been moved off now for, what, fifteen years? You can turn him in and he won't figure it out, and even if he did, you're way off gone, and he can't push you around. Everbody here's scared of him."

I understood his point, but I had nothing to report. The police, SLED, or the FBI would consider anything from me just rumor.

"That's why you got to look in that building. Here." Purvis took my hand and placed into it two keys on a ring. "He's going to Aiken tomorrow afternoon after the funeral to see one of his *associates*. The guy's in the horse business and always takes Rembert out for a big night, then puts him up. He won't be back 'til next day. Those keys will get you into the fence and into the building. And don't worry about them dogs. They's just like they always was."

"Purvis, I don't know. I don't know if I want to know what the hell he's up to."

"Marijuana, for one thing—a couple of special kinds he found on one of his trips that's the most powerful in the world. He seeds it in that garage and then plants it in with the corn. One kind that come from the Amazon or somewhere even grows down in the swamp. Then he crops it and takes it back to the garage to cure it."

"Big goddamn deal, Purvis. He grows pot."

"That ain't all. The thing is, this stuff's so powerful that while it's growing and harvested and hung up in that garage to dry—that takes a couple of weeks—and then chopped up and soaked in some kind of shit before it's ready to smoke, it's poisonous. You ain't supposed to get *near* it 'til it's done been processed. Right now, he's got a crop in yonder ready to be cut up and treated and bagged."

"So what you're worried about is how potent this stuff is? Does it hook people and kill them, like crack?"

"No, huh-uh. *Smoking* it don't kill 'em," Purvis said, and he looked around the corner again. "*Working* it does. He can't use regular people to harvest it and all."

"Who does he use?"

"Zombies," he said, nodding to reassure me that I had heard correctly. His necklace bounced on his chest. The pendant was an alligator/roach clip.

"Purvis, this is insane. What the hell do you mean, *zombies*?"

"Like I said, zombies. You know, they ain't got no souls, but they still walk the Earth. Him and Forty-Four gets 'em from down in Mexico or some damn place. They ship 'em up here when it's time to plant or harvest or whatever. Them what ain't kilt by the poison they send back, where I reckon they die, or die *again*."

He looked as if he was going to say something else, but then he got this scared look on his face, like he'd just been caught doing what he was sure Rembert was up to, and slipped around the side of the house without another word. I turned around, but all I saw was Calhoun Funderburk, whom I remembered seeing up close only three or four times, and all before I was twelve.

I started back towards the fire when I was met by Rembert, Spessard, DeWayne, Markley, Cecil, and Grossman. Armageddon must be on intermission, I thought.

"Come on, Greazy," Grossman said excitedly. "Uncle Rembert's going to show us his exotica."

"He better not," Spessard said. The others were already laughing. "I might have to lop it off."

✺

The old barn held a vestige of the aroma of curing tobacco—a scent I loved as a child, even though it put me on the verge of nausea—mixed with the odors of dust, old leather, and several types of woods, none freshly cut, to produce a mahogany colored disk, which was bumpy like Braille. Among the clutter were animal heads protruding from large plaques (a zebra, a cape buffalo, a wildebeest), other parts put to mundane use (an elephant leg coffee table, a chair with lion leg armrests), whole animals stuffed (a twenty-foot anaconda, a komodo dragon, a baboon, a toucan), furniture (a camel-hide divan from Syria, a rattan bed from Indonesia, rosewood table and chairs from Kashmir), stacks of unopened crates, and what attracted the most attention—a collection of knives and swords. On one table, everything was a foot or more long—sabers, scimitars, cutlasses, rapiers, bayonets, execution axes. The smaller ones—ritualistic animal-sacrifice throat slicers, ornamental circumcision blades, dozens of sheath and folding knives—were in a large wooden box. With each new item, DeWayne asked, "How much you want for it?" until Spessard saw that Rembert was about to lose patience and gave DeWayne a one-raised-eyebrow stare that apparently still held power over him.

"I got some old books you might want to look at, Slick," Rembert said as the others ogled a Russian saber. "Picked 'em up in Europe."

He opened a trunk and pulled out a dusty stack of books. Some had cracked leather covers. Others were detached or missing altogether. Some were in English, some French, and a number in Spanish. I did not recognize any of the titles, and the only author's name I knew was a Spanish writer named Ibáñez, who wrote around the turn of the twentieth century. Even if these were first editions, I doubted they would be worth much, since nearly all were by obscure writers and in fairly bad condition.

"Look at this 'un," Rembert said, showing me a blue and gold Crown Royal bag. He loosened the drawstrings to pull out a small book with a deep red, soft leather cover with a few bare spots on the corners and spine. "Got it in Spain, but it ain't writ in Spanish. The feller I got it from said it was a thousand years old, but he wa'n't there then, so I don't reckon he knowed for sure."

The book was written in Hebrew or Arabic in a simple, unadorned style—it even looked like handwriting—on heavy paper, probably parchment. "Saul," I said. He was admiring the etching on a scimitar blade. "Take a look at this." He came over and I handed him the book.

"It's Arabic," he said and buried his nose in it.

"Now this is something real special," Rembert said. "I won this in a bar bet in Alabama." He handed me another Crown Royal bag from a trunk across the room. Inside the bag was an old Coca Cola bottle, itself probably collectable, with a sheet of paper rolled up inside. On one side of the paper was a menu, and on the other was handwriting.

"That there's an original Hank Williams song, never recorded," Rembert said, sniffing in a big breath. "The feller I took it from said Hank and his band stopped in his little café in 1950 on their way to a concert. It was late and they was the only ones in there. They sot there real quiet and had sandwiches and coffee and a couple of Co-Colers.

Hank was drinking something from a paper bag he had stuffed in his pocket."

"Greazy," said Grossman, pulling on my jacket sleeve. "Look at this."

"Just a minute," I said and turned back to Rembert.

"He said Hank was singing to hisself the whole time and writing on the back of the menu. Then some sort of fuss started between Hank and one of the band, and Hank hollered over to the feller what run the place, 'Hey Mister, tell me if you think this song's any good,' and he *sung* the song to him right there. The feller said he liked it. What the hell else would he say, it Hank Williams and all? Hank said, 'Well then, you can have it,' and stuck the menu in this Co-Coler bottle and left."

"Greazy," Grossman said again, "this is fascinating."

"Just *one* minute." I held the bottle up to see the paper better. At the top was a title, "I'll Never Know," and slanting across the bottom was "Hiram Williams." I could decipher a portion of the visible lyrics that I took to be the chorus:

I thought I understood your heart
Until I watched you go
Did you ever, ever love me, dear
I guess I'll never know

If only Lucian were here to see this, I thought. Not only did he adore old Hank, he could whip up a melody in an instant to fit these lyrics. I had a stack of recordings of Lucian fiddling, much of it old bluegrass, country, some rock, and even a few soul tunes (he especially liked Al Green and Jackie Wilson). He wrote songs as well and would introduce them on tape with something like, "I call this one 'Don't Got Words Cause I Can't Sing No Way,'" and he might play it three or four times in a row with slight variations or in different keys.

"So how'd you end up with it?" I asked Rembert.

"Son, if they's something you want in this world, you can get it one way or another, mostly another. Oh, I nearly 'bout forgot this 'un." Rembert pulled something else from the first Crown Royal bag. "It come from India."

Smaller than the first book, it was wrapped in blue and yellow wool instead of an ordinary cover. I opened it to find unbound pages of a material similar to papyrus folded together with writing in a language I did not recognize—perhaps Sanskrit.

Grossman stuck his book up to my face. "Greazy, this is astonishing. Look."

"You know I can't read Arabic."

"It says it's by Ibn Rushd."

"No shit? You think it's old?"

"Very. This style of binding—the sewing—went out of fashion centuries ago. And the script is very odd."

"How do you know this stuff?"

"My grandfather collected antiquarian books."

"The rebbe again?"

"Yes. And this is interesting: the first page says it's Ibn Rushd's commentary on Aristotle's work on comedy."

"Bull*shit*!" I snatched the book from Grossman's hands and stared at the first page as if the marks would suddenly become decipherable to me. Aristotle's analysis of comedy, supposedly a companion to or another portion of his *Poetics*, which is on tragedy, was mentioned by ancient sources and has been the stuff of legend since antiquity. Jackie Armstrong had said that Ibn Rushd was acquainted with some of Aristotle's writings unavailable to the modern reader, so if this book was what Grossman said it was and it wasn't some sort of hoax, then Rembert had tucked away in his barn the most significant find in philosophy since the Crusaders dumped an ass-load of Aristotle, again thanks to preservation and commentary by Arab philosophers, into Europe in the twelfth century. "Saul, do you realize what this could mean?"

"We'd better get back to that hog, boys," Rembert said.

"Right!" Grossman said as he spun towards the door. Somehow, the barbeque took precedence over the ancient book he'd been entranced by just a moment before. Sometimes, I really couldn't understand that guy.

The others began replacing the swords into a neat line. I needed to take the book to the conference the next day to get Armstrong's opinion on it, and maybe the guy who read the paper on Buddhism and skepticism could tell me something about the other book.

"Uncle Rembert," I said. He was putting the possible Hank Williams song back into the trunk on the far end of the room. "I'd like to show these books to a couple of fellers who could tell us—you—something about them. Mind if I take them to my conference tomorrow?"

He stroked his chin a couple of times. Rembert had always been generous, but at the same time he was quite protective of his property. "I tell you what," he said, removing a leaf from the Indian book and handing it to me. "Take this," he said, and then took the Arabic book from me. "And this." He *ripped* a page from it! I almost shat as he handed me the leaf with the frazzled edge.

"You let me know when you want to get rid of that Russian saber," DeWayne said.

"Give it up, for Godsake," Markley said.

We left the barn, and Rembert clanked the padlock through the latch that connected the creaky double doors. It was just for appearance's sake. The latch was barely held in place by loose, rusty screws. In the fence around the big garage some thirty yards away, the dogs lay quietly and unalarmed, smelling Rembert's presence. Beyond the garage, I could see the Hume Shipping truck. A *kalunk* noise seemed to come from inside the garage.

"Somebody back there, Rembert?" Spessard asked.

"Naw," Rembert said. "Just them damn sooners."

※

I placed the two pages on the backseat of Saul's Volvo and then joined the others at the fire. Everyone, even Lula Mae and Bernice, was outside. More had just arrived, all of whom must have been related to me in some way—it was too late for non-relatives to be coming. I thought I should head back home, too, since my paper was scheduled for nine in the morning. After that, I would try to find Armstrong and

Parathpanamnda, then get back to the funeral at three. Someone was playing a fiddle, and partially obstructed by the flames, I made out an older cousin everyone called Uncle Lum, whose given name was Christopher Columbus Hume and who, especially in his little snap-brim hat, looked just like Strother Martin in *Cool Hand Luke*. Near him were his children—my third cousins, Stetson, Levi, and Grace—with their children and spouses, and other cousins, some whose names I remembered, more I did not. Lum was playing a lilting old tune called "Maiden's Prayer."

Someone took my shoulder, and I turned to see Spessard holding out DeWayne's guitar to me. The strings were old but still had some life in them, and it even had a capo, the elastic kind, strapped around the neck, to facilitate key changes. I walked over to Lum amid approving comments of "Now we getting it going" and "Sing one, Greaze" and shook his hand and nodded to the others. He drew out a couple of notes I used to tune the guitar. I capoed up to play in the fiddler-friendly key of A, and he lit into something he called "Mustache Millie," which was a bit like "Ragtime Annie" and easy for me to follow. Rembert turned down the TV, and when DeWayne grumbled and turned the volume back up even higher, unplugged the set. Lum did a couple mid-tempo tunes I had never heard with names like "Hind Tit" and "Hard Row to Hoe." He handed a fiddle to the Old Man, who was sitting beside him, picked up a second one, told me it was in E, and played a slow, lurching number I don't think even had a name.

"Sing us one, Greazy," a couple of people said, more because they were getting bummed out by the slow fiddle tunes, I thought, than really wanting to hear me.

"Do that 'Copenhagen' snuff song," Purvis said.

"Don't do that, Legare," said Arlene. "That thing makes me noxious."

Lum and I agreed on A again. He swapped fiddles with the Old Man, and we did several old bluegrass songs, up-tempo despite their gloomy topics of dead children and live children longing for heavenly reunion with dead mothers. I had not played much in weeks, and my voice hadn't warmed up, but feet tapped and hands clapped along just the same. I sang, and Lum played breaks. He was quite good, had a perfect sense of timing, and anticipated chord changes flawlessly. I sang "Wandering Boy," a mother's lament for her prodigal son that was a fast song nevertheless. Having finally screwed up the nerve to play a solo, I finished and saw Mama dabbing her eyes with her tissue.

DeWayne could not stand it any longer, and he was suddenly on his feet doing "When You're Hot, You're Hot." It was more talked than sung, so it did not really matter what key I tried to follow along in. He did only the Jerry Reed parts, so he would go silent for a measure or two when he got to the chorus, imagining the background singers coming in. Several people, trying not to look too rude, took this as an opportunity to go get pie. Rembert dug up another bottle of Crown Royal.

"Sing us something *pretty*, Greazy," said Arlene, by which I knew she meant something slow and sad.

I did one by folksinger Si Kahn called "Aragon Mill," about textile mills closing, and the narrator has nowhere to go and nothing to do but be haunted by the wind that sounds like looms used to. Lum's mournful fiddle break caught the mood of the song exactly. By the time I did the chorus for the third time, a dozen or more folks were singing along. No one applauded afterwards, as if following a hymn.

"How 'bout old Roy Acuff?" said Baron. So Lum and I did "Wabash Cannonball" to lift the spirits some. "Do another'n!" Baron hollered, and before I knew what I was doing, I was singing Acuff's sappy and moralizing "Wreck on the Highway" about a fatal car crash. I was surprised to hear so many approving comments when I was done. They considered it perfectly appropriate.

Someone wanted Hank Williams, so we did "Lonesome Whistle Blues." Mama had made it through "Wabash Cannonball" with no problem, but this was one train song too many, and she was sobbing away by the second time she heard the lo-wah-a-wahn-some whistle refrain. I thought of Chalmers's noon-time confusion Wednesday and was tempted to sing about *no* whistle being heard but decided it might not be appreciated. Several wanted to hear something by Ol' Possum, and I remembered George Jones's "Walk Through This World with Me," which Lum said was one of his favorites. I was not sure whether there were more than two verses, but Lum kept giving me the keep-going sign, so, I sang the two verses I knew three times each.

When I was nearly done, I noticed that attention was focused behind me. I looked around and discovered why Lum wanted to stretch it out: near the house, directly under the soft blue glow of a mercury vapor light, Grossman and Willie were slow dancing. They were barely moving their feet, Grossman's hands on Willie's shoulders, hers clasped together at the small of his back, her head in the groove of his neck. When we finished the song, everyone clapped for the dancers. Willie smiled and did an exaggerated curtsy, but Grossman looked mortified. Willie took his hand and led him into the back door of the house.

Behind me, a fiddle began playing tentatively, searching for the melody. I turned to see the Old Man leaning back in his chair, his legs crossed, the bow clasped in an uneasy grip. He wandered through a few notes until the tune emerged—"Bonaparte's Retreat," one of Lucian's favorites. Lucian had used it as a showcase piece, playing it incredibly fast, and unleashing all his virtuosity. But the Old Man was playing it in a different key with an old-timey, modal sound, dark and somber. Others sitting around recognized it as something from way back in the old days, and the mood changed to nearly reverential. I sat down by the Old Man, he said "D," and I followed. As far as I knew, he had not played for twenty years and was out of practice, but there was a feeling, a texture to his playing that bore no relation to technical proficiency. He looked directly at me during the song, played the B part an extra time at the end, and finally ended with a simple, fading tag.

It was more than he had said to me in years.

"I better quit before I tear up my fingers," he said.

"Do something sacred," I heard Lula Mae or Bernice say. "Yeah," said several others.

Miriam walked over and sat beside me. "Y'all know 'Were You There?'" The Monroe Brothers, Bill and Charlie, had made it famous back in the thirties. I said I did.

"That's a good 'un," Lum said.

"You do a verse, and I'll do a verse," Miriam said to me.

Lum kicked it off, and I did the first verse—"Were you there when they crucified my Lord?"—which is similar to the others, each repeating its line, then segueing into the chorus, in which the instruments stop playing and whoever has the highest part sings "Awww, sometimes, it causes me to tremble," with the other voices each adding a "tremble." The finish had all the instruments coming back in as the verse line is repeated. I tried a risky, Bill Monroe-style counter-tenor for the chorus, and surprised myself when it came out on exactly the right note. Miriam joined in with the second "tremble," Lum added a bass "tremble," and *damn*, we sounded like pros.

When Miriam did the second verse—"Were you there when they nailed him to the cross?"—her voice took on a life of its own. It was soulful and husky, like Mavis Staple's, with "Mm, hm"s and "Good Lord"s. She grabbed that old gospel tune that used to give me the heebie-jeebies as a boy and wrang new sense from it—a saucy, hip-grinding cake walk, a nighttime revival by the river, the "let's all get dunked and then sneak off into the bushes as the spirit moves us in more imminent ways" version. We did the chorus the same way as before, and then I nodded to her to do the next verse—"Were you there when they laid him in the tomb?" (I imagined Rembert answering each query with, "No, and you weren't neither.") The song ended, and she returned to her demure self, acting a little embarrassed she had gotten caught up in the moment and lost control.

At midnight, Lum said he had enjoyed the music-making but had to get going and made to pack away the fiddles. Several begged for one more, and he finally agreed.

"Do one we all can sing," Mama said.

Someone had asked earlier for something by the Carter Family, and that gave me an idea. I whispered to Lum. He nodded and played a short kick-off, then I sang "Will the Circle Be Unbroken?" When I reached the chorus, a number of people joined in. I sang each verse alone, and with each chorus we picked up more voices in a sound reminiscent of shape-note singing. It came time for Lum to play a last fiddle break before we ended with a final chorus, but he took a step backward and nodded, and another fiddle began playing. For an instant, I thought it was the Old Man again, but even before I turned my head to look, I could tell it was somebody else. Standing very still, his heels together and staring far off into the night, Saul Grossman was playing achingly, beautifully, in an unmistakable Eastern-European way. A. P., Sara, and Maybelle Carter could never have foreseen this, I thought. His duct-taped glasses sagged at the temples to give him a sad-eyed, Basset hound look. He soloed through three verses and choruses, in the Grossman trance, meandering off from the melody and threatening to modulate before sliding back into the groove and right on the beat. He suddenly nodded to me, signifying he was done, and I led the chorus one last time.

The whole family, many holding hands, had shifted, almost as a single body, the few yards from the fire to stand under the canopy of the chinaberry tree and around the roasting pig. The embers flickered orange patches on their faces as specks of ash and sparks from the fire rose over their heads. Something was being acted out, something expressible only in this form, not further analyzable, not translatable *salva veritate*. The voices lifted, raw yet thoroughly blended in their very primitiveness.

> *Will the circle be unbroken*
> *By and by, Lord, by and by?*
> *There's a better home a-waiting*
> *In the sky, Lord, in the sky.*

"Chalmers woulda loved to been here for that," Miriam said.

"Naw," Rembert said. "He always went to bed early."

NINE
The Allegory of the Cave

The things around us that we ordinarily take as real—mountains, horses, head lice, our very flesh and bone—are illusions, Plato thought. The ideas, *eidos*, or forms of those items—mountainhood, horseness—are real, but what we call objects are insubstantial copies, shadows, or reflections of the inhabitants of his ideal world. The lover of wisdom mistrusts the senses' wildly misleading reports and accepts only what reason establishes.

Plato likened the human predicament to cave dwellers shackled and facing the back of a cave so that the only sights they behold are shadows cast upon the wall from people and objects passing before the cave's entrance. Having never seen the cave opening or the stuff outside, Plato's troglodytes would naturally believe the shadows to be reality.

Suppose, by some great effort, one prisoner escapes his bonds and wanders out to see the puppet show. Plato says the mole man would at first be stunned by the blinding light, but when his eyes adjust and he gets over his bewilderment, he will figure out that his entire life has been one big hoodwinking. Like a fool, he had believed the shadows to exist in their own right, but now he knows they are ontologically derivative and only ersatz simulacra to the originals that he, through breaking his Earthly chains, experiences directly.

When ex-cave man returns to the dim world of his benighted friends to enlighten them, the complacent prisoners will hear nothing of the good news about the world outside but will instead tell the escape artist to shut the hell up, find a seat, and watch the show, or else we'll kill you. Such is the fate of the philosopher, warned Plato: nobody wants to hear the truth, and if you try to push it on them, you might get Socratesed.

I do not know what truths I have discovered that the world does not want to hear. I am not sure that any contemporary philosopher would be audacious enough to say that he or she or anybody else in the entire history of philosophy has wrestled any philosophical problem through all its protean evasive maneuvers until it came to rest in its true form. (This despite the mystics out there who will tell you they have found the truth, perhaps through an out-of-body journey, but they cannot convey it until you, too, have been initiated and introduced to the mysteries, which they can guide you through for $500 per weekly session, plus book purchases and maybe a blowjob.) *The single exception?* This one lustrous gem, uncovered from the bones and detritus in a long-abandoned cave at an APA conference in Charleston, South Carolina, where Saul Grossman settled philosophy's most son-of-a-bitching problem by showing it was unsolvable and thus not really a problem at all. He led us out of the cave, and this meant, in part, that those attending my paper that morning would still be struggling to contract their pupils from what had happened in the past two days.

My session would be like sleepwalking.

༄

Grossman was completely at ease having coffee in the hall, joking with admirers and signing programs, a changed man from the one I'd smuggled away from the same sycophants two days earlier. Several kept dragging him away to a table for a serious talk. One of them was Marty Girdlemuller, my old undergraduate professor from the College of Charleston. I was about to say hello to Marty when Parathpanamnda walked by. I snagged him and tried to show him the page Rembert had said was from India.

"A bloody great match last night, yes?" he asked.

"I wasn't there."

"Oh, a misfortune, my friend! Such a great show, and an entire section set aside for philosophers. Five hundred of us! And those chaps in the ... what do you call it? Ring, yes, despite being square. They were pummeling and kicking and tossing one another. Bleeding and losing consciousness as well. Makes all this talk-talk-talk we do here seem very boring indeed, yes?"

I liked his British-trained, Indian (or thereabouts) accent, but it was nearly time for my session. I handed him the sheet from the book, and he skimmed it while continuing to tell me about Armageddon.

"Afterwards, we were invited to go backstage and meet the wrestling gentlemen, but it was much too crowded to squeeze-squeeze-squeeze us all in, so I returned. My colleague stayed and did not return to the hotel until," his voice became fainter, "four A . . . M . . . this . . . morn—Where the bloody hell did you get this?"

His voice scaled up an octave. "It's Pali, and a form used by Buddhist monks in the first century." He squinted, removed his glasses, and put his face two inches from the leaf, which was about twelve by six inches, folded in the middle, with writing in a tiny script on only one side.

"This is bark—birch, I think—the inner layer dried and pressed." He pecked at a spot on the sheet with a long-nailed index finger. "Amazing. See this word?" They were just curly lines to me. "It's *Issa*."

He stared at me, waiting, I supposed, for me to feel the full force of the pronouncement.

"What's that?" I asked.

"Christ! Issa, that's *Jesus*! My friend, this is about Jesus Christ."

He told me of a legend that dates back to at least the third century about Jesus in India. One version says he was there as a young man studying Buddhism. Another version, preferred by the Muslims of Kashmir, has him appear after the crucifixion—which he escaped through divine intervention—to live out the rest of his years. If the writing was indeed from the first century, as it appeared to be, it would be the most amazing find in religious studies since the Dead Sea Scrolls.

"Our idea of Jesus, the man and the message," he said, "and of Buddhism, for God's bloody sake, would be totally buggered-buggered-buggered."

Sitting in the audience now, at my reading, Parathpanamnda stared at the little sheet almost continuously, pausing occasionally to glance at me with a gigantic grin and flash me the thumbs-up sign. He returned to the sheet just as the door opened, and Jackie Armstrong, fashionably late, entered wearing large sunglasses. Could she, too, have been slumming with the wrestlers? I was happy she was there in any condition so I could show her the possible Ibn Rushd page as soon as my session was over.

I was four pages into reading my paper when, for the first time, I saw the man in the black overcoat change seats. He was about forty, red hair, maybe six feet tall, and even more noticeable because of his limp—more an exaggerated hesitation in his left leg, as if it were an ill-fitting prosthetic. As he moved from one side of the room to the other and two rows closer to the front, I took note of who was in the audience. Attendees were spaced across a checkered carpet that looked like an oversized game board, which somehow aggravated my headache. Only those few who were less hungover than I, I suspected, had shown up for the conference's morning sessions. Among those at my session, aside from Parathpanamnda and Jackie Armstrong, were Grossman (a glob of epoxy from the Old Man's shed holding his broken glass frames together at the nose bridge), Meierson, Gary Winters, an old man in a wheelchair, and six or eight who had followed Grossman in like groupies and were sitting around him. For a moment, I half hoped T. A. Gallagher was among them, but I really did not need another reminder of my nutlessness. I could smell something like WD-40, white, marbled with charcoal, and shifting from hexagonal to rhomboid.

The man chairing the session left and returned with two cups of coffee. He stopped to offer one to the old man in the wheelchair. When the old man raised his head to smile and politely wave him off, I recognized the face from book covers: Chauncey Hartley. The recognition threw me off track, causing me to lose my place for a second. I took off my jacket to stall while I got back into gear. I started reading again and looked up to see the limping guy sitting beside Hartley. The guy's eyes were narrow, and his chin jutted out like it was pointing at me. Meierson, Winters, and Armstrong all smiled at me. Gilbert was missing. Perhaps he had overdone it the previous day.

I was nearing my conclusion and still trying to decide whether to read my original ending about not finding Hartley's version of the argument valid or replace it with comments about having lately changed my mind. Driving to Charleston earlier that morning, I had believed I would go with the first ending, but during the course of reading the paper and hearing my own voice recount Hartley's argument, the objection by the guy from Duke, and my rebuttal to the objection, I realized that all of us—believers, non-believers, and theological fence-straddlers—had committed a fundamental blunder. Paul Tillich said it is perfectly sensible for a believer to say that God does not exist, for only beings exist, and God is not *a* being but Being itself. I doubt that Tillich himself knew exactly what he meant by that, but at least his way of thinking frees us from the burden of proving and disproving God's existence. My notion was that—and I am sure somebody else must have said this—God is a metaphor. Now, I am not quite sure what God is a metaphor for. But the idea of God is the only way for some people to make sense of *some*thing. If you do not need—are not genetically inclined—to make sense of that *je ne sais quoi*, then you have no use for the metaphor. I needed to think about it some more, but I was considering throwing it on the table at the end of my paper. What the hell!

With only two pages to go, I was wrapping up my argument when the restless man with the limp stood up, peeled off his coat, and pulled a rifle from his left pants leg. He pressed the muzzle of the gun against Hartley's temple.

"No!" the gunman shouted. "It can't be!"

Audience members hit the floor. Some screamed. Some crawled toward the door. The rifleman turned toward me. He was wearing his name tag, and I could see "DUKE" in large letters and, after a bit of squinting, "Bishop" in smaller letters above it—the guy whose paper I was criticizing in mine.

"Deny it! Say your argument fails or I'll blow your damn head off!"

The centenarian Hartley, looking regal with a blanket draped over his shoulders like a cape, said in a thin voice, "Go ahead," and hee-heed at calling Bishop's bluff.

"You, too, you apologist son of a bitch!" Bishop now aimed the gun at me. I thought *I* was obsessed with the ontological argument. This might be the day, I thought, that Camus was really proved wrong.

The chair of the session, a guy named Knight from Notre Dame, peeked over the top of the table he had ducked under. "Now see here," he said, "as chair of these proceedings, I insist you put away that weapon and allow Professor Hume to continue with his paper."

"Shut the fuck up!" Bishop said.

Knight did.

"This is shameful," Armstrong said from where she lay on the floor. "You must expect disagreement in this profession. You should never have entered academia if you cannot weather the criticism that comes with the free exchange of ideas."

"So true," Parathpanamnda said. He lay prostrate, his face on the floor muffling his voice. "Not a career for the thin-thin-thin-skinned."

"That's not it, goddamnit," said Bishop.

"Look what you're doing to your career," Gary Winters said. "A job at a prestigious university, for Christ's sake. Are you tenured by any chance?"

"*Every*body shut the fuck up!" Bishop demanded. Everybody did. "I can take it with the best of them, but this is different. Hartley's argument for God is the best one ever constructed, and my criticism is the only one that might work. If this Hume son of a bitch is right, then my criticism fails, and that means we're all doomed. Don't any of you bastards *see* that?"

"I don't think that follows at all," Armstrong said. She rose to her knees and crawled a couple of steps forward. "Hume's paper only attacks your criticism of Hartley. It doesn't conclude that the argument is sound. Right, young Hume?"

"That's right," I said. "If you'll just let me finish—"

"Liar!" Bishop yelled.

"Even if the argument works, and I do not think it does," Parathpanamnda said, sitting up to peek around a chair, "why would it mean we are all doomed-doomed-doomed?"

"Sophists! Anselmites!" Bishop said. "Don't try to make a sucker of me. You think this is a game?" He pointed the rifle at Hartley's head again. "Recant!"

"Can't you put that phallus extension away?" Meierson said, trying to hide a smirk.

Parathpanamnda crawled forward across two of the carpet squares to flank Bishop. "Come-come-come now, mate. We philosophers already have such a bad-bad-bad reputation for being too serious. Where's your sense of humor?"

Bishop scowled and pumped the lever several times. *Several times?*

I took a gambit and stepped down from the dais.

"Stop right there!" he yelled.

I did not. He shot, and a BB sank into my shoulder. It stung like a snakebite, but I continued to move toward him. He jacked the lever again. Suddenly, Grossman was standing on a chair, and before I could yell, "No!" Grossman screamed "IIIEEEEEEE!" and sailed onto Bishop's back like Cousin Lymon onto Miss Amelia. Bishop doubled over quickly, and Grossman went flipping to the floor. For an instant, I expected Bishop to fall onto him and go for the pin. Instead, he shot from a kneeling position, and the BB popped me right on my forehead wound.

That one hurt far more than the first. Little patches of blue, in shades I had never before imagined, danced before me. My left eye slammed shut by reflex and would not open. I was motionless for a second or two, not from being stunned by the pain, but from trying to calculate the odds of the BB's striking right there. I could do it, I thought, if I knew the area of the front of my body, which was facing Bishop, and determined that, say, four BBs could fit into a square centimeter. So, it would be about one in however many square centimeters the front of me is—times four.

I took three more steps. He was pumping the lever. I grabbed the barrel and yanked the air rifle out of his hands. He threw his hands up and "Waaahhh"ed like a child who had lost toy privileges.

I whipped the air rifle back like a baseball bat and was about to try to crack his skull when another, much larger body sailed through the air. This one belonged to Peter Boykin/Gyges, philosopher/wrestler on-the-spot. His elbow caught Bishop on the jaw. I heard the bone crack. Bishop spun around and dropped like a straw man.

Two security guards ran in. I still held the BB gun. They threw *me* to the floor. Voices yelled that they had tackled the wrong guy. They figured it out and handcuffed Bishop, who was still out cold. I sat up. Blood was on my shirt. Grossman, Winters, and several others hovered over me, asking if I was all right. I could hear Hartley having the last laugh.

༄

"Are you awake?"

I was disoriented but calm for the few moments it took me to recognize Grossman's face. Opening my right eye was an effort, and the left remained shut. Also recognizing Grossman's voice, I heard him explaining that I was in the emergency room. I thought I smelled celery and witch-hazel, running and twisted back on itself like a muscadine or scuppernong vine, whichever one has the green grapes. I reached up to feel the bandages on my forehead and shoulder. A nurse looked into my good eye and checked my pulse and blood pressure. She said the doctor would see me in a minute.

"Greazy, you're a hero," Grossman said. "They arrested the guy who shot you. He was the philosopher you attacked in your paper. Did you know that?"

I nodded.

"The television news people want to interview you, like they interviewed me." He grinned, glanced away, and then back. The old Grossman would have been horrified by the possibility of being on TV. "Oh, an officer left his card. Said you should call him as soon as you're up to it."

The card was from a SLED agent. Scribbled on the back was:

"Great job! Been working with FBI on this guy. He's suspected in other crimes. Please call."

"I'm getting the hell out of here," I said. The wall clock across the room said twelve. "Where's my jacket?" Perhaps I could get back to the conference and show the page of Arabic, if it remained in my jacket, to Armstrong and still have time to make it to the funeral at three.

"On the chair over there. By the way, I showed Jackie Armstrong the Ibn Rushd piece. I found it in your jacket when we had to go through your pockets to get your insurance information."

"Well?"

"We found it in your wallet."

"No, goddammit! What did Armstrong say?"

"She thinks it's authentic, written by Ibn Rushd himself. She's very excited. She said, 'This is extraordinary, most extraordinary. I can't . . . can't believe what I am . . . The style is exactly what . . .'" He was quoting her verbatim. ". . . Only Ibn Rushd himself could have—"

"OK, I get it. What did she say we should do about it?"

"She left a few minutes ago, but would like us to bring her the entire manuscript. She'll be visiting her sister at 1126 High Winds Road on the Isle of Palms, area code 843-5—"

"All right. Did you get the page back from her?"

"Yes, in your jacket, along with the one from the Indian guy. He would like to see the rest of that manuscript as well."

"You didn't call my folks, did you?"

"No." He lifted his head high. Then he bent near me and cupped his hand by his mouth. "The hospital staff doesn't know you're staying with your family. They know only that you're from Florida. I thought you would like that." He was grinning like a mule eating briars. He had, without coercion from me, knowingly deceived. This was a major moment.

"Saul Grossman, I'll dance at your wedding."

"I hope it's soon," he said and blushed.

The doctor came in, looked me over, showed me the BBs she had removed from just under my skin, and said that, because I had not bled enough to cause me to lose consciousness for that long, I should stay for further observation. I said the hell with that and threw my jacket over my bare back—I reckoned that my bloodied shirt had been ditched—and checked out. Grossman pointed out the TV reporter in the waiting area, and we dodged him.

On the way home, Grossman talked nonstop about the "hostage situation," a phrase he probably picked up from the TV people. My memories of the event's images were uncommonly sharp, but two qualities of my experience struck me as more significant. First, I remembered experiencing the incident as if it were naturally playing itself out, like watching a movie whose conclusion is *fait accompli*, yet I was at the same time fully engaged in directing the actions from *within*. It was a peculiar and elusive aspect of my memory of the experience that I tried hard to reconstruct but could not fully reproduce. I know that, in highly excited states, we can experience events in odd ways, but I was never excited, nor was I ever (this is the second quality) afraid. Even before I saw that Bishop was wielding only a BB gun (what kind of pansy-ass was he?), I felt I could not be harmed. I do not mean I believed I could suffer no injury. The BBs hurt, and obviously a thirty-ought-six would have blown me away.

Somehow an experience that should have scared me shitless produced not so much a belief or knowledge claim but more a *feeling* of euphoria, a confidence that nothing could really hurt me, that I knew exactly what to do, and that I would accomplish it without fail. I still felt some of that power. Now, why would that cause me to pass out, other than the sheer novelty, given my usual pissantness?

۶

The smell of the flowers was nearly unbearable: thin and flaky like butterfly wings, orange, and with innumerable variations on sick-sweetness that made me nauseated. Attending the graveside services were most of the people who had come to Rembert's house the night before—many of them in hangover-hiding sunglasses today—and some who had not. Lula Mae and Bernice were front row center of the ribboned-off family section. Flanking them were Miriam and Rembert (who had held things up a moment to answer his cell phone) on one side, the Old Man and Mama on the other. Nieces and nephews sat behind them, and everybody else stood around the grave. All were filling up on the bullshit-banquet the preacher was dishing out about God calling his child, another purpose in heaven, this world is not our home, boom-shacka-lacka. Every once in a while, someone would add a "Praise the Lord" or "Amen." Afterward, they would all comment, "I mean to tell you, *son*, hit were *beau*tiful."

My left eye had opened but was watery, and I was wearing the Old Man's shirt and shiny polyester tie. Ordinary bandages were enough to cover the BB holes. I claimed to have tripped and fallen from the dais after my talk, hit my head on a chair, and poked my shoulder with an ink pen and had to throw the shirt away. But Grossman could not stand it and insisted on describing the hostage situation in detail, acting out the parts of all the players and even jumping onto and falling off the couch to recreate his attack on Bishop. He leaped onto the couch again as Gyges, saying *karack* as a sound effect for the elbow-to-jaw collision. Mama cringed through it all and started crying when he reached the part in which I took the first BB. Unitas gasped, laughed, and hopped, begging Grossman to tell the story again when he was done. Willie watched Grossman like a proud mother seeing her child recite lines in the second grade end-of-the-year play in an echoing cafetorium. When Grossman told them the incident would be on the news, all eyes lit up. They were proud of me—as much as they could be of a man who had overpowered a BB-gun-wielding assailant. But appearing on the national news meant I was shit on a stick.

Miriam replaced the preacher and a cappella-ed "Precious Memories," but I was too concerned about those manuscripts to listen. When I gave the pages back to Rembert just before the service and told him about Armstrong's and Parapanamnda's evaluations and how they needed to examine the entire works, he made quite a show, as I expected, of how important they were to him and how he could not trust just anybody with them but that he would, in classic Rembert style, think about it.

In 1947, a goatherd boy found the Dead Sea Scrolls when he chucked a rock into a cave to scare out a dogie. An illiterate Egyptian scraping up guano found the Nag Hammadi codices in 1945, only to have his mother burn who-knows-how-much-of-them for kindling. I could play a part in this stuff-of-legend scholarship. But questions of propriety arise: What is owed the scholarly community? Who should have access? Who gets to translate? Who gets the right to publish the first article—the most eminent Aristotle scholar or the most distinguished Ibn Rushd scholar? Will the Greeks, Arabs, or Spanish claim some rights by heritage? Will the Buddhists claim first crack at the Pali writing? Will Christians want to suppress it? These sorts of fights had delayed translation of the Dead Sea Scrolls for decades. A pile of money could be made by selling them—a Sotheby's auction, anyone?—to a museum, if they turned out to be authentic. And what about the Hank Williams song? Would Hank, Jr., or his half-sister, Jett, claim it? The affair could turn into a monkey's paw.

If Rembert would part with only one, which one would *I* choose? Which would mean more to the world, and which meant more to me: a lost book by the world's greatest philosopher, a work that would change our picture of the founder of the world's largest religion, or an unknown tune from the greatest songwriter in country—hell, the greatest American songwriter in history?

What about my tenure? I had read a paper at the APA conference, and AmWorld would honor the hero who disarmed the gunman shit. They would give me a nice raise, a bigger office, or name a ride after me. Then again, I did not have to accept tenure. I did not have to go back to Tally, assuming she'd have me back. Whatever I did, it would not be because I had to.

Miriam finished the song, and the preacher asked if anyone would like to say a few words. The entire front row turned around and looked at me. They ignored my "Huh-uh"s.

"Go on, Legare," Mama said. "You know your father and Rembert can't get up there."

My aunts, because they were women, were automatically exempt, of course. Willie elbowed me. The Old Man looked at me as he never had: not the typical commanding stare, but a sincere request; not a duty, but a favor. I had to go. No—I wanted to.

The preacher stepped aside, and I stood at the head of the grave. The mound of fresh dirt smelled sweet and warm and safe and a little like bream fried in cornmeal, spherical with ripples around the surface.

"All of us here are connected by blood or friendship, as we each were to Chalmers. We mean things to each other, as we did to Chalmers, and as Chalmers did to us. The world we live in *is* that network of interlaced, interdependent, overlapping meanings, an organic, organismic whole mirroring the self-transcending aspects—us—of itself. In certain special moments, perhaps a time of emergency, or in a peculiar sound or smell, we glimpse the world in all its self-transcendence. The course of Chalmers's life runs like a meandering creek through us all, adds to the flow of our lives as we pass through stronger currents together, lap upon banks alone, and return to the deep channels that no droplets can avoid."

I was carried away by my watery metaphor, and actually a little proud of it, but also thinking that I needed to be more concrete, when I looked beyond the group to see two men standing by a pickup truck. Both were wearing khaki pants and denim jackets. One was rather tall with an extended gut and a wide-brimmed hat like those state troopers wear. They were the Hume Shipping truck drivers. I looked at Rembert and may have caught him shooting a glance at the men. The taller guy, carrying a small bag, box, or envelope to Rembert's truck, leaned into the passenger's side window, came out, and returned to the other man. They talked for a moment, leaned against the front of the truck facing the funeral, perhaps looking for a sign from Rembert, then got into the truck and drove away.

"What part of Chalmers will flow most strongly through me?" I continued. "Chalmers accepted things just as they appeared to him. His world was what it was, nothing more." I expected Grossman to consider that a tautology and thus trivial.

"His was a world of meaning, of highest purposes created by him, by us, with us, through us. This world was his home, as it is indeed ours. He occupied it, as do we, because our blood occupies our veins. We are what Chalmers was—subjective fields of meaning whose every temporal movement toward the future is an interpretive harvesting of the past. Chalmers is now, as we shall all be, an objective, factual, but resonant datum drawn along in the wakes and eddies of our lives. Chalmers is not in that casket, nor has he risen to some supernatural abode. He is an undeniable force in the structure of the world, like a bone cell in our skeletons."

Well, they asked for it. No—I had something to say, and I said it. I doubt that anyone had the slightest idea what the hell I was talking about. I'm not so sure I did. Clarity, after all, is not all it's cracked up to be.

The preacher smiled, patted my back, and said, "God bless you, son." I felt like popping him one, but I merely stepped away as the casket was lowered. Relatives filed past and told me how pretty my talking was. Lula Mae said I sounded like one of them preachers off the television, and Bernice said she could tell I had an education. Arlene said it was an eloquent "panegoric." Some told me how much they enjoyed my picking and singing the night before, and others informed me of what I should have played: "Bo, you don't know no Alabama?" and "You gotta like some Eagles, buddy roe. I can't bel*iev*e you didn't sing air one of they songs."

Willie walked toward me with a couple I had not seen at the setting-up. The woman looked to be my age and the man about ten years older with a long, sad face like one of Spessard's cypress knee sculptures.

"Legare, you remember Martha Umphlett, don't you?" Willie said. I sure did. We shook hands and said nice to see you. I did not tell her that she'd retained her blue-black hair and preference for older men.

"It's Martha Bombardi now," she said. "This is my husband, Tom."

I shook hands with him, pleased to meet you. He looked familiar.

"They own the frame store next to my shop," Willie said.

"I found your eulogy quite interesting," Tom said. "Undercurrents, if you will, of process thought."

"Are you a philosopher?" I asked.

"No, but in another life I had an interest in theology and did quite a bit of reading where the two fields overlap."

"Another life? In seminary, perhaps?"

"You could say that, and nearby," he said with a smile, "but rather reclusive."

I understood. "We've met, haven't we?"

"I think we did, years ago." As a young monk, he'd discovered me spying at the abbey twenty years earlier. Now, he had forsaken the life of the spirit for the life of the flesh—a walking movie of the week. "Did you ever find what you were looking for?" he said.

"Pretty close," I said. "You?"

"Same with me. Closer than in the other life."

"Nice to hear your voice this time," I said.

People gathered around the back of Rembert's truck as he handed out tinfoil-wrapped paper plates of barbeque from two large coolers. Ordinarily everyone would have come to his house at noon to feed on the animal that had cooked all night, but a family council must have decided that such a gathering would have risked interfering with the funeral schedule, or that no one would be in the mood for a feast after a funeral.

Someone asked Flolene where John the Baptist was, and she said he'd gone out for cigarettes at noon and never come back. "Lord knows how I'da got chere if Arlene ha'n'ta been home when I callt her on the telephone," she said.

"You coulda just called somebody else," Markley said. "Somebody'da come for you."

"I don't know they woulda. You don't never know about people—your own people," she said, smoothing the petals of the white corsage pinned under her chin.

Rembert joked that if the barbeque "ain't no good, y'all blame him." He pointed at Grossman, who blushed at being given some credit for the product.

Willie kissed Grossman on the cheek.

※

"I think I understand what you were trying to say," Grossman said on the way home from the graveyard. I was behind the wheel, Willie and Unitas in the back—one big happy family. "I've felt connectedness, with people. I've just never thought of it as anything more than an odd sensation, the milieu of religious mystics, certainly not something open to philosophical analysis."

I gave him a mini-lecture on how he had been trained to see through the lens or with the blinders of analytic philosophy, which dices the world up into discrete, atomic bits.

"Your characterization of the Western epistemological enterprise is interesting," he said, "especially the tendency to separate our perceptions into sense-data of either colors, shapes, or sounds, which seems inaccurate when we have perceptions of mixed form, like hearing a shape."

My foot yanked away from the accelerator. "Saul, are you telling me you hear shapes—that you experience synaesthesia?"

"Not often. Sometimes I hear a shape or color, particularly with music."

"Give me an example."

"Last night, when you were singing about the circle being unbroken, I heard the song as a wavy loop, like a Möbius strip trying to close itself. That's why I had to play the violin, to aid in its resolution."

"That's beautiful, Saul," Willie said. "And did it?"

"Yes, which is why I stopped playing. When everyone sang together at the end, the strip shrank and faded."

"How do you know how to play the fiddle, Mr. Gross Man?" Unitas asked.

"My grandfather taught me."

"The jeweler, rare book dealer, rebbe grandfather?" I asked.

"Yes."

"Let me guess? He bought Stradivariuses, or is it *Stradivarii*?, with all the money he made."

"No. He sent me to college."

We pulled into the yard just ahead of Spessard and Arlene. The Old Man and Mama were not yet back, but Willie had a key to the trailer. We talked about how nice the weather had been for a funeral, how pretty the flowers were, and how sweet my talk had been. Unitas took Grossman to examine the guineas. Wynonna, with some encouragement from Willie, asked me to read her a book version of *Froggy Went A-Courting*. The Old Man and Mama came in, and Wynonna helped in the kitchen like a big girl. Willie and I moved to the porch as Unitas gave Grossman a tour of the dog pens.

"He asked me to marry him," Willie said.

"Godamighty, didn't I warn you? When'd he do that?"

"In a poem I found at the shop yesterday morning. Must have slipped it through the mail slot." She folded her legs under her in the swing and smoothed her dress around her knees.

"A love letter? Like a high school kid?"

"Bubba, it was sweet. He's a very sensitive man. I don't think you've ever seen, or *tried* to see, that side of him."

"What did you say? Y'all must have discussed it last night."

She laid her head over the back of the swing and stared at the porch ceiling. "I told him it was the sweetest thing anyone had ever said to me, and I love his company, but I won't be ready to marry anyone for a long while. He said he understood, and could be as patient as I needed."

"That's good, being two states apart."

"You're not listening. I like him. I'm not in love with him, but he cares about me. I miss that, Bubba. Maybe every now and then, the kids and I could come down and visit you and Tally—that is, if you get your ass in gear, and she lets you come home."

Mama stuck her head out the door and called us in to eat.

"Y'all leaving tomorrow?" Willie asked.

"Probably late morning," I said. "No hurry, since maybe I won't be *let* back home."

"I want to talk to you before you leave, maybe after supper. There's something else I need to tell you."

I stood up. "OK, we can settle this whole thing then."

"Honestly."

⟡

I doctored up some two-day-old purlieu with some garlic (salt, that is, and happy to find that) and pickled cayennes the Old Man called "cheyennes"—he'd grown them in his little garden. The rest ate barbeque, praised it as the best they'd ever put in their mouths, and watched the six o'clock news. The lead story was of a man who ran off a bridge near Moncks Corner. The on-the-scene footage showed a car being pulled from the canal as the voice-over explained that fishermen helped the driver, who was unharmed, from the water. Next we saw a black man speaking.

"We been sitting right there by the bridge catching redbreast when they was a great big splash. Phonzo, he run up the hill, but I seen that cyar going under." The camera panned the canal. "Wa'n't but 'bout thutty, let's see, 'bout thutty foot out there. I call Phonzo back and just when that hind bumper was all sunk, that white boy come bobbing scraight up. He swum a piece, then grab on my cyane pole."

"I be dog, that's old Bunkus Manigault," Spessard said.

A connection was made between the man who drove off the bridge and the driver involved in a recent hit-and-run, who had to be the one that killed Chalmers. The picture changed from a view of the bridge to a shot of a shirtless man being handcuffed.

"Look at J. B.!" Unitas shouted.

"I'll be John Brown," the Old Man said.

John the Baptist had run over Chalmers. That explained the dent in the car we'd seen the night before, and why he hadn't had the nerve to get out of the car to view the body.

"That is one sorry shitass in this *world*," Spessard said, which, for once, summed it up perfectly.

"A bizarre hostage situation took place at the Charles Towne Convention Center during the annual conference of the American Philosophical Association," the anchor continued. "A deranged man with a BB gun threatened a room full of people until he was disarmed by one of the philosophers." On the screen was someone I took to be Bishop being loaded from a gurney onto the ambulance.

"It's the Gross Man!" Unitas squealed and fell over laughing.

Grossman was speaking into a microphone, but the anchor's voice was still saying something about Bishop being from Duke. Just behind Grossman stood Sennet, who was talking with Boykin/Gyges. Under Grossman's face, the caption read, "Paul Grossman. Apprehended the Gunman."

"What?" said Grossman. "I never said I did that."

Then Grossman's voice came from the television. ". . . simply extracted the weapon from his hands, rendering him powerless . . ." That was it, and the anchor moved on to the weather—record high temperatures expected to continue. Arlene said, "Mmm, mm."

"I was telling them about *you*, Greazy!" said Grossman. "This is outrageous!"

"Saul, I mean, Paul," I said, "I know you told them the truth. But nobody wants truth—they want stories. You did fine."

۞

Until Triple Six and Azrael sneaked past the referee and turned the tide, the apostles were beating the Four Horsemen. The Wrath of God nearly pinned Beelzebub until a chair hit him across the back of the head—thrown by Scourge. The forces of good were having a bad night, and the arena fans as well as those sitting with me in Cordesville were having a rapturous time befitting the final hours. Between matches, the cameras went backstage, where some hoopla was brewing over an unregistered newcomer. The silent wrestler, dressed in a flowing white robe and heavily made-up so his face seemed to glow—anyone should have recognized him as Gyges in a new role—left the negotiations and threats to his new manager, none other than Sam Sennet! Sennet wore a long black coat (exactly like Bishop's), ribbon tie, and porkpie hat and called himself the Parson. When officials challenged the right of his client (as yet unnamed) to enter the ring, Sennet took swings at them with an oversized Bible.

"Heathen!" he hollered. "You'll soon taste a hotter fury than mine!"

I announced I was taking a quick ride, knowing that the ladies would be uninterested, and the men would not invite themselves along and risk missing the final rounds of Armageddon. I slipped out the back door to avoid Willie and Grossman on the front porch so that (i) I would not disturb them if they were having the serious discussion I'd hoped they would have or (ii) Grossman would not have the opportunity to invite himself, perhaps to avoid the serious discussion. I grabbed a flashlight from the tool shed and an old shovel handle, in case I had to crack one of Rembert's sooners over the head.

I drove the Volvo out to Flippo's—he was not there and probably would not have recognized me anyway. There, I bought a ten-pound bag of chicken necks, usually used for crabbing, to occupy the dogs. No one was supposed to be at Rembert's, but just to be safe, I took the next limestone road over—it twisted back around, and dead-ended at the edge of the swamp behind the old barn, just a short walk through the woods. The moon was full, the ground was spongy—must have been high tide—and the swamp smelled deep blue, mossy, and ciliary like a paramecium. Up through the cypress and sweet gum limbs, I could see Betelgeuse below Orion's Belt—the hunter was ass-end up. The night was perfect for breaking and entering.

A slight breeze met me from the direction of the dogs, which I smelled before they sensed me and yelped. One bayed in a low tongue—exactly as I remembered Rounder, Rembert's mostly bluetick, had done twenty years before. I passed the barn and got to the dogs' side of the fence surrounding the garage. I cut through the top of the plastic chicken necks bag with the Barlow knife I'd carried since Rembert gave it to me on my twelfth birthday. The curs smelled the chicken—did the necks smell greenish brown and like wobbly rectangles too?—and switched to whimpers and whines. I threw a few handfuls over the fence, saving a couple in case I needed to appease them on the way out, and after some scuffling, each dog settled down with its own bony chew. They would have opened the gate for me if they had thumbs and a key, both of which I had. So I passed the Hume Shipping truck and the rusted dumpster that smelled like burned paper and meat, opened the lock on the double gates, and in I went.

Two big garage doors took up half of the building's long side, which faced me. I tried the key in the small door beside them, and it opened to an office that looked fairly ordinary: a couple of filing cabinets (which I doubted contained copies of tax returns); a desk with pencils, an ash tray, and a stack of ledgers; and a State Farm Insurance calendar picturing a family frozen in July at their backyard, Independence Day cookout on the wall beside a pre-Soviet Union breakup world map.

I opened the door that led from the office into the warehouse and was hit by a yellow, scaly, caustic odor that made my eyes water and burned my nostrils. The back of my palate felt scratchy, and I cleared my throat several times, but it did not help. I flicked on the fluorescent tube lights, which sputtered a couple of seconds before illuminating an immaculate, assembly-line style workroom with shiny, white walls and floors like a hospital lab. Along one wall stood a row of five deep, stainless steel sinks with dozens of gallon-size plastic jugs under them. The other wall was lined with tables and neatly assorted knives, scissors, tweezers, boxes, bags, bottles, bowls, magnifying glasses, and weights and measures.

Most of the room, though, reminded me of a tobacco barn, for tied to metal racks attached to the ceiling and rigged to chain blocks to raise and lower the racks easily were greenish brown plants suspended upside down. Space heaters sat on the floor to dry them faster or more evenly, I guessed. Under each plant was a tray that collected liquid dripping from the tips. The liquid was dark brown, and I could not tell if it was sap or some kind of chemical sprayed on the leaves to cure them, detoxify them, or what. I did not know how much pot sold for, but a fortune surely was hanging from that ceiling.

At the far end of the warehouse was a door I knew did not open to the outside. Coming closer, I saw that a heavy bolt latched the door. I opened it and was greeted by another strong scent—this one organic, a purplish orange plank of sweat, mildewed laundry, and shit. I switched on the light and jumped back, dropping the flashlight, which rolled across the floor.

The room was a barracks—with six sets of bunk beds where black men lay. One had raised up onto an elbow to squint at me, but I thought I saw other open eyes taking no notice of me. I cut off the light and squatted and listened for anyone else waking up. I crawled a few feet and groped around for the flashlight. The floor was wet and gritty, a contrast to the antiseptic atmosphere of the big room, whose light through the bunkroom's cracked door, as my pupils dilated, gave shape to the eight forms on the beds. Someone moved. The man who had risen up had lain back down, apparently from lack of interest. The room was full of sleeping men, yet there was no snoring, no deep breathing, and hardly a sign of life in the eight immobile bodies.

I left the flashlight, locked up the bunkroom, cut off the light, went back out through the office, locked the outside door, tossed the remaining chicken necks to the dogs, closed the gate, and returned to the Volvo. The temperature had dropped a couple of degrees, but it was still warm. Frogs, crickets, and other insects were raising hell.

On a warm winter night just like this one more than twenty years earlier, Lucian, DeWayne, Purvis, and I camped out to go duck hunting. Just before daybreak the next morning, we positioned ourselves at the area of the creek we had baited with cracked corn for weeks: Lucian and DeWayne on the bank, Purvis and me in the jon boat. I had never shot from a boat, so when a couple of mallards flew overhead, I flipped over backwards and into the cold, tannin-dark water. My hip boots filled from water in the ten-foot deep creek. Purvis stuck down a paddle for me to grab, which I did, but in so doing, dropped my sixteen gauge Browning. I sat in the boat drenched and shivering for the next hour as the others shot ducks, then paddled around for a half hour searching for dead birds Purvis swore he had hit. Finally, I dried off and warmed up some by the fire back at the tent while the others cleaned the ducks.

After my return home, the Old Man called Billy Spoade, a frequent customer of the gun shop and the official scuba diver for the county rescue service, and asked if he would try to retrieve the shotgun. Spoade did, although not by himself as the Old Man had assumed—two other rescue guys, with nothing else to do, used the fire truck to help, which got magistrate Mutt Furman's attention. Spoade came up with the gun and handed it to me. I turned it upside down and poured out the water—and a procession of corn, which also got Furman's attention. He "confiscated" the gun (took it to the Old Man) and had Jimmy Wyndam, the game warden, come to our house and make a show of not casting Spessard and the Old Man into prison. DeWayne and Purvis sneered until we were sentenced to no hunting of any kind until deer season started in August. They and Lucian turned icy gazes toward me. Purvis said he bet I would not drop my gun if it were up my ass.

I had seen what Purvis had told me was in Rembert's warehouse, which at best were illegal drugs being manufactured for distribution by illegal aliens, at worst, that plus kidnapping and slavery and, according to Purvis, soul theft, against which there probably was a law on the books in South Carolina, right beside one forbidding a woman to cut her hair, for it is her *glo*ry. What to do? Call the sheriff? FBI? Forget the whole damn thing?

I opened the car door, which felt too low. The tires sunk into the soft, high-tide absorbent earth. I couldn't take much more excitement. I thought I would barf. I cranked up the car, but the tires just spun. The swampy ground was lit well enough by the full moon and stars for me to gather up some fallen limbs to wedge under the tires for traction. I cranked the car and put it into gear, and it lurched backward an inch, rocked forward, and still spun. I got out and restacked the limbs and sticks. The car climbed a little higher and rocked ahead even farther, but not back again.

I was looking the situation over and thinking of returning to the garage to hunt up a come-along (or chain jack, I was never sure if there was a difference) when I heard an automobile engine and the dogs barking and saw headlights through the trees coming from the direction of Rembert's house. They ran the perimeter of the field on the other side of the patch of woods from me, disappeared when obscured by the barn, then reappeared as taillights when the vehicle moved to the garage.

The engine cut off. I crept to the other side of the woods as the dogs hushed and the gate creaked open. I could not see around the garage and wasn't close enough to hear what was being said, assuming they had been talking. I stayed along the edge of the trees and sidled towards the back until I saw the same pickup truck, parked half in shadows, that Rembert's two men had driven to the funeral. I moved another ten yards to look around the Hume Shipping truck and could see that the door to the office was open and the light was on. Perhaps they were checking on the temperature, fudging the ledgers, or answering an alarm I had unknowingly tripped.

I crouched and eased up to the pickup. The windows were up, and hardly any of the mercury vapor light's soft glow shone directly into the cab. I cupped my hands around my eyes and placed my face against the passenger's window. The inside was nearly bare—maybe a newspaper on the floorboard and a towel on the seat. A pair of sunglasses hooked over the rear-view mirror. I looked into the back—two shovels.

Something just inside the garage shuffled, slid, and bumped against a wall. I scuttled back to the tree line. The men were pushing or rolling something that seemed to be wedged in the office door. Someone spoke, then the inside light went off and the door shut. One guy opened the gate while the tall man wearing the wide-brimmed hat came out with what looked like a large sack thrown across his shoulder. A third man followed, limping and examining something in his hands. As the first guy locked the gate, the tall man tossed his burden into the back of the truck, got into the front, cranked up, and waited for the others to join him.

One crawled in to sit in the middle of the cab, while the third man hesitated at the passenger door. He hooked his left hand under his knee and yanked his leg up and onto the seat. I saw a flashlight in his hand. Was it the one I had dropped in there? As he scooted around to twist himself onto the shotgun side of the seat, the dim mercury vapor light splashed across the pink face of Forty-Four. The recognition startled me, and I had a nearly irrepressible and inexplicable urge to call his name, but I fought it off. They drove out onto the highway.

I went back into the garage. The dogs jumped up around me and whimpered but never barked or growled. I tried to hurry—in case the men came back—and I managed to find a grubbing hoe I later used to dig out the tires and escape the bog. The only sign around the warehouse that the men had been in there was a rolling cart, which had been moved. That or whatever was on it must not have fit through the office door. I stared at the far end of the warehouse.

I walked across the room, opened the bunkroom door, and flicked on the light. Seven men lay motionless in their beds.

❦

"Find what you were looking for?" Willie asked upon my return.

"Yeah. I mean . . . what?" Immediately after getting back, I'd brushed off my muddy shoes and changed into sweat pants and a sweatshirt. Grossman had gone inside to watch Armageddon. Willie must have told him to give her and me some time alone.

"You snuck off by yourself. I figured it was a nostalgia drive, searching for your lost youth or something pathetic like that."

"Yeah, pathetic is right. Some things never change." I did not mention anything about Rembert's place. In the morning, I decided, I would call the SLED agent who had left his card at the hospital. I just hoped the men in the pickup wouldn't come looking for me first.

"Bubba, I'm not sure you're ready to hear this. But you're a big boy." She sipped her coffee. "You remember how Lucian used to tease you that you're adopted and call you 'Little Chalmers'?"

"You can't be serious."

"No, no, you're not adopted. The point is that Lucian may have joked about it, but he feared being the outsider. He told me he had heard a rumor, but wouldn't say what it was. I pushed Arlene until I squeezed it out of her."

"What rumor?"

Unitas came to the door. "Uncle Greazy, it's almost the end! Come on!"

"I'll be there in a minute, U." Unitas went back inside.

Willie thumped her coffee cup. "The story is that Mama couldn't get pregnant and went to Forty-Four for a potion. I guess her wanting a child overcame her holy-roller notion of those 'devil's doings.'"

"She went to Forty-Four?"

"Arlene took her. She told Daddy she was going, and he said she was out of her mind. Well, she got pregnant right afterwards, and Spessard and Arlene teased her that it was Forty-Four's baby."

"He does have a reputation." Remnants of the acrid smell from Rembert's lab lingered around me, but it was now more brownish and stringy.

"Daddy, as you can guess, didn't think it was very funny. He partly believed the potion had worked. In his mind, Lucian was, at least symbolically, Forty-Four's baby. Lucian picked up on this and was tormented he might be the unwanted product of the woodpile."

"Something's not adding up here," I said. I really wanted a beer, but I was afraid Willie would accuse me of running away if I left for the kitchen. "First, if you're saying Lucian believed that Forty-Four was his real father, you're wrong. Lucian never placed any stock in rumors generally, and I don't think he would have ultimately cared *who* his father was. Second, he never mentioned feeling unwanted to me at all."

"First," Willie said, mocking me, "you're not listening. I didn't say he thought anyone other than Daddy was his father. Second, he told *me* many times he felt unloved and unwanted. Mama and Daddy never treated him in any way different from how they treated us, but he still *felt* they did. There was nothing rational about it. I think he felt that way long before he caught wind of Spessard and Arlene's joke, but he latched onto it as some kind of excuse."

"Well, he never said anything to me about it." Far off in the direction of Rembert's house, I heard a screech owl's lonesome cry—something I hadn't realized I missed so much. I would lie in bed and try to imitate the night birds' stark songs that found their way out from deep in the swamp. My favorite was the whippoorwill, a bird I had never seen but whose estranged call Lucian, when he could not sleep, which was often, would ask me to mimic. Could a whippoorwill's heartbreaking call really attract a mate? No wonder Hank Williams wrote about it.

"I don't think you should close your mind off so quickly to the idea that these feelings contributed to his suicide."

Grossman came to the door. "Greazy, you don't want to miss this, bo!" *Bo?*

"OK, Saul. In a minute." One of the Old Man's hunting dogs began to bay mournfully. Another dog far through the woods answered. "I'm not closing my mind," I said.

Dogs in every direction, perhaps miles away, had joined in the howling. When I was a kid, I would hear their late night exchange and imagine they were commiserating about their captivity or bragging about their hunting exploits through an untranslatable song. Wittgenstein said that if a lion could speak, we could not understand him. Wittgenstein could speak, but perhaps no better than lions or dogs.

"You're a case. You know that?" She took my hand and pressed it to her cheek. "It's just that you've closed your mind to so much else—like the times Lucian covered for you."

"What are you talking about?"

"He was always smoothing things over when you got into trouble. He would lie to Mama and Daddy or whoever the right person was—"

"Like, Goddammit, when?"

"Like all those fights at school."

"I had only a couple, and the Old Man would go talk to the asshishtant principal—"

"Or when y'all were baiting them ducks and Lucian took the blame."

"He did not!"

"Or when you took Martha Umphlett to the girlie show . . ."

"I did fucking not!" My head suddenly started pounding. I sensed a buzzing sound, like gnats swarming around me.

". . . and he had to keep her daddy from killing you. Or when you and your sorry fraternity buddies tore up the graveyard at Bullhead Chapel."

"Thatsh a damn lie! Lucian was never . . . we didn't do anything wrong." I hadn't done anything wrong, and no one had to do anything for me. My life was my own.

Willie sighed. "Don't get so defensive, Greazy. You've just been so disconnected for so long."

The door flung open. "Uncle Greazy," said Unitas, "don't you want to know how it all's gonna end?"

Grossman stuck his head out, too. "Uncle Spessard says it's getting hotter'n a two-peckered owl!" His impersonation of Spessard was uncanny.

"Get in there," Willie said. "Maybe you can save Saul from them."

I wanted to punch somebody. Instead, I kissed Willie on the head.

"And don't forget to work on yourself, too," she added.

☙

Pandemonium was in the ring. Announcers screamed their hoarse disbelief. No spectator sat. Wrestlers alternated climbing into the ring and being ejected into the stands, as did the six referees, who tried to create order from the meleé. Every minute or two following a trumpet or air horn blast, a complex, not-easily-locatable shift in the combatants' relative positions rolled through the mass of muscle and sweat and reverberated through the crowd. With a sandled foot on a post and the other on the turnbuckle, Gyges, who in my absence had apparently gotten himself a new name, which Unitas couldn't remember, seemed to direct wrestlers, spectators, camera and lighting operators, or somebody else behind the scenes with elaborate hand signs, like a Tibetan Buddhist monk's mudras, and in a vague, maybe even involuntary way, they all seemed to respond.

Through the cheers of the crowd and the frenzied yelling of the announcers came the barely audible voice of Sam Sennet babbling pentacostically. The TV screen occasionally showed the ringside table where Sennet jammed his red face between the wide-eyed announcers and tried to steal a microphone while hopping and spitting and reading from a book he sometimes used to bludgeon a flipped-from-the-ring wrestler. The cameras outside the arena showed waiting police cars and ambulances, while overhead the blimp circled Charleston saying, "Elixir: Get The Spirit!"

I had begun to settle down, and my head no longer throbbed. "Saul," I said to en-Gross-ed-man, hopping with an excitement to match Sennet's, "listen to Sennet. Isn't that *koine* Greek?"

I thought I recognized *ouranou* for "from the sky" or "from heaven" and *abussou* for "abyss" and something about smoke and the dark sun and locusts.

"You mean the Parson?" He closed his eyes and cocked his head. "Yes. He's talking about locusts that look like horses with armor and crowns and faces like men—"

"That's from *Revelations*," Mama said. "He's reading the Bible but the Spirit's speaking it through him in the Lord's tongue."

"He done gone ecstatical and got the Holy Ghost," Arlene said.

"He done gone fool and 'bout to get his ass whipped," Spessard said. "He ain't supposed to be there no way with his man propped up on the ropes what ain't registered."

"Well, I think they're all blaspheming," Arlene said, "and desecarating the Word."

"The Word ain't been *desecarated*," Spessard said. "He's in there getting whomped up, but he ain't been desecarated." He, the Old Man, Unitas, and Grossman had a hearty laugh over that one. Arlene pursed her lips and shook her head.

The lights in the arena blinked, eliciting a gasp from the spectators and a pause from the fighters. Sparks fell from the ceiling. Smoke grew around the ring and in the stands. Some in the audience panicked and rushed the exits; others reveled in the chaos. Sennet the Parson yelled, "I told you! Taste the fury!" The wrestlers went back to work. Gyges (or Messiah or Son-o-Man or whatever name he had adopted) spread out his arms and fell into the writhing mound of battlers. The referees jumped toward the middle at once, and several of their hands signaled for someone to ring the bell. The announcers confessed their confusion: "Is it over? Has the end finally come?"

Wrestlers backed up to the ropes, leaving each of the referees holding up the victorious hand of six different wrestlers—three good guys: Gyges/Messiah, the Word, and the Wrath of God; and three bad: Beelzebub, Azrael, and Triple Six. The non-winners shouted protests, the candidates looked bewildered, the spectators tossed their Elixir cups into the ring, and the referees commenced to fight.

"It looks like that's the end, folks," said an announcer.

"What a climax!" said the other. "That came like a thief in the night!"

"What the hell was that?" asked Spessard. "Who won?"

"I think nobody won," Unitas said.

"They's got to be a winner," said the Old Man.

"That was patently ridiculous!" said Grossman. His hand clutched his head, and I worried he would rip out handfuls of hair. "Tournaments imply closure. It can't be left unresolved—just *incomplete*."

"Vould you prefer to have it inconsistent, Herr Doktor Professor Grossman?" I asked in an affected German accent.

Grossman looked at me, squinted, and clutched his beard. Then he fell back onto the couch laughing. The others did not understand the joke but joined in the laughter just the same. No one laughed harder than I. It felt good to release the tension of the most bizarre week of my life. After breakfast in the morning, I would slip off and make my phone call to the law, tell everyone goodbye, then head back home to Tally, who surely by now was penitent. I would still have two weeks before the spring semester to relax and get in some fishing.

I had another life to slip back to.

TEN
Buridan's Ass

Imagine a hungry donkey equidistant from two indistinguishable haystacks. No wind blows to enhance the aroma of one over the other, no sunbeam illuminates one more than the other, and the donkey has no feature that would make him find one more attractive than the other (that is, he sees equally well from both eyes, he is neither left- nor right-hoofed, etc.). If there truly is no difference between the options, nothing to create a preference, could the donkey choose, or would he starve?

Aristotle gave a similar illustration, but the puzzle is known as Buridan's Ass, named for the fourteenth-century philosopher Jean Buridan, although the problem does not appear in Buridan's available writings and may have been an opponent's *reductio ad absurdum* criticism of Buridan's notion that reason and will are the same. Buridan was a student of parsimonious blade-slinger William of Ockham, famous for his advice on the swift, surgical removal of all metaphysical tumors, malignant or benign. So we should not be surprised that Buridan would find a head housing reason and a will crowded. But if there is no irrational will to light a fire under muley reason balked by twin options, Buridan cannot get his ass in gear.

During most of my life, I had lacked the ability to make a selection between even radically unequal choices. I had been the unwitting but exemplary Taoist, letting things happen, allowing Being to be, and riding waves of the Tao like flotsam. If you just go with the flow, the river, sooner or later, will deposit you on a bank. I had relied upon this alluvial acquiescence for a little too long. It was time to work the current to reach a landing of my choosing, maybe even go against the stream—hell, even dig a canal. I would be a swimmer, not a floater; a full-bellied donkey, not a starving ass.

I lay in bed, proud of my increasing resoluteness. I had stood up to the air rifleman. It was not as if I'd taken a couple of .44 magnum slugs, but it was a start. I had gone to Rembert's to check out his operation. I expected no one to be there, of course, but nobody made me go. And I did not have to creep through the woods to spy on Forty-Four and the henchmen. Maybe I was growing some balls, and when I wanted to, as Willie said, I could get on the stick. The icy waters of wife and job have shrunk many a priapic pendant, but I could work on my backstroke when I got back to Florida.

I thought of Lucian. If Willie was right, then beneath his veneer of confidence and independence—a personality contrasting with my pissantness—my brother struggled and lost his fight with self-doubt. The listlessness, the drifting lack of purpose after his accident that we attributed to brain damage or a guilty and broken heart may have been due to an unfounded, though no less strong, feeling of not belonging, of being *in* but not *of* the world. It was a perverted notion to begin with, especially when smugly proclaimed through shit-eating Pauline grins by believers who have no idea how desperate a state the phrase can describe, and a fatally inverted one when made bitterly concrete by Lucian. Though anyone can kill you, only you can take your own life. Thus, I had nearly made a monument of his suicide as the freest, most authentically individualistic, and paradoxically most life-affirming, act he could perform—regrettable, indeed, yet a seamlessly rational and willful response to a Unamuno-style tragic sense of life. But Willie had shaken the foundation of my shrine to self-affirmation and instead threatened to topple it into a confused heap of broken images of self-pity. I had to decide about him, too.

And if she was right about that, was she right about my inaccurate memories? Had I constructed a delusional story of my life, a narrative trajectory more hyperbolic than parabolic? If she was right, Lucian hadn't been individualistic, it seems, and neither had I.

I still had to deal with the ontological argument, but in a more manageable way. I was convinced that the argument presented a powerful case for the necessary existence of *some*thing, but that something was not the omnipotent, omniscient, omni-etc. bogeyman of traditional theism. I had more important things to think about.

Through the window behind my head, the full moon washed over my stomach. I usually slept spiraled up on my side, with Tally taking up twenty percent more than her allotment of the bed. But here I lay supine and sank into the old mattress like mud.

I dreamt I was eating hay.

෴

"Fire!"

I jumped out of bed, ran out of the room, stumbled into my sweat pants, and yelled again, "Fire!"

Someone flicked on a light, and the Old Man in his boxer shorts, Mama in a terrycloth robe, Grossman in red and black hounds-tooth flannel pajamas, and Unitas in an oversized T-shirt showing the Wrath of God drinking from a massive bottle of Elixir met me in the living room. All looked bewildered and more sleepy than frightened. "What? Where?" they asked. I held up my palms to signal "stop."

The clock over the TV read 5:02. I closed my eyes and inhaled slowly through my nose. The smell of ammonia, other astringent chemicals, a trace of rubber, and an unmistakable, smoky leaf blended into a yellowish brown, and I knew exactly what was burning.

"Rembert's," I said. "Call the fire department and rescue squad. I'm going out there."

I threw on a shirt and my shoes and remembered the SLED agent's card. I gave it to the Old Man and told him to call the number and report drug manufacturing. I was getting into the Volvo before I realized that Grossman, still in his pajamas, was outside too. I had no time to argue with him and was soon speeding backwards out the driveway with him trying to close his door and telling me to buckle up. I turned on the radio long enough to hear a verse of some twenty-year-old dickweed's up-tempo and mutilated version of Gram Parson's "Hickory

Wind" and swore I would track him down one day and as Spessard would say, beat his ass to a frazzle and then beat the frazzle's ass.

Threads of smoke wisped across the red moon. With the window down, the smell of burning pot was so strong I was afraid I'd be too high to do anything once we arrived at Rembert's. As we got to the back, I slammed on the brakes to stop right beside the henchmen's truck. I had expected to see the place ablaze, but only small flashes of flames darted around the roof of the garage—too few, it seemed, to produce the amount of smoke rolling over the trees. Dogs ran around the open field. A big dualie was parked near one end of the garage.

I told Grossman to stay in the car, and as I stepped out, two dogs jumped up on me to play. I heard voices across the field, then two pops from a pistol. Someone was near the end of the garage opposite the dualie, and an unknown voice yelled, "Get on outa hyere!" I took it to be directed at me.

From near the dualie came another voice, "Go on, son, before you get hurt." *Funderburk—had he set the fire?*

"I'm coming to get those men out," I shouted. "I don't give a damn what happens to the pot and drugs and shit in there, and you can all kill each other, for all I care. But I'm getting them out."

I walked across the field. No one spoke. No one fired. I neared the side opposite the dualie and saw Rembert's thugs squatting behind an old tractor. Turned onto its side was a big tank, which Rembert used for dipping his dogs in Happy Jack and burnt motor oil. The smaller man stared at me with his mouth open and turned to watch each step I took. His bulkier accomplice adjusted his wide-brim hat and slowly shook his head.

I went around the fence and through the gate to one of the big doors. The key that opened the office worked. When I pushed the rolling door up, I was slapped by a hot, multi-faceted odor as caustic as tear gas. The room smelled crimson and black and dangerously inviting to the touch, like one of those big red velvet ants that's really a wingless wasp you have to stomp and grind repeatedly, thinking you will never kill it, all the while hearing the muffled buzzing and feeling its vibrations run so sharply up through your heel you think you've been stung. I coughed and gagged and fought my way in. Through watery eyes, I could see that the source of the fire at the other end of the garage was a pile of wooden crates whose flames, because of a pool of chemicals or fuel, maybe kerosene, had spread across much of the floor and were hopping into sinks and wrapping around tables. Half of the hanging plants were smoldering.

I yanked the bolt on the bunkroom door. Someone yelled something outside, and I heard the deep blast of a shotgun and the *pank!* of the pellets against metal. Some light from the fire flickered into the room—the zombies were still lying on the beds, motionless. I yelled at them and grabbed one from the nearest bottom bunk. He sluggishly rose to his feet, but oblivious to the smoke, smell, and heat, did not take a step. I pushed him, and he moved a few feet into the doorway, then stood as if awaiting further encouragement. A flashlight beam broke into the room, and a voice only a few feet away shouted something that sounded like *Move et vous* and other phrases in a Pepe Le Pew-style pidgin French. The wide-brim hat guy replaced the zombie in the doorway, and the others eased out of their beds, lined up, and in what seemed like an hour, shuffled through the door and out the building. The fire was eating into the bunkroom by the time we finally cleared everybody out. The big guy and I coughed and gagged, but the zombies made no sounds.

"Let's get 'em through the woods yonder," I said. I figured he would not want to chance parading them by Funderburk. "There's a road that dead ends just through those trees. They ought to be safe there." I indicated the direction with the flattened-hand-perpendicular-to-ground point of country men. Flames were now leaping high into the night sky.

He barked something at them, then turned to me. "I tolt 'em where to go. Now, you'd better get on, specially before your uncle gets here. He's gonna kill that other'n and liable to take out whoever else is around."

Other'n? Grossman?

In the shootout, the wide-brim hat guy took his place by his partner, and I lit out across the field. Headlights approached the house.

"Greazy, who else you brought?" Purvis yelled from the dualie.

That stupid bastard must be a part of this. He and Funderburk must have set the fire. Why had he dragged me into this? Had he set me up?

"Who's that coming yonder?" Purvis asked.

Had he counted on my bringing others?

I was near the Volvo when a truck pulled into the yard. I looked around and saw that the fire had jumped to the roof of the old barn. I turned and ran across the field toward it.

Another shot. I glanced back to see Rembert steadying his rifle across the hood of the truck and aiming in the dualie's direction. A pistol pop came from the direction of the henchmen. Funderburk fired back. Someone got out of the passenger side of Rembert's truck and limped toward the Volvo. Grossman jumped from the car.

A blast from the dualie. Forty-Four fell. Grossman ran toward me and between Rembert and Funderburk. Rembert shot. Grossman fell.

"Dammit, boy!" Rembert shouted to Grossman. "What the hell you doing?"

"Stop shooting, Rembert!" Funderburk yelled.

"Get him and go, Greazy," Rembert said.

Grossman was sitting up, holding his left knee, when I grabbed under his arms and lifted him to his feet. More headlights approached.

"You'll be all right, Saul," I said. "Let's get you out of the line of fire." I put his arm around my shoulder and helped him to the edge of the field.

"How common is this sort of stuff in your family?" he asked as we hobbled into the trees.

"What, too sophisticated for you?" I said and sat him down. "Wait for me right here."

I ran back into the field and toward the barn. I glanced toward the house to see the Old Man getting out of his truck with a shotgun. He and Rembert yelled at each other, both demanding explanations.

Funderburk yelled for the Old Man to leave before Rembert shot him like he had "that boy." In the distance, I heard a fire engine's siren. The Volvo cranked.

I pulled hard on the barn door, and the rusty screws in the latch fell out. Fire was quickly consuming the rough old wood, but the air was not as smoky and acrid as the garage had been. In fact, it smelled sweet—probably from the years of tobacco—and felt smooth, elongated, and translucently green like a glass bottle. A central beam holding the roof had fallen to the floor and become a flaming partition, forking the room into a trunk-holding-old-manuscripts side and a Hank-Williams-song side. The rest of the roof would surely collapse any second.

"God*damm*it!" I said. This literal trial by fire was too much for me. "God*damm*it!" My head was pounding. I stood, shaky, everything within and without my grasp. I felt dizzy.

I moved. The heat was horrific. The metal lip around the trunk lid blistered my hand. Coughing, I fumbled around until I found the velvety Crown Royal bag. I turned and coughed again, fighting the vertigo. Someone was in the barn doorway.

I fell.

☙

"Are you awake?"

I tried to answer, but my mouth would not cooperate. My eyes were open, but I saw only milky forms vaguely resembling faces. I thought I heard Robert Earl Keen singing "Going Nowhere Blues."

"Greazy, do you hear me?" asked the same muffled, female voice.

I held up my hand and made the OK sign as someone else said she would get a nurse. I tried to talk again. Like the rest of me, my mouth felt tired and unwilling, and I said *merrlaah*, which was nothing like the "Get me a beer" I intended. Just as the shapes in the room were coming into focus, fingers spread my right eye open and shoved a bright light up to it. I tried to say "Son of a bitch" but *sukbus* spilled out instead.

"Dr. Hume, can you move your fingers?"

I raised my middle finger. Someone giggled.

"Looks like you can. Now, can you raise as many fingers as you see?"

They were blurry, but I saw two. I raised two.

She congratulated me on the correct answer and said my surgeon would soon be in to explain everything to me. She left, and another face moved into my narrow field of vision. My focus was already much better, but I had to blink a couple of times to be sure.

Tally sat on the edge of my bed and held my hand.

"Greazy, honey, you feel OK?" She looked sleepless. I released my hand from hers and pantomimed writing. She turned away a moment, someone said, "Here" (maybe Willie), and then she placed a pen and a "M[edical]U[niversity of]S[outh]C[arolina]" memo pad into my hands. Somebody else, whom I could not see, was mumbling on the other side of the bed, and I thought I heard, "Thank you, Jesus"—it was Mama.

My fingers felt like sausages and the pen needle thin. After a moment, I was able to scribble, "Who invite you?"

Tally cleared her throat. "I've been here a week. You were in a coma."

"Coma?" I scribbled.

"You were unconscious for two days when they gave you a CAT scan and found a brain tumor. The doctor said it must have been growing for years. The surgery was five days ago. We didn't know if you were going to wake up."

"No such luck," I wrote.

Clinching her eyes, she did a hiccup-like sob. I heard Wynonna ask if they could go get ice cream now. Mama shushed her.

"You slept through Christmas, Uncle Greazy," said Unitas, somewhere out of view.

"Grossman?" I wrote.

"He's fine," Tally said. "They operated on his leg, put a big metal brace around it. He'll probably have a limp. He went with your father to the state prison in Walterboro to straighten out some things with

Rembert."

"prison?"

"Rembert's in jail on a slew of charges, including murder. Bail's too high for him to get out."

The surgeon came in, looked into my eyes, had me watch his moving finger, and had me move my fingers and toes. Then he held my head in both his hands and swiveled it in a gentle figure-eight. He showed me a sketch of a brain and shaded in a portion that looked like a curled-up, grotesque little man to show where the massive tumor had been. He thought he had got it all, he said, but there was some damage, and he could not accurately predict how it would manifest itself. My speech problem was, however, expected and temporary.

"Can I have it?" I scribbled.

"What's that?" he asked.

"I get my bad parts from auto mechanic—get same from you?"

He contracted his bushy gray eyebrows into a puzzled look.

"Joke!" I wrote. "Vision and hearing nearly normal but something odd. Senses incomplete."

"You're lucky to have your sight at all. There was a great deal of pressure on the perceptual centers in your brain. Removing the tumor and simply relieving that pressure caused some shock to portions of your brain, like a series of tiny concussions." I heard Mama say, "Mmm, mm."

He looked into my eyes again. "Your senses will take some re-adjusting, but I doubt it'll be anything permanent."

"paralysis?" I wrote.

"I don't expect any, but I'm afraid nothing is certain."

Nothing is certain. I am a philosopher named Hume, and *he* was telling *me* nothing is certain? He said I would need observation for a couple of days and perhaps some physical therapy before they could "safely discharge" me. I tried to laugh, and it sounded almost normal. He got up and asked Tally to step outside with him.

Willie sat on the edge of the bed. Robert Earl Keen whined from the headphones of the tape player she had forgotten to turn off.

She picked up my hand and kissed it. "Hey, Bubba. Some Christmas, huh?"

I moved an imaginary pen, and she put the pen and pad back into my hands.

"What happened?" I wrote.

"There's a lot we still haven't figured out—maybe never will," she said. "Saul and Daddy have been trying to piece it all together, and they think Purvis wanted out or had it in for Rembert but was so scared of him and scared of going to prison that he just didn't know what to do. Maybe if Funderburk turned Rembert in, he thought, he could get out of it. But Funderburk decided his idea of revenge or punishment for Rembert was to burn the place down. Purvis got scared and thought Rembert would blame him, and that's why, we think, he wanted you out there, thinking you would call the law and get Rembert arrested before Funderburk arrived to set the fire."

"Why Rembert came back?" I wrote.

"We don't really know. Daddy thinks Purvis may have been trying to cover his ass and called him in Aiken when he realized you hadn't told the police yet. Maybe he hoped everything would get burnt up and Rembert would get arrested and not suspect that Purvis was playing double-agent. He didn't count on Rembert getting back as soon as he did, and he didn't count on those other guys showing up."

"Tally said murder," I wrote.

"Rembert shot Funderburk. Killed him."

"Purvis?"

"They arrested him, and he's been too terrified to say a word to anybody. Those two guys from Florida who worked for Rembert got arrested, too."

"zombies?"

"What?" Probably Purvis and I were the only ones who called them that, but Willie quickly figured out who I was talking about. "They were here until a couple of days ago," she said. "The SLED agents tracked down their families. I guess they sent them back to Cuba or Haiti or wherever they're from. Some of them may have brain damage because Forty-Four, we think, kept them doped up. Seems there's an international slave trade of that sort of thing going on."

"Forty-Four?"

"Nobody knows. Daddy says Forty-Four tried to get away by jumping into the Volvo, but he drove all around the field with the dogs chasing the car, and finally crashed it into a tree. They found his wooden leg somehow wedged between the brake and the clutch—something about the foot pedals—and when his foot got caught in there, he lost control and couldn't stop. There was a lot of blood in the car, and they tracked him a ways into the swamp, but he's disappeared."

I laughed. "Will it fit Saul?" I wrote.

"Yeah, very funny."

"Who got me out?"

"Who'd you think? Daddy. Seconds later, Saul said, the whole roof fell in. That's when Funderburk started walking towards Rembert. The sheriff and rescue squad and all'd just pulled up, so maybe Funderburk thought Rembert wouldn't do anything stupid then. He was wrong."

"Bag?" I wrote.

"What?"

"Crown Royal."

"Oh, I've got it at the house. Saul said you'd wrapped the drawstring around your wrist. But he said it was the wrong one—whatever that means—and he's going to ask Rembert where the other one is."

"What's in bag?"

"A Co-Cola bottle with paper in it."

I smiled and wrote, "Not wrong one."

۞

By evening, I could mumble a few words. I even got out of bed, took a few steps, and sat in a chair. Everything seemed to work, just weakly and slowly. I finally got Tally to hand me a mirror. My entire head was bandaged, my eyes looked like someone had punched them, and my lips and nostrils were chapped and cracked. I was still on the IV but could drink water through a straw. I was so unquenchably thirsty I even accepted a few sips of Elixir, which, despite its invitation to "Taste the Fury," was flat.

The Old Man and Saul returned with a family-size bucket of fried chicken. They both threw their arms around me and wept when they saw me awake. With some effort, I managed to call them pansies. Saul showed me a paper bag and grinned and hopped like an excited child. I opened it: a bottle of Blenheim's Extra Hot ginger ale. I laughed, Saul slapped his knee, and Tally poured the ginger ale into a beige plastic cup with some crushed ice from the beige plastic pitcher indigenous to hospitals. I had a sip. The ginger ale had more flavor than the Elixir but was not nearly as powerful as it should have been. I realized then that I could not smell the chicken.

"Get doc—" I tried to talk but inhaled some Blenheim's and began coughing and gagging. Tally ran for the nurse, Mama patted my back, and Grossman paced. Two nurses came in with an oxygen tank and shoved the mask over my mouth. I stopped coughing, and they checked my pulse and blood pressure as I asked repeatedly for the doctor. The assisting surgeon showed up fifteen minutes later.

"No smell," I said. "No smell."

The doctor explained that my brain had suffered some damage, and perhaps this was one of the effects. He could not say whether it would be permanent.

"CAT scan?" I asked, grabbing his sleeve.

"No way to tell," he said. He looked nervous. He left and took Tally with him.

The Old Man reported that Rembert was in good spirits, sent his apology that I had to get messed up in his dealings, and said the song was now mine.

"I asked Uncle Rembert about the Ibn Rushd and the Buddhist manuscripts," said Grossman. He cut his eyes at Willie, who had smiled when he'd said "Uncle." "He took them with him that night and sold them to his business associate in Aachen."

"Aiken," the Old Man said.

"Aiken. So they weren't even in the barn when you went after them. He wouldn't tell us how to track them down. That wouldn't be good business," he said. Grossman said this matter-of-factly, as if reading aloud from the newspaper. "Oh, and one more thing. Uncle Rembert said to tell you you've got some boils."

"Balls," the Old Man said.

Unitas and Wynonna told me about their Christmas toys.

Tally returned and sat on the bed. One moment she was smiling, the next sniffling. Mama said the weather had changed to cold, said we might even see snow, then murmured an eschatological "Lordy, Lord." The Old Man said the odor of the burned pot still lingered around Cordesville, and he had taken Rembert's dogs to Poitier Prioleau to be "vetted." Mama and the Old Man quickly found homes for most of the sooners.

Spessard and Arlene then dropped in. Spessard said it was "about time they found something in a Hume's head."

Half speaking and half writing, I thanked Grossman for hanging around with me, but because Tally had come, I would ride back with her. Besides, I pointed out, my stay here might be indefinite. If his car had been fixed, he could return to Florida.

"I'm not going back, Greazy," he said with a smirk, and glanced at Willie.

"He's taken a job at the University of Charleston," Willie said. "We've already started looking for an apartment for him near campus."

"I was offered the position by your old teacher, Girdlemuller," Grossman said. "I start teaching in two weeks. Tenure, full professor. I called Dean Warden, and he said there might be a problem with my tenure at AmWorld anyway. Since I did not actually read the paper that had been accepted for the APA program, I am technically still without an appearance at an academic conference. Isn't that ironic?"

"Strictly speaking, no," I wrote. "Typical," I said.

"Warden said they were all excited to hear about you, though—the hostage situation, that is, not the surgery. When you get back, the

Board of Directors is going to give you an award and would like you to deliver the commencement address on the theme of education as self-direction."

"Whoopie," I said.

"Oh, I forgot," Grossman said. "Your friend Bartholomew Gilbert died."

"Honestly," Willie said, elbowing Saul in the arm. "That could have waited."

Grossman rubbed his arm. "He had been very ill for a long time, I was told, and stopped taking his medication."

My God. He was so energetic after *I* told him the lie that convinced him to stop taking his meds.

"Cancer killed him," I wrote, then tried to speak. "The cancer, right?"

"Of course," Grossman said, "although causation is a complex—"

"Saul," Willie said. "We need to go." She turned to Tally and shot her an eyebrow cue. "Speaking of news . . . Tally?" Willie led the others from the room.

This is it, I thought—the bad news they've decided I'm finally ready to hear. Maybe they removed the brain tumor but found something worse. Maybe I'm impotent.

Tally took my hand. "Greazy, honey. I'm pregnant." She began to cry. I guessed immediately (and correctly, I found out later) that Willie had known all along, which would explain why she was giving me those heart-to-hearts about the rumors—her way of dragging me into maturity.

"I found out the day you told me you were leaving for the conference," Tally said. "I wanted to surprise you over a candlelight dinner that night. I was even going to use our best china."

I laughed.

Tally sighed. "I thought being pregnant would make the extra effort worthwhile. I thought you might change. But, Greazy, you are what you are. Ironic, isn't it?"

"Yes," I said, and I laughed a long, low, painful, cleansing laugh.

❧

The wind is raising big waves on Tampa Bay as I drive north on the Howard Franklin Bridge and Hurricane Kurt creeps towards St. Petersburg. Mandatory evacuation orders have not been issued, but I figured that I and David Lucian Hume, now almost a year old, should get out. Tally hadn't been all that happy when I went by her apartment last night to pick him up, announcing I'd skip a few days of classes to take David on his first trip to South Carolina instead of letting her take him to her mother's. She gave in, since it is, after all, my week to have him, and besides, she and I get along fairly well now, given our new appreciation for the tautology: she is what she is; I am what I am. Not that we see each other that much, but at least nothing is hurled—neither foul names nor household items.

I got tenure the semester after returning from the APA conference and took sabbatical the next year, giving me plenty of time to learn to be a single father. My concern with duty these days has less to do with the Kantian categorical imperative and more with tidying my bona fide family room and changing dirty diapers, which is not so bad, since I no longer can detect odors. My speech has not completely returned to normal either. I leave out a syllable here or there, occasionally get a verb tense wrong, and sometimes shibboleth. I stopped dipping snuff entirely; much of my taste is lost anyway.

I had time also to draw out some philosophical implications of my temporary synaesthesia. The key to the meaning of our being-in-the-world, I think, is something like a connectedness, a relatedness, a groundedness more immediately and causally felt in the first shovelful than reflectively and thematically known by auguring beneath the surface. Florida Scholarly Press is interested in the book I've been working on; the tentative title is *Making Scents*. The philosophy editor is worried that my ruminations are too inconclusive for a philosophical audience accustomed to consuming the world by ripping and bolting.

In the meantime, my parents made their first visit to Florida—in a brand new Oldsmobile—and stayed for a week just after David was born. They came back over Christmas and even brought Spessard and Arlene. The shootout at Rembert's had a deep effect on the Old Man, but I can't exactly say what it is. He talks about tall cypresses, red-cockaded woodpeckers, and thick-necked bucks that steal the corn he plants for them in Rembert's field.

Saul spends his time fighting off the heavyweight universities that still try to lure him away from his position at the University of Charleston. He sees Willie, her children, and my parents once or twice a week. Unitas calls him Gross Man, while Wynonna prefers Goat Man. He attended this past December's APA conference, hosted by his alma mater Columbia, where three symposia were held in his honor. The conference took place without incident. Willie drove him to New York; even she couldn't get him to fly. She did, however, make him visit his family for an awkward reunion. His father was most unforgiving about Saul's having shaved his beard. The rebbe grandfather, unbeknownst to Saul, had recently died, leaving a stack of unenveloped and unmailed letters he had written to Saul over the years, each beginning as a commentary on a Torah passage but ending as an expression of encouragement and love for Saul.

Chauncey Hartley died at the age of 101. He had begun a new book—seventy years after his first one on the subject—that criticized his own approaches to the ontological argument and cast doubt upon its validity. For him, the existence of God was less a problem to be solved than a project to be pursued, a flowering shrub whose branches are lopped off, only to encourage more complex growth, a lusty and many-headed hydra whose newly budding faces are more vicious, fiery, and endearing than before.

Bart Gilbert's funeral took place while I was still in the hospital. Joyce sent me a letter thanking me for convincing him to quit his chemotherapy and giving him perhaps the happiest (final) four days of his life. I started a letter explaining that I had not intended to help him, that I told him a damn lie for no reason at all, and that I should have tried to change his mind. I wanted to tell her what a pissant I was. I tore up the letter.

Pissant, indeed.

After legal battles and some finagling, the Hank Williams song "I'll Never Know" belonged to me. I put it to music from one of the tunes Lucian had recorded so many years ago. RCA bought the song and promised it would go platinum. They released it as a single by that kid whose ass I swore I would beat to a frazzle. It sold about a dozen copies. A couple of the studio musicians who worked on the album asked to hear some more of Lucian's tunes. *What the hell.*

The storm's low pressure has excited the gulls. They're tacking against the air currents and banking just in time to dodge the bridge rails when the gusts hit. Perhaps it's just the biometeorological effect of the low pressure, but at least for the moment, a couple of things seem clear to me: (1) I will never have a complete understanding of Lucian's inner life, but I somehow know him better now than when he was alive, and I believe that, in some way only he could ever know, he died fulfilled. I will try better to appreciate that. (2) God is, for me, a former poltergeist that stomped on stairs and scared me shitless in the middle of the night, but now is only a shift in corner shadows, and a fluttering at the visual periphery that disappears, like a dim light, when looked at directly.

David hums in his sleep, almost to the beat of "Time of the Season" playing on the oldies station. I roll down the window a bit and feel the gale force winds. For once in St. Pete, the air on the first day of fall is cool and invigorating. I suck in a lungful through my nose. I feel a twitch, a stir in the sinuses. I breathe deeply again. Do I detect a slight olfactory awakening? If I concentrate, I can smell something.

It think it's purlieu.

ACKNOWLEDGEMENTS

Everyone who has ever meant something to me appears somewhere in this book. My parents, grandparents, aunts, and uncles filled my youth with an abundance of stories bound to find their way onto the page. This novel is the result of their beautiful voices coursing through my memory.

I owe special thanks to: Paul Allen, for his tireless work at trying to make me a writer; Nan Morrison, who made me into a reader; Garrison Somers, for nearly thirty years of friendship and guidance; Amy Mangan, for being the best writing buddy I could ever hope to find; Martin Perlmutter, for stirring up thoughts of becoming a philosopher; Bruce Wilshire, for making me into one; philosophers like Eugene Long, Rosamond Kent Sprague, Brian McLaughlin, Ernie Lepore, Peter Klein, Martha Bolton, John Lachs, and Ed Casey, whose teaching or acquaintance inspired me in many ways; Rebecca Goldstein, who, like Iris Murdoch before her, proved that philosophy can make great novels and philosophers can make great novelists; Bruce Bortz, for seeing something worth taking a gamble on in these pages; Harrison Demchick, for his astonishing editorial insights; and above all my wife Sandra, my critic, muse, and reason for everything I do.

ABOUT THE AUTHOR

A South Carolina native, Ron Cooper received a Ph.D. in philosophy from Rutgers University and now teaches at Central Florida Community College.

He is the author of a number of philosophical essays in academic journals, such as the *Journal of Speculative Philosophy and Philosophy Today*, as well as the book *Heidegger and Whitehead: A Phenomenological Examination into the Intelligibility of Experience* (Ohio University Press). His short stories have appeared in *Yalobusha Review, Timber Creek Review, Apostrophe,* and *The Blotter.*

With *Hume's Fork*, which is his first published novel, he was a finalist for the Bread Loaf Conference's Bakeless Literary Prize.

A bluegrass enthusiast, he lives in Ocala, Florida, with his wife and three children.

ABOUT THE AUTHOR

A South Carolina native, Ron Cooper received a Ph.D. in philosophy from Rutgers University and now teaches at Central Florida Community College.

He is the author of a number of philosophical essays in academic journals, such as the *Journal of Speculative Philosophy and Philosophy Today*, as well as the book *Heidegger and Whitehead: A Phenomenological Examination into the Intelligibility of Experience* (Ohio University Press). His short stories have appeared in *Yalobusha Review, Timber Creek Review, Apostrophe*, and *The Blotter*.

With *Hume's Fork*, which is his first published novel, he was a finalist for the Bread Loaf Conference's Bakeless Literary Prize.

A bluegrass enthusiast, he lives in Ocala, Florida, with his wife and three children.